"You are X M...

"I am called that," X Man admitted.

"From what land do you hail?"

"It is called Novum Eboracum."

Ham frowned. "*Novum* means 'new.' But I fail to place the name Eboracum."

Doc's trilling came again. "Eboracum," he told Monk and Ham, not taking his eyes off X Man's still face, "was the name of a fort in Roman Britannia."

"That don't make no sense," Monk grunted. "All them Roman forts are ruins now. This guy can't be some ancient Roman who's been hangin' around since the days of Cæsar, can he?"

Doc Savage demanded, "Is Novum Eboracum in Britannia?"

X Man shook his head. "It lies on the Lake of Smoke, in the shadow of Vulcan's Forge," he said hollowly.

The New Adventures of Doc Savage
Ask your bookseller for the books you have missed.

THE FORGOTTEN REALM

Kenneth Robeson

BANTAM BOOKS
NEW YORK • TORONTO • LONDON • SYDNEY • AUCKLAND

THE FORGOTTEN REALM

A Bantam Spectra Book / November 1993

ISBN 0-553-29555-1

Published simultaneously in the United States and Canada

*Bantam Books are published by Bantam Books, a division of Bantam
Doubleday Dell Publishing Group, Inc. Its trademark, consisting of the
words "Bantam Books" and the portrayal of a rooster, is Registered in
U.S. Patent and Trademark Office and in other countries. Marca Regis-
trada. Bantam Books, 1540 Broadway, New York, New York 10036.*

PRINTED IN THE UNITED STATES OF AMERICA

OPM   0 9 8 7 6 5 4 3 2 1

DOC

Doc Savage—born Clark Savage, Jr.—was raised from the cradle for his task in life—his job of flitting about the globe righting wrongs, helping the oppressed, smashing the guilty. He is a physician and surgeon—and a mighty good one, the tops in his line. He has the best and most modern equipment at his command, for he has limitless wealth. His main headquarters are in New York, but he has his Fortress of Solitude at a place unknown to anyone, where he goes at periodic intervals to increase his knowledge and concentrate. He's foiled countless crooks, and changed many of them into honest, useful citizens. The world would be a great place if there were more Doc Savages. But there's only one.

HAM

You'd never think a gentleman named Brigadier General Theodore Marley Brooks would be called Ham—would you? But Monk, Ham's pal, had a reason for giving him the nickname. He thought it would irritate the dapper Brigadier General Brooks—and that alone was regarded as a good reason by Monk. Ham is a knockout dresser and a knockout fighter, too. There's very little of the law that he doesn't know down to about six decimal places. But in a fight, the main law that he thinks about is the law of self-preservation, although most of his battles have been in the interest of folks too weak to fight for themselves. His slender black swordcane is something to avoid.

MONK

When you look at this picture, you can understand very
well why the subject is called Monk. Hardly any other nickname would fit him as well. He's a tough hombre. His arms
are six inches longer than his legs, and with this gorilla
build he seldom stacks up against any opponent who's
more than a brief workout for him. No one ever calls him
by his real name of Andrew Blodgett Mayfair. And maybe
they'd better not! There's a ring to it that Monk might not
like! Yet Monk has a keen brain as well as a strong body,
and is reputed to be one of the world's greatest chemists.
His combination of body and brain makes him a big asset
to Doc Savage's intrepid little band of crusaders.

RENNY

If you know him well, you can call him Renny. If you want to be formal, it's Colonel John Renwick. He's a giant of a man. A six-footer would have to look up at him. He weighs well over two hundred, and while he doesn't throw his weight around, he knows how to use it in a fight.

His fists—and they are very big and bony—are very bad on faces. They can actually shatter the solid panel of a heavy door. Renny is an engineer, and tops in his line.

LONG TOM

Major Thomas J. Roberts—Long Tom to his friends—is the electrical wizard of Doc Savage's little group of adventurers. In spite of his nickname, he is not so tall. Doesn't weigh so much, either, and the appearance of his skin gives the impression that he might not be in the best of health.

That skin, however, has been misleading to anybody who ever picked on Long Tom for a set-up. Try taking a cougar's cubs away, but don't ever shove around Long Tom. He's as fast as light, and a terrific socker.

JOHNNY

Few persons would take Johnny—whose real name is William Harper Littlejohn—for a scrapper. He's quite studious. He's an archæologist of worldwide reputation.

Anybody who picked on Johnny, however, would be making quite a big mistake. He can fight like a wounded panther when he's aroused. Like a great many gaunt men, he has an inexhaustible reservoir of strength. He's an important member of Doc Savage's little group.

PAT

Pat Savage is a cousin to the man of bronze. She has Doc's metallic coloring—bronze skin, flake-gold eyes—and is extremely attractive. Pat operates one of New York's most exclusive beauty salons, and constantly yearns for excitement. Though highly capable, her participation in the adventures of Doc and his aids is usually against Doc's wishes, for he believes the work of his group too dangerous for a girl.

Contents

I

THE MAN IN THE MADHOUSE

The mystery got started in a madhouse.

When those involved in the matter later looked back upon it, they realized that, like a storm, the mystery had been gathering for some time before the madhouse incident. The madhouse was simply where the mystery broke loose, roaring and snarling like some black, unstoppable cyclone.

Compared to the institutions for the deranged common in the last century, the Wyndmoor Asylum for the Brain Impaired—situated in a green suburb of Scotland—was a humane establishment. Most of the inhabitants had private rooms. The medieval device called a strait-jacket was seldom resorted to.

The one exception to this rule was confined to a cell-like room where the walls were cushioned with quilted padding to prevent him from inflicting injury upon himself. Mental patients sometimes fell into the distressing habit of repeatedly banging their heads against walls and other solid objects.

There was a name on the door to this cell. A strange name—but very fitting considering the strangeness that was to come. The name was:

X MAN

It was the only name by which the individual—around whom the tremendous mystery revolved—was known. His true identity was a mystery. There was some doubt that he even had a former identity. When asked his name, he had stated, "I am X Man." His voice had been hollow, as if all the life had been sucked out of it.

1

It was noted that in scientific parlance, X stood for the unknown. Thus, X Man might mean an unknown individual. It was as good a name as any.

X Man had been a model patient for a time. Ever since he had been found, wandering and half starved, in the Scottish countryside and declared insane by examining doctors. He had been dressed as a citizen of ancient Rome. While he spoke English after a fashion, he was often overheard talking to himself in a tongue the more learned recognized as Classical Latin.

"Stone daft," as one doctor had put it to another.

"But a nice chap, after all," replied his colleague.

"Certainly not violent."

And so X Man had been committed to Wyndmoor and given a pleasant private room with pretty nurses to attend to his needs. All the nurses in attendance at Wyndmoor were pretty, it being well known that there is nothing like a very snappy-looking young lass to make a depressed man feel like going on living.

On the contrary, the unfortunate lunatic appeared all but oblivious to feminine charms. This was taken as further proof of his mental instability.

The only interest he had shown was to request a number of potted plants to brighten up his room. This he did in acceptable but toneless English.

Upon receiving the potted plants, he had promptly uprooted some and thrown them away. But he had kept others. The empty flowerpots were set on the window sills with the others and within weeks, new plants had begun growing.

No one thought much of this.

One summer's morn, a window had been left open. The smell of breakfast kippers had evidently attracted a stray cat. The cat had leaped onto the sill of X Man's private room. Bars were not considered necessary for the windows of Wyndmoor. The patients—not inmates—were so pampered that escapes were almost unheard of.

As later reconstructed, the strange hollow-faced patient had fled the room screaming that the feline was trying to devour him.

He was found huddled in a utility closet, shivering and whimpering, Fear was in his eyes like whipped kittens.

That was when the strait-jacket had been taken out of storage and the hospital administrator reluctantly unlocked the seldom-used padded room as two burly orderlies dragged the man into it.

The tiny black seeds came to light at this time.

They discovered these in the odd garment that X Man had been wearing since his incarceration. It was a tunic of some sort, white but bordered in gold. X Man had been wearing it when first found by Scottish authorities and had proven so attached to it that he had been allowed to wear it except when the garment required washing. He had had to be wrestled out of the white tunic in order for the strait-jacket to be wrapped around his struggling body.

The orderly who discovered the seeds brought them to the head of the asylum, a Dr. John Gilchrist, who was considered a "guid fellow" in the parlance of his fellow Scotsmen.

"You say these seeds were on his person?" Dr. Gilchrist asked, taking the seeds in his palm.

"Aye, and it was a brawn battle to get him to part with them," the orderly reported.

Dr. Gilchrist examined the seeds. They were so tiny they might have been unusually large grains of pepper. But they were seeds. Dr. Gilchrist, who tended a garden in back of the asylum, was certain of this fact. But the type of seed, and the kind of plant they might produce if allowed to germinate, baffled him.

He was not aware of the plants growing in the flowerpots from which X Man had uprooted other plants.

Dr. Gilchrist brought the seeds with him the next time he looked in on X Man in the padded room he had been so loath to use.

"Has this man been violent?" Dr. Gilchrist asked the nurse who was in charge of this particular floor of the madhouse.

"No," said the nurse, who, in keeping with the policy of such institutions when dealing directly with the dangerously deranged, was a man.

"I would like to speak with X Man," said Dr. Gilchrist.

A large brass key grated the lock mechanism and the door was opened.

X Man lay on a cot, on his back, his eyes fixated on the ceiling, which was the only surface not padded because it was hung twelve feet above the head of even the tallest man.

"Are you up to a chat?" the doctor asked in a coaxing tone.

When no answer was forthcoming, Dr. Gilchrist restated his question in Latin.

The man continued to stare at the ceiling. He was, Dr. Gilchrist reflected, not a hopeless case. At least, so it had appeared until the incident with the tabby cat. Privately, the doctor—he was a psychologist, educated in Edinburgh and Vienna—had wondered if X Man might not be suffering from some form of traumatic amnesia, rather than a delusion. But the man insisted he knew who he was. He was X Man. He had been quite definite on that score.

Beyond that, he offered little enough about himself. He evidenced none of the more common delusions, such as did those patients who had become convinced they were famous individuals such as Napoleon or Oliver Cromwell. There were two Cromwells currently residing in Wyndmoor. The resident Napoleon had succumbed during the Spanish influenza outbreak that had been such a scourge during the Great War.

Dr. Gilchrist had found no historical personage known by the name X Man.

He looked down at the silent man on the cot, studying his features. They were strong and surprisingly dark for a man who had been confined to a madhouse for going on a year now. He seemed not to be a fair-skinned Britisher at all. His eyes were quite black, like olives. And his hair, shorn close to the skull, was intensely black and tended toward masculine curls.

"I understand we had a wee bit of a run-in with a stray cat," Dr. Gilchrist said. X Man continued staring at the ceiling. Dr. Gilchrist passed one hand over the patient's eyes. This technique worked. The man's trance was broken. X Man blinked his deeply black eyes and his gaze sought the doctor's.

"Do you remember the cat?" Dr. Gilchrist asked. "He came to steal your kippers and milk?"

X Man's voice was thin and lifeless, much as it had been when the poor unfortunate had first been brought to Wyndmoor.

"Yes," he said in English. His lean features began to twist.

Dr. Gilchrist smiled. "Good. What else do you recall?"

X Man mumbled, "They said the lord mayor dropped dead when he heard about it."

Dr. Gilchrist blinked wonderingly.

"Those little birds on the ceiling," X Man intoned, pointing with his clefted chin. "One of them can talk. He speaks English and French with a Spanish accent."

Dr. Gilchrist looked up involuntarily, although he knew there would be no linguistic birds on the ceiling. He took a breath.

"And these little birds, what are they saying to you?"

X Man turned his face to the wall. His voice was twisted with anguish. "They—they are begging for their lives. Pleading that the—the cats not—eat—them." He swallowed hard. "I don't want them to eat me, either," he said thinly.

Hearing these words, Dr. Gilchrist let a shudder shake its way down his white-coated body. He understood that for the human mind to remain healthy, such reactions should not be kept in.

When the nervous convulsion had spent itself, the psychologist asked, "Is there anything I can get for you?"

"My plants. My plants will protect me from the cats who want to eat me."

"They will?"

"That is why I grow them. I remember now. Before I —couldn't."

"I see," said Dr. Gilchrist, who did not see at all. In fact, he was quite worried now. In the year X Man had been in his charge, he had shown no tendency to hallucinate. Now he was seeing imaginary birds and was frightened of simple country mousers.

"What else do you remember?"

"I—I remember who I am."

Dr. Gilchrist started. "Indeed! Laddie, who are you then?"

"I dare not tell you."

Dr. Gilchrist frowned. "Why not?"

"Because if Imperator Kizan hears that I am still alive, he will send his cats across the Lake of Smoke to hunt me."

"Kizan? And who is Imperator Kizan?"

"A devil." And it was X Man's turn to shudder. He closed his eyes tightly. The shudder seemed to start at the man's bare toes, work its way up his wiry legs, and shake his torso so mercilessly that the man's head jittered on his shoulders until Dr. Gilchrist was forced to leave the cell. His own shuddering had commenced once more.

That night, Dr. John Gilchrist got out the medical file that was marked with the name X Man and changed the diagnosis of the patient from that of a possible amnesiac to definitely delusional.

It was unfortunate, he reflected grimly. Such patients had a poor prognosis. X Man would probably live out the remainder of his days at Wyndmoor.

As an afterthought, Dr. Gilchrist added the word "ailurophobic" to his notations and put the file away.

The next morning, as instructed, X Man's plants were brought into the padded cell and arranged so that the patient could enjoy their sight and smell, as much as was possible under the circumstances.

It was necessary to loosen the patient's strait-jacket twice a day to insure no harmful loss of blood flow, and that was when the cyclone broke loose irrevocably.

Two orderlies had the task. They went about it with firm gentleness as X Man sat on the edge of his cot, staring rather dazedly at his potted plants.

The door had not been completely closed, and while the attention of the orderlies was focused on the brass snaps that secured the ridiculously long canvas sleeves that wrapped around the patient's body, the door pushed open slightly.

The timing could not have been more unfortunate.

The last snaps had just come free and they were pulling the strait-jacket off the man, as if it were some absurd jersey.

When it at last came loose, X Man noticed the cat.

Judged by its tawny coloration, it was certainly the same tabby that had given X Man his earlier fright. But that incident was nothing compared to the eruption that transpired when the dark-skinned mental patient's eyes fell upon the prowling mouser.

He gave out a long, ripping shriek and with the strength that sometimes comes to madmen, threw off the burly orderlies as if they were children.

X Man came off the cot, his dark face working into gullies of horror.

"Get away! Get away!" he shrieked.

Startled, the tabby leaped straight up into the air and came back down, hackling, arching, hissing, and spitting.

X Man fell upon the potted plants and began hurling them at the cat. The tabby took the hint and whipped out the crack of the open door.

X Man stood watching the door, chest heaving, eyes showing white all around, and was oblivious to the two orderlies coming to their feet directly behind him.

The touch of one meaty hand on his shoulder brought an instant reaction from X Man.

The agitated man was clutching a plant.

X Man whirled and broke the flowerpot—it was of thick orange clay—over one man's head. He went down, falling so as to upset the other.

X Man was out the door while the orderly who had held on to his senses was getting himself organized. The fleeing one hardly paused to scoop up one of the surviving potted plants.

By the time the orderly was out in the white-walled corridor, there was no sign of the escaped man. He started down a likely direction and soon encountered a female nurse who had pressed herself up against a wall and was pointing to a slowly closing door.

"He—he went that way!" she squeaked.

The orderly had had his eye on that particular nurse for some weeks. The notion of impressing her got the better of his judgment. He swaggered over to the door and flung it open.

And a flowerpot crashed down upon his thick skull. The orderly became a tangle of flapping arms and legs rolling down two flights of stone steps.

The unimpressed nurse ran for, she thought, her life.

An alarm was sounded. Instantly, the big institution was full of smooth action.

There were procedures for escapes, but it had been so long since a patient had attempted to flee the idyllic place that was the Wyndmoor Asylum for the Brain Impaired, that the staff was more than a little rusty.

Rooms were searched, as were the spacious and well-manicured grounds. It was quickly established that the grounds were bare of escaped patients.

"He must still be on the premises," concluded Dr. Gilchrist, who had taken over the direction of the search effort. "Search high and low, laddies. Donna stop until he turns up."

The search went on. Every closet and storage space was examined. Patients were locked in their rooms once these had been searched, to foreclose on the possibility that X Man would slip into an already-searched room and thus escape detection.

Gradually, the searching narrowed down to the kitchen and the laundry room, both of which were huge.

In the latter, soiled clothing lay heaped in wheeled carts, awaiting their turns at the very modern washing machines. Orderlies went among these, looking between the cast-iron legs and behind the carts. Hands were plunged into the carts, searchingly, but the odious nature of the task forced the searchers to resort to probing the laundry stacks with broom handles.

When this operation produced no response, they emptied out of the laundry room, locking it after themselves.

Moments later, a pile of clothing lifted and separated —and a black-haired head came into view. Dark eyes searched the surroundings.

Then, unfolding his lean, wiry arms, X Man stepped out, massaging the ribs of his right side. He was clutching a garment, which he pulled on. It was white and bordered in gold and left his legs bare. Tunic was the only appropriate word for the strange garment.

So attired, X Man worked one of the windows open and squeezed through the narrow aperture to the outside.

The asylum grounds were a marvel of shrubbery and hedge rows. It was a simple enough matter for the patient to make his way from one to the other, working his way to the low fieldstone wall that marked the outermost periphery of the hospital.

There, crouching in the lee of the wall, X Man paused to catch his breath. A strange expression crossed his sunken face.

Digging into his exotic garment, his fingers sought an inner pocket. They came away, all but empty. One black and hard speck clung to a fingertip.

It was a seed, so small that even in sunlight, it was difficult to make out its true nature.

Muttering under his breath, X Man dug deeper into his hidden pocket. Finding nothing, he turned it inside out.

A look of profound disappointment came over his features then.

Carefully, so as not to drop it, X Man restored the solitary seed to the secret pocket as if it were a grain of pure gold.

His eyes darted this way and that. They were haunted eyes, full of a dark light.

Had Dr. Gilchrist been able to observe his patient now, he would have been forced to reconsider his most recent diagnosis.

For X Man's eyes were not full of madness, but cunning.

Then he moved on, a fantastic apparition in the Scottish countryside.

II

THE SCOTTISH SPOOK

William Harper Littlejohn was the next man to be sucked into the ravenous cyclone of events.

In many respects, William Harper Littlejohn resembled a tall, gangling scarecrow that might have pulled itself free of its wooden stake and gone shambling off in search of a square meal. He was a long skeleton of an individual, being in the neighborhood of seven feet. William Harper Littlejohn's intimates frequently described him as looking like the advance agent for a famine. He appeared thinner than any human being could be and still go on living.

In the realms of archæology and geology, William Harper Littlejohn was a name to conjure with, a cognomen which was spoken with fitting respect. This was in spite of the distressing fact that when he took the lecture podium to address students, scientists, and other experts, he resembled an empty suit of clothing waiting for its owner to take up habitation within. He wore his hair long, in the fashion of scholars, and on his coat lapel a monocle glittered whenever the gaunt archæologist grew animated in his discourse. He had never been known to wear the eyepiece. As a matter of truth, the monocle was a strong magnifier which was carried thus for convenience. His vision was perfectly sound.

William Harper Littlejohn could hold the most erudite gathering of geologists and archæologists spellbound.

He could also daze a layman with his big words, for William Harper Littlejohn never used a small word when he had time to think of a big one. He was a walking dictionary of words of more than three syllables. Usually, the average person could not understand him.

Renown is a strange thing. Although William Harper

Littlejohn was undisputably tops in his chosen field, most people would not have recognized him for his discoveries in ancient ruins and musty tombs. The common man often found such matters of but passing interest, usually for only as long as it took to read a newspaper item or watch a newsreel.

It was as an associate of Doc Savage that William Harper Littlejohn found his greatest fame, oddly enough.

Doc Savage was a man who was fast becoming famous in the world. Doc—Clark Savage, Jr., to use his full name—was an archæologist of note himself. His discoveries in that area outclassed even those of William Harper Littlejohn. This alone would have made Doc Savage a name for the history books.

In truth, his archæological achievements might have been among Doc Savage's least famous accomplishments. That hinted at what kind of a man was Doc Savage.

When William Harper Littlejohn returned to his London hotel from a late-night lecture session of the Fellowhood of Scientists, the doorman bowed deeply and said, "Good night, Mr. William Harper Littlejohn," and the clerk at the desk said, "No mail for you, Mr. William Harper Littlejohn," while the elevator boy murmured, "Hi 'opes you 'as a pleasant night, Mr. William 'Arper Littlejohn."

When William Harper Littlejohn was in his room, he gave an overstuffed chair a terrific kick, then sat down hastily to massage his tingling foot. He was tired of hearing that name. Everybody in London called him William Harper Littlejohn, adding sometimes an "Honorable" or a "Sir." Sir William Harper Littlejohn particularly irked him, although the title was real, he having been knighted for outstanding accomplishments in his field.

If some one would only call him "Johnny," it would help. But nobody did. Nobody would think of calling such a distinguished scholar by a nickname; not in London, anyway.

London was getting in Johnny's hair. He had been lecturing for several weeks now, and he was fed up.

For days, Johnny had been longing for a good fight.

He had even considered socking a certain eminent archæologist whom he had found to be a bore, just to see what would happen.

Johnny was a strange fellow. He had the make-up of a profound scholar, but he loved excitement. He liked a fight better than the most pugilistic dock worker in London's East End, and despite his emaciated appearance, could hold his own in a scrap with the toughest of these gentry. Johnny's body make-up was deceiving.

This love of adventure was another quality that Johnny had in common with Doc Savage.

Doc Savage had cabled Johnny that he intended to visit in London, and Johnny's hopes for action had arisen, only to subside when he learned Doc's visit was of a scientific nature. Doc was also going to lecture before the Fellowhood of Scientists, which was one of the greatest organizations of learned men in existence.

Johnny was the geology-archæology expert in Doc Savage's group of five assistants. Johnny was associated with Doc Savage for two reasons—he loved excitement, and there was usually plenty of that around Doc; and there was something about Doc Savage that commanded allegiance. Doc was the sort of being at whom one never ceased to marvel. Johnny, who was a mental Hercules himself, considered Doc Savage a mental wizard.

Disgusted, Johnny picked up the evening paper. He had read an item about Doc Savage's imminent arrival at Croydon Air Field, then turned to other stories.

He found the London paper as dry as his unsatisfactory day had been. Most of the front page was devoted to the effects of what was being dubbed the "American business slump" on Europe.

Finally, one particular yarn seized his attention.

Johnny reread the bit several times. It was short and contained only bare details:

"X MAN" ESCAPES SANITARIUM

The baffling escape of a patient from the renowned Wyndmoor Asylum for the Brain Impaired this day has laid bare a greater mystery—the identity of the escaped madman who was known to the staff only as "X Man."

Dr. John Gilchrist, in charge of the sanitarium, internationally celebrated for its humane treatment of the lunatics housed behind its cheerful walls, declared to police that he had no inkling of the true name of the mysterious patient, who had been under his care for nearly a year.

Readers of this newspaper will easily recall the commotion that attended the discovery late last year of a man, outlandishly attired in the tunic of a Roman of Cæsar's day, found by constables wandering the ruins of the Roman Legionary Fortress at Stirling and reciting, in Classical Latin, the famous speech given by Marc Antony in the third act of Shakespeare's famed play "The Tragedy of Julius Cæsar."

Taken to the Wyndmoor Asylum, the man professed no recollection of his past and was determined by the staff to be suffering from some hitherto-unknown form of dementia. Of only one fact did this fellow seem certain: that his name was "X Man."

In the absence of a proper name, the hospital staff accepted this curious appellation.

According to Dr. Gilchrist, X Man passed his days in apparent contentment, showing little interest in life outside the asylum except to pass his days engaged in the growing of certain plants, which he cultivated with great care.

This tranquil existence was disrupted by the appearance of a common tabby cat who, it is believed, attracted by the fragrance of a breakfast consisting of kippers, entered X Man's private room, severely upsetting the patient's mental equilibrium.

Upon being committed to a cell, the unfortunate became violently disposed and escaped at the first opportunity that presented itself.

The local constabulary is putting forth strenuous efforts to locate X Man and restore him to the asylum. He is not considered dangerous, but all persons in the locality are advised to take precautions against forcible entry of their domiciles, for it is certain that the escaped madman will seek out food where he can.

* * *

Johnny consulted an expensive watch which had been presented to him by the graduating class of a famous United States university in which he had once held a chair of Natural Science Research. It was nearly midnight.

One of Johnny's thin hands drifted for the telephone. Doc Savage was not due in London until the following afternoon. The urge to do something, to do anything, had seized the bony archæologist. He had his fill of dry scientific lectures.

"Apprise me of the most linear path to the principality of Stirling," he advised the front desk.

"I beg your pardon, sir. May I assist you?"

Frowning, Johnny recast his statement in more colloquial English.

"Stirling, Scotland. I would like to go there."

"To-night?"

"Immediately," Johnny said.

"At this late hour, sir, I believe a motor coach from Victoria Station is your only hope."

"Summon a hack."

"Beg pardon?"

"A taxicab."

"At once, sir."

Johnny was out of his hotel room less than a minute later. He took only the clipping relating the events of the lunatic X Man's escape, which he violently tore from the newspaper and stuffed into a special padded pocket of his coat where he was wont to secrete his monocle magnifier when there was danger of it being broken.

Victoria Station is to the heart of London what Grand Central Station is to New York City. It is the crossroads of the city, from which a traveler might make the proper connections by motor coach or passenger train to any point on the verdant isle that was England.

The motor coach to Stirling was of the double-decker variety, red as the coats of the Beefeater guardsmen who inhabit Buckingham Palace, and, as the hour was late, there were few passengers. Johnny Littlejohn had the upper deck entirely to himself.

Ordinarily, the disappearance of a mental patient from an asylum would not have been sufficient to stir a hair on the bony geologist's shaggy head, but the fact that the individual known only as X Man had first been found in a Roman ruin, attired as if for the Roman senate, had piqued Johnny's curiosity.

The Romans, Johnny knew, had conquered the isle of Britannia in the days following Cæsar and the Roman republic. That was in 81 A.D.—many centuries ago. The last of the Romans had departed over four hundred years ago, and if there were any left they were more likely to be engaged in the running of spaghetti houses than in addressing a long-buried senate.

Still, it was a mystery. If nothing more, Johnny hoped to help return the unfortunate X Man to his proper place.

As he watched the sleepy thatched cottages of the London suburbs go marching past, the lanky archæologist had no way of knowing it, but he was destined to restore the man he sought to his proper place in the world. But that place was not the Wyndmoor Asylum for the Brain Impaired. In fact, it was not anywhere on the damp island whose name had come down from the Roman word "Britannia."

But before he could accomplish that, Johnny Littlejohn had to wade his long legs through a cyclone of violence and death.

Having no inkling of what lay in store for him, the gaunt geologist dozed off as the motor coach rumbled along in the night.

The cry "Last stop, Govn'r!" roused Johnny Littlejohn. He came awake, blinking his eyes.

"Is this Stirling?" he remarked.

"Righto."

"Thank you," said Johnny, clambering down the gangway stairs to the lower deck, stooping in order to exit the machine.

The station was barely that. A tiny structure with a thatched roof no different from those decorating the cottages of the Scottish countryside. Testing the door, Johnny found it locked.

The driver was closing up his bus. Johnny accosted him.

"Is there somewhere I can hire a taxi?" he asked, using small words because he was impatient to be on his way.

"Not at this hour," he was told.

"Point me in the direction of Wyndmoor Asylum."

"Wyndmoor? That would be northerly, as the crow flies."

Johnny thanked the man and set off at a brisk, long-legged stride.

As it turned out, Scottish crows do not fly in particularly undeviating lines. At least, Johnny was forced to walk around hills and once a body of water that was probably a loch—as the Scots call their lakes.

Beyond the loch, Johnny came to the Roman ruin, as he knew he would. Johnny knew Roman Britain better than he knew the modern version.

There he paused. Not because he needed rest—the contrary. Although he gave the appearance of a scholar, his endurance was legendary. Had there been no other way, it was conceivable that the skeleton-thin archæologist could have made the long trek from London to Stirling on foot, stopping only for nourishment—and not often for that purpose, either.

Johnny Littlejohn had another reason for loitering at the dilapidated ruin. He was, in his way, something of a psychologist.

The escaped patient who might or might not be a lunatic had been found in this very ruin. It was conceivable that the first thing he might do upon escaping from a year-long confinement would be to return to this very spot.

As he tramped about the forlorn remnants of the northernmost point of Roman Caledonia—a worn-down line of building foundations overgrown by rhododendron bushes and fragrant purple heather—Johnny hunted signs of recent encampment.

He was rewarded when the smell of charred wood brought him to a loose pile of dirt. Knocking this mound apart, he uncovered fragments of burned twigs and the unmistakable signs of a hare which had furnished some one a recent meal.

Johnny reburied the half-eaten hare with a shod foot and continued his search.

"Crepusculescence is imminently millennial," he murmured.

Which, had there been anyone with a dictionary to overhear, meant that it lacked but a few hours to sunrise. Two hours without light. But also two hours in which he was unlikely to meet interference. If the local constabulary was still engaged in hunting the escaped X Man, they were likely to be fast asleep, their search put off until first light.

Johnny took a chance and from a coat pocket extracted a tiny spring-generator flashlight he habitually carried. He gave it a wind and thumbed on the light.

An exceedingly bright thread of illumination sprang out, creating angular shadows in the old Roman fort. Holding the beam close to the ground, Johnny continued his search.

Scuffings of feet came to light. Johnny paused, determined their likely direction, and picked up the trail.

The moon came out from under a cloud, shedding additional light.

He came upon the sleeping figure quite unexpectedly.

Instantly, the lanky archæologist doused the light. He held his breath. He had luck. The sleeping figure had not been awakened by the light.

Cupping a bony hand over the lense, Johnny turned on the light once more. His hand glowed like a tiny basket of bones with a burning coal in it.

The crimson glow shed sufficient light to show the man's features. But Johnny's eyes barely flicked over these. He was looking at the garment that barely served as covering for the slumbering man's long form.

"I'll be superamalgamated!" Johnny exploded.

He couldn't help himself. The garment had that effect on him. The oath—or what passed for an oath in the long-worded archæologist's vocabulary of jaw-breakers—jumped out of him before he could stifle the ejaculation.

The figure in the gold-and-white tunic catapulted from his slumber as if propelled by springs.

He leaped up, in the darkness seizing on the only

source of light—the warm glow of Johnny's nearly fleshless hand.

"Wait!" Johnny bleated, surprise getting the better of his defensive instincts.

But there was no waiting. The man in the tunic began flailing away. Johnny's hands were both wrapped around his flash, so his chin was unprotected.

A solid blow glanced off the point of the bony archæologist's jaw, rocking him backward. He let go of the flash lense then—and the intensely white light splashed into his eyes.

Johnny kept his feet, but he had to stumble backward nearly three yards before he got his daddy-longlegs lower limbs untangled.

By that time, the strange figure was running low, dodging amid the ruins.

"Wait!" Johnny called.

The figure continued to weave and run.

On a hunch, Johnny called out again.

"Siste, viator!"

This had a marked effect. The figure abruptly stopped, wheeled, and made a watchful shape in the darkness.

Excitement rising in his throat, Johnny called again.

"Homo X es?"

"Metho Regulus sum! Quis es?"

Before the gaunt archæologist could answer, the sound of an automobile bouncing and rattling along deep ruts disturbed the night.

Johnny turned—and the blaze of automobile headlamps smote his gaze.

Throwing a bony arm across his eyes, he shrank from the too-bright illumination. Muttering unscholarly imprecations, Johnny proceeded to blink his vision back to normalcy.

When the spots in his eyes were no longer as big as planets, he scanned the heather where the tunic-clad figure had fled.

There was no sign of the man. Johnny started to follow, his flashlight coming on. He was fast. But the other had too much of a head start.

Dejectedly, Johnny trudged back to the automobile, which had stopped where the dirt road had petered out.

A man approached. For a moment Johnny's hopes rose, for the man's silhouette was not unlike that of the fleeing man who had worn the gold-and-white tunic.

This new arrival was not wearing a tunic, however. It was a kilt. He helped himself along with a gnarled thornwood walking stick that an Irishman would have called a shillalah. He might have been a sleepless local out for a nocturnal ramble.

"And what would ye be doing out on the heather at this hour, my guid fellow?" the kilted one called in a thick burr.

"My name is William Harper Littlejohn," said Johnny, panting a little from excitement. "I wonder if you could—"

"Littlejohn!" the other exploded. "Not the Professor Littlejohn who is an associate of Doc Savage?"

"Yes," Johnny said excitedly.

"Be ye looking for that escaped lunatic they're calling X Man?"

"Unquestionably," said Johnny, thinking that perhaps he could talk the Scotsman into the loan of his auto.

The thought stayed in his excited brain long enough for the shadowy Scot to clump up and brain Johnny with the thick end of his upraised walking stick. Johnny fell.

"Damn ye for sticking your nose where it don't belong," said the Scotsman, his burr dwindling to a faint growl. "Now I have to take care of ye, too."

Among other things, William Harper Littlejohn was remarkably hard-headed. He was not entirely knocked out. His struggles, however, were feeble.

So for good measure, the Scot laid the thick end of his walking stick against the side of the squirming archæologist's head, aiming for a forehead vein which pulsed threadily.

Johnny's long form relaxed completely, and the man stooped and gathered up the long-limbed archæologist, throwing him over his shoulder as if he were a loose sack of salt.

Walking stick in hand, the Scotsman hiked back to his waiting auto.

When he entered the glare of his own headlights, his face became washed by the electric glow. It was a wide face, made wider by a fringe of muttonchop whiskers.

From a low hiding place, a white-clad figure lifted up his head curiously. Eyes the color of black olives took in the sight of a rough profile and grim lips parted to hiss a single word:

"Brutus."

He might have been been speaking the other's name. If it was, the man in the kilt failed to register it.

Depositing Johnny Littlejohn in the rear seat of a touring car, the kilted one then got behind the wheel and sent the machine jouncing back along the unpaved road.

When he reached the point where there was room to turn the machine around, he sent the car in a circle. Then, gathering speed, the auto raced away.

But not before a figure, moving low so as not to be seen, caught up with the boot and, after a running leap, attached himself to the tire carrier.

The night swallowed the touring car and the clinging passenger who called himself X Man.

III

"NOVUM EBORACUM"

A person unfamiliar with William Harper Littlejohn's history with the tiny coterie that comprised Doc Savage's band of adventurers might have been forgiven for thinking the gaunt archæologist suffered from a brittle constitution. Johnny was wonderfully bony, and this very quality caused many a rogue to mistake him for a pushover.

Johnny had been knocked on the head twice. Once is usually sufficient to put an ordinary man out for the better part of a day.

But it was less than forty minutes since the lanky archæologist had experienced the concussion that had laid him low. Forty minutes and already his eyelids were fluttering.

When they opened, Johnny calmly took stock of his surroundings. He lay on the floorboards of a moving auto. It ran, Johnny decided, with the smoothness of a twelve-cylinder motor. He made a mental note of this.

The road was paved and the shocks good, because there was little enough bumping to their progress.

Which was fortunate, Johnny discovered when he lifted his head. It throbbed, the throbbing growing in intensity until it blossomed into a splitting headache.

Johnny stifled a low groan, pushing it deep into his dry throat. The sponge in his mouth aided his efforts.

When he had gotten the agony under control, he tried movement again. His hands were bound behind his back, although his legs felt unrestrained. There was a distressing rubberiness about the knees, however.

Careful not to make any betraying sound, the bony archæologist endeavored to poke his head up to the level of the rear passenger window.

He succeeded—although the effort came at the cost of gritted teeth and infinite pain deep in his long skull.

Through the window, the somewhat spectral tableau of the Scottish night met to his bleary eyes. There was a full moon, and it washed the moors until they shone like silver. Lochs marched by, an amazing number of them. They resembled a scattering of mirrors under the cold moon glow.

Balancing on his knees, Johnny set his chin on the door handle, testing its give. He was too weak to force it up, and the door open.

The speed of the auto argued for the wisdom of not leaping from the door, even if it could be opened.

Johnny settled for watching intently. He hoped to recognize landmarks, and ascertain his whereabouts.

The automobile traveled rapidly for a long time. Catching sight of a grillework of girders on either side at one time, William Harper Littlejohn knew that he had crossed a river or narrow loch. He mentally computed the time it took to cross the span.

At least the last ten minutes of the journey was through sparsely settled country, and the very tail end of the trip over a road that was unpaved, rough. The car stopped and Johnny slipped back to the floorboards to feign unconsciousness. His ears were very alert, however.

The driver got out, after which came the loud grating of rusty hinges that told an iron gate was being opened. The driver returned and they rode into what seemed to be a modest estate, as Johnny discovered when the machine rolled to a halt and the driver got out again to yank open the door before Johnny's surprised face.

"Awake, eh?" the man gritted.

"Mumph—"

Whatever words Johnny might have spoken, they never got past the dryish sponge in his mouth. A blindfold was quickly snapped over his eyes—but not before the archæologist caught a brief glimpse of a sizable stone house and beyond it a body of moonlit water.

The kilted abductor laid rough hands on Johnny's skeletal form and lifted him out of the auto.

To Johnny's ears came the gritting of shoes on gravel, the distinctive clatter of a door being unlocked, and then the air became cooler and a trifle damp. Johnny had the sensation of being in an enclosed space.

When he was set down, it was not on a floor or a cot, but in a musty box of some sort that was not long enough for his elongated form.

The sponge was yanked from his mouth with such suddenness, he wondered about his front teeth. His searching tongue brought assurances of their intactness.

"What is the meaning of this?" Johnny demanded.

"Shut up!" the voice of his captor snarled. "I will ask the questions here."

"I would like to know who I am addressing," Johnny said, sullen-voiced.

The blindfold was whipped from his eyes. Johnny found himself almost nose to nose with his captor.

The man possessed the meaty girth of a side of beef. His hide was like dried meat—tobacco-colored and almost devoid of health. His face was that way too. Except for the eyes. They were very much alive and they glittered.

His muttonchop whiskers would have seemed profusely comical had it not been for those unpleasant orbs. They gave the man the aspect of a ferocious, angry hedgehog.

Johnny looked away—and his eyes came to rest on an upright shape he recognized. It was of wood, but bore a face that stared at him with painted eyes. An ancient sarcophagus.

Johnny had taken no more authentic specimen from the tombs of Egyptian pharaohs. These cases had usually held mummies. William Harper Littlejohn had never been particularly enthusiastic about mummies. In fact, he considered them the most horrible, macabre things with which he was acquainted.

Then he remembered the malodorous box in which he had been deposited.

"Am I in a—coffin?" he gulped, coming erect in his horror.

"I told ye that I ask the bleeding questions here!" the man resembling beef jerky snapped.

Johnny was smacked in the nose for his pains, and fell back, half blinded with anguish.

"Ye should be proud, Professor Littlejohn," the man said. "The last occupant of that box inhabited it for two thousand years."

That seemed to confirm the gaunt archæologist's worst suspicions—that he had been laid out in a sarcophagus.

"I demand to know what is the meaning of this abduction!" Johnny shouted.

"Where does Doc Savage come off mixing into my business?" the other shot back.

"I do not know what you are talking about."

A heavy hiking shoe lashed out and punished the row of ribs along one of Johnny's sides.

"Talk!"

"You are mistaken," Johnny bit out.

The man grew incensed and reached down to take Johnny by his coat lapel. One thumb snagged the black ribbon that anchored his monocle magnifier to the lapel. The magnifier came out of the padded pocket where Johnny was wont to stow the eyepiece at times when he feared for its fragility, along with a folded newspaper cutting.

The man dropped Johnny with a hollow thud. He picked the cutting open with eager fingers. His glittery eyes narrowed as they read along, then returned to Johnny's face.

"Mistaken, am I?" he snarled.

Johnny was kicked again, was directed, "Spill!"

"Hell with you!" Johnny exploded.

"Ye know what X Man really is, don't ye?"

Johnny said nothing.

The other shoved his jaw out. "Of course, ye'd be the one to show up first. Ye know where X Man comes from, too. Ye've figured it out, blast ye! Ye want him to guide you through the Veil of Silence so that your name will go down in history. Well, I've thwarted that little scheme, now, haven't I? It will be a fine day indeed when that comes to pass, let me tell ye! It will be my name that schoolchildren will be memorizin' thousands of years from to-day!"

William Harper Littlejohn was an interested listener to all of this. Not only was he interested, but he was vastly puzzled. The man seemed a little addled in his ravings. Perhaps he, too, was an escaped lunatic.

The man ruminated onward. "To step through the mists of time, to see how great civilizations existed when they were young. This has been the dream since mankind first pondered its past. And I—I alone—have accomplished this. No other will steal the glory from me. Not even ye, Professor Littlejohn. Ye hear me?"

The man gave the box in which Johnny lay a swift kick. Then he resumed his pacing, muttering darkly of long-ago times.

Listening, Johnny lay there and wondered what it all meant. He had an agile brain and he put it through its best paces. The net result of his cogitation was a disgusting zero.

Johnny was utterly baffled.

"Somehow, Savage has figured out the whole thing," the man was saying in a bitter, distracted voice.

Johnny's eyes sought the room. Off in one corner he saw a case which held a tablet covered with hieroglyphics. There were shadowy faces on the wall. They were not Egyptian, but of a character infinitely more barabaric.

"Or maybe—" The man's voice sank into thoughtfulness. His entire demeanor changed then. His glittery eyes grew crafty. "Or maybe Savage ain't wise at all. Maybe it's just ye. Maybe—"

Johnny had faced death before. Many times, in fact. He saw cold murder in the dark eyes of the man now.

Abruptly, the man turned on his heel and went to a door. Flinging it open, he tramped up a flight of creaky wooden steps.

Johnny knew he would not be long. He had gone to get some instrument for inflicting death—whether a gun, knife, or other he did not know, nor did he care.

The bony archæologist understood only that his best hope lay in quick action. His feet were still free, and he endeavored to gain them.

It was no simple task. Johnny was agile for all his

gangling length, but he was still weak from the double blow to his head and the punishment inflicted on the rest of him.

He squirmed on the dirt floor of the cramped space that seemed to have once been a root cellar, but that now was given over to a display of artifacts that could not be real, unless they were priceless.

Then, the rasp of a hasp came. Johnny started. A door, evidently to the house above, stood ajar. But there was no one there. The bony archæologist rotated his head and zeroed in on the sound, which repeated.

Johnny saw the door then. Small, and closed by a hasp arrangement. There was no padlock. Someone was trying to enter—enter furtively.

Playing a hunch, Johnny redoubled his efforts. He found to his feet, swayed. Nausea came to his stomach and water to his eyes.

Then he stumbled over to the door and, turning about, found the hasp with the fingers of his bound hands. He pulled. The effort landed him on his face. He rolled, bringing his long feet up to defend himself, if need be.

Johnny Littlejohn found himself staring up at the strange figure he had earlier encountered—the escaped lunatic, X Man.

There was nothing lunatic in the man's olive-hued eyes. A finger lifted to the figure's lips, admonishing silence.

Johnny, scarce believing his own optics, complied.

X Man fell upon him and picked at his bonds.

"Too strong." The man's voice was hollow.

"Clasp knife in my coat," Johnny hissed.

The man reached in and pulled out the knife. He seemed not to know what to do with it at first. His eyes were doubtful.

"Pull open the blade!" Johnny hissed.

The man, after some fumbling, succeeded. The blade was superlatively sharp. X Man had only to touch it to the hemp and the strands began parting.

Johnny did the rest. His long, bony frame concealed stringy muscles that were immensely powerful. He burst his bonds and came to his feet.

"We must escape Brutus," X Man undertoned.

"Brutus?"

"The freeman who captured you. My enemy."

Johnny blinked. A freeman, he knew, was the name given to a citizen of Imperial Rome. Then he remembered that this man had escaped from a madhouse.

"Why are you helping me?" Johnny demanded.

"You speak the tongue of my people, even though you are an outlander."

"People?"

"Yes. I must return to them. You will help me?"

"How?"

"You understand how to make the chariot that does not need horses go?"

Johnny blinked. Then it came to him. "The car?"

"Yes."

"I can."

"You will go where I tell you?"

"Where?"

"Novum Eboracum."

This time Johnny's long jaw dropped as if his cheek muscles had been severed.

"Novum Eboracum?"

"Yes, it is there that I come from. I must return, for time is running short. The Veil of Silence is thinning and soon the Black Ones will—"

A sound cut off the man's words.

Johnny wheeled.

At the door, the kilted abductor stood framed. There was a dagger in his hand. It looked like an ornamental Scottish dagger.

He brought the blade up and started forward.

X Man hissed, "Brutus!"

"Damn ye!" he cried. "Why did ye not stay in that asylum, where ye belonged!"

X Man was quicker. He let fly with Johnny's clasp knife and the blade buried itself in the thick portion of the man's exposed thigh.

Brutus gave a horrible shriek, and began hopping in place.

"Come!" X Man shouted, pulling Johnny along.

"Hold on," Johnny said. "I want to get to the bottom of this."

"There is no time! The waters are cooling on the Lake of Smoke. If I do not return, Princess Namora may be sacrificed next."

Johnny paid the man's raving no heed. He started for the man in the kilt who had been called Brutus.

It was a mistake. For all his hulking appearance, the muttonchop-whiskered Brutus possessed speed. He reached down and with a grunt, yanked the clasp knife from his leg. Crimson flowed.

Johnny moved in to take the weapon from him. Blows were struck. They made meaty smacking sounds.

Ordinarily, the bony archæologist was the equal to almost any man in a fight. But not after the damage that had been inflicted on him.

"Lend a hand!" Johnny shouted over his shoulder.

There came no response. As the tussle moved him about the strange root cellar, Johnny caught a glimpse of the open door that led outside.

There was no one there. X Man had run off.

The sight did more than dishearten the fighting archæologist; it cost him the battle. In the moment when his attention was focused elsewhere, a brown fist came up and rapped the point of his chin.

Johnny Littlejohn's teeth came together with the dry click of a skeleton snapping shut his jaws. A sigh leaked out from between them.

Then, knees buckling in opposite directions, the bony archæologist sank to the floor.

His conqueror stepped over him, muttering, "I'll settle ye after I'm done with that bleedin' toff."

IV

THE MAN OF MYSTERY

London's Croydon Air Field attracts passengers from all over the globe. Men of distinction alight into its bustle with monotonous regularity, for Croydon is the chief stopping point between America and the Continent—as certain people insist upon calling greater Europe—for the flying public.

To-day, there was more bustle at Croydon than usual. The commotion took the form of representatives of Fleet Street, the catch-all name that has come to describe the London press as a class.

The press milled about the tarmac, eyes searching the western sky. All afternoon long they had been waiting, and although it was a good summery day for London—plenty of sunshine and none of the relentless damp and fog that blights life in the staid city—the waiting journalists were growing impatient with the grim monotony of their task.

Just when they were at their most subdued, the throaty drone of an airplane would fill the air and the pressmen abruptly snapped into life, throwing off listless attitudes and stamping out cigarettes underfoot.

"Zounds!" one grumbled. "This 'ad better be the bloke, now."

"To be sure," added another.

An elderly passenger who had just deplaned chanced to overhear this remark and, intrigued by the sudden life that had come into the assembled press, walked up to one reporter to ask, "Is the King expected?"

The reporter, one eye on the blue sky, grunted out a sound too coarse to be a laugh and said, "Bigger than the bloomin' King, I'd say."

"Is that so? And who would be bigger than the King of England, if a body might inquire?"

"Doc Savage," snapped the reporter. "That's who."

This statement set wrinkles gathering around the elderly air traveler's mouth. "In my day, the only recognition a doctor got was when a patient decided to pay his bill," he quavered.

The scribe turned and said, "Is it possible you have not heard of Doc Savage?"

"Not until just now."

"I *am* surprised!"

"If you knew the kind of a place I've been in the last ten years, you wouldn't be."

The reporter finished stubbing out his discarded cigarette on the warm tarmac. "In hell, my dear fellow, they know about Doc Savage. And just about every other place, hot or cold. He is perhaps the most famous of living men."

"You do not say," the elderly man said thinly.

"In fact, Doc Savage is probably the most amazing chap of all time," the reporter added expansively.

"I do not understand," the elderly gent said. "What has he done?"

"A great many things. You name it, Doc Savage has done it. And you say you've not heard of him, eh?"

"No."

The reporter expanded his chest and grew enthusiastic about his subject.

"Doc Savage is a very powerful man," he explained. "His muscular strength is said to be among the greatest in the world. Big fellow, a physical freak, almost."

"I see. Another Sandow."

"Not a bit of it!" the journalist retorted. "Doc Savage is not what you would call a *professional* strongman. He has a brain even more remarkable than his body. They claim he's what you might call a mental wizard. Does some surprising things with his wits. He is a scientific product, according to stories I hear. He has been trained from childhood for his career of helping others out of trouble. That is his profession. His parents, remarkable people, decided at his birth to make him what he is. The greatest men in such professions as chemistry, engineering, electricity, medicine, surgery, contributed to his training, so that today he is a nearly unbelievable combination of knowledge and muscular—"

"Pardon me, old top," interrupted the elderly listener. "But I do not think I quite caught the part about this Doctor Savage's profession."

"Why, that's what makes him so famous. Savage is in truth a doctor; the man is responsible for some of the greatest surgical discoveries in use today. But his chief claim to fame is that he helps people who need it. People in trouble."

"But how does he make that pay off?" the elderly man asked, his fading eyes scanning the patch of sky from whence came the motor drone that had drawn the gazes of the restless contingent of reporters.

It had proven to be a mail plane. Their watchfulness subsided. Fresh cigarettes were set alight.

"No one seems to know," replied the talkative reporter. "They say the bronze man is very wealthy. And his aids are also wealthy men."

"Aids?"

"Five men, experts in five different professions, who help him. They are probably with him on the plane. Look! Here it comes now!"

The old man's entire face bunched up in puckery wrinkles. There was a dot in the western sky, sure enough, but no engine rumble. Only after a moment did a sound reach their ears—a shrill hissing unlike that of any airplane engine imaginable.

Soon, the dot developed wings and showed itself to be an aircraft. A tri-motor, but of unique design.

"My eyes aren't what they once were," the old man complained. "How can you tell this is that Savage fellow's plane?"

"It's bronze. See? They call Doc Savage the Man of Bronze. So that must be his plane."

As the subdued sound of three synchronized engines came closer, the elderly man finally made out the bronze shape of the downward-slanting plane. It was an amphibian, broad of wing and evidently an æronautical marvel. Two streamlined engines were set in the great wing and a third was mounted between them, on a pylon over the wing, and back of the cockpit.

Flashbulbs popped. Photographic plates were hastily swapped in and out of big cameras.

Abruptly, the elderly man swallowed hard and began to slink away.

The talkative reporter noticed this and asked, "You mean to tell me, old dear, you aren't going to stay for a glimpse of Doc Savage, the most famous bloke in all the jolly world?"

"Decidedly not," said the elderly man in a dismal croak.

"And why not?"

"Recall I told you I had been away for ten years?"

"I do."

"I have been in a South African prison, over a little misunderstanding the authorities chanced to call embezzlement, and from what you say of this Doc Savage, I do not think he is the sort who would look favorably upon a man of my background."

At that, the elderly man betook himself away.

Shrugging, the reporter redirected his attention to the approaching bronze plane. It was coming in for a landing now.

Air wheels cranked down from the smooth, boat-shaped hull preparatory to landing. The silence of the great engines was remarkable, even at close range.

It was a transatlantic job. There was no doubt about it.

And the hand at the control wheel was practiced. The plump wheels kissed the tarmac, and held it as if magnetized. The great æronautical marvel failed to bounce once.

Engines ticking over, the air giant rolled to a confident stop.

The representatives of Fleet Street received a welcome, if unexpected, break. The pilot was guiding the tri-motor in their direction.

"A break for us, wot?" exclaimed one.

"Odd," murmured another. "I have heard the bronze man does not go in for publicity, ordinarily."

"Perhaps he has not seen us," offered a third.

The second scribe—the one who knew a lot about Doc Savage—looked about. If the pilot had not noticed the pack of jostling newsmen, his eyes were bad and his license ought to be pulled, he decided.

At last the craft came to a jolting stop and the reporters, respectful of the great turning propellers, waited for them to snap into quiescence before the rush for the sliding hull door commenced.

They arrayed themselves about the door. A few shutterbugs snapped photos of the sleek marvel of a tri-motor. It was painted a solid bronze color—a certain indication of Doc Savage's ownership.

So when, a few moments later, the sliding door rolled open and a towering figure appeared in the hatchway, flashbulbs splashed light before anyone stopped to ascertain the identity of the man in the plane.

The blinding bulbs illuminated a fantastic human hulk of a figure.

He was gigantic. There was no question of that. His head, square around the jaw and coming to a bulletlike peak, grazed the top of the hatch. Even then, he was not as huge so much as he was outsized. There was hair on the back of his hands—bright red hair—but none on his head.

Freckles paraded across his rather bovine physiognomy, seeming to avoid his flaring nostrils. The press had cause to note those generous nostrils a moment later.

As the flashbulbs continued to pop, the hulking figure loitered at the open hatch, blowing smoke from first one nostril, and then the other.

Source of the smoke was a long cigar clamped between strong white teeth.

But now his mouth opened and his cigar fell into his hand, which was conveniently waiting. He juggled the hot end of the cigar away from his palm, twirling it smartly in a technique a Wild West gunfighter would have called a road agent's spin. Then he demonstrated the border transfer, passing the cigar back and forth between his hands.

This feat of legerdemain held the press momentarily speechless. Then one scribe found his tongue.

"I say, are you Doc Savage?" he asked doubtfully.

The big fellow flipped the cigar upward, catching it in his mouth. He chewed his stogie amiably and nodded acquiescence.

His shirt was open at the throat and the triangle of chest that lay exposed seemed to have caught fire from a fugitive cigar ash. Closer examination showed that the fiery material was simply more of the too-red hair that furred the giant's hands. Both pockets of the shirt were stuffed with fat cigars.

"He is not!" another journalist exploded.

The giant spoke up.

"Am so," he said. His voice was a coarse whisper.

"Blather," sniffed another. "Doc Savage is a handsome chap, whose skin is bronze as a blinkin' statue."

The huge whispering giant seemed incapable of shouting—instead he made a sound like steam escaping.

"You sayin' I ain't?"

"You do not fit the description."

"I just landed his plane, didn't I?"

This was a good point, and it caused the assembled journalists to scratch their heads, both figuratively and literally.

"I know!" exploded one scribe. "The bloke must be Monk Mayfair, the chemist of Savage's jolly band."

"Right," chimed in another. "Mayfair has red hair, as I hear it." The newsman called up. "Is that so? Are you Andrew Blodgett Mayfair?"

The bald giant blinked, opened his mouth, closed it absently, and scratched in the red fur at the open neck of his shirt.

"Nope," he said.

"Perhaps he is Renwick, the engineer. I understand he is a rather imposing lad."

"Wrong again," said the furry giant.

"You aren't Long Tom, the electrical wizard," he was told. "Long Tom is a thin, poorly-looking fellow. And you aren't Johnny, the archæologist, nor Ham, the solicitor. Just who are you then?"

"I told you: Doc Savage." The man clamped his cigar back between his very white teeth and his lips peeled back in a welcoming grin. "Who wants to interview me for starters?"

A man raised a copy pencil eagerly. Another pushed it down angrily, saying, "Do not be a fool. That is not Doc Savage. He is notoriously chary of the press."

"Maybe I've changed my ways," the giant who called himself Doc Savage said huskily. He kicked a set of folding steps at his feet and they locked into place. He started down. The steps groaned audibly under his weight.

"I'll take you one at a time or all at once," he announced. "What'll it be, gents?"

The press hesitated. The skepticism on their faces darkened to open hostility.

"You ought to be arrested, my good man," a reporter said indignantly.

"For what?" the cigar-smoking individual asked innocently. He possessed bright blue eyes, and they twinkled merrily.

"For impersonating one of the greatest men since Richard the Lion-Hearted, that is what!"

"Richard the Lion-Hearted," the bald one mused, his face screwing up in pleasure. "I kinda like that. Will you put that in the story when you write me up?"

"We are not writing you up, you-you unmitigated glory-seeking fraud! Come on, lads, let's be off. Doc Savage—the true Doc Savage—is bound to arrive any moment now."

The press fell back from the great tri-motor. Some threw their undeveloped photographic plates away, which broke on the tarmac with sounds like plate glass shattering.

None looked back at that moment. Which was fortunate. For out from between the legs of the unlovely apparition who had claimed the name and fame of Doc Savage, scooted an equally unlovely creature.

With a speed belying his hulking lines, the bald giant bent at the waist and scooped up the squealing animal, tucking it under one muscular arm. Then, with a silence that was eerie, he withdrew into the plane's curtained confines.

A squeaky voice asked, "It worked, huh?"

"So it would seem," returned the hulking bald giant in

a voice that was markedly different from the husky whisper he had been affecting. The voice was deep, cultured, and remarkably toned. It had also a compelling power that did not fit the giant's happy-go-lucky personality.

"No thanks to you, you homely gossoon!" a snappish voice snarled. "Your fool hog almost gave the entire imposture away."

"You leave my hog alone, you ambulance chaser!"

"It might be advisable," interposed the rough giant with the well-modulated voice, "to lower your voices. The representatives of the press might overhear."

Instantly, the quarrelsome pair ceased their arguing. They were an odd duo. The possessor of the childlike voice was a squat, apish man who reached out long, hairy arms to accept the offered animal.

Intimates knew him as Monk, but his stationery was headed by the impressive-sounding name "Lieutenant Colonel Andrew Blodgett Mayfair." He was an industrial chemist. Possibly the tops in his field. A person meeting him for the first time could be forgiven for doubting that claim.

For Monk Mayfair looked like nothing so much as a human gorilla. He was almost as wide as tall, and furred over with hair resembling shingle nails gone to rust. His eyes were very small and twinkled in pits of gristle with a humorous light. His arms were so long he could conceivably tie his shoes without stooping.

Monk gathered up the squealing animal lovingly, showing it to be a pig—but no ordinary member of the shoat family.

The pig had long passed the age where most of his kind become breakfast bacon, yet he was no larger than he had been a few weeks after his advent. Something had stunted him.

The pig was Habeas Corpus, Monk's pet. Monk had traded Habeas off an Arab in Arabia, the Arab having claimed Habeas was catching wild desert hyenas and dragging the carcasses into camp, where they were a nuisance. Desert Arabs of the tribe were notorious liars, yet Habeas had his qualities. His ears came near being those of an elephant; he had the long legs of a dog, a snout built for inquiring into deep holes of small diameter—and the rest of him was negligible.

The other man, Brigadier General Theodore Marley Brooks—called Ham by those who were close enough friends to dare to do so—was conceded to be one of the most clever lawyers Harvard had ever turned out. He was carefully honing the razor-sharp edge of his sword cane. On the tip of the blade he had daubed a sticky compound. This was a drug, the presence of a slight quantity of which in an open wound would produce instant unconsciousness. Ham's sword cane had merely to inflict a tiny cut on a foe to drop the fellow senseless.

"I understand bacon is a popular breakfast dish here in England," he murmured, eying the pig. "Come the morrow, I might whack off a slab to go with my eggs."

"You touch one bristle on Habeas's head," Monk warned, "and I'll turn that ape of yours into a coonskin cap and make you wear it!"

Ham frowned, and began looking around. "Where *is* Chemistry?"

A moment later a chattering pint-sized edition of Monk Mayfair ambled out from behind some equipment cases, where he had been cowering. It was of some species of runt ape. Just to what branch of the monkey family Chemistry belonged was a question which might have given an expert some puzzled moments.

Chemistry took one look at the bald ogre who had called himself Doc Savage and retreated, chattering excitedly.

"Get a load of that!" Monk roared. "That numbskull monkey of Ham's is afraid of you, Doc."

"And why not?" Ham blazed indignantly. "That is a perfect disguise. It would fool anyone."

Monk snorted derisively. The pair glowered. They were a study in contrast, the pleasantly homely Monk and the suave, chisel-featured Ham, who was attired in faultless morning coat and striped trousers. It was said that when Ham Brooks strolled down Park Avenue, his passing drew sighs from the best tailors, who took delight in seeing clothes worn as they should be worn.

If a well-dressed-men-in-America poll had appeared without Ham's name among the leaders, it would have been a calamity.

With Johnny Littlejohn, they were part of Doc Savage's group of aids. The remaining assistants, Colonel John "Renny" Renwick, an engineer of international repute, and Major Thomas J. "Long Tom" Roberts, the renowned electrical magician, were in other parts of the world, pursuing their respective vocations.

Long Tom was at the moment in Europe, endeavoring to assemble a supply of a rare mineral, rhenium, very necessary in the manufacture of a new type of X-ray tube which promised to revolutionize surgery, while Renny was busy surveying a Malaysian rubber plantation with an eye to laying track for a rail line needed to transport its product to market.

"We had best hangar our ship before heading into the city," said the red-furred monster who had been addressed as Doc.

He strode toward the cockpit and dropped his bulk behind the pilot's wheel. A crash of the self-starters brought the great engines roaring back to life.

There was a hangar whose door lay open and he sent the tri-motor bouncing into its unlighted confines.

As soon as the tail cleared the door, Monk and Ham leaped from the open hatch and ran the door closed.

A grease monkey, grinning with anticipation, hustled up to the hatch.

"I say, where is 'e?"

"Is who?" Monk asked, suspicious.

"The American, Doc Savage."

"What makes you think Doc Savage is on board that bus?"

"I overheard 'em talkin' about hit at the operations building, 'at's 'ow!"

"It was," Ham inserted, "supposed to be a secret."

"Blimey, hit cawn't be a secret hif 'Oratio 'Arris knows about hit, now cawn hit?"

"So you're the bird that squealed on us!" Monk gritted.

"Beggin' your pardon?"

"Some one informed the press of Doc's arrival," Ham said pointedly.

"That was me. Share the wealth, I always say."

Then the bald giant poked his head out. He reached up to one of two shirt pockets which resembled short bandoliers, except they were stuffed with cigars and not bullets.

He extracted a cheroot and brought it up to his mouth. Biting off the end, he spat the remnant to the hangar floor.

The grease monkey named Horatio Harris took an involuntary step back.

"Well, love a duck! Who in the name of the King are you?" he blurted.

"That's Doc Savage," Monk said casually.

"Don't you recognize him?" added Ham, his dark eyes humorously aglow.

"Cor, that hain't Doc. I saw a picture of 'im once. E's a strappin' chap, with eyes like two gold Jimmy O'Goblin's, or so they say." Horatio Harris scowled. "Who are you—the bloomin' Cardiff Giant?"

"You might," said the giant, reverting to his husky, whispery manner of speaking, "call me Bell."

"Bell?"

"Behemoth Bell."

"Never 'eard of you!"

"You might say he's the new man in our group," Monk inserted.

"Pleased to myke your acquaintance—I think," Horatio stammered. "But hif I may be so bold as to hinquire, where is Doc Savage?"

The giant who called himself Behemoth Bell stepped from the plane.

"He's not on board," he said.

A statement which, technically, did not overstep the truth.

"G'wan! I 'eard 'em talkin' about hit."

Behemoth shrugged amiably. "See for yourself."

The Cockney grease monkey took Behemoth Bell up

on the invitation. He was not in the plane very long. He returned, his face abashed.

"You were speakin' the 'onest truth, you were."

"Told you," said Behemoth Bell.

"Now go tell those nosey scribblers you gave them a bum steer," Monk growled. "And maybe that'll teach you not to repeat stories that ain't so."

"Right you are, sir. Right you are."

Horatio Harris quitted the hangar, the picture of dejection.

After he was gone, Monk's huge mouth split into a grin.

"That Behemoth, he's sure a swell bit of apparatus to have around."

Ham Brooks added, "As much as I hate to agree with Monk, Doc, this is the second time that disguise has come in handy. That mystery of the Man in the Moon a few months ago would not have been solved had you not invented him."*

In contrast to his good-natured behavior around the newsmen and the snoopy grease monkey, the disguised Doc Savage—for the self-styled "Behemoth" was the Man of Bronze—did not share in his aids' pleasure.

"We must be going," he said.

Their pets in tow, Monk and Ham followed the red-furred giant. They took pains to steer clear of the pack of reporters, who were busily engaged in chasing after every plane that happened to land in the vain hope of buttonholing Doc Savage.

A taxicab took them to a hotel near Hyde Park, where soapbox orators, after a long tradition, held forth on matters of importance, both actual and perceived.

Monk and Ham were pleased to find that Doc Savage had registered himself as the fictitious Behemoth Bell. They took possession of their rooms, pronounced them satisfactory, and joined Doc in his.

"Gonna give Johnny a call, Doc?" Monk asked.

"I made a point of telling Johnny that the purpose of

---

* Devil on the Moon.

my visit to London was to address the Fellowhood of Scientists. I did not want to get his expectations aroused."

Monk stared at his bronze chief. "That's what you told us, too," he muttered.

Ham unjointed his sword cane thoughtfully. "Yes, but you asked that we join you anyway. I rather thought it was suspicious."

"My true reason for coming to London may or may not lead to action," said Doc, beginning to peel his scalp away. It exposed smooth hair that was the color of bronze and as close-fitting as a skullcap.

Transparent shells that gave Behemoth Bell's eyes their merry blue coloring came out, to expose optics of a startling character.

They were like pools of flake-gold, always in motion. There was something hypnotic, compelling in the way the gold flakes seemed to be stirred by tiny, restless winds. These were eyes that could alternately calm or disconcert anyone gazing into their aureate depths, depending on the owner's mood.

From a grip came chemicals, the application of which rubbed the freckles from Doc Savage's features. With them came the reddish cast of his skin. The fine-textured flesh revealed was also of bronze—although somewhat lighter than the hue of his hair.

As he worked, Doc Savage seemed to grow in carriage. Wire rims came out of his nostrils, returning them to normalcy. Removal of putty restored the flattish nose to its correct contours. Extracted dentures took away the squareness of his jaw, and the teeth that remained in his head would have disappointed an avaricious dentist.

Removal of make-up effected a change that was nothing less than startling.

Doc Savage was a giant of a man, but there was nothing beefy about his build. His neck sinews, the tendons in the backs of his long-fingered hands, looked as supple as bundles of violin string. There was a flowing ease about his movements that indicated great agility and Herculean strength. His stature, his unusually regular features, the distinctive bronze color of his skin—a result of long exposure to tropical sun—created a distinctive and arresting picture.

The general result was that Doc Savage was as conspicuous as if he carried a flag.

Hence the need—tiresome as it was—to at times resort to elaborate disguises to avoid troublesome situations, not the least of which were members of the Fourth Estate. Doc Savage had many enemies.

Doc turned from the mirror. He set aside the cigars; he did not smoke, as a general rule.

"You might," he said, "ring Johnny's hotel."

"Glad to," said hairy Monk. He scooped up the telephone instrument, and the front desk made the connection.

"What's that you say?" he squeaked upon asking to be connected with Johnny Littlejohn's room. "Johnny ain't been seen since yesterday?"

Dapper Ham drew closer, an interested listener.

"And he ain't showed for his lecture to-day?" Monk added.

Doc Savage made, very softly so that it was hardly audible within the hotel room, a small trilling sound. The note was exotic, as weird as the song of some tropical bird, or the vagaries of a wind in a waste of arctic ice pinnacles. The most peculiar quality of the trilling was the way it seemed to come from everywhere, rather than from any definite spot in the room; it was distinctly ventriloquial.

The sound was a small unconscious thing which Doc Savage made in moments of mental stress, or when he was contemplating unusual action, or was very puzzled.

Doc glided over to the telephone and took the instrument from Monk's hand as if Monk, who could bend silver dollars between thumb and forefinger, possessed but the strength of a child.

"For how long has Johnny been missing?" Doc demanded.

"Since midnight last," the desk man informed him.

"Has his room been searched?"

"No. This is not yet a police matter."

"Touch nothing in his room. We shall be there momentarily," Doc rapped, hanging up.

"Do you think something happened to old Johnny?" Monk wondered.

"Johnny is not the kind to miss a lecture without good reason—or at least excusing himself," Doc imparted.

"Then let's go!" Monk whooped.

A taxicab dumped them off before a hotel in the Earl's Court sector of London. They entered the place and attempted to engage the desk man in conversation, presenting a striking sight to staid British eyes.

After the desk man had finished putting his eyes back in his head, he stammered out a response to Doc's question.

"Sir William had not returned from his lecturing while I was on duty yesterday," he said.

"Sir William?" Monk muttered.

Ham snapped, "Johnny, you dope! Didn't you know they knighted him?"

"You lay off me and I'll go that one better," Monk warned.

"Eh?"

"I'll crown you, you notary public."

Monk and Ham had a peculiar trait; invariably, it seemed as if each was trying to rid the world of the other's presence, giving the impression of a hostile cat and dog thrown in close and unwilling association. Yet when something serious developed, they worked together in perfect unison. It had been demonstrated that if anything actually threatened Ham's safety, hairy Monk would risk his life to help his partner. And Ham would do the same thing.

Doc Savage said, "We would like the key to Johnny's room."

The key was promptly surrendered and they took a creaking elevator three stories to the room that had been Johnny's.

They found little enough. No signs of struggle. No notes.

Monk took from a coat pocket a tiny device not unlike a folding box camera. It had a lens that was purplish-black in color. He threw a switch. Nothing happened, but the absence of visible light seemed not to perturb the hairy chemist.

He circled the room, directing the lens on the walls, hardwood floor, and other flat surfaces, homely features wrinkling in concentration.

He paid particular attention to the windows and washroom mirror.

Ham asked, "Anything, you ape?"

"Nope," said Monk, cutting the switch. "Johnny didn't leave no message with our special chalk that glows when exposed to ultra-violet light."

Ham Brooks stood in the middle of the room, fuming.

"Dash it all," he grumbled. "This isn't like Johnny."

"Maybe you oughta cut out that Harvard accent, shyster."

"Why is that?"

"In these parts, you sound like an imitation Englishman."

Ham purpled, seemed on the verge of saying something, when Doc Savage suddenly reached into a wastepaper basket and extracted a discarded newspaper. The paper was neatly folded.

"Johnny discarded this," Doc said.

Monk eyed the paper. "Yep. Just like that bag of bones to go and fold a paper so neat before stuffing it into a wastepaper basket."

Doc unfolded the paper, his flake-gold eyes scanning the masthead. "Yesterday evening's edition," he said.

"Maybe Johnny read something that set him off," Monk hazarded.

"My thought exactly," said Doc, leafing through the paper.

The ripped-out section was on page four.

They fell to searching for the absent item. Monk peered into the basket and Ham looked under the bed.

"No clipping," Monk announced.

"The clue might be in what was cut." Doc turned the page. The other side was an advertisement. The missing item had been on page four, without doubt.

Doc went to the telephone and asked the exchange to

connect him with the publisher of the London newspaper in question.

After Doc had identified himself, the publisher said, "How the deuce did you slip past my man at the airport?"

"Not important," said Doc. "I would like information on an article that was printed on the first column of page four in your late-evening edition."

"Will you consent to an interview if I oblige?"

"No," returned Doc.

"Then I do not see why I should help."

"It concerns the possible disappearance of one of my aids, Johnny Littlejohn."

That made a difference. "Sir William? Why didn't you say so, my good man? One moment." The publisher returned and against a background of rustling newsprint proceeded to read the report of the disappearance of the mysterious X Man from a Scottish madhouse.

"Thank you," said Doc, hanging up.

Monk and Ham had been eager listeners to all this.

"Doc," said Ham, "do you think Johnny lit out after this X Man fellow?"

"It should be possible to determine with certainty," Doc said. He started for the door. It was closed, and a sharp rapping rattled the panel before the bronze man could lay a hand on the doorknob.

He threw the door open. It was the desk man.

"Beggin' your pardon," stammered the desk man, "but I have just had a telephone conversation with the night man."

"Go ahead," directed Doc.

"It seems Sir William inquired after directions to a little Scottish town at about the midnight hour last night."

"Stirling the name of the town?" asked Doc.

The desk man lifted a surprised eyebrow. "Cor, but it is. However did you know?"

"Please call a taxicab," requested Doc.

"What destination shall I say?"

"Croydon Air Field."

"I guess," Monk said to Ham, "that means we're going to Stirling. And Doc ain't even got around to telling us the real reason we come to London."

Nor did the bronze man enlighten them as they quitted the room that had been the missing archæologist's.

The cyclone had collected its latest victims.

V

MINT

The arrival of Doc Savage and his two aids at the Wyndmoor Asylum for the Brain Impaired was the cause of great commotion.

Nurses, very neat in white uniforms, halted and stared as they entered the ivy-covered edifice. Their scarlet mouths came roundly open.

"You are expected," said a guard in a properly impressed tone of voice. "Come this way."

They followed the guard through hospital-white corridor walls. From the outside, Wyndmoor had the flavor of a Scottish manor, but inside the decor was thoroughly modern, and along the lines of the better hospitals of New York City.

"Some joint, huh?" Monk muttered as they walked along.

"I fancy it will do," Ham said approvingly.

"Do? For what?"

"Why, for your retirement. I am certain they have a suitable cage for a dim-witted ape such as yourself."

"Watch it, shyster," Monk growled, "or I might take a notion to find out if your head is detachable."

Doc Savage inserted, "This place was formerly a mansion, but the family that owned it was forced to sell during the worldwide business slump. It was converted into a model institution for the treatment of mental cases."

Monk grunted. Neither man questioned Doc Savage's remarkable knowledge of an obscure Scottish sanitarium. The bronze man had an amazing memory, thanks to a routine of exercises which he took two hours each day. They were responsible for his astonishing physical development,

47

as well as his heightened senses and the retentive power of his mind.

They came to the end of a corridor and a frosted-glass door on which was the gold-lettered legend:

DR. JOHN GILCHRIST
ADMINISTRATOR

The guard announced them and withdrew.

Dr. Gilchrist was no dour Scot after the popular impression, but a ruddy-cheeked and rotound little man with an affecting smile.

"Dr. Savage," he said effusively, rising from his desk. "I canna tell you how glad I am that you have come to visit my wee asylum. But as I told you over the telephone, I know nothing of your man, Sir William."

"There's that Sir William stuff again," Monk undertoned to Ham. "Remind me to razz Johnny about that when we find him."

Surreptitiously, the dapper lawyer whacked the homely chemist on the knee with the heavy handle of his dark cane.

Monk bared his teeth in a remarkably monkeylike grimace, and a slow hiss escaped his tightly held teeth.

Doc Savage was saying, "There is reason to believe that Johnny set out for this destination at approximately midnight yesterday."

Dr. Gilchrist took his plump chin in hand and made a concerned face. "You donna say. And pray tell why would he?"

"Interest in the escaped patient, X Man."

The psychologist fell to rubbing the red color out of his cheeks, but this only served to bring out more of their ripe apple hue.

"Now he was a puzzle, that one," he muttered. "I had never seen the like. Had been a model patient for near to a year—and the sight of a tabby cat unbalanced him completely."

"Ailurophobia?" Doc asked.

"Aye, fear of felines. Such is what I noted in his file.

But why would your Professor Littlejohn take an interest in him?"

"According to the paper, X Man, as you call him, was discovered roaming a Roman ruin, dressed in a tunic and reciting Shakespeare in the Latin tongue."

"A not uncommon delusion, as you know. Thinking that one is not one's own self, that is."

"Yes," Doc agreed. "But to Johnny, an archæologist, it would easily have aroused his interest."

"I see. Weel, we havna seen the poor addled laddie since he got away. And I canna tell where he got to. It was as if the fellow was washed down the drainpipe."

"I would like to examine the tunic he wore, if it is available," Doc requested.

"Sure, and I can have it fetched up here," said Dr. Gilchrist.

They waited patiently and a guard soon reported that the tunic was missing from the laundry room.

"Was there no sign of it?" Dr. Gilchrist demanded.

"No, Doctor," the guard answered. "But this was found at the bottom of one of the carts filled with soiled clothing."

The guard extended a broad hand. In the palm, so small as to be barely discernible, was a tiny black speck.

Dr. Gilchrist brightened. "Ah, one of the mystery seeds."

"Seeds?" asked Doc.

"Yes. Our X Man had a horticultural bent. Liked to grow plants. A harmless habit, which we encouraged. Had a bit of a green thumb, he did. Go on, have a look."

Doc accepted the seed from the guard. Monk and Ham crowded near. Monk shoved his nose close to the bronze man's palm and blinked. "That don't look like no seed I ever laid eyes on," he muttered.

"Of course it is a seed," Ham said sharply. But he frowned and made doubtful faces.

From a pocket under his coat, Doc Savage extracted a telescoping tube no thicker than a pencil which, by changing lenses, could become a small monocular, periscope, microscope, or other optical device. He removed a lense, pocketed the rest, and fell to an examination of the supposed seed.

His striking golden eyes were intent, but he gave no indication that his examination had gleaned results.

Doc turned to Dr. Gilchrist.

"I would like to examine X Man's plants," he said.

"To be sure."

They were taken to the padded cell which had been X Man's last room before his escape.

"There was a bit of a row," Dr. Gilchrist explained, "so some of the broken ones had to be discarded. These are all that survived."

Kneeling, Doc made an examination of the plants, touching green leaves between metallic thumb and forefinger. From time to time, he broke off samples and brought them to his nostrils.

The exercises that were responsible for his amazing development had augmented the bronze man's sense of smell, too. But he offered no pronouncement.

Curious, Monk reached down and broke off a leaf. He rolled it between his thick fingers and took a long sniff.

"Minty," he muttered.

Frowning, Ham unsheathed his sword cane and with an upward flourish snapped off the tip of a stalk. It sailed high and he snagged it in an elegant hand.

"Show-off!" Monk snorted.

Ham sniffed of the leafage delicately, frowned. "I smell nothing," he complained.

"Gotta crush it," Monk advised.

Ham did.

"Spearmint," he opined.

"Hah! It's peppermint, you disgrace to the bar."

"This is definitely spearmint," Ham snapped. "Smell it."

Monk allowed the dapper Ham to place the crushed leaf under his broad, flat nose.

"Dang! It *is* spearmint."

"They are all varieties of mint," said Doc, coming to his feet.

Dr. Gilchrist offered, "X Man claimed that the plants

would protect him from the cats who, he feared, would devour him. He was quite emphatic on this point."

"Poor devil," Ham said sympathetically.

"Haw. He *was* nuts," snorted Monk.

"Would you believe it," Dr. Gilchrist said, "but he tried to take one of the plants with him?"

Doc eyed the psychologist.

"Would have gotten away with it, too," Dr. Gilchrist elaborated, "but a guard happened upon him and X Man elected to brain him with it."

"I would like to see that particular plant," Doc requested.

"It has been consigned to the trash bin."

"Nevertheless, I would like to see it," Doc stated.

The plant was found and brought to Doc Savage at Dr. Gilchrist's office in less than twenty minutes.

"It is a sorry sight," said Dr. Gilchrist, shaking his head at the plant, now clinging to a clump of dark soil and surrounded by the remnants of its crockery flowerpot, after it was laid on his desk.

Doc did not use his magnifying device this time. With fingers that exhibited great sensitivity despite their metallic cast, he prodded the limp and dying plant.

It was predominantly green, with spade-shaped leaves that were saw-toothed at the edges and covered with tiny veinings.

The stems did not grow straight, but bent and twisted, as if they had grown in some confined space, and shaded to purple in spots. They were covered with fine white hairs—or what resembled hairs to the unaided eye. They brought to mind insect hairs.

"Don't look much like the others," Monk muttered.

"Dope!" Ham snapped. "The others did not all look alike, either."

"Still, this is different somehow."

Doc Savage plucked a wilted leaf, crushed it, and this brought forth a strong scent.

Monk and Ham leaned closer to capture the fragrance.

"Smells kinda minty, too," Monk ventured.

"But I can't place it," added Ham.

"Nor do I," said Dr. Gilchrist.

Everyone looked to Doc Savage for an answer. Instead of providing one, the bronze man began harvesting the leaves. He plucked a goodly assortment, and from inside his coat extracted a glass phial with a rubber stopper. Rolled tightly, the leaves went into this and, stoppered again, the phial was returned to a pocket deep in Doc Savage's person.

"What more can you tell me of the patient, X Man?" Doc queried.

Dr. Gilchrist pondered the question. "It was a strange way he came to Wyndmoor, it was," he allowed.

"Strange?"

"A man called to report X Man wandering where we found him, in the Roman Legionary Fortress."

"Nothing unusual in that. Tourists often visit such ruins."

"Aye, but the caller dinna call the authorities, but myself personally. He never identified himself, but I have often thought that it was the caller's wish that X Man be confined to this institution in particular. For the life of me, though, I canna understand why."

"The patient had no identification on him?" Doc asked.

"None whatsoever." Dr. Gilchrist reached into his desk drawer and brought forth an envelope, which was not sealed.

"These are the strange seeds which I confiscated," he declared, handing them over.

Doc undid the flap and glanced inside briefly.

"Are those leaves from seeds such as those?" asked Dr. Gilchrist.

"They are," said Doc, pocketing the envelope. He offered nothing more on the subject, but stated, "I would like to remain here with my assistants."

"For what purpose?"

"There is every reason to believe that my missing aid, Johnny Littlejohn, might yet show up."

"It is to be devoutly hoped," said Dr. Gilchrist sympathetically.

"And there is the distinct possibility that X Man will return," Doc added.

"But—why would he do that? He was obviously keen to escape."

"To recover this plant."

"You are more than welcome to stay," said Dr. Gilchrist, plainly puzzled.

Several minutes later, Monk and Ham went out to the rented car to check on their pets, Habeas and Chemistry, who had been left there so as not to agitate the inmates of the asylum.

Monk muttered, "Poor Habeas. He must be awfully lonesome sittin' in that car with a corpse."

"Corpse?"

"Yep. Your pet What-is-it, Chemistry. Habeas has probably assassinated him by now."

"You dope," Ham said, yanking open the car door.

The animals made delight noises and climbed over their respective owners, after which they took the first opportunity to get into a fight.

"Doc says we should keep a sharp eye for either Johnny or this X Man loon," said Monk after he had separated the animals by nudging Habeas in the ribs with a toe.

"The place is certainly big," Ham commented, looking about.

"Yeah," Monk agreed. "Watchin' it will be about like watchin' a whole town. Specially now that it's gettin' dark."

"Well, at least we seem to have stumbled onto some excitement."

"Yeah," said Monk. Then he snapped his fingers.

"What is it, you lop-eared missing link?" Ham asked unkindly.

"I just remembered somethin'. Doc ain't yet told us why he dragged us to London with him."

"Doc has a good reason, I'll wager."

"What'd I tell you about that fake Harvard accent of yours?"

"It is not fake!" Ham retorted.

"Tell it to a real Englishman," Monk jeered. "But like I was sayin', Doc asked us to tag along even though he was only supposed to lecture to that Fellowhood of Scientists. But once we got to town, he hinted something else might be up."

"Doc will tell us when he is ready."

Monk scratched his bristly nubbin of a head. "Yeah. But my curiosity's kinda up right now. And what can those plants mean?"

"I, for one, am less interested in the mystery of this X Man unfortunate than I am in Johnny's present whereabouts. It is unlike him to disappear so thoroughly."

"You want my opinion, Johnny is the disappearingest member of our group. With him gallivantin' around all corners of the world on his lonesome, poking into tombs and digging up old bones and things, it's a wonder he ain't disappeared on us permanent-like before this."

"I shudder at the thought," said Ham.

Night was falling. Somewhere, in the far distance, came the actual skirling of bagpipes. Some Scottish swain courting a bonnie lass, more than likely. The pirboch sank into a haunting, doleful strain.

Chemistry placed his hands over his ears. Habeas's long elephantine ears lifted at right angles to his head in a manner so preposterous it sent dignified Ham Brooks into convulsions of mirth.

"That fool hog of yours looks like he's about to fly back to where he came from," Ham chortled. Sobering, he added, "Not that I would complain if he did."

Habeas began to make snuffling sounds.

Hands resting on knees, Monk bent down. "What d'you smell, Habeas?"

The pig grunted, his intelligent eyes fixed on a privet hedge some yards distant.

"Habeas smells somethin'," Monk muttered, his own piglike eyes squinting.

"If he smells something, why are his ears sticking out?"

"That's his way of tellin' me there's danger," Monk said, low-voiced. "He's a bloodhog, Habeas is."

"Bosh!"

"I'll prove it." Monk addressed the shoat. "Habeas! Go get 'em!"

On spindly legs, the scrawny pig took off toward the privet hedge. He ran like a dog, snout to the ground.

Monk and Ham followed, with Chemistry knuckling along at the rear.

"My hog," Monk was bragging, "is a mixture of bloodhound, falcon, and Hindoo gooblestuffer. You know what a Hindoo gooblestuffer is?"

"Shut up!" Ham requested. "I'm not interested."

"A gooblestuffer is something that don't like lawyers," Monk explained. "The Hindoo variety of—"

Ham yelled, "Cut out that child humor, or I'll hit you so hard your nose'll have to go over to Ireland to find your face!"

"You caress me," Monk invited, "and you'll become a grease spot. Presto! Just like that."

They paused, glared at each other ferociously, then broke into a dead run as commotion sounds came out of the privet hedge into which the ungainly shoat had disappeared.

Pig squealing followed.

"Habeas!"

Pumping his bandy legs, Monk howled and ran. He soon outdistanced Ham Brooks.

Tucking his sword cane under an elbow, Ham produced from an armpit holster a weapon which had much the appearance of an oversize automatic, except that it was equipped with a drum cartridge magazine. This was a machine pistol which Doc Savage had devised. It was capable of discharging shells at a horrendous rate.

While Ham preferred to depend on his sword cane in hand-to-hand combat, he was not loath to have the machine pistol in his hand. Ham shared none of Doc Savage's scruples about carrying firearms. Doc believed that carrying a gun tended to make the one who carried it more helpless when not in possession of a weapon. For his part, the dapper lawyer preferred the helpless feeling to the risk of being unarmed.

Monk leaped into the hedge. It was like most English shrubbery—very tall and thick. It could conceal a man easily.

It completely swallowed Monk, who was broader than

most men and whose chest was as big around as a rain barrel.

"Chase him out, you misbegotten tree-man!" Ham howled, trying to pick out a target in the commotion.

"I'm trying!" Monk roared back. "I can't find him!"

Then the hairy chemist did find his quarry. He had been using his long, thick arms to separate shubbery when they encountered, abruptly, a physical form.

"Ye-eo-w!" Monk squawled.

The howl came out of him as he landed on his spine, the breath *whoofing* out of his capacious lungs. He lay dazed for only a moment, then jumped to his feet.

When he was mad, or in a fight, Monk preferred a lot of noise. "Blazes!" he said. "Blast the blankety-blank blazes!" And some more.

When he became extremely aggravated, he was inclined to jump and squawl. He did a little of that now.

It did him little good.

The hairy chemist knew a lot of rough and tumble, as well as some jujutsu taught him by Doc Savage himself. His darksome opponent was using neither. Yet somehow Monk found himself being thrown to the ground every time he attempted to rise.

It hurt his proud soul to admit it, but he needed help.

"Help!" Monk howled.

"I'm coming!" called Ham, his voice ripping with concern.

Monk had a little luck then. One hairy hand snagged an ankle. He gave a twist, and upset his foe. And promptly received a thumb in his left eye. Monk howled anew. Ham could be heard crashing amid the shrubbery, all but trampling it into ruins.

Then the dapper lawyer yelled, "There he is! On the other side of the hedge!" And he cut loose with his machine pistol. It made a sound that might have come from a bullfiddle as big as a house, if there could be such an instrument.

"I got the blighter!" Ham shouted.

Monk froze, waiting for his foe to topple inert.

When it didn't happen, Monk yelled, "I thought you said you got him!"

"I did!" Ham called back. "He's falling."

"He is not! He's on top of me!"

"Then who did I—"

"Oh no!" Ham wailed, sounding like a minister who had unexpectedly awoken to find himself residing in Hades. "It's Doc! I've shot Doc Savage!"

VI

DELUSION?

Monk Mayfair found his strength then. He had his foeman's wrist, the one that was attached to the thumb punishing his eye, and bent it in a way not intended by nature.

A scream ripped through his eardrums and Monk rolled his opponent off him.

"One side, guy!" he gritted. "Doc needs me."

The foe seemed as willing to break off conflict as Monk. He scuttled off.

The hairy chemist snapped branches as he crashed in the direction of Ham's anguished cry.

He located Ham Brooks, supermachine pistol in hand, kneeling over the prostrate form of the bronze man. Ham looked up, his chiseled features twisted.

"Monk! Hurry! You know what to do!"

"Comin'!" Monk puffed.

He dropped beside Doc, saw that the bronze man's eyelids were fluttering.

"Mercy bullets?"

"Of course."

Monk grunted. The tiny superfirers were amazingly versatile, and could fire lead, gas, or explosive shells. Usually, however, they were charged with so-called "mercy" bullets—thinned-walled metal capsules which broke the skin and so introduced a fast-acting chemical anæsthetic into the victim's bloodstream.

Sure enough, there was a slight wound at the back of the bronze man's neck. The dapper lawyer had indeed discharged his tiny weapon at Doc, not realizing in the darkness that the bronze man had been making his stealthy way through the shrubbery.

Monk yanked open Doc Savage's coat and shirt, exposing an inner vest that was constructed of leather and covered with many pockets. Monk fumbled one of these open and extracted a hypo needle and charged it from a phial.

"This oughta bring him around," Monk said, injecting the bronze man at a point above his wrist. "It's a counteractant to the chemical anæsthetic we use in our mercy bullets."

After a moment, the flutter of Doc Savage's eyes settled down and the bronze man lay on his back, staring up at the stars.

His flake-gold eyes were odd; they seemed unaware of what they were looking at. His regular features were blank and metallic.

Then, as if gathering themselves, his great sinews and neck cords tightened. The bronze man sat up abruptly.

"What happened?" he asked, his voice odd.

"You don't know?" Ham gulped.

"I heard commotion and came out to investigate," Doc related. "I was circling the hedges—and that is the last I recall."

Monk started to say, "This legal eagle—"

"I'll tell it!" Ham snapped.

Doc looked at the dapper lawyer. "Go ahead."

Ham swallowed. His sword cane twisted in nervous fingers.

"I shot you by accident," he admitted, thick-voiced. "Mistook you for Monk's prowler."

The bronze man was silent as this sank in. "I should have been more careful," Doc said quietly, getting to his feet. "It will be a lesson to be more alert in the future."

Ham looked relieved. Monk thought he detected a rare trace of embarrassment in the bronze man's manner. It was not often Doc Savage was caught flat-footed like this.

Doc Savage noticed Monk's bruised eye then.

"I hope the other fellow got the worst of it," he remarked.

"I wish he had, Doc," Monk said sheepishly. "Whoever he is, he knows his stuff. It was all I could do to keep him from turning me into a pretzel."

"Strong?"

"Naw. Just sneaky."

The bronze man was looking around.

"He cannot have gotten far," he said.

"Habeas will find him," Monk boasted.

"You said that last time," Ham sneered.

"And I was right. Habeas found him. Only he didn't hold on to him so good."

The apish chemist got to his feet, looking around. The queer-looking pets, the big-eared, spindle-legged Habeas Corpus and the strange monkey Chemistry, stood nearby.

"Habeas, go get 'im!"

The shoat lifted his snout to the air, took a few sample sniffs, and set off at a trot. The others followed, Doc moving a little unsteadily. The stimulant Monk had dispensed had not fully taken hold.

"Nice goin', shyster," Monk undertoned when he noticed this.

"Shut up!" snapped Ham, coloring.

Habeas trotted down a path between two identical hedge rows. He disappeared around a turn. When they reached the bend, they discovered another hedge-bordered path. Farther along, the path split into opposite forks. They looked up and down these. Habeas had taken the right-hand fork.

"What is this?"

"English maze," said Doc.

"Maze?"

"It is a British custom to plant hedge rows so they form an outdoor labyrinth," the bronze man explained. "Evidently, the asylum has maintained this one, which might be several decades old, for the benefit of patients and staff. Or possibly to ensnare escaped patients long enough for easy capture."

"A maze," Monk muttered, pulling out his machine pistol. "I don't like this."

They liked it even less when farther along, Habeas suddenly plunged into one hedge.

"Here we go again," Monk complained.

Doc rapped out quick orders. "Monk, backtrack. Ham, you go on ahead."

"Righto," said Ham. "What about you?"

The bronze man apparently did not hear. He might have been so dulled by the effects of the mercy bullet that the query had not registered, but the dapper lawyer knew better. Doc Savage had a small habit when he didn't want to hear a question—he just seemed not to hear the inquiry. It was aggravating, and often puzzling, but the bronze man frequently did things that were mystifying, but which turned out all right in the end.

Doc shook his head, as if to clear it, and plunged into the hedge after Habeas Corpus. The shrubbery seemed to part before him and take him into its leafy embrace.

A slight sound was the only noise of his going—and even that was unusual. The bronze man frequently displayed the stealth of a stalking panther. It was this uncanniness of movement that possibly explained how he had fallen victim to Ham's reckless firing. In motion, Doc could resemble a fugitive shadow.

Monk and Ham went in opposite directions.

The interval between Doc's disappearance and the results of his taking to the trail was short. Possibly less than two minutes. It seemed an eternity to Monk and Ham as they made their way along the hedge maze, seeking any sign of their mysterious quarry.

Then came a crashing of brush, the slap of bare feet on grass, and a piggy squeal.

Monk, nearest to the commotion, simply tore through the hedge. He emerged on the other side, looked both ways, and caught the tail end of what must have been a very short battle.

Doc Savage had hold of a figure. A man—or perhaps a girl. It wore a skirt. But it fought like a man, raining hard blows on the bronze man's chest and face.

Doc simply took them, resolute as the metal that had given him his cognomen, Man of Bronze.

And he continued squeezing his foe's throat until the latter gave a visible shudder and went limp in the bronze man's unshakable grip.

Ham was arriving as Doc Savage lowered the figure onto the greensward. He stopped dead.

Monk gave out a grunt when he saw what Ham had seen.

It was a man. He lay on his face, his eyes open, but as rigid as if turned to flesh-colored stone. That was not what held their interest, however. The phenomenon was simply the result of a technique Doc Savage employed—one which was capable of rendering a foe immobile, but entirely conscious and aware of surroundings. It was accomplished by an application of pressure on a person's spinal nerve centers.

The thing that held them in shock was the odd garment that swathed the man's lean physique. A tunic, it had been called. It had a skirtlike cut, with the legs left bare. It was white, edged in gold.

It was also obviously homespun. Ham, whose knowledge of clothing was perhaps as extensive as his knowledge of the law, saw that immediately.

"No factory made that!" he blurted.

Doc nodded. He was fingering the weave. "Great care went into the construction of this garment," he said. "It is not cotton or linen, but some tough plant fiber."

"So what?" Monk said.

"So this, you ape," Ham retorted. "This is no costume-shop Roman gag outfit."

Monk frowned. "Kinda skinny for all the trouble he gave us."

"You mean he gave *you*," Ham said hotly. It was clear that the dapper lawyer was still smarting over the incident in which he had mistakenly filled Doc Savage. His neck was still crimson.

Monk blew out his cheeks and prepared to explode.

The bronze man caught the hairy chemist's eye and indicated discretion.

Monk promptly subsided.

"Well, one thing for sure," he allowed, "this here's X Man."

Doc Savage put a hand on the man's jaw and used this to move his face back and forth. He was evidently studying the man's left and right profiles, committing the contours to memory.

For a moment, his trilling came briefly. It held a curious note before trailing off.

Before Monk and Ham could question him, Doc said, "I am going to release you from the spell you are under. Do not resist. I have the power to reduce you to this state again."

Doc began kneading a spot at the back of the man's neck, just below the juncture of the skull.

Monk watched intently. The hairy chemist had never quite figured out how Doc induced the strange paralysis. Neither could Monk bring a victim out of the spell. Doc did that with pressure also, was doing it now.

The bronze man's hand came away.

"Dang!" Monk grunted. He'd missed catching how it was done again.

X Man—assuming it was he—lay still while he tested his ability to move. He made fists with his hands several times. He wriggled his toes—he wore no footgear, so this was visible to all. Next, he moved his head from side to side experimentally.

Satisfied that he was still intact, he lay still a moment. His olive-hued eyes shut and his face became a blank.

Monk and Ham were taken by surprise by what happened next.

Not Doc Savage. He had caught some imperceptible sign and was ready for the quick hands that sprang to his throat.

Doc allowed the fingers to gain purchase. It would keep them out of the way. With his own corded hands, the bronze man slammed his attacker back against the ground.

It was a short, irresistible gesture. And it took all the fight out of X Man. The air blew out of his lungs, and the fire went out of his eyes. His fingers released the bronze man's neck without leaving any marks.

X Man lay on the grass, chest heaving.

Ham had his sword cane unsheathed and ready. He had been on the point of sticking X Man with it, but Doc's sudden quelling of the situation had come before the dapper lawyer could take action.

Doc Savage stood up. "When you have your wind back," he told X Man, "we will hear what you have to say."

"Nice goin', Doc," said Monk approvingly. "This baby is docile as a little lamb."

Doc let the comment slide past. He was examining X Man in a manner that suggested great curiosity—except for the utterly impassive cast of his metallic features. It was not his way to express emotion. It had been schooled out of him—that is, the facial reactions that accompanied curiosity. The outward signs of fear, anger, and other strong emotions had been trained away, but not the underlying emotions themselves.

To one who knew him well, it was plain the bronze man found X Man a very intriguing specimen. It showed in the way Doc canted his head and in a slight agitation of his restless flake-gold eyes.

At length, X Man's breathing rhythms resumed their normal pattern.

"You are X Man," Doc Savage stated.

"I am called that," X Man admitted.

"What were you called before you became known as X Man?"

The thin man said nothing.

"Talk!" Ham urged.

Monk said fiercely, "Let me sock him one, Doc."

Doc admonished silence.

"X Man, from what land do you hail?" he asked.

"It is called Novum Eboracum."

Doc's strange sound, the low, exotic note that meant his mind was excited, was briefly audible, then drifted away to nothingness.

"What is it?" Ham demanded.

"Sound familiar to you?" Doc prompted.

Ham fretted his smooth brow.

"Reflect on your schoolboy Latin," Doc suggested.

"Novum—Novum means 'new'! But I fail to place the name 'Eboracum.'"

"Eboracum," said Doc, not taking his eyes off X Man's still face, "was the name of a fort in Roman Britain."

Monk grunted. "I don't get it. All them Roman forts

are ruins now. This guy ain't some ancient Roman who's been hanging around since the days of Cæsar, is he?"

"His tunic appears authentic," Doc pointed out.

"Jove!" Ham breathed.

"That don't make no sense," Monk complained.

"It does not," Doc agreed. "And even less sense when you realize that Eboracum was the name for what is now modern York."

Monk scratched the back of a furry arm. "York? So?"

Ham said, "Simplewits! Don't you see? When he says Novum Eboracum, this fellow is trying to tell us he hails from New York!"

That seemed to stun the homely chemist.

"This is screwy," he muttered. "First, he's a dang Roman. Now he's a Gothamite. I say he's a loon and let it go at that."

Doc asked X Man, "What is the purpose of the seeds?"

"The seeds will protect me when I return to Novum Eboracum," the strange captive replied.

"From what?"

X Man showed a first hint of human emotion then. He shuddered. "From the cats that devour men," he said thickly.

"Screwier and screwier," Monk opined.

"Do you know where you are now?" Doc asked the man.

"Truly. Britannia."

"That's the old Roman name for Britain," Ham said slowly. A peculiar flicker touched the dapper lawyer's chiseled features. "I say, could this man be from—the past?"

That disturbing thought hung in the night air until the Man of Bronze put forth another question.

"Is Novum Eboracum in Britannia?" Doc asked.

X Man shook his head.

"Where is it?"

"It lies beyond the Veil of Silence, in the shadow of Vulcan's Forge, on the Lake of Smoke."

"Now we're gettin' somewheres," Monk said sarcastically.

"Shut up!" Ham snapped.

"We are seeking a friend of ours," Doc interposed. "His name is Johnny Littlejohn."

"I do not know him."

"He is a tall man, Johnny is," Doc pressed. "His hair is worn long and his looks are lean. Have you encountered such a man?"

X Man was a long time in replying.

"Yes."

"Where is he?"

"Brutus has captured him."

"Who is Brutus?"

"My enemy, formerly my friend."

Doc asked, "Can you take us to our comrade, Johnny?"

"Why should I do this for you?"

"Suppose I give you something in return?"

X Man's dark eyes narrowed slowly. "What?"

"The leaves from the plant that is so important to you," said Doc, extracting from his equipment vest the glass phial containing the leaves he had plucked from the ruined plant and holding it before the other's eyes.

X Man displayed life then. For the first time, his dark eyes sought the bronze man's.

"Homo Metallicus, I will do anything you ask in return for those," he said with a grave earnestness.

"What did he call Doc?" Monk wanted to know.

"Man of Metal," Ham explained.

Doc Savage uncorked the phial and waved the open mouth under X Man's nose.

"Satisfied?" Doc asked.

"Yes."

"Then let us be on our way."

Doc Savage offered his hand, and X Man accepted it. His clasp was firm as Doc pulled him to his feet.

For the first time, he regarded Monk and Ham. His eyes passed over the sartorially perfect Ham with a measure of disdain. Monk's apish form brought a blurted question.

"Que es simia hic?"

Ham abruptly doubled over.

"What's so blamed funny?" Monk demanded.

Ham tried to answer. He was holding his sides. He sat down.

Doc Savage said, dryly, "He asked, 'Who is this ape?'"

Ham's mirth laid him out in the sward. Chemistry copied the posture with monkeylike fidelity and began chattering.

Monk eyed X Man and cocked a thumb at his own chest, saying, "They call me Monk." Indicating Ham with a finger, he added, "And that there is—Porcus."

Ham couldn't have stopped laughing faster if he had been slapped. He sat up, Chemistry following suit.

"Porcus!" he howled.

Monk grinned broadly. "Yeah. It means swine, in case you don't know."

Ham grew red with rage at this apparently simple remark. Reference to pigs was one thing that was guaranteed to touch Ham deeply. Ham hated any reference to porkers. This loathing dated back to the Great War, when he had been unjustly framed on a charge of stealing pork. That Monk had done this framing, Ham was still convinced, the motive being revenge for a practical joke which Ham had played upon the homely chemist. The incident had given Ham his nickname.

As Ham Brooks picked himself up off the grass, it was abundantly clear that he detested the latinized form of Ham as much as the nickname itself.

He separated his sword cane. Monk blew on his furry fists.

Before any violence could transpire, sounds began filtering down from the asylum itself.

"Looks like they got a search party worked up," Monk offered.

"Explanations will take too long," Doc rapped. "We will be on our way." He turned to X Man. "Can we count on your cooperation?"

X Man nodded.

Doc motioned the others to follow him. Ham brought up the rear, his sword cane unsheathed and ready to bring down the strangely garbed X Man should he take flight.

* * *

They got into the maze. Doc reached out to snap hedge branches, deliberately made noise to draw pursuit. When sounds told them that the search party had gotten into the maze of shrubbery, the bronze man urged them along until they emerged at an exit.

"How'd you know the right path to take?" Monk muttered.

"A map of the maze was prominent on Dr. Gilchrist's office wall," Doc explained.

Monk grunted. A simple explanation, that, but he had not noticed the map himself. It was typical of Doc Savage to overlook nothing.

The bronze man led them back to where they had parked their rented car.

X Man allowed himself to be placed in back. When Monk started to climb in back with him, he shrank a little.

"Ham, you will sit in back," directed Doc.

Monk relinquished his claim to a back seat and reached down to pull Habeas off his feet by one ear. The pig gave out a contented grunt. He seemed to enjoy being toted by one ear.

Doc and Monk took seats up front while Chemistry found a place on Ham's immaculately creased lap, and they got under way.

They passed through the gates before any one could organize pursuit.

"That Dr. Gilchrist will have words for us," Monk muttered.

"We will square matters with him after Johnny has been found," Doc said. He did not sound perturbed at all.

"So," Monk said, "where do we start?"

"At our plane."

"Why?"

"Truth serum," Doc explained.

Monk looked back at X Man and grinned. He hadn't believed X Man's strange story, and truth serum should tell whether or not X Man believed it himself. The serum, while not magical, should at least reveal whether X Man was telling them incredible and mystifying lies, as they were inclined to believe he was.

Monk made muttering noises while he considered the

situation. X Man lying? The man sounded as if he told the truth. But then, there are good liars, just as there are expert acrobats. And the whole thing was not exactly the kind of stuff that could be readily believed—which was perhaps the reason they found it difficult to accept the story. Suppose, after all, it was true?

On the other hand, X Man *was* an escaped lunatic.

"I give up," Monk grumbled. And then, suddenly, he gave a jump. He remembered something. He leaned over and whispered to Doc Savage.

"Listen, Doc," Monk breathed. "I just remembered somethin'. We ain't got no truth serum left."

"What became of it?" Doc asked.

Monk grimaced sheepishly. "I gave it to Ham the other day, when he wasn't looking, in his coffee. Then I asked him a lot of questions and made a phonograph record of his answers. It was a gag."

"You gave Ham truth serum?"

Monk shook with laughter. "It was a joke. After the truth serum got hold of Ham, I asked all kinds of personal questions. I asked him if he loved me, and he said he did—like a brother. That'll burn him up. I found out he's carrying a torch for a Broadway chorus girl. I asked him what pet name he called her, and he told me. Boy, oh, boy! Such goofy love-talk. It's all on the phonograph recording. The next time Ham pulls one of those things on me he calls a practical joke, I'm going to spring the record on him. Will he be mortified! Anyway, the truth serum is all gone."

Doc Savage was silent. One of the bronze man's characteristics, that of saying very little, was evident. The stupefying chemical from the mercy bullet was having some effect on him, but his strange flake-gold eyes were alive and vital. Even in repose, and half drugged, the qualities that had given him an enormous reputation were evident.

Curiosity got the best of Ham Brooks. He leaned forward.

"What is happening?" he demanded querulously.

"Nothin'," Monk said. "Doc and me were just havin' a private conversation, is all."

Ham frowned darkly, but said nothing more.

Doc Savage spoke up. His words were directed toward

the hollow-faced individual who had claimed the mystifying identity of X Man. He spoke carefully, as if to someone to whom the English tongue was not natural.

"In which direction lies our friend?"

"East. Toward the water."

Doc Savage piloted the car east.

"There will be a bridge of a metal harder than iron," X Man added.

"Such a bridge lies over the River Forth," Doc stated. His knowledge of such minute geographic details aroused no especial comment.

They drove for some time, at last came to a steel bridge, and rattled over it.

"Where now?" asked Doc.

"There will be a farm on which sheep with black faces graze," X Man told him.

There was. Blackface sheep were numerous in this, the lowlands of Scotland.

"Go left," X Man said after they had passed the grazing land.

Doc obliged. The macadam petered out and became sod.

Through the open windows, the smell of salt water came. They were close to the shore—or one of the great inlets the Scots call firths, which extend far inland.

"We are very near now," intoned X Man.

Abruptly, Doc Savage pulled the car off the road and killed the motor. He turned in his seat and fixed X Man with his flake-gold eyes.

"Walking distance?"

X Man nodded.

"Then we will walk."

They got out, and began walking.

The night was pitch and what moon there was consisted of a fingernail slice that seemed to attract the fast-scudding clouds.

They walked down the dirt road single file, Doc in the lead, Ham Brooks bringing up the rear.

Monk hovered close to X Man, his hairy arms swinging jauntily. It seemed a natural way for the apish chemist to ambulate. In fact, his swinging motions were calculated to enable him to seize X Man in an unbreakable bear hug if the latter should bolt.

X Man did not bolt. He appeared content to walk along. One hand clutched the phial Doc had surrendered. His grasping knuckles were very white. From time to time, he took a deep sniff of the phial, as if he found the minty scent reassuring.

They came, after a while, upon a stone manor, quite substantial, which perched on the lip of an inlet of some size. Beside the house stood a boathouse. Not as substantial, but quite large. It had evidently fallen into disuse. At least, there was no wharf or docking slip on the water end of the structure.

From the house came a terrific shriek.

They froze on the trail.

"Did that—isn't that—I mean—" Ham gulped.

"Yes—Johnny," Doc said grimly.

Monk Mayfair went slack-jawed. "Sounded like he was—dyin'!"

VII

DEATH'S DOMAIN

William Harper Littlejohn was not dying.

But from the sounds emanating from his throat, he was giving a credible imitation of a man in the final moments of expiring.

These sounds were being encouraged out of the lank archæologist by his captor, the kilted worthy with the muttonchop facial adornment who had as yet not provided his identity.

"Blast Doc Savage and his meddlers," the Scotsman was saying. "It's answers I want, and I'll get them if I have to stave in every one of your meatless ribs! Now spill!"

Johnny spilled. He opened his mouth and howled out raw sound. In truth, he was not as anguished as he made out. The extreme volume and agony were for effect. It is well known that the more satisfaction one gives a sadist, the less he is likely to inflict further punishment. Too, Johnny hoped that his howls would be heard.

And so he howled in a box on the floor.

But he told his captor nothing. The man drew back a foot, and evidently tiring of his fruitless endeavors, withdrew from the root cellar, leaving Johnny Littlejohn bound on the floor and coughing spasmodically.

It had been thus for nearly a day now. Johnny had been left alone only once for any appreciable measure of time. That had been when the bewhiskered Scot had left Johnny to pursue the fleeing X Man.

Three hours had passed and then the Scot had returned, fuming and scowling, the picture of defeat. He had attempted to extract words out of the bony archæologist, but to no avail.

Threats were made—horrible promises of slow, agonizing death. These, it became obvious, were but a bluff. Whoever his captor was, Johnny concluded, he seemed reluctant to take the gaunt archæologist's life until he had extracted from him the truth of what Doc Savage knew.

"One last chance, before the worst," the man grated.

"Go peddle your papers," Johnny shot back.

That slangy retort had done the trick. The Scot stormed off.

Thereafter, his visits had been few and far between, but each one was occasioned by hard questions and a harder toe in Johnny's lathy ribs.

In the quieter intervals, Johnny had heard sounds from beyond the house above. Hollow clangings. The hammer of metal upon ringing metal. Once, a hissing, as of steam escaping from a broken valve.

No steam-heat radiator had made that sound, and when the Scot had next appeared in the strange root cellar, he was red-faced from exertion and sweaty of brow.

The Scot had offered no explanation for his exertions —not that Johnny had asked.

Lying quietly now, hoarse from yelling, Johnny listened for the sounds, but the clanging and ringing commotion did not come again. Johnny decided his captor must have turned in for the night, so he set about trying to escape.

Johnny sat up. It was difficult, inasmuch as his skinny arms were bound behind his back, but after some gritting of teeth he succeeded.

It was possible to see about the root cellar, owing to some light shed by the half-closed door leading to the dwelling above.

The wan light limned fantastic sights—African masks, Egyptian artifacts, short swords and shields. Johnny had been particularly intrigued by an array of weapons of a distinctly Roman character. The workmanship appeared authentic, but these specimens had not come out of any ruin. Unlike the other items, they appeared new.

It was very puzzling, but Johnny's thoughts now were focused on escape, not the weirdness of antiques belonging in museums being stored in a Scottish root cellar.

He sat up in the grisly coffin, and began rocking to

and fro. It was not, as he had feared, an Egyptian sarcophagus, but a one of more recent vintage.

The coffin was stout. It was no carven showpiece such as funeral parlors offer, but was constructed of stout pine board. The nails holding the boards together were square-headed, old-fashioned cut nails. The boards squeaked like disconsolate mice.

He gave it up, and lay back—as comfortably as it was possible to do so in the cramped container.

Abruptly, there was a hissing sound. Johnny sat bolt upright.

From the padlocked door that led to the grounds, harsh white light was spilling. Johnny was forced to turn away to avoid injuring sensitive optic nerves.

But his heart leaped high, for he recognized the hissing sound. Thermit!

The door was suddenly hanging by its padlock and hasp; the hinge pins were now hot, dripping slag.

And in the square of star-sprinkled night sky, was framed a towering figure.

"Doc!" Johnny breathed.

The bronze man glided forward. His strong hands seized Johnny's chafed wrists and separated them slightly, as if testing the resistance of the hempen bonds. He snapped them together and apart again with sudden violence.

The hemp made snarling sounds and fell loose.

"Can you stand?" asked Doc, going to Johnny's ankles.

"I do not know," Johnny gasped truthfully, using small words, as he did with the bronze man.

"Try," said Doc, his metallic fingers pulling the knots apart.

Johnny tried. With Doc's help, he got to his feet, then swayed and collapsed into the bronze man's waiting hands.

"Sorry," Johnny mumbled. "Blood circulation is bad."

Doc hoisted the gaunt archæologist in his arms and started to bear him toward the gaping door.

"Wait!" Johnny implored.

Doc stopped. "What is it?"

"Look about this place."

Doc Savage laid Johnny on the dirt floor and extracted one of the tiny spring-generator flashlights of his own invention. He moved to the ajar door that led above and eased it shut. The bronze man thumbed on the flash, shielding the light with one big hand.

The light picked out the array of weird ceremonial objects. Doc roved the cellar, touching this, examining that.

For a moment, his eerie trilling permeated the close, musty space. Abruptly, it ceased. The bronze man had realized he was making the trillation, and had stifled it.

"Are they real?" Johnny moaned.

"Some of these appear authentic. Others are obviously of recent manufacture."

"Except for that, they would pass as the real McCoy," Johnny said. He paused as if a thought had just entered his scholarly head. "Do you think this is some kind of counterfeit artifact racket?"

The bronze man was a long time in answering. His ray was picking out details on the Egyptian mummy case that had so unnerved Johnny when first he had laid eyes upon it.

"No," he said. Then the beam collapsed and Johnny found himself being lifted off the dirt floor.

"Monk and Ham are outside, with the one called X Man," advised Doc.

What Johnny Littlejohn might have said in reply was not to be known, for a moment later a cry came to their ears.

It was more of a bellow, actually. Both men recognized the author of that inhuman sound.

"That was Monk!" Doc rapped.

"But what could—"

The bellow came again. Simultaneously, booted feet began pounding down the cellar steps.

Johnny firmly in hand, Doc Savage flashed through the cellar opening. There was clear space before them— rolling lawn. No shelter. Doc adopted the broken-field running tactics of a football linebacker, zigging this way, then zagging.

He cleared several yards, then came a twang from the

house. A long, thin quill appeared a short distance to their left. In the moonlight it was difficult to make it out. It might have been a booby trap springing out of the earth.

Doc veered, put on speed.

From the vicinity of the root cellar, Johnny heard another sharp twang.

And without warning, Doc Savage was flung forward as if by a monster fist. The bronze man tried to move with the impact, but it was too great. He upset. Johnny tumbled from his suddenly lifeless grasp, to lie sprawled and helpless in the grass.

When the bony archæologist got himself organized, he saw the bronze man lying on the ground, a shaft quivering in his back.

"Doc!" Johnny howled. "No!"

The bronze man was not moving. It did not look as if he would ever move again.

Then a shadow fell over him—a cold shadow.

Johnny turned his head and never saw the fist that struck his jaw. He was not knocked out, but in his condition, the blow was enough to stun him.

Johnny Littlejohn was dimly aware of rough hands lifting his long length and placing him on a shoulder. The sensation of undulating movement was his predominant impression for several moments thereafter.

"Blasted meddlers!" a harsh voice rasped. "Now I have to take ye with me, for ye know too much!"

After that, there was no question of who had seized him—the muttonchopped Scot with the strange name, Brutus.

That seemed too much for the skeletal archæologist to handle. He had been cruelly abused and denied nourishment for a day now. His vast reservoir of stamina finally gave out, and he swooned.

When Johnny Littlejohn came to, he was on his back in a dark space. He had the dim impression of machinery. His eyes attempted to pierce the gloom and he detected the dim white faces of dials and gauges. Oddly, they were calibrated not in Arabic-style numbers, but in Roman numerals. There were pipes. His groping hands encountered a slick surface that was cold and metallic.

Johnny continued blinking the cobwebs out of his optics. He saw that he was not alone in the dark.

A man moved at the far end of the long chamber in which the gaunt archæologist had awakened. The chamber was, by rough estimate, perhaps thirty or so feet in length. What little light there was came from above. It shed enough illumination to make it plain that the hunched figure was Brutus. He was throwing levers and tripping switches, entirely oblivious to the fact that his captive had awakened.

Then, the chamber began vibrating alarmingly. Many sounds attended this unnerving vibration. Hissings that were fierce. A growing whine.

Johnny took advantage of the racket to struggle to his feet. He noted the light coming down from above. He saw a growing mist. It was framed by a circular opening like a porthole without glass.

And as the noises grew in volume, the bony archæologist reached up, took hold of the edge, and levered himself up.

He was immediately sorry that he had.

He seemed to have intruded into a realm of mist—warm, clinging stuff that made his skin flush.

Through the mist, not three feet from his nose, a face stared at him.

No human face was this. Indeed, no face that man had ever beheld since he had emerged from the caves of prehistory.

It was green and serpentine, the skin ridged and horny. The snout was a beak, and there were two eyes, dark and glassy, without pupils. It seemed to regard him with a baleful contempt. It was the face of a dragon of some unknown species.

Johnny's feet rested on piping, and he turned about.

Now he was staring at a row of the saurian heads. They were facing away from him, the farthest ones dim in the ghost-white mists.

As Johnny swallowed, hard and silently, hoping the things would not hear him, there came a procession of grating sounds from below, and the nearest dragon head swiveled on its blunt neck so that its dark eyes met Johnny's widening gaze.

Then the jaws separated, exposing rows of needle teeth.

The lanky geologist attempted to scramble away, but out of the ugly maw came a slow hissing. The hot breath of the thing was a vaporous yellow and smelled of rotten eggs and other, less pleasant, aromas.

The exhalation took Johnny's senses to some high realm from which there seemed no returning.

His first chaotic thought was that he was about to be devoured alive. In his final feeble moments of consciousness, the gaunt archæologist did a strange thing.

He ripped off his tie and began writing on it with a piece of chalk scrounged from a coat pocket. Oddly, the chalk left no visible mark.

When he felt hands gripping his ankles, he hastily flung the tie as far as he could.

The last thing he heard was a harsh voice saying, "Ye fool! 'Tis death to breathe the Mists of Time!"

VIII

MONSTER WRAPPED IN MIST

The first thing Monk Mayfair had done upon hearing Johnny Littlejohn's cries in the night was to uncoil out a hairy arm and snag X Man by the wrist.

"Not so fast, you," he warned.

X Man strained against the hairy chemist's unbreakable grip.

Doc Savage said, "Monk. Ham. Stay with X Man."

"Righto, Doc," breathed Ham Brooks.

And the bronze man had melted into the night.

They had waited in the darkness, crouched low so as not to be seen from the windows of the dark house, confident that the bronze man would reconnoiter Johnny's location successfully.

"This won't take long," Monk said, tightening his grip on X Man's wrist. It felt like a narrow plank covered in loose chicken skin.

Kneeling carefully so as not to acquire grass stains on his immaculate attire, Ham Brooks clutched his sword cane tightly and watched with alert eyes.

"Whatcha see, shyster?"

"Nothing so far."

"That means Doc ain't lost his touch none."

It was true. For among the succession of scientists and other experts who had taken a hand in rearing the bronze man were expert trackers and masters of stealth. Doc could move like a vagrant breeze when he wished, and no eye could follow his uncanny progress.

Time passed. It seemed an eternity.

Somewhere, an owl hooted.

"I am going to move closer," Ham murmured.

"You heard what Doc said," Monk cautioned.

"It is taking longer than it should."

Monk clipped his lips together. He understood that the dapper lawyer, stung by his embarassment, wished to acquit himself of his earlier mistake. He let Ham go.

Turning to X Man, Monk growled, "Don't you get restless on me."

X Man said nothing, but his eyes were haunted. Monk squeezed his captive's wrists more firmly, eliciting a grimace of pain.

"That's for givin' me a rough time before," Monk said. "And when we get back to our plane, we're gonna wring some truth out of you!" he added fiercely.

The hairy chemist was soon to regret that crack, for after Ham had passed into the murk, X Man, crouching behind Monk, reached around to jab a thumb into the homely chemist's windpipe.

It was only the beginning. Monk squawled, lashed back one furry beam of an arm, and found himself in the equivalent of a cat-and-dog fight in a matter of seconds.

"Not this time, you don't!" he raged, terrible hands gripping.

But it was not as simple as brute strength. The wiry X Man knew some science of fighting that the apish chemist had never before encountered. Nerve centers were jabbed expertly. His opponent's legs scissored around Monk's own, inhibiting movement. His ears were twisted painfully.

Monk roared his rage—and the flat of a hand caught him in the nose. He was slammed back.

Around and around on the ground they rolled, and the simian chemist, in the red rage of combat, was oblivious to all other sounds.

Monk was still rolling when his opponent went suddenly limp in his arms.

Abruptly, the hairy chemist threw him off.

"Hah!" he said. "He wasn't so tough, after all!"

"Not when he has a worthy opponent," drawled a cool voice.

Monk blinked, looked up. There, calmly sheathing the fine steel of his sword cane, stood wasp-waisted Ham Brooks, a pleased expression on his handsome, chiseled features.

"You stick him with that thing?" Monk demanded.

"My dear man," Ham drawled. "It was the only way to preserve you from the thrashing of your life."

Baring his teeth, Monk bounced to his feet.

"You ambulance-chasing polecat! I almost had him licked until you butted in!"

"He was besting you," Ham said calmly. "I saw that clearly. Another minute and he would have unjointed one of your arms."

"Liar!"

"Accident of nature!"

The two comrades in arms glowered at one another and violence seemed to impend.

Then something split the night and dispelled all thought of fighting.

They heard a sound—a sliding, rasping, slithering sound. Any one hearing that eerie agglomeration of mushy noises coming out of the night would be a long time forgetting them.

"What's that?" Ham muttered uneasily, looking around.

"I dunno," Monk admitted. "Sounds like it's comin' from that boathouse, though."

Monk's guess was proven correct a moment later when, with a prodigious splintering, the water end of the boathouse exploded outward.

They heard it, but from their vantage point, they could see little. Just an exhalation of dense, smoky mist, like something incredible had exhaled after a thousand-year sleep.

"Come on!" Monk howled.

Ham Brooks following, the homely chemist charged for the boathouse. The noises—the slitherings and slidings that were so uncannily horrible in the darkness—continued and changed character. It became a great bubbling, rapid and hideous to hear.

"There's somethin' going into the water!" Monk bellowed.

Something was. Something big. It surged into the inlet, trailing writhing billows of opalescent mist. The water swallowed the conglomeration of sounds like a maw of silence.

They arrived at the water's edge in time to see a horrific sight.

The back end of the boathouse was wood—or had been. Now it gaped as if a primordial dinosaur had broken loose. Board lay scattered all about. Much of it had been chewed up underfoot by whatever had slid into the water. Mist clung to everything.

The inlet waters were roiling, regathering themselves after the thing had gone under the surface. Fragments of wood floated on the surface. Misty tendrils clinging to the water made it seem as if something fantastically hot lurked below sight.

Monk screwed up his unlovely face and peered out over the dark water.

"I don't see nothin', do you?"

Ham did. "There!" he said, stabbing the air with his cane.

"Where?"

"About fifty yards out!"

And then Monk saw it. Or them. There were five or perhaps six of them. Heads, triangular, with horns on each forehead, and swimming away from shore in single file. They smoked faintly. There was a single wake trailing behind the school—if it was a school—of heads.

Monk gaped. "I heard tell of sea serpents in these Scottish lochs," he gulped. "But I never believed them yarns until to-day."

"I don't believe it now," Ham muttered in a disbelieving tone of voice.

But the evidence was before their eyes.

Monk brought out his flashlight and thumbed it on. A cone of light popped. He raced it along the dark waters.

He caught sight of the heads just as they were submerging.

Then the creatures were gone. They might not ever have existed, except for a misty exhalation which still clung to the troubled waters. That and the fact that Monk and Ham stood amid the ruins of the boathouse in which they had been, evidently, imprisoned.

A disturbed bird or two fluttered in the brush, and on the inlet, cloud images resembled great, vile monsters that seemed somehow to lurk over the tiny light points of the stars. There was nothing else.

"We'd better find Doc," Monk mumbled. "He'll want to know about this."

The pair turned, and had a brief contest to see who could jump out of his shoes faster.

"Doc!" Ham exclaimed.

"You scared me out of five years' growth!" Monk added.

"I have been watching," the bronze man said. His voice was dull. He seemed strangely passive.

"You O.K., Doc?" Monk asked worriedly.

Instead of replying, the bronze man began removing his coat. He had some trouble with the simple operation, and finally grasped the tail and tore the garment up the back.

They saw why a moment later.

There was an arrow sticking out of the bronze man's broad back. It had struck low and embedded itself. Strangely, except for a noticeable deliberateness in his motions, Doc Savage showed no trace of obvious discomfort.

Doc removed his shirt by the simple expedient of shredding it in his strong, capable hands until his many-pocketed undervest was exposed.

He undid the zipper, and when the vest came off his back the arrow came with it. The vest—leather on the outside—was lined with a chain-mesh alloy strong enough to turn bullets. In this case, the fine point of the arrow had managed to work between two of the links, but not penetrate very deeply.

The smooth bronze skin of Doc's back was broken in one spot and there was minor leakage of bodily fluid, but the injury could not in any sense be termed a serious wound.

Yanking the shaft free, Doc donned the trick vest, his features grim. It was clear that the impact of the shaft had left him in a stunned condition—a situation that might have been aggravated by his earlier mishap in being felled by one of his own mercy bullets.

"Where's Johnny?" Monk asked.

"Taken away."

"To where?"

"Boathouse."

Monk's ample mouth fell open. "That—that whatcha-macallit thing came out of the boathouse!" he blurted.

They investigated the boathouse.

It was dank and spacious and there were tools about. Not simple tools such as a country squire might own, but welding torches, a large lathe, drills, and other implements more appropriate to a machine shop.

Doc examined these carefully, then followed the trail of wreckage back to the water. The ground was chewed up severely—by what it was impossible to say.

Of Johnny Littlejohn, there was no sign.

"Maybe he didn't come this way after all," Monk said hopefully.

"His captor—the one who shot the arrow—carried him in this direction," Doc insisted. "I could tell by the crushed grass made by his footsteps."

Doc returned to the boathouse. His flake-gold eyes were fixed upon the stone flooring. It was set in flags—shale, cracked in many places as if from a great weight.

"Monk, have you your ultra-violet lantern?"

"Sure, Doc."

"Let me have it."

Monk pulled the tiny device from a pocket and gave it to the bronze man. Doc touched a switch and a whirring came from the thing. He directed the purplish lense about the floor.

Almost at once, electric-blue letters sprang out on one of the flags.

SCYL

"Johnny was here," Doc announced.

"Sure," Monk agreed. "Johnny made that. Probably with that special chalk we use, which glows under the black light."

"Is that a word?" Ham mumbled thickly. "Scyl?"

"Part of one," Doc said, eying the eerie letters.

"Any idea what it means?"

The bronze man knelt and pushed away some debris. It was revealed that the message had been written on a discarded necktie. There was no more to it than the four letters revealed by the black light. The rest was a luminous smear.

"Johnny did not have time to finish," he said, "and the thing that slid into the water obliterated some of what he attempted to write, but there is only one word he could have been essaying."

They waited for him to enlighten them.

"Scylla."

Monk and Ham exchanged blank looks.

"A sea monster in Roman mythology," Doc explained, "supposed to have six heads and twelve legs."

"That—thing we saw had at least five heads—that I saw," Monk muttered.

Doc nodded. "Obviously, Johnny recognized the creature—if it was such."

"If it wasn't a creature, what would it have been?" Ham wondered, not unreasonably.

Characteristically, Doc Savage did not say. He switched off the black-light device and the letters faded instantly, leaving no trace discernible to the naked eye. They had been written with a chalk composed of a substance which, in common with aspirin and petroleum jelly, glowed when bathed in ultra-violet light.

Doc turned. "Where is X Man?"

Monk cocked a thumb. "In the grass yonder. He and me got into a scrap."

"Which I ended with a timely stab of my stick," Ham added quickly.

"I would have had him tied in knots in another second," Monk boasted.

"Nonsense. He was more than a match for you, you furry freak. You must be slipping."

"Not in a million years," Monk returned angrily. "You take that back, you unsaddled clothes horse."

But Ham did not and Monk did not pursue the argument. Monk did not look that well. The expression on his face as he and Ham followed the bronze man out into the night, suggested the simian chemist was wondering if he was indeed slipping.

They found X Man where he had been left. Doc Savage revived him with a stimulant taken from his handy equipment vest.

"What do you know of Scylla?" asked Doc, once clarity had come into X Man's olive-black eyes.

"A fearsome beast."

"Real?"

X Man shook his head. "A fable."

Monk snorted. "Hah! Change your tune, guy. We just saw him gallop into the water, big as life."

X Man looked at the apish chemist as if the latter were not in his right mind. "Did you find your friend?" he asked Doc Savage.

No one knew quite how to answer that, so no one did.

They marched X Man into the house.

It was homey, but not well heated, as there was only a single fieldstone fireplace in the gloomy sitting room.

Doc found some personal papers in a roll-top desk.

"The occupant appears to be an individual named Bruce O'Neil," he imparted.

"That tells us a lot," Monk muttered unhappily.

The upper floors were unremarkable as to personal effects and other items. There was not much in the way of furnishings. The owner lived a rather frugal life, it seemed.

Doc Savage led them to the cramped root cellar, where their flash rays illuminated the bizarre collection of artifacts until they discovered a light switch that brought wan illumination.

Monk and Ham, neither of them experts in antiquities, made doubtful faces at the exotic collection.

Monk had collected the arrow that Doc had extracted from his vest, and was examining it. He remarked, "This here's some kinda dried hay or grass tied on the back end so it'll fly straight. Not feathers. Maybe it's prehistoric."

"You should know," Ham sneered.

"If you're referring to your private opinion that I look like a prehistoric cave man," Monk said, "please be advised I'm not in the mood for much of your sass. I'll snatch an ear from you."

"It is fur off a lion's mane," said Doc, referring to the adornment on the arrow's end.

The bronze man spent some time poring over the various specimens.

"Some of this stuff appears of recent manufacture," Ham hazarded.

"It is," Doc said. The bronze man was holding a vicious-looking short sword whose double-edged blade was of iron. He examined it critically, appeared to be testing it for heft and balance.

Doc turned to X Man. "Do you recognize this?" he asked.

X Man nodded. "It is a gladius."

"Yours?"

"It belonged to Brutus."

"Brutus the man who took Johnny prisoner?"

"Yes."

"According to papers, a Bruce O'Neil owns this house. Does that name mean anything to you?"

X Man frowned. "In Novum Eboracum, he was known as Brutus Otho."

"What the heck is *that* supposed to mean?" Monk wanted to know.

X Man did not enlighten him, and Doc Savage did not pursue the matter.

They conducted a general search for Johnny Littlejohn, with no encouraging results whatsoever.

Once they had reorganized, Ham started to say, "You don't—" He swallowed. "You don't suppose one of those sea serpents—ah, devoured him?"

No one offered any comment. The idea of losing Johnny and his big words conveyed horror itself.

At that point Doc Savage began removing his outer clothing, quickly stripping down to a pair of black silk bathing trunks he habitually wore in lieu of shorts.

He waded into the inlet, let the cold water come up to his chest, and fell into a powerful overhand stroke that took him to the approximate spot where the many serpentine heads had slipped from sight.

The bronze man had retained one of his waterproof spring-generator flashlights and he thumbed it on. Then he sank from sight.

Doc Savage followed the beam to the muddy bottom of the inlet. There were salmon present. Not many. But no other signs of life.

On the bottom, there were footprints—multitudinous tracks as if some gargantuan herd of creatures had plodded along the mud, single file, leaving a shallow trench that might have been made by a heavy, dragging belly. Driftwood lay splintered along the path, where tendrils of disturbed mud hung and drifted in the current.

Holding his breath, Doc followed the tracks. They went on for some rods. Gripping driftwood projections and the occasional slime-coated rocky jut, he helped himself along; otherwise his natural buoyancy would have brought him to the surface.

Progress was slow, and the bronze man appeared somewhat sluggish in his movements. Too, he was concentrating on holding his breath. He could do this for prodigious lengths of time, having learned the art of underwater swimming from the masters of that particular art—the pearl divers of the South Seas.

It was clear, Doc saw, that the tracks were leading east —toward the sea. Catching up would not be possible, not for a lone swimmer, and it was unclear what would be accomplished by attempting such a feat.

There was no indication—neither scrap of clothing nor fragment of human remains—to indicate Johnny Littlejohn's fate.

Doc Savage broke the surface and gulped in lungfuls of bracing air. His skin and hair, it could be seen, immediately began shedding moisture—a quality that brought to mind the waterproof down of a duck.

Doc Savage swam for shore, and upon reaching it, lay down and got his breath, secretly wondering if he could be getting old and feeble or something. It was not often a swim winded him. It might, he reflected, be the result of the inadvertent dosing with anæsthetic mercy bullets he had gotten earlier. That would also explain, he preferred to think, the abysmal lack of progress in the evening's activities.

Monk and Ham—X Man in tow—trotted up a few minutes later. They had spotted Doc making his way to shore. The bronze man stood up.

The faces of his two aids mixed hope and horror. Doc spoke before they could get the question stuck in their throats worked loose.

"No sign of Johnny."

"Blazes," Monk gulped. Ham twisted his sword cane wordlessly.

Coming erect, Doc Savage reclaimed his clothes from Monk and began climbing into them.

"What about this Bruce O'Neil?" Ham interjected. "He went into that boathouse, and out came some unnatural creature. How can that be?"

Doc Savage drifted up to X Man.

"Do you know where the one you call Brutus Otho has gone?"

"I do not."

"Or our friend, Johnny?"

"No."

"This guy ain't exactly no information bureau," Monk muttered. "Let me twist his arms a little, Doc."

Flake-gold eyes on X Man's hollow features, Doc Savage seemed to consider the homely chemist's offer for some moments.

"X Man is not your true name," he said. It was not a question, but a statement of fact.

"This is so."

"What is your true name?"

The man threw out his chest with a trace of pride. "In Novum Eboracum," he said, "I was known as Prince Metho."

"Prince!" Monk exploded.

Doc gestured for silence.

X Man—or Prince Metho, as he styled himself now— went on. "I ruled Novum Eboracum until the arrival of Brutus Otho, the freeman. It was he who turned my people against me, and Imperator Kizan banished us both from the Veil of Silence. I—I have been lost ever since."

"You wish to return?"

"More than anything," admitted the self-proclaimed Prince Metho.

"This is squirrel talk," Monk muttered.

Because he had made it a policy never to agree with anything the apish chemist said, Ham Brooks said, "He sounds perfectly sincere to me."

"He's an escaped lunatic. Naturally, he sounds sincere. He probably believes every dang word he's sayin'. But I don't. It's—what do they call hooey over here?"

"Rot," said Ham.

"It's rot. Unvarnished rot."

"If you will help us find our friend Johnny," Doc Savage offered, "I will do everything in my power to return you to Novum Eboracum."

Prince Metho searched the bronze man's impassive features.

"I believe you mean what you say, Homo Metallicus."

"I do," Doc stated. "Do we have an understanding?"

Prince Metho leaked a sigh and hung his head. His shoulders sagged.

"I—I do not know where Novum Eboracum is," he said disconsolately.

"That tears it," Monk said. "He's a phony."

"Quiet," Ham snapped. "Can't you see the poor beggar is depressed?"

"How did you come here to Britannia, Prince Metho?" Doc Savage asked, no hint of doubt in his steady voice.

"Brutus brought me here. I do not know how. We were banished by Imperator Kizan, and left to die on the Lake of Smoke. There was no going back, for we were warned that the great cats would dine upon our living bodies if we returned."

"What did you do then?"

"It was a trek of many suns through jungle and savage tribes. Somewhere—somewhere on that trek, I lost my mind. I remember almost nothing after that."

Prince Metho's dark eyes seemed to retreat into his

skull, as if recoiling from memory of his hardships, whether real or imagined.

"Then what?" Doc prompted gently.

"I was in a dark place for a long time. Brutus fed me. The dark place was never still and I was often sick. The air had a terrible smell, not like the clean air of Novum Eboracum. When I was very sick, Brutus would give me potions so that I would sleep."

"Do you remember how you came to the place of ruins?" Doc inquired.

"No. I awoke there. Before, the last thing I recall was the voice of Brutus, telling me that he would come for me when he was ready."

"I say, Doc," Ham inserted. "Dr. Gilchrist told us that some one called to alert the authorities that this fellow had been seen wandering the old Roman ruins. Do you suppose it was this Brutus chap?"

"It is reasonable to assume so."

"But why?"

"Brutus had cause to believe that in his present mental condition, X Man, or Prince Metho, would be indefinitely confined, his story not believed."

Monk confronted Prince Metho, "O.K., guy, answer me this: Why'd you call yourself X Man?"

"I—I do not remember. I did not recall that I was Prince Metho until the little leo came to my room. I remembered Novum Eboracum, and that I must return there, but not who I was."

Monk made grimacing faces. He tugged on a cauliflowered ear thoughtfully, but said nothing more.

Doc asked, "What else do you remember about Novum Eboracum?"

"That it is a place where time does not exist."

"Blazes," Monk squeaked. "How can time not exist?"

Doc asked, "Describe Novum Eboracum, please."

"It is a great city, always surrounded by the Mist of Never."

"Mist?"

"I do not know, but I believe it is the mist that keeps away time. It is impossible to see beyond the mist, which is called the Veil of Silence, although men have penetrated it and stepped into this world of yours. Some never to return."

"How did you expect to return if you do not know the way?" the bronze man asked.

"Brutus. I intended to force Brutus Otho to take me back, for only he knew the way. But now he is gone, too, and I have no hope."

The man's demeanor was so unutterably piteous that Doc Savage and his men offered no comment. Even Monk Mayfair held his tongue.

Doc Savage moved Monk and Ham off to one side and engaged them in earnest conversation.

"X Man, or whoever he is, is convinced of the veracity of his own statements."

"But that don't make them true," Monk retorted. "I mean, he's talking about a place where time ain't operatin' and people speak Latin, like in ancient Rome."

"Ancient Rome is exactly what he is describing," Ham offered. "He spoke of an Imperator Kizan. If I recall my ancient history, an imperator is the Roman equivalent of an emperor."

"Correct," said Doc. Then, changing the subject, he said, "There is nothing more to be accomplished here."

"Where are we going?" Ham wondered.

"Back to London."

"London? What about Johnny?"

"Wherever Johnny is, we cannot hope to locate him alone. The British authorities might be able to render some assistance in the search."

"If you say so, Doc," Ham said unhappily.

They trudged back to their car, a dejected group. Even their pets, who had camped out by the water, were hunkered down in attitudes that could only be described as mournful.

As they approached their waiting machine, a bubbling came from the nearby inlet.

"What's that?" Ham asked.

"Sounds like one of the noises them dang sea serpents made," Monk breathed.

Doc went to investigate, but it was only a salmon leaping. It did, however, appear unusually agitated.

They drove in silence to the bronze man's plane, which they had left on a great treeless moor.

At sight of the bronze-colored air giant, Prince Metho grew alarmed.

"What's the matter?" Ham wondered.

"I have never seen such a bird," Prince Metho said nervously. "It is greater than an eagle."

"Eagle!" Monk exploded. "Ain't you ever seen an airplane before?"

It became evident that the hollow-faced man had not. For as they walked him toward the plane, he endeavored to escape.

Monk and Ham fell on him simultaneously, and quickly found themselves on the ground, Prince Metho's thin arms and legs tangled with theirs.

The bronze man reached his hands into the knot of limbs, found the spinal nerve centers in Prince Metho's neck, and rendered him insensate.

Monk and Ham sat up, looking sheepish.

"This is embarrassin'," Monk muttered thickly.

"If you had not gotten in the way," Ham charged, "I could have bested him."

"He must've got his start fightin' octopuses," Monk complained. "That's how he fights—worse than a dang octopus. I never saw anything like it."

"Wrestling," Doc said.

"Huh?"

"The Romans were expert wrestlers," Doc explained. "Prince Metho was employing wrestling holds of a type never before seen in modern times."

"That wasn't like any wrestlin' I ever saw," Monk added.

"A mere wrestler," Ham sneered. "You *are* getting soft."

They continued their argument as Doc Savage bore Prince Metho into the tri-motor and laid him in a cargo net.

"I will be only a moment," he said, abruptly quitting the craft.

Curious, Monk and Ham pressed their faces to portholes and watched as in the darkness, Doc Savage roved a patch of weeds until he found whatever it was he sought. He knelt down.

Using tweezers taken from his vest, Doc harvested a number of leaves and, careful not to touch them directly, stuffed them into a glass phial.

When he came back, he swapped the new phial with the one Prince Metho had inserted into a secret pocket of his tunic.

Monk and Ham watched this operation in silent fascination.

When the bronze man declined to explain his actions, they prepared to take off.

"Hey," Monk said as the motors roared into life, prop wash flattening the heather into a rippling purple carpet, "what about our rental machine?"

"We will apprise the rental concern of its whereabouts from London," Doc said, throwing the throttles forward.

They bumped along, gathering momentum, the tail lifted, and they were soon in the air.

Below, moonlight sparkled on the jet expanse of the Firth of Forth. Their eyes were continually drawn to it, but Monk and Ham detected no trace of any sea creatures, and soon began to doubt the memory of what they had witnessed.

IX

THE STYGIAN SHORE

When contacted by radio, the British Admiralty was only too happy to lend the bronze man aid. The famous Doc Savage, they said with un-British effusiveness, had only to tender his request and all manner of assistance would be rendered. After all, had not Doc Savage done the Crown a good turn or two in the past? He had indeed. And did he not also hold an honorary commission with Scotland Yard, in recognition of those services? It was so. All that remained was for the request to be set before the admiralty.

Doc Savage explained, in as few words as possible, his needs. They chiefly consisted of sending coastwise British naval vessels to patrol the waters of the Firth of Forth and report any sea monster sightings.

Came the doubtful reply, "Sea monsters, did you say?"

Doc launched into a description of the horned heads sighted less than an hour before.

There was a protracted silence over the tri-motor's cabin radio, seasoned by a surprising minimum of static.

At last, "This will be done, of course."

Doc next explained that Sir William Harper Littlejohn was missing, and asked that Scotland Yard be put on the matter.

This, too, was promised.

An hour later, Doc set his tri-motor down on Croydon Air Field. They had to assist X Man—or Prince Metho— from the machine. The flight had evidently terrified the man. After releasing him from the chiropractic paralysis, Doc was forced to administer a sedative of short duration in order to pour him into a taxi with minimum fuss.

"This man acts as if modern civilization is completely foreign to him," Ham observed as they piled into a cab.

"He's just nuts," Monk scoffed.

At their hotel, they allowed the supposed Prince Metho to sleep while Doc Savage reestablished contact with the British authorities by telephone.

"Sea serpents have indeed been sighted," an official with the British Admiralty reported in a tone that indicated he scarcely believed his own words. "A veritable herd of them, it appears."

"Where?"

The official named three points along the eastern coast of England.

"They appear to be moving south," Doc suggested.

The official agreed that this was the trend of the sightings, and rang off.

Scotland Yard was next, but it offered little enough in the way of information on the missing archæologist, Johnny Littlejohn.

"We fully expect results shortly," reported a Scotland Yard official, after giving his summation.

Doc Savage was hanging up when Monk and Ham burst into the room. They had been engaged in making calls from their own rooms.

"We got a line on Bruce O'Neil," Monk announced, sounding pleased with himself.

"We had to call nearly every police station in England and Scotland," Ham added. "But it was worth it."

"The only Bruce O'Neil we could find," Monk continued, "that seemed like he might have any connection with a lost land or such was a half-baked explorer who has been poking around Africa for a long time. What makes this O'Neil look interesting is the fact that nothing has been heard from him for a couple of years."

Ham added, "This O'Neil chap has an odd nickname: Waterloo. Seems he was something of an inventor in his past, but of the crackpot sort."

"Crackpot?"

"At one time, he announced that he was going to circumnavigate the poles in a dirigible. At another, there was talk that he was working on a radical new kind of submersible designed for the exploration of undersea caves. Nothing was ever seen of these contraptions. That's how he acquired the nickname Waterloo. He was a big bust."

"We haven't much dope here on Waterloo O'Neil," Monk said. "Only that he's middle-aged, or maybe an elderly man—it depends on what you call fifty years old. An examination of Waterloo O'Neil's past work shows us that he once visited the lost city of Zimbabwe, so called, in Africa. Zimbabwe ain't really a lost city, seein' as how tourists have been going there for years. It's just a ruined place, and wouldn't have any connection with any place called Novum Eboracum. Say, there's a lot of stories that this Waterloo had kind of a tomb robber racket going on a while back."

Doc's flake-gold eyes showed a flicker of interest. "Tomb robber?"

"Yeah. He got caught rifling some tombs and was thrown out of Egypt some time back. Seems he was always chasing' after lost cities and not findin' any, frequently goin' broke tryin', so he musta turned robber."

"That could explain some of the artifacts found in Bruce O'Neil's root cellar," Doc stated.

"And some of them were too recent to be authentic," Ham added. "I guess that puts to rest any of this wild talk of time-travel. All that junk was looted or copies of actual artifacts."

Doc Savage said nothing. Instead, he went to check on Prince Metho.

The man slumbered. Doc checked his pulse, seemed satisfied that Prince Metho would not awaken for some time, and stood up.

"Up for a ride?" he asked.

Monk looked interested. "Where to?"

"To follow through on my original reason for coming to London."

Monk grinned. "I was kinda wondering if that got forgotten in all the hullabaloo."

Ham looked concerned. "But what about poor Johnny?"

"Scotland Yard has every available man searching," Doc replied. "Without leads, we can accomplish little."

And so they left the hotel.

Outside on the curb, Doc waved them into a waiting taxicab.

"Crowninshield, Kent," Doc instructed the driver.

As the machine leaped from the curb, Ham Brooks frowned darkly.

"I do not recall a village by the name of Crowninshield hereabouts," he said.

"Crowninshield," the bronze man explained, "is the name of a mansion in the town of Kent. Outside the city, in the more sparsely settled areas, prominent houses have names instead of addresses."

"Who lives there, Doc?" Monk asked.

"Alexander Abercrombie Nade," Doc Savage said. "Otherwise, Lord Nade."

"Seems I have heard that name," Ham said vaguely.

"Alexander Abercrombie Nade was once an explorer of some repute," Doc Savage said.

"That's right!" Ham exclaimed. "Wasn't he the Lord Nade who discovered a mysterious Egyptian tomb a long time ago?"

"The same."

"What's he to you, Doc?" Monk wanted to know.

"Alexander Abercrombie Nade was a friend of my father's," Doc imparted.

Silence followed that admission. It was rare that the bronze man spoke of his father, the man who had placed him in the hands of scientists in order that he embark upon the strange career he now followed. Clark Savage, Sr., had himself been an explorer of some renown. It logically followed that he would number among his acquaintances men of like accomplishment.

"Courtesy call?" Ham asked.

The bronze man shook his head somberly.

"Alexander Abercrombie Nade heard that I was to arrive in London and sent a radiogram asking that I call upon him. He did not say why, but suggested it was a matter of some importance."

"Know him well?"

"The contrary," Doc Savage stated. "I have never had the pleasure of making his acquaintance."

Crowninshield was a name that might have been originally applied to one of the many brooding castles that dot the English countryside. The dwelling—it was more manor than mansion—seemed to have been built of the sundered stone blocks of a traditional castle. The architecture was sixteenth century. Jacobean. Probably there were only twenty or thirty rooms. The cars were kept in converted stables, and the whinnying of horses could be heard from out back.

The taxi deposited them on the imposing front door and Doc Savage gave the lion-shaped knocker a single sharp rap.

They expected a butler—veddy British and redolent of tea and crumpets.

The door opened instead on a swart butterball of a Hindu who looked at them with intensely black jewellike eyes and announced in a doleful voice, "You are too late, *sahibs*—as I have foretold."

"Too late?"

The Hindu bowed his turbaned head so that a square emerald mounted on the front winked at them. He affected native costume, and the hues were not subtle.

"I am Goona Bey, and I see all events before Fate's loom reveals them. I informed Alexander Abercrombie Nade that to summon the great Doc Savage was foolhardy because the gods had determined that the threads of his life had all but unraveled."

Doc asked sharply, "Lord Nade is dead?"

"*Nahin, sahib.* No. He has but passed beyond. For no one truly dies. Perhaps he is now a butterfly or a fox. But he is not dead."

"Show us."

The Hindu Goona Bey pursed small, pouty lips and his eyes grew veiled.

"Enter," he said at last.

They stepped into a vestibule in which the stillness was broken by an ancient grandfather clock whose monotonous ticking might have marked the toiling progress of the unseen mechanism of time itself.

Goona Bey preceded them through paneled rooms that were dark with age and staining. Walls hung with trophies of all sorts. Tigers' heads. Elephant tusks. Ceremonial masks. Native artifacts. The colorful acquisitions of a globe-trotter's active life.

"Some of this stuff reminds me of the junk we saw in that O'Neil's cellar," Monk undertoned.

Ham said nothing. Doc Savage was very quiet as he strode along, his face unusually set. The soft sound of the Hindu's slippers *whisk-whisking* along seemed unnaturally intrusive in the stillness.

Servants peered out of ajar doors, only to retreat at their approach.

At last, Goona Bey brought them to a great double set of carven oak doors and pulled them open.

A smell of must wafted out and they entered.

It was a bedroom, the master bedroom of the hoary mansion. The bed was a four-poster, easily a century old. A man not much younger than the bed lay in it, covers tucked up to his chin. His eyes were open but there was no life in them. Death had pulled dryish lips back from yellowing, peglike teeth.

Doc Savage touched the man's wrinkled face. His metallic fingers slowly withdrew when they encountered obviously cool flesh. He pulled the covers over the dead man's head, flake-gold eyes filled with eerie stirrings.

He faced Goona Bey.

"How long ago?" the bronze man asked quietly.

"Within the hour."

Doc said nothing. He might have been reflecting on the delaying events of the last few hours and the opportunity to converse with a friend of his late father's, now lost forever.

His voice was very subdued when he spoke next.

"Lord Nade hinted that he wished to see me on an unspecified matter," Doc related.

"It is so," the Hindu intoned. "I assured Lord Nade that he should but trust in the gods and they would provide. But his heart ached with longing too much for patience. And it was too weak from age to beat beyond this day." The Hindu bowed his turbaned head. "*Affaf!* Alas! I have done what I could. No man can do more—not even one who can see across the River Styx to what those of the West call the Stygian Shore."

"See here, my good man," Ham put in. "You are not making sense. Why did Lord Nade wish to see Doc Savage?"

"It was the master's wish that the white bronze man enter into a futile quest on his behalf, one in which the bronze one is destined to play no role."

"Quest?" asked Doc.

"Alexander Abercrombie Nade had a son," related Goona Bey. "Matthew Anthony Nade by name. He has been missing for over six years. All hope had been lost. In his grief, the father turned to Goona Bey, the All-Seeing, and I have counseled him for these many bitter months. I beseeched him to be patient, but Lord Nade could not. And now he is dead."

"What happened to Matthew Anthony Nade?"

The Hindu shrugged elaborately. "What happens to many first-born sons. He attempted to follow in his father's footsteps and lost his way."

"Meaning?"

"To the Dark Continent, which is rightfully named, Matthew Anthony Nade ventured. The son plunged into the Congo jungle to show his father that he could become as great an explorer as he. The son has not been heard from since."

"Matthew Anthony Nade is lost in the African interior?" the bronze man demanded.

The Hindu lifted a plump finger. "No more. For the shades of the netherworld have whispered in my ear of the son's imminent return. Alas, too late to gladden the father's heart."

"I see what this is about," Ham Brooks said testily. "Doc, this fat fake was pulling the old spiritualism racket on Lord Nade. You know how it works. They play on the victim's sympathies and extort money in return for empty promises of future success or solace."

"I have never accepted a single ha'penny from Alexander Abercrombie Nade," Goona Bey said with injured pride.

"Hah!" Monk snorted. "Prove it!"

Goona Bey did. He clapped his hands together once sharply, and the peremptory report brought snappy results. The servants of the house began appearing at the bedroom door.

Monk cocked a rusty thumb at the Hindu.

"This guy been chiseling money from Lord Nade?" he demanded of them.

The servants murmured denials. They were quite vehement on that score. A few brushed tears from eyes and suggested that in his last days Alexander Abercrombie Nade had no finer counsel than the esteemed seer, Goona Bey.

"I don't believe it," Monk roared.

They separated swart Goona Bey from the household staff and Doc Savage interviewed the latter, individually and together. The end result was the same. There was no confidence trick being pulled. At least not an obvious one.

In fact, a maid informed them that she had lost a ring and had sought Goona Bey's advice.

"Sor, that ring was right where he told me it would be," the maid averred. "Under an armoire."

When Doc Savage again confronted Goona Bey, he put to the Hindu a direct question.

"Earlier, you said something about Matthew Nade's return."

Goona Bey placed plump fingers together and smiled broadly. "*Han, sahib.* It is so. The spirits who inhabit the other world have informed me that this day will mark the return of Matthew Anthony Nade to claim his birthright."

"To-day?"

The Hindu closed his eyes. He might have been communing with the dieties he claimed contact with.

"By sunset. It has been so written for a thousand years."

"Hokum," scoffed Monk. "Unvarnished, unmitigated hokum."

"For once I agree with this hairy lunk," Ham chorused.

"What say the shyster and I unwind this fraud's turban and strangle some truth out of him?" Monk suggested.

Goona Bey grabbed hold of his turban as if it were precious to him. His dark liquid eyes widened.

Ham Brooks unsheathed his sword cane and was on the point of spearing the turban when the maid who had vouched for Goona Bey's supernatural claims came running into the room.

"It has just come over the radio!" she cried.

Everyone turned to look at her. The maid placed a hand upon her heart, caught her breath, and tried again.

"The young master has been found!" she panted. "He is alive! Oh, but it is a sad thing, what with his father just passed on."

"Matthew Anthony Nade has been found?" Doc said, his flake-gold eyes whirling.

The maid beckoned frantically. "Come! Come! They are speaking of it even now!"

They rushed into a sitting room where a great console radio sat, its tubes filling the room with a warm glow.

Out of the speaker was coming the dulcet tones of a British radio announcer.

"—given up for lost these many years. According to early reports, Matthew Anthony Nade has just to-day surfaced, after spending six years as a captive of a hostile tribe, deep in the Congo. The young explorer is happily none the worse for his long ordeal. He is expected in Southampton on the morrow."

Doc Savage turned off the radio. There was a mantel over the fieldstone fireplace and the bronze man went to it.

In the center was a framed portrait of Alexander Abercrombie Nade, and beside it, that of a young woman whom Doc presumed to be the explorer's late wife. On the side, there was a portrait of a young man of perhaps twenty-four years. He seemed to take more after his mother than his father. The elder Nade had, even in the portrait, a rugged, athletic air. Matthew A. Nade, on the other hand, looked fair-haired, well fed, and even somewhat soft. It was difficult to see in his features the fortitude that would have impelled him to brave the African interior in search of adventure.

"This is Matthew Anthony Nade?" Doc asked the maid.

"It is, sor."

Doc examined the portrait some moments, as if memorizing the lost explorer's features. Then, he replaced it on the mantel.

Goona Bey stood regarding the scene, his placid features quite satisfied.

"Now do you believe in the power of the spirit world?"

Ham made a skeptical noise deep in his throat.

"Coincidence," he sniffed.

Normally, Monk would have echoed those skeptical sentiments, but agreeing with the dapper lawyer was something to be avoided.

"Maybe there is something to this mumbo jumbo after all," he allowed. "You hear a lot of strange stories out of India. Mental telepathy. Second sight. Yogis climbing ropes that are not attached to any visible support and then disappearing once they reach the top."

"If you think there is something to these wild claims," Ham suggested haughtily, "why don't you ask him where Johnny is?"

Reluctantly, Monk did.

"Your friend," replied Goona Bey sonorously, "has passed on."

A cold chill settled on them with those words.

"We must be going," Doc said abruptly.

"I am sorry that evil planets have thrown their dark shadows over your visit," purred Goona Bey. "I will convey your condolences to young Matthew Anthony Nade upon his return."

"Not necessary," said Doc.

"No?"

"We are going to Southampton," explained the bronze man, "to meet Matthew Nade."

Goona Bey swallowed noticeably and essayed a broad smile that was quite white and dazzling but otherwise conveyed no warm feeling.

X

MATTHEW ANTHONY, LORD NADE

The first word of the lost son of Alexander Abercrombie Nade came from an unexpected source—the British passenger steamship *Numidia* as she steamed from the Belgian Congo to Britain.

The announcement was made in mid-ocean by a rangy young blond man who had come aboard in Boma, the chief Congolese seaport. The blond man had quietly booked passage and kept much to himself during the early portion of the ocean voyage, taking his meals in his stateroom, along with a traveling companion.

"I am Matthew Anthony Nade," he told the ship's captain upon encountering the latter on the promenade deck of the steamer, "and I have spent six frightful years lost in the African Congo."

This bald statement, coming as it did during a lull in the voyage, produced considerable shock.

"But, if you are Lord Nade's lost son, why have you kept your identity a secret?" the steamer captain demanded.

"I have said nothing of myself until now because I required rest before revealing my identity," the subdued young man explained.

Instantly, the young man had become a shipboard celebrity.

Passenger steamship lines are always delighted to have celebrities on their vessels, for it publicizes their craft. Matthew Anthony Nade had been interviewed aboard the passenger steamer and had been courteous enough to tell his tale. This, together with the news of his discovery, had been radioed to London. As a result, a swarm of reporters and cameramen were on hand to greet Nade when the *Numidia* docked at Southampton.

"I can only spare a few moments," he said, when asked if he could answer a few questions. "I'm in rawther of a hurry to get to London and be reunited with my fawther."

"How was your trek out of the Congo to the steamer?" he was asked.

"Quite uneventful."

"Where have you been these six long years?"

"I fell captive to a tribe of natives and only managed to escape a fortnight ago, thanks to a mail pilot who landed in the bush owing to fortuitous engine troubles. Hearing the sound of his craft, I managed to escape my captors—with some success, obviously—and make my way to the plane, just as repairs had been completed. We managed to take off despite a hail of spears and war clubs."

"Were you scared?"

Young Matthew Anthony Nade laughed and said, "Perhaps you had better ask the pilot who rescued me." He indicated his traveling companion.

The pilot—he was distinguished by a lack of space between his eyes and an overabundance of jaw, and gave his name as Mulligan—was asked.

"Matthew Anthony Nade has iron nerve," declared the pilot.

Matthew Anthony Nade looked properly abashed under such praise, and murmured, "I shall have to be going now. I'm in rawther of a hurry, you know."

But the Southampton authorities had other ideas.

Two men in plain-clothes, with a blue-uniformed bobby standing deferentially behind them, shoved forward and showed identification.

"You are Matthew Anthony Nade, the explorer?" one demanded.

"I am."

"We have been awaiting your arrival," he was told. "Scotland Yard would like to interview you on your mysterious absence."

Matthew Anthony Nade looked nervous. "Is this necessary?" he asked. "I would prefer to hurry home to London."

The two Scotland Yard men were polite but firm.

"We are afraid is it," said the one who had not spoken. "Now, if you will come along. A motor car awaits."

Matthew Anthony Nade allowed himself to be escorted to the waiting car. The British press gave back politely and did not follow. Instead, they descended on the heroic mail pilot, Mulligan, and began plying him with shouted questions.

Once the young explorer was safely ensconced in the back of the car, the news was broken to him.

"We are sorry to inform you that your father passed on only yesterday."

Matthew Anthony Nade lived up to advance notices then. Only a slight ripple of shock was visible on his lean, fair-haired features. His shoulders shrank and he settled his slight weight more deeply into the cushions.

"I have kept body and soul together these many years in part because of my fierce determination to be reunited with my father," he said in a voice sucked dry of all feeling.

The Scotland Yard men said nothing. The driver engaged the auto and pulled away from the docks.

In the back seat, their passenger nursed his grief in utter silence.

Not many minutes later, Matthew Anthony Nade was being interviewed in the local police station. He took a seat beside a large window which gave a view of blaring Southampton traffic and a cluster of sooty buildings.

The Scotland Yard men assured the young explorer they would keep him no longer than necessary, and then one said:

"Please accept our condolences upon the death of your father, Lord Nade, but we must ask you some questions."

"Such as?"

"Such as are necessary to establish your identity."

The new Lord Nade cocked an astonished eyebrow. "Why, of course I am he."

"Of course," the Yard man agreed. "But as a matter of form, we would like to make sure."

"What do you mean?"

"You have been missing for some six years now," the young explorer was informed. "It is, of course, highly desirable that you be identified beyond a reasonable doubt."

"How can I make my identification more complete?" queried the young man.

"Finger prints," smiled the Scotland Yard man. "When you were a youth, your father took the precaution of having you finger-printed. That was so you could be identified in case of anything like a kidnaping. As you know, many prominent men now have themselves and their families finger-printed."

"Oh, yes," said the young man who had presented himself as Matthew Anthony Nade. "I remember it now."

He did not sound very happy.

A bobby was directed to bring Matthew Anthony Nade's youthful finger prints, and a print expert, to the room. The officer departed on his mission.

A few newsmen loitered beyond the open door, hopeful of catching a quotable morsel or two. One had been regarding the seated figure of Matthew Anthony Nade in silence.

"I say," he muttered to a brother scribe. "His Nibs appears to be jolly healthy for one who has spent six years in a bloomin' African jungle."

The other squinted. "Now that you mention it, you're right."

"And wasn't Matthew Nade a rather roly-poly sort to start with?"

"Perhaps the African jungle agreed with him, wot?"

"You could be right," the first reporter admitted. "It could be that he shed some poundage while a captive of that tribe of savages. After all, he was quite the young swain when he first set out for the jungle. Time enough for him to lose his baby fat, wot?"

"Yeah, perhaps that's it," agreed the second reporter.

The door was shut and the reporters went away to hunt up quotes from others.

They could not help but notice a rather striking individual loitering about the station. He had been asking questions of various constables and reporters, at the same time taking care not to be seen from the room in which Matthew A. Nade was being interviewed. It would have been difficult not to notice the man. He was a big bull of a fellow, bald on the top and very red and hirsute everywhere else.

"Who the deuce are you?" one newsman asked, awestruck by the apparition.

"I'm Bell, with the New York *Comet,*" said the giant, who was actually Doc Savage, once more in the outlandish guise of Behemoth Bell.

"Reporter?"

"Naw," the giant grinned. "I own the sheet."

"You don't say," said the reporter, dismissing the man as a boastful American reporter. As a matter of fact, Doc Savage did own a share of the paper in question.

"Where did that pilot, Mulligan, get to?" he asked of no one in particular.

The question seemed to not have occurred to the press before then and they hunted up a constable, who informed them that the man in question had not been taken into custody.

Hearing this, Behemoth quitted the building. He went directly to a telephone box and placed a call. He was not particularly missed.

The finger-print expert now appeared. With him he brought printing materials and the card which bore Matthew Anthony Nade's youthful finger prints. The equipment was spread out on a table in front of a large window, where there was light.

"You will press your fingers to the inky pads," the print man explained. "Then place them on this card, one at a time."

Matthew A. Nade nodded and, without the slightest hesitation, got the ink on his finger tips. He leaned forward to press his hand on the card. But before he could touch the card, the unexpected happened.

Came a loud smacking noise. Breaking glass jangled.

Glittering fragments of the window sprayed across the room.

"Hell's bells!" yelled a bobby. "Some one has shot through the blinkin' window!"

British policemen are not accustomed to having bullets come into their own headquarters. There was an uproar. Constables shouted and dashed about. Newspapermen knocked each other down, getting to cover lest there be other bullets.

"The shot came from that building two blocks away!" barked a bobby, pointing at a structure which housed one of the city's smaller hotels.

Bobbies raced for the building, nightsticks in hand. A radio patrol car was directed to go to the scene as soon as possible.

Young Matthew A. Nade was carefully wiping the ink off his finger tips when the questioning got around to him again. He pointed at the record card, which now bore a set of freshly inked finger prints.

"There you are," he said in an unruffled tone of voice.

The finger-print man started his comparison.

"You're a cool one," a newspaperman told young Matthew A. Nade. "If you asked, I'd say that bullet was fired at you."

"But why should it be?" young Nade countered. "I have no enemies."

They had found the spot where the bullet had struck in the wall opposite the window. They calculated its probable course, and decided it had indeed been fired at Matthew A. Nade. It had not missed him by a great deal.

The bullet was excavated and scrutinized.

"Came out of an army rifle," one of the two Scotland Yard inspectors decided aloud.

The finger-print expert straightened.

"This man is unquestionably Matthew Anthony Nade," he declared. "Finger-print markings do not change appreciably from childhood. His present prints, and those taken when he was a tyke, jibe absolutely."

"There is no doubt?" Matthew A. Nade asked dryly, as if piqued by the elaborateness of the identification.

"Not the slightest," asserted the expert.

A telephone report came in from the small hotel where the shot had been fired. The sharpshooter had escaped, thanks to the fact that he had lost no time whatever in fleeing after firing his shot. The hotel was one which did not pay a great deal of attention to its patrons. So only a sketchy description of the rifleman was available. He had been a lean-hipped man in plus fours and wearing a knit tam-o'-shanter on his head. His face had not been seen clearly.

The chief constable did some swearing, when he heard this. Unless they could unearth some further clue, it was likely that the sniper would make good his escape. The marksman had carried his rifle out in a golf bag. So an order was issued to stop all men seen carrying golf bags, and to search the bags.

Meanwhile, the man who had been positively identified as Matthew Anthony Nade was taking his leave of the Southampton police station.

He had declined an offered ride to the train station, saying that he wished to be alone with his thoughts.

The reporters present accosted him on the station steps.

"Is there anything you would like to say regarding the passing of Lord Nade, your father?"

Matthew Anthony Nade drew in a ragged breath. His eyes looked hot.

"My father," he said, "will be remembered for his exploratory endeavors long after my own name is forgotten."

It was a good quote, and copy pencils began scratching it onto note pads.

One who did not was the giant figure of Behemoth Bell. He was loitering around the corner, out of sight, but within earshot of the exchange.

"I imagine you will come into quite an inheritance, wot?" a scribe asked next.

"I trust so," returned Matthew Anthony Nade. "But it will in no wise make up for the loss of my dear pater. Now I must be going."

He strode out of police headquarters in a perfectly natural manner, but as soon as he was on the street, he began to act rather strangely. He walked slowly, stopping often to peer in shop windows, endeavoring to pick those which held mirrors in which he could observe those who passed him without it being too apparent that he was watching. He became satisfied that no one was following him.

Next, the rather athletic young man went to a telephone box. He dialed a number and apparently recognized the voice which answered, for no names were exchanged.

"Everything is going all right?" asked Matthew Anthony Nade.

"How did the finger-print business come out?" demanded the voice on the other end of the wire.

"Excellently," said Matthew A. Nade. "Your shot broke the window at just the right moment. I was able to slip those rubber caps bearing the fake finger prints over my fingers and get the false prints on the card. No one saw that in the excitement."

The man on the other end of the wire laughed.

"Good show," he complimented.

"Are you in the clear?"

"I think so. The Yard lads are looking for a Scot."

"A Scot?"

The other chuckled. "Carrying an army rifle in a golf bag."

The man who had succeeded in passing himself off as Matthew Anthony, Lord Nade smiled grimly.

"You have rented an auto?"

"I have. Shall we rendezvous at the foot of High Street, as planned?"

"Quite so." And the impostor hung up.

He looked both ways as he exited the telephone box, and although he was exceedingly careful in the manner in which he made his way to the docks, pausing from time to time to check a heavy pocket timepiece, he failed to detect the interesting fact that he was being followed every step of the way by a giant figure with no hair on his head and an abundant matting of red fur on his arms and at his open collar.

The figure walked with a long cigar clamped between strong teeth, but was not smoking.

At one point in the perambulation, the giant figure paused to look into the window display of an apothecary shop, and took up a position beside a scruffy Cockney sort in threadbare tweeds with a cap pulled low over his sharp features.

"He is going to rendezvous with an accomplice at the end of High Street," he informed the scruffy one.

"Know what this is about yet?"

"No. Where is Monk?"

"That ape is tooling about in the car, where he won't scare children."

"Get word to him, and meet me there."

"Righto," said the scruffy sort, shuffling off. He walked with his right hand clenched and held high, as if toting a walking stick that had been absent-mindedly left behind.

The scruffy Cockney was Ham Brooks, for once bereft of his ever-present sword cane.

The end of High Street—there seems to be one so named in almost every large British city—was not much distant from Southampton Common. And it was away from that center of public recreation that the false Lord Nade stopped and once again checked his timepiece.

He looked about with quick, nervous glances, eying passing traffic—motor cars, the ubiquitous London taxis, and the occasional trundling lorry—anticipation tightening his fair features. And so when a great grinning monster of a man loomed up behind him and placed a Brobdingnagian paw on his shoulder, the man's feet all but left the cobbles.

"This where Mulligan said to meet?" he asked in a good-natured whisper.

The spurious Lord Nade whirled and found himself looking directly at an open shirt front matted with bright red hair. He looked up. His neck immediately hurt.

"I beg your pardon," he gulped. "Who are you?"

"Goona Bey sent me."

"I am not certain I place the name. Could you repeat it?"

"Don't act cute. Goona Bey sent me here to watch out for you two."

When the false Lord Nade continued to stare blankly, the giant took the cigar out of his mouth and leaned over.

"Goona told me the whole lay."

"Did he now?"

"That's right. How you've been set up to pass for Alexander Abercrombie Nade's lost son, Matthew, cash in on the inheritance, and divvy up the swag. Have I got it straight?"

"Ye-es," the other admitted jerkily. "You have some conception of what is behind this, I will admit."

"Good. They call me Behemoth Bell, from the States."

"But I am bewildered," confessed the false Matthew Anthony Nade. "Why has Goona brought you in?"

"Does it matter?"

"It most certainly does," snapped the blond young impostor. "I demand an explanation!"

"I'm your protection."

"Against what?"

"Doc Savage."

The false Matthew Nade looked close to swooning then. He caught himself, swayed on rubber legs, and passed a white silk handkerchief over his suddenly moist forehead.

"How did that rotter get into this?" he demanded.

"Seems the old top knew Savage's father, and sent him a radiogram," related Behemoth Bell. "Goona couldn't stop Savage from coming, so he sent for me."

"Doc Savage has a reputation."

Behemoth grinned. "So have I—I'm from Chicago."

This impressed the false Matthew Nade sufficiently to reinvigorate his courage. He had heard a great deal about Chicago gangsters from the British press.

Behemoth pulled a cigar out of one pocket and offered it.

"Don't mind if I do," drawled the blond young man, taking the fragrant weed.

From somewhere—it seemed to appear between his thick thumb and forefinger by magic—Behemoth Bell produced a wooden match. He flicked it to flame with a thumbnail and applied it to the cigar firmly clasped between his teeth.

The fake Matthew Nade leaned his cigar into the offered match and the two men stood smoking for some moments, the bald giant falling into his playful habit of expelling smoke from alternate nostrils.

"Learned the trick in Alcatraz," he offered good-naturedly. "I escaped."

Matthew Nade blinked. "I thought no one had ever escaped from that fearful place."

Behemoth shrugged unconcernedly. "Guess they haven't missed me yet."

This startling revelation kept Matthew Nade occupied in thought while a long dark sedan muttered up High Street and drew to a stop directly behind him.

"Psst!"

The supposed Matthew Nade turned—and found himself looking into the homeliest face he had ever beheld.

Then he fainted.

Doc Savage caught him and boosted him into the sedan's back seat, which Ham Brooks—still dressed in Cockney tweeds—had pushed open.

"The drugged cigar worked, huh, Doc?" Monk asked.

Doc pulled the door shut, and got behind the wheel. Monk shoved over, incidentally crowding a slumped figure.

Monk reached down to the floorboards and pulled the slumped figure's head up by the hair.

"Meet Mulligan," he said broadly. "He gave me and Ham an argument when we pulled him over, so we took out our frustrations on him."

Doc sent the sedan scooting away from the curb and said nothing. Monk was often rough on crooks.

From in back, Ham asked, "Did you learn what is behind this, Doc?"

"The fake Matthew Nade confirmed my surmises," the bronze man said.

"So he *is* a phony," Ham murmured.

"And so is that Goona Bey!" Monk howled. "But what's it all about?"

"An elaborate confidence trick," Doc explained. "The plan was to pass this impostor off as the new Lord Nade and seize control of the inheritance."

"But wouldn't somebody recognize this guy as a fake?" Monk demanded.

"Remember, Lord Nade is now deceased, and there are no close relatives left to detect fraud. Since Matthew Nade might be expected to have changed somewhat during a six-year absence, that fact, and a loss of weight that would be blamed on his difficult ordeal, meant that the pretender's deceit would probably go unrecognized."

Ham said, "I knew it all along. These fakirs are all of a type. No doubt Goona Bey secretly misplaced that gullible maid's ring just so he could pretend to find it and establish his so-called mystic powers."

Doc nodded. "That is how the groundwork for these schemes is often laid."

"I can hardly wait to see the look on that smug Goona Bey's puss when we all barge in on him," Monk chortled.

XI

COMMON CAUSE

Right at that moment, Goona Bey was wearing the expression of an individual who had gone for a woodland walk and heard the steely snap of a bear trap in the vicinity of his right foot.

The Hindu's normally-sallow visage was distinctly pale. Perspiration was profuse upon his fat features, giving them the aspect of cooking molasses.

Goona Bey was standing in the doorway of Crowninshield, having just opened the front door, his mouth open and nothing coming out.

The reason was clear. A fat Webley pistol was prodding his voluminous native costume in the area of his ample stomach.

The impressive pistol was nestled in the big hand of a caller notable for his burly physique and bristling profusion of muttonchop whiskers. He resembled a hedgehog.

The gruff voice of the caller demanded, "Who the devil are ye?"

"I am known as Goona Bey," said the Hindu, his plump hands floating uselessly at his sides. "And you might answer your own question, *sahib.*"

"Never ye mind, ye fat heathen. I have come for Lord Nade."

"Accept my profound regrets, *sahib.* Old Lord Nade has this day departed for a higher sphere."

"I don't mean the old man. I want the blasted son."

"He—he has not yet arrived," the Hindu stammered.

The Webley increased the alarming dent in the Hindu's belly.

"I will wait," the other said, prodding the gun muzzle.

"As you wish, friend," purred Goona Bey, his facial

117

perspiration like rain on a windowpane now. He backed into the gloomy vestibule on slippered feet that whispered with each cautious step.

The muttonchopped one looked around cautiously. "Servants?"

"*Han, sahib.* But what—"

"Shut up, dammit! Get them out here."

"I am wont to clap my hands and they come."

"Then clap and mind ye don't provoke a bullet in yer fat gut."

The Hindu bowed with his turban-burdened head, and brought his fat hands together.

The servants came, stopped, and their reactions ranged from hands leaping over widening mouths to that of an elderly cook, who fainted onto a decorative chair when she saw the pistol.

"Every one of ye will do exactly what I tell ye or I will puncture this damn Hindu," the gunman warned.

"I have foreseen your coming," Goona Bey announced in a voice made loud.

"And what did ye see?"

"That this ordeal will pass without harm to anyone," Goona Bey said with a note of hope quivering in his voice.

"That's where ye're wrong," said the invader, lifting the heavy snout of the Webley and bringing it lashing down on the Hindu's head.

Squeals from the staff. The cook who had fainted came to, took one look at the tableau, and draped herself over the chair onto which she had fainted in the first place.

"But he—he has never been wrong before!" the maid squealed.

"Always a first time, it 'tis," the gunman snapped.

The Hindu, Goona Bey, had lost his colorful turban in falling, revealing a thick thatch of black hair in which some crimson seepage was already showing.

The household staff just stared. No one knew what to do. But they were suitably cowed and allowed themselves to be prodded and herded into a back room, which was promptly locked with an iron key.

The gunman then went to a washroom and filled a

porcelain pitcher with icy-cold tap water and dashed it onto the face of the insensate Hindu, Goona Bey.

Goona's dark eyes remained closed even after he revived, shaking his round head of water droplets like a dog slinking in from a thunderstorm.

"Let's have yer name, skurlie," the intruder snarled.

Goona Bey was having trouble collecting his wits, so the gunman went to work testing the elasticity of the Hindu's ribs with his boot toe.

"Spill, damn ye!"

Goona Bey found his wits with alacrity.

"What do you want of me?" he whined, his voice losing its oily purr.

"Your name, to start."

"Goona Bey, *sahib.*"

"Just what is yer game, Goona Bey?"

The Hindu swallowed uncomfortably. The hard prod of a boot tip under his lowermost ribs coaxed additional words out of him.

"By trade, I am what some call a confidence man," Goona Bey admitted grudgingly.

"One of those, eh? So what's yer scheme?"

A resigned sigh emerged from deep within the Hindu's oblate bulk. "I suppose the game is over anyway now that Doc Savage has stuck his nose into it," he said.

"Savage! What has *he* to do with ye?"

Goona Bey took up his turban and unraveled it enough to begin wiping the sweat off his round features. The skin remained moist, and a trifle paler than before.

"*Sahib* Savage has just gone to meet Matthew Anthony Nade at the Southampton docks—he thinks."

"Unriddle yer words, damn ye. What do ye mean—thinks?"

"Savage is under the impression that Lord Nade's lost son has just returned from Africa," said Goona Bey.

"That so? I just happen to know that Matthew Anthony Nade died in the African interior."

The Hindu smiled weakly. "Most labor under that impression, *sahib.* It is why my associates and myself hit upon as sweet a swindle as the human mind has ever conjured.

We were going to pass off an actor as the lost son and divide the inheritance among ourselves."

"Happy coincidence, the father dying to-day," the gunman growled meaningly.

"A subtle poison hastened the inevitable," the Hindu admitted sheepishly.

"Hah! A rogue after me own bleeding heart!"

Goona Bey looked suddenly interested. But he kept his own counsel.

"Savage have any one with him?" the gunman demanded.

"Two, *sahib*. What you might call a well-dressed toff and a human gorilla."

"That's all?"

"All I beheld."

The muttonchopped one took a fistful of his whiskers and twisted them in thought. "Hmmm," he said thoughtfully. "They must have stashed him."

"Who?"

"A very important person who is sometimes known as X Man."

"A curious name—if it is a name," Goona Bey said.

"Prince Metho is his other name."

"I know of many princes—by reputation, of course. But no Prince Metho."

The burly gunman seemed not to register the Hindu's words. "If Savage hasn't got Prince Metho with him," he murmured, "that means he's stashed somewhere."

"I do not follow."

The gunman came out of his reverie very suddenly.

"How would ye like to be cut in on something bigger than Lord Nade's inheritance?" he asked suddenly.

"*Sahib,* whom do I have to poison?"

"No one—if there is no need of it. I am a man not partial to wanton bloodshed."

"Blood and murder are different things, *sahib,*" Goona Bey answered, reverting to his oily purr. He touched the square emerald that decorated his askew turban. It popped down on a hinged setting, revealing a whitish powder.

"Poison?"

The Hindu nodded. "Untraceable, as I have said."

The bewhiskered gunman broke out into a crooked grin. "You might come in handy, after all. Your blokes—how many do ye have?"

"Two. Mulligan and one Leo Corby, now passing for Matthew Anthony, Lord Nade. They're handy lads to have in a row, as you might put it."

"I trust so. For where we are going will require toughness and wiles. But at the end of the journey lies riches undreamed of in this sorry time."

"Time?"

"Never mind that now. We must prepare for Savage's arrival."

"One who seeks the end of the rainbow," the Hindu suggested, "first must know what is contained in the pot that is buried there."

"Exactly what should be expected."

"Gold?"

From a pocket, the gunman plucked a fat coin. Holding it between two fingers, he brought it level with the Hindu's widening eyes. There was a profile and inscription, but the Hindu had eyes only for the unmistakable yellow gleam. Gold, sure enough. Simon pure, from the teeth marks embedded in the rim.

"I have never before beheld the like," Goona Bey said softly.

" 'Tis a gold dinarius. There's sackfuls more where this came from."

"What do I call you, master of my destiny?" wondered Goona Bey suddenly.

" 'Tis Waterloo."

"I devoutly hope that name is no omen," the Hindu said blandly.

The two rogues fell into low, earnest whispers.

XII

PAROXYSM

Doc Savage killed the sedan motor as they neared Crowninshield. The machine coasted to a gradual stop and the bronze man got out.

The two prisoners—the false Matthew A. Nade and the pilot, Mulligan—were still unconscious.

Monk blew on a furry fist. "I'm itchin' to go to town on that Goona Bey."

"Not necessary," Doc said. "You and Ham remain with the prisoners."

Monk began to protest. "But what about—"

"Doc can handle one overfed rogue," Ham pointed out.

Unhappy, Monk subsided. He settled back in the cushions and jabbed a hard elbow into the ribs of the still-sleeping Mulligan.

"Fear not," Ham informed Doc as the bronze man alighted from the machine. "I am prepared to administer the proper sedative if anyone should become restless."

"These guys," Monk snorted derisively, "are dead to the dang world."

"I was referring to a certain hirsute anthropoid," Ham sniffed.

Doc Savage drifted away from the idle machine as the muffled sounds of another argument grew heated.

He approached the house with care, but once within sight of the front door, shed all stealth. He had not removed his Behemoth disguise; and he stood out alarmingly in the gathering dusk.

The bronze man had good reason for exposing himself to the occupants of Crowninshield so recklessly. Goona Bey, assuming the conniving Hindu had remained in the manor to bluff out the arrival of his confederates, would be expecting Doc Savage to accompany the others, Mulligan and the fake Matthew A. Nade.

He would not recognize the nonexistent Behemoth Bell, nor would he be likely to be unduly alarmed by his turning up on the front door of Crowninshield.

So Doc Savage, blissfully unaware of what awaited him, approached the great doors with confident, rolling steps, as befitted his assumed personality.

He lifted the brass knocker, and the door, obviously unlocked, fell inward.

A suffocating and unmistakable odor billowed out and into his bovine features.

Illuminating gas!

Doc Savage took at least two hours of scientific training each and every day. Each muscle in his splendid physique, every individual nerve and brain cell were tested, stimulated, and improved until they were at the peak of human possibility. His senses, reactions to stress and peril, and the all-important ability to handle the challenges of his fantastic career were continually attuned.

Not the least of which were his reflexes. From the time he had learned to walk, Doc had honed his reflexes by the deceptively simple expedient of snatching bits of cheese off a mousetrap before it could snap and catch his fingers. The first few times he attempted the feat taught him a painful lesson; thereafter, he became proficient with both hands. Later, he learned to do the trick with his wonderfully prehensile toes.

At the first split-second awareness of danger, Doc Savage's reflexes began functioning with lightning efficiency.

The bronze man hastily backpedaled. He had a cigar in his mouth. Simultaneously, he brought one huge hand over the lit end. His hands were covered with a chemical dye to mask their normal distinctive bronze hue. The dye was, fortunately, somewhat fireproof.

Doc smothered the glowing tip with no significant damage to his palm. He flung the cigar into the grass and whipped out a gas mask of his own devising, consisting of goggles, nose clip, and a chemical breath filter fitting between the teeth.

He clapped the goggles over his eyes, pinched his nose with the clip, and took mouthfuls of filter.

Then he plunged into the open door.

Every wall fixture had been turned on, he saw. The manor was a gigantic tinderbox!

Doc Savage began moving from room to room, his features tight, cheeks flat with strain. The chemical sponge inhibited speech, and there was a frenzied way about Doc's movements as he pushed doors open, seeking possible gas victims.

The bronze giant found them huddled on the floor of a closet. The household staff. They were unmoving. Chests still rose and fell in respiratory distress, however.

Doc swept back, and into the handiest bedroom. He began throwing up window sashes, and shoved out his head, the sponge filter popping out of his mouth.

Doc shouted rapid words in a foreign tongue. The lingo was Mayan; Doc Savage and his aids were almost the only persons in the so-called civilized world who spoke and understood this particular Mayan vernacular. They had learned it during the course of a fantastic adventure in a lost city in Central America.

The bronze man had summoned Monk and Ham to help carry the gas victims to fresh air.

Doc returned to those victims now, haste apparent in every movement of his great leonine body.

Lifting two limp forms, one under each arm, he bore them into the bedroom, now filling with fresh air. Laying them on the bed, Doc returned and collected two more.

He was working on the third pair when Monk and Ham, gas masks in their own mouths, burst in. Doc made hand signals for the two aids to pitch in. He employed the deaf-and-dumb sign language all his aids understood, and which came in handy at times when speech was difficult or impossible.

A bullet snarled in through an open window, embedding itself in a plaster wall under an ornamental metal shield. The bullet made an ugly chucking sound drilling the hole—but that was not what stopped their hearts in their chests.

They understood that had the bullet struck the shield and snapped loose a spark, the gas would have ignited with horrific results.

Then another bullet came. It, too, missed its target.

Monk Mayfair did a brave thing then. He got in front of the window through which the two bullets had come. Ham Brooks, seeing this, leaped to place his waspish body before that of the hairy chemist's.

They began pushing one another aside, vying for the privilege of being the human shield that would stop the next bullet—and it came.

Whistling, the bullet angled in through a different window and struck the shield head-on.

There was probably a noise attending the tremendous explosion that followed. No one heard it. Their eardrums took such terrific concussion punishment that they became instantly oblivious to all sound.

The manor was sandstone—good, substantial material. TNT might move those blocks. Illumination gas is not TNT.

Still, every pane of glass in the entire house blew out in a coruscation of flame and violence.

Monk and Ham blew out, too. Doc Savage, one hand coming up to shield his flake-gold eyes, lost sight of the pair in the ensuing paroxysm.

After that, he was too busy fighting the flames with his doffed coat—which had fire-retarding qualities too—and easing the unconscious members of the household staff out the shattered windows.

He had luck. The air in the room had sufficiently cleared by the time of the conflagration that the bedroom was not engulfed in the mass of flames that overtook the rest of the old manor.

After the last victim had been laid out on the lawn, Doc Savage began hunting Monk and Ham, oblivious to the crackling of fire and the grayish-black worms of smoke funneling out of every broken window of Crowninshield.

He found them. Monk had lost some hair. At least the

top of his bullet head looked somewhat singed. Ham's prematurely white hair, which was never subjected to anything less than a five-dollar haircut, was not even mussed, oddly enough.

They came around after a little while.

"What happened?" Monk muttered, his tiny eyes blinking.

"You failed to catch the bullet, you ape," Ham said tartly, sitting up.

"Catch it! In what—my teeth?"

"Wasn't that what you were trying to do?"

"No, I was—I was . . ." Monk let the sentence trail off. Although each man had obviously been willing to sacrifice his life for the other, it was not something they ever spoke of. The opposite, in fact. They had seldom been heard to speak a kind word of each other, unless one believed the other to be dead.

Monk clambered to his feet, and said, "Trap, huh?"

"It would appear so," Doc said. The flames had started melting the flesh-colored rubberized cap that had made his head appear bald. With careful fingers, the bronze man began stripping himself of the adornments that made him Behemoth Bell.

Ham looked around his feet, at first with concern; then, evidently not finding what he sought, he began making flapping hand motions, suggesting incipient panic.

"What is it?" Doc asked.

"My stick!" Ham bleated. "I had it in my hand."

They fell to searching. Ham's stick was not to be found. That was when Monk Mayfair noticed that one pocket of his trousers was hanging out. He shoved a big paw into it and made nose-wrinkling faces.

"I think somethin' musta dropped out of my pocket," he complained, "but I'll be hanged if I can remember what."

"You should be hanged on general principles," Ham said unkindly.

They searched the ground for anything the apish chemist might have dropped, but found nothing in the grass.

Doc Savage suddenly knelt and his flake-gold eyes grew animated.

"Monk's pocket was picked," he said suddenly.

Monk and Ham studied the piece of turf the bronze man was scrutinizing. Here and there, it was flattened by many overlapping footprints.

"This compressed area of grass is where you both landed," indicated Doc. "See these prints? They belong to none of us."

Monk wondered, "But who would've done that?"

"Look closer, you monkey," Ham snapped. "This footprint shows no demarcation between sole and heel."

Monk seemed not to get it at first.

"Goona!" he howled. "It was that fat heathen, Goona Bey! He wears native slippers instead of shoes."

"Goona Bey, without a doubt," Doc said, coming erect. "He doubtless set the gas trap and fired the shots intended to kill us all."

"That doesn't make sense," Ham offered. "Why not simply escape before we arrived?"

Doc Savage did not answer directly. Instead, he suddenly made for the parked car.

It was no longer there.

"Got away with his two pals," Ham said bitterly. "And my cane."

Doc, examining the ground, said, "There was a fourth man."

"Yeah?" Monk said.

"This one wearing ordinary shoes." Doc stooped, and his hands, coming up, held a gold coin balanced between metallic forefinger and thumb.

Examining it, the bronze man's trilling came. This time it was distinctly puzzled. Crowding closer, Monk and Ham saw that one side was stamped—hand-stamped, for no machine had cut that profile—with the face of a man with a distinctly Roman nose and a garland in his hair. Under the profile was a short inscription:

IX HISPANA

"Never saw a coin like that," Monk muttered.

The clanging of arriving fire engines smote their ears before they could further examine the strange gold coin.

Doc greeted the fire chief—or whatever the English equivalent was—and explained the events of the last few minutes. His explanations were accepted with some skepticism inasmuch as he was still partially in the Behemoth Bell disguise. He was discarding what he could of it—he lacked the chemical dye remover at the moment—when the local police arrived.

The bronze man did better with his explanations then.

"You say it was a Hindu that done this?" a constable asked.

"The household staff might corroborate my surmise," Doc offered.

They—or at least the Irish maid, the first to come to—did. After a fashion.

"Sor, a man came to the door and waylaid poor Goona Bey."

"Then what transpired?" the constable prompted.

"We were made to hide in a closet. The two spoke for some time but the door was too stout for their words to be overheard. Then the awful smell of the gas came."

The maid closed her fear-sickened eyes at the recollection.

"We all got onto the floor and after that, there is no remembering what happened."

"Who would this new person be?" Ham demanded of no one in particular.

Monk, who had been fishing in his pockets throughout the recitation, came to a sudden unpleasant discovery.

"Hey! There *is* somethin' missin' from my pocket!"

They all looked at him.

Monk turned both pockets inside out.

"My dang hotel room key! It's gone! But—why would they take *that*?"

"The key had the crest of our hotel stamped upon it," Doc rapped. He turned on the constable. "The use of your auto might prevent additional complications."

"We will be pleased to drive you wherever you wish," the constable declared without hesitation.

*   *   *

As it turned out, Doc Savage did the driving, with the constable seated beside him and Monk and Ham in the rear. The remaining bobbies, not wishing to be left behind, stood on the running boards and clung to the window posts, trying to retain life and limb as Doc Savage, driving with a controlled fury that seemed reckless, showed himself to be a veritable wizard behind the wheel.

There was already much commotion outside the hotel when they arrived. A milling crowd. Two representatives of Scotland Yard were questioning hotel staff.

Doc shoved through the crowd, which parted as if they were water and the bronze giant the prow of some boat.

"It seems several blokes barged in, carrying the trussed body of a man," a Scotland Yard man informed Doc, after the bronze man had presented him with an identification card indicating a high honorary commission with the Yard.

"Carried the body in?" Doc asked sharply.

"And carried him out again not five minutes later, according to reports. We are now attempting to ascertain precisely which room they invaded. None appear to be jimmied."

Doc flashed up the stairs, the others trailing like steel filings pursuing a lodestone.

The bronze man reached their suite of rooms, stopping before Monk's closed door.

Before they went in, or even touched the knob, Doc Savage uncorked a small phial and held it under the doorknob. Vapor from the phial caused greenish spots to appear on the knob.

Monk, the chemist, knew what caused the phenomenon. Doc had wiped the knob before he left. Some one had taken hold of it since, and the person's hand had left minute deposits of the oil which is always on the human skin. The chemical vapor from the phial had reacted with this oil, making a visible stain.

"They went in there all right," Monk breathed. "But, dang it, why?"

Doc Savage moved to the door adjoining Monk's. It was his own.

Inserting a key, he got the door open and went in. The others followed. They saw that the connecting door lay open.

Doc went to the suite bedroom where he had left the slumbering X Man—or Prince Metho, as he claimed to be.

"Blazes!" Monk squawled.

A figure lay on the bed. It was not the mysterious X Man.

The bound man tried to sit up, but he was trussed too expertly. He made only a flopping on the bed like a beached fish. There was plaster tape over his mouth and he was trying to talk through this.

Doc seized one corner and ripped the plaster tape free.

"—malgamated!" the man said. Then added a fervent, "Ouch!"

"Who is this individual?" a Scotland Yard man demanded.

"This," Doc Savage said, "is the missing William Harper Littlejohn."

XIII

FACES ON A COIN

William Harper Littlejohn sat up, blinked, blinked again, and looked around.

"Where am I?" he asked.

"Our London hotel suite," Doc related.

"Londinium," Johnny said in a tiny voice. Then evidently remembering his words, added, "An indiscriptibilitive nonexpectation."

The Scotland Yard men looked befuddled.

"What did he say?" one asked.

"Sounded like London," said Monk.

"Of course," the Yard man said impatiently. "Londinium was the Roman name for this city. I meant the rest of it."

"He said this is a complete surprise to him," translated Monk. "You'll get used to his words after you've been around him a while."

"I trust not," the Yard man said dryly.

Doc Savage was working on Johnny's bonds and asking questions.

"Remember how you got here?"

"No," Johnny admitted.

"What do you remember?" Ham asked.

Johnny noticed the dapper lawyer's empty hands, frowned, and asked, "Where is your stick?"

Instead of answering, Ham chose to seek out his pet ape, Chemistry. Habeas Corpus had trotted out from under the bed whereupon he took up a sitting position beside his master, and collected unblinking stares from the police.

Doc continued the questioning.

"Waterloo O'Neil carried you into the boathouse," he stated. "Recall that?"

"Yes, I—" Johnny's brow furrowed up. "What name did you say?"

"Bruce O'Neil, sometimes called Waterloo."

"There is a scoundrel by that name who has been rifling ancient tombs for years," Johnny remarked. "Is he the same fellow who was called Brutus?"

"The very same."

Johnny's long face bunched up in disapproval. As an archæologist, he placed tomb-robbing on the same shelf of wickedness as cannibalism.

Then a queer expression crossed his face.

"I remember waking up in a dark chamber filled with machinery," he said hollowly. "I tried to escape and found the chamber was surrounded by mists—and creatures." The gaunt archæologist shuddered. "They—they made me think of dragons."

"You had time to write out a word," Doc reminded.

"Scylla! The row of dragon heads looked exactly like the classical description of the sea monster called Scylla in old Roman texts. It was supposed to possess six beaked heads, a dozen legs, and a great body. It was a crazy thing to write, but it was all I could think of when—"

"When what?" Doc prompted.

"When it opened one of its heads to—breathe some foul exhalation upon me," Johnny said weakly.

The Scotland Yard men exchanged dubious looks. Even Monk Mayfair scratched the exact top of his nubbin head with some perplexity.

"A multiheaded creature such as you describe was seen escaping the boathouse," Doc Savage related, golden eyes searching the bony archæologist's face.

"I recall nothing of that," Johnny admitted, clearly uncomfortable with the subject. "The next I recall, I was back in the strange . . . chamber. There were dials and gauges, lights, and I had the distinct sensation I was floating inside some sort of machine in transit." Johnny closed his eyes, shuddered.

"Machine?" said Ham, who had returned, leading the grotesque runt ape, Chemistry, by one hand.

"My impressions are fuzzy," Johnny admitted. "I lost consciousness after a time. Then I woke up here."

"Doc, could Johnny have been inside a—a time machine?" Monk exploded.

"Time machine?" Johnny said. "Now that you mention it, that Brutus fellow—I mean, Waterloo O'Neil—insisted that we were on a journey through what he called the Mists of Time into the past. But that does not explain the creature that resembled Scylla. It is a myth, not prehistoric."

"I wonder," Ham said thoughtfully, rubbing his jaw.

They all looked at him.

"Could it be that Johnny was transported back through time, and the tear in the fabric of history allowed this creature to escape into our present time?"

Doc said, "The events seem to have happened in impossible order."

Monk winced. "What's possible about them?"

"See here now," the Scotland Yard man broke in. "What sort of nonsense talk is this?"

"Conjecture," Doc told them. "We have no proof of any of this."

"Well then, let's get down to brass tacks. Who was the man who was abducted from this room?"

"He is an escaped mental patient who was known as X Man," Doc supplied.

"X Man, you say?"

"Later, he told us he was Prince Metho of Novum Eboracum," Ham added.

"Novum—Novum—" The Yard man soon found the words he was evidently groping for. "New York!"

Doc nodded. "That is what he told us. We cannot explain any of it to our own satisfaction."

"What has this to do with the fire at Crowninshield, Lord Nade's residence?"

Doc explained, "We believe Waterloo O'Neil hooked up with Goona Bey and his confederates, for what purpose we cannot say with any certainty."

The Scotland Yard men withdrew into a corner and conferred at some length. They returned no more satisfied of expression than before.

"It is clear to us that this has all been the work of confidence men," one of them announced in an important tone, "and we will cast out a dragnet, as you Americans call it, until we apprehend the blighters."

"Look for some one with a terrible insatiable itch," Doc suggested.

"Itch?"

Doc nodded. "It will be impossible to disguise the itching problem, no matter how these men attempt to conceal their identities."

And with that morsel of data to be digested, the Yard men went off to pursue the hunt.

Johnny tried standing up and experienced no more success than he had when Doc Savage had last encountered him.

The bronze man allowed him to fall back onto the bed and helped him get his feet up on the covers.

"Do you—do you think is possible?" the bony archæologist wondered, his eyes upon the ceiling. "I mean, that I have traveled through time? That somewhere in the past there is a Roman city called Novum Eboracum, which is possible to visit at will?"

"If there is," Doc stated, "the secret of this machine would be of inestimable value to science and history."

"Think of it," Johnny breathed. "To travel back into time. To meet with Cæsar. See the pyramids being built and solve the riddle of their construction. I'll be superamalgamated."

"Danged if I believe any of it yet," Monk said.

Instead of replying directly, Doc produced the gold coin he had found on the lawn of Crowninshield and held it before Johnny's dazed eyes.

The gaunt archæologist came bolt upright and he fumbled from his concealed pocket his monocle magnifier, which had miraculously survived his travels intact.

"Where did you get this?" he blurted.

"Waterloo O'Neil dropped it—evidently," said Doc.

Johnny murmured, "It looks as if it were minted yesterday. There is no tarnishing, no wear at all. I have examined Roman coins of every era and I have never seen one like this."

Ham Brooks came closer and his dark eyes fell on the coin. There was a profile on one side, distinguished by a decidedly Roman nose. Doc Savage flipped the coin and the gasp that came from his three aids sounded like air being sipped.

For the other side also boasted a profile—one they all recognized. A legend under the coin said:

METHO REGVLVS

"Jove—or should I say, Jupiter!" Ham blurted. "Unless my Latin has gotten rusty, Metho Regulus—those *V*'s are actually *U*'s—means Prince Metho."

"That is what X Man called himself when I first encountered him," Johnny put in. "I thought he was insane."

"Does kinda look like the guy," Monk admitted in a small voice.

"Roman coins," Johnny breathed, "simply do not survive to the present day without collecting wear and tarnish. I would say this specimen could have been minted no more than ten years ago!"

"My estimation as well," Doc stated without emotion.

"For the love of mud!" Monk squawled. "Are you sayin' what I think you're sayin'? That this coin came from the past without layin' in the ground all these years?"

"There is no date stamped on either side," Doc said. "So it is not possible to say anything for certain. The faces on each side of the coin are not of any of the known Roman emperors, and the name of Metho has likewise not come down through history."

Johnny indicated the face on the other side with an elongated digit.

"I do not recognize this name either," he mused. "Dux Lucius Optimus Dentatus Africanus. Hm-m-m. Dux is a military rank, meaning general. And Africanus is an honorific title, indicating one who served in Africa. The rest of it is the man's full name."

"Ain't that a date there?" Monk wondered, referring to the inscription under the man's profile which read IX HISPANA.

"No," said Doc. "IX Hispana can only refer to the Ninth Hispana Legion of Rome, who were one of the legions involved in conquering ancient Britannia. They were stationed at one time in Scotland. And at the Legionary Fortress at Eboracum, now York."

"Blazes," Monk gulped again.

"Shouldn't that give us a clue as to the time period from whence this coin originated?" Ham queried.

"That's the problem," Johnny muttered.

They looked at him.

"The Ninth Hispana Legion," said the bony archæologist, "was transferred out of Britannia to other duty in the Roman Empire. No one knows where."

Monk grunted. "Yeah? Why the heck not?"

"The Ninth Hispana," Doc Savage stated, "completely disappeared from the history books around the end of the first century A.D. One persistent rumor insists they never left Britannia at all, but were destroyed in the year 117 A.D."

That statement left them in stunned silence.

"Another theory," Johnny added, "was that they were transferred to Mesopotamia or what is now modern Germany—both of which were part of the Roman Empire, which was then at its height. The north coast of the African continent, possibly Cyrenaica, or Africa itself, as one of the Roman-controlled African provinces was known, has also been given as the spot in which they met their mysterious fate."

Monk made a face. "Africa, Britannia, Londinium. Ain't there no place on earth that them old Romans *didn't* name?"

No one answered Monk's possibly rhetorical question. They were too busy trying to grapple with the conundrum presented by the mysterious golden coin.

"What do you make of this, Doc?" Monk asked.

"It seems somewhat fantastic," the bronze man admitted.

Ham sniffed, "That is a mild word for it."

"Somebody," said Monk, eying Johnny, "is tellin' some whoppin' lies."

Johnny Littlejohn, who seldom had occasion to have his veracity questioned, snapped, "I'll be superamalgamated. An imperspicuous and enigmatical adumbration of facts."

Ham Brooks looked slightly dazed by the words.

"Sir William means that the whole thing kind of has him baffled," Monk explained. "I presume he means that he ain't tellin' no stretchers."

"You can also presume," Johnny told Monk indignantly, "that referring to me as Sir William is a request for a ventriductal encrustation."

When everyone simply stared at him, Johnny explained, "Another way of saying a scab on the end of your nose."

They spent the next several days hunting for Waterloo O'Neil, Goona Bey, Mulligan, the impostor Matthew A. Nade, and the missing X Man, whom they were beginning to conclude really was a Roman prince of some sort. No trace of any of them was discovered. Even Scotland Yard had drawn a blank.

The body of Alexander Abercrombie Nade had been subjected to an autopsy, and the verdict was death from natural causes.

Doc asked to have a look at the body. He took with him a wonderfully compact chemical laboratory that Monk was in the habit of toting with him on long trips. After some testing of tissues, the bronze man pronounced the cause of death to be a subtle poison, difficult to detect unless one knew what to look for.

Thereafter, the hunt for Goona Bey was intensified.

There was some trouble over the bronze man's spiriting away of the mysterious X Man from the Wyndmoor Asylum for the Brain Impaired and then losing him, but a telephone conversation with Dr. John Gilchrist put the matter to rest, at least temporarily.

On the third day, they got a break. Of sorts. As breaks go, it was late coming out of the gate. But it was better than nothing.

Doc Savage, much to the British Admiralty's increasing annoyance, had persisted in his interest in sea serpent sightings.

There had been a few. One remarkably close to Southampton. It was the most recent of the sightings and brought the bronze man and his aids—Johnny had by this time recuperated sufficiently to be ambulatory—to the bustling port city.

At the police station where the fake Matthew A. Nade had bluffed his way through his finger-print test—Doc proved the prints were false after using a chemical reagent to show there was no oil residue in the ink, and the rest was simple enough to deduce—a Scotland Yard chief inspector explained that a sea creature had beached itself north of Southampton.

They went to the spot. It was sandy and although the tide had come in and it was three days later, there were still tracks—a wide swath edged in centipedelike prints.

"Exactly like those left on the bottom of the Firth of Forth," Doc told them.

The Scotland Yard man snorted derisively. "Sea serpents! Bah! Poppycock!"

They attempted to follow the tracks inland, but lost them over hard ground and rocks. The only structure in the area was a warehouse. It was deserted. They found some tools laying about, but that was all.

No one, it turned out, had sighted the creature after it had taken to land. Those who had beheld it beaching itself had promptly run away, but nonetheless gave remarkable descriptions of it. Remarkable in the sense that the details were wonderfully fanciful: an elongated green turtle of a thing with six heads and an excess of legs.

"Scylla," Johnny murmured.

"If this Scylla is just a dang myth, how could it come forward in time?" Monk wanted to know.

Doc turned to the Scotland Yard man and said, "It might be advisable to transfer our search to the docks."

"What would a sea serpent—if there is such a creature—want with the docks?" was the not-unreasonable retort.

"Our search for the missing men, Waterloo O'Neil and the others," Doc explained.

They went to the docks.

*   *   *

The Southampton water front is a sprawling line of wharves, dockage, and piers. It was busy. But then, it is always busy, being one of the most active seaports in the world.

Doc and his aids split up and began asking around.

It was Monk who discovered the *X* scrawled on the side of a steamship pier. He immediately called the others on his pocket radio transceiver, a wonderfully compact device about the size of a cigar case, which enabled Doc and his men to communicate over short distances.

"I'm at Pier Twelve," the hairy chemist shouted into the transceiver's square loud-speaker grille. "Come runnin'! I think I found somethin' important!"

They came.

"It's just an *X*," Ham complained contrarily, when he laid eyes on the marking.

Monk grinned. "*X* for X Man."

Ham looked doubtful. "It might just be an *X*."

"Or a Roman numeral," Johnny interposed. "They are still in common use."

"Yeah? Well, I know my Roman numerals. *X* is ten, right? And this is Pier Twelve, not Pier Ten."

Monk and Ham fell into a heated argument, so Doc Savage went to the ticket office.

"What ships have left this pier in the last three days?" Doc asked the ticket agent.

The man consulted a thick ledger. "The liners *Berengaria* and *Empress of Britain* and the steamer *Numidia*."

"When did the *Numidia* sail?" Doc asked.

"Two days ago," he was told. Doc presented his Scotland Yard identification card and requested, "I would like to see the passenger list."

It was brought to him. The bronze man ran his strange golden eyes down the list.

None of the names meant anything to him, but he knew it was possible to book passage using fictitious names.

"Did any of the passengers display a propensity for scratching themselves?" Doc asked next.

"Not that I recall. And I sell all the tickets here."

"Thank you," said Doc, moving away.

Johnny asked, "Why are you interested in the *Numidia*?"

"The *Numidia*," Doc explained, "is the ship that brought the false Matthew Nade and his pilot to England."

Doc next sought out the radio room and asked to be put into contact with the captain of the *Numidia*.

"Yes, as a matter of fact my ship's doctor *did* report an outbreak of poison ivy on board," the captain related.

"Poison ivy?" Monk blurted.

Ham hissed, "That must have been what Doc substituted for those strange mint leaves, that time he picked some plants up in Scotland."

A light of understanding dawned in the apish chemist's tiny eyes. Well he knew of the irritable properties of the poison ivy plant.

The captain was speaking. "We put those passengers off at Boma, along with their freight."

"Freight?"

"Crate after crate of some sort. According to my manifest, they contained heavy machinery."

"Thank you," said Doc. He addressed his men. "Waterloo, Goona Bey, and the others have unquestionably gone to Africa."

This took a while to sink in. When it did, Monk muttered, "This is startin' to throw cold water on this time-travel notion."

"Not necessarily," put in Johnny. "If Waterloo had gone back into time to Novum Eboracum, and brought back that gold coin, it stands to reason, rogue that he is, he would want more."

"Yeah?"

"Stealing gold from a well-defended Roman treasury is not something lightly undertaken," he added. "But if he had learned the location of Novum Eboracum, it might make sense to find out where it used to be, and excavate the ruins in the hope of locating abandoned treasure."

Monk smacked one furry fist into the other.

"That makes sense! He's gone to the ruin to dig up the gold."

Ham, squeezing his empty hands—he seemed lost

without his cane—asked, "But why take X Man? I mean, Prince Metho?"

"Possibly to help with the search," Johnny suggested. "After so many centuries, the city would be overgrown with jungle. Who better to help scout out the landmarks than a man who grew up in that area?"

It all made perfect, if astounding, sense, and when Doc Savage did not offer a contradictory theory, they assumed it had to be so, preposterous as it sounded.

Monk grinned broadly. "I guess this means we light out for Africa!" He sounded beside himself with joy over the prospect.

XIV

"NEPETA CATARI"

Doc Savage ran the leviathan tri-motor with the throttles open. They were over the Atlantic Ocean now. Owing to the recent Spanish troubles, it had been necessary to circumvent the bulging land mass of Spain. This detour cost precious time, which the bronze man was anxious to make up.

From time to time, Monk or Ham—both were accomplished pilots in their own right—would spell Doc.

During one of these periods, Johnny Littlejohn—whose remarkable constitution was reasserting itself after his long ordeal—approached the bronze man.

"Say, Doc," Johnny said, using small words as was his habit when conversing with his bronze chief, "Ham informs me that you confiscated a number of peculiar leaves which X Man had in his possession."

Doc produced the phial and uncorked it. Johnny accepted it and brought the glass mouth to his nostrils. He sniffed for some moments.

"It is not poison ivy," he pronounced. "It appears to be some species of mint."

"Recognize it?"

Johnny sniffed again. He made faces. In his work as an archæologist and geologist, knowledge of botany ofttimes came in handy.

"I don't—wait a minute! Is this *nepeta catari*?"

"By the scent, it would seem so," the bronze man confirmed.

"I'll be superamalgamated! Why would X Man be growing *nepeta cataria*?"

Monk Mayfair chanced to overhear this conversation

—the air giant was wonderfully soundproofed, even running at full speed—and demanded, "Them words—nep—"

"Nepeta catari," Johnny supplied.

"They Latin? I don't recognize 'em."

"Fully half the words in the English and related languages derive from Latin," Johnny informed him.

"That don't answer my question."

Johnny, still miffed at the Sir William slur, returned the phial to Doc, who stoppered it once more.

No more was said about the mysterious leaves, not even when Doc took Monk's compact chemical laboratory to the rear of the plane and began conducting some experiment with a sample of the leafage that involved squeezing a pale green juice from the sampling. He transferred the extract to a trio of smaller phials, which he stoppered and stowed at various places on his person.

It was obvious that the bronze man considered this extract very important.

They arrived at Boma by nightfall, and were greeted by an official representative of the government of the Belgian Congo, who wore tropical whites and spoke English with a decided French accent.

"Oui, M'sieu Savage," he informed Doc. "We have conducted a search, as you requested by radio. Sadly, we have discovered little."

"But Waterloo O'Neil and his crowd had disembarked here on Boma?" Doc countered.

"Mais oui! We have established this, *vraiment.* But we find zey have registered at no hotel nor have zey been seen by anyone. Zey might have vanished into—how you say?— zin air."

"I would like to examine the *Numidia's* berth," Doc requested.

They were soon whisked to the water front. It was not much. One covered pier long enough to accommodate a medium-sized passenger line. There were smaller wharves and berths for the rusty tramp steamers that continually ply the coasts of Africa.

Ham Brooks was rubbing his chin with the head of his elegant cane. The dapper lawyer owned a dozen of the sticks, and fortunately had had the foresight to have brought along a spare. He was muttering, "This is deuced strange. They could not simply vanish—four white men in an African port. They would stick out like bally sore thumbs."

Doc addressed the Belgian official. "They were reported to have been packing a substantial cargo of machinery."

"Oui? All cargo meant for transshipment into the interior is transferred to rail."

"Could this be done without especial notice being taken?"

"It is possible," the official confirmed. "For the spur is not one hundred yards from here."

They were escorted to the spur, a single set of tracks rusting in the oppressive humidity of the African night. There was no activity in the tiny freight yard.

Doc asked, "The *Numidia* docked by night, did she not?"

"*Oui*, but what—"

"But it would be possible to transfer large quantities of cargo by night without attracting much notice?" Doc suggested.

"Perhaps the yardmaster might tell us things," said the official, now growing concerned.

The yardmaster was white, nervous, and fidgety. Everyone noticed this when they approached him in his tiny office.

"I do not understand," he said, upon being accosted by Doc Savage and his men. "What is it you want?" This made them even more suspicious, since they had yet to ask the man any questions.

"We are seeking four men who may have transferred some cargo off ze liner *Numidia* ze other night," the Belgian official said. "What can you tell us?"

"Nothing," the yardmaster said almost before the question had been gotten out.

They stared at him in silence.

The man was squirming on his feet. Perspiration oozed from his low forehead. He took one loose-fingered hand in the other and began knotting his digits.

"We know Waterloo O'Neil bribed you to facilitate the transfer of his cargo," said Doc Savage in a very steady voice.

The yardmaster looked about ready to buckle at the knees and began to blubber. Perhaps he would have done exactly that, but from somewhere inside his cowardly soul, he found a shred of courage.

He was shaking all over. That's why they were fooled. Perhaps only Doc Savage noticed that he shook his right hand more than any other portion of his quivering anatomy.

Came a clattery sound and up flashed his hand, clutching a dagger that appeared as if by magic. He drove for the nearest man—the Belgian official. The latter took a step backward and yanked a revolver from his belt holster.

Doc lunged for the weapon, brought it up, and the bullet made a crack in the ceiling, which leaked plaster.

Monk and Ham, meanwhile, closed in. Ham had his sword cane out. That made the difference. The man looked at the long blade, at his own blade, and decided that he was outclassed.

"Surrender at once, my good man," Ham suggested.

The railroad man seemed to drain of all life then. The dagger fell from his loosened fingers. But it did not fall far. It stopped at about the level of the man's knees, and swung there.

Monk Mayfair wrestled the man's hand upward, and hauled down his sleeve, exposing a metal bracelet to which was attached a fine silver chain. The other end of the chain was affixed to the dangling dagger's hilt. There was a leather sheath attached to the bracelet where the dagger would repose when not in use.

"Never saw a rig like this before," Monk muttered, wrenching the bracelet off the man's wrists.

"African bracelet dagger," Doc supplied. "A vicious tool when employed to catch a man unawares."

The Belgian official had his pistol trained on the man —Doc had relinquished his obdurate grip after Monk had subdued the yardmaster—and demanded, "Speak, *cochon!*"

The railroad man did. He told of having arranged a

flat car to be waiting for Waterloo O'Neil and his accomplices. He had been contacted by O'Neil, he explained, a year ago and money had changed hands in anticipation of O'Neil's return to Africa.

Doc Savage had only one question, "Was there a dark-eyed man with them?"

"*Oui*," the yardmaster admitted. "A very dark-eyed man in an odd garment. He was very frightened."

"X Man," Ham breathed.

After the crooked yardmaster had been taken away, Doc asked the official, "Where do the tracks go?"

"From here, *M'sieu* Savage, zey go to Léopoldville, ze capital, and from zere branch out to ze north and to ze east, deep into ze interior."

"Then they could have gone in either direction?" Ham said.

"I am afraid so. However, it might be possible to determine zeir destination by telegraphing stations zroughout ze Congo."

This was done. The results were a profound disappointment.

"It is very mysterious," the official reported around the hour of dawn the next morning. "No engineer, no station manager, no yardmaster recalls a flat car carrying large crates."

"Impossible!" Ham protested. "Such a car could not simply vanish!"

But it had. All efforts were made to locate it, on a siding or elsewhere. No missing flat car—empty or otherwise—turned up.

"But what about that O'Neil and the birds who were with him?" Monk demanded.

"They have covered their trail," the bronze man replied. "And if we remained here searching for them, the chances are we would not find them."

"You think they've cleared out?"

"They have, or they intend to. Why else would they want a flat car, unless it was to reach some remote spot."

"Novum Eboracum?"

"It is reasonable to think so."

Monk exploded, "Then why don't we jump in our airplane and light out for the place? Our bus is capable of a hop clear across Africa, if necessary."

"It would be an excellent idea," Doc told him. "Except for one obstacle."

"Eh?"

"Where is Novum Eboracum?"

Monk scratched his head. "Yeah, that's right."

"A Senegambian imponderability," Johnny remarked, running long fingers through his even longer hair.

"We can't just give up," Ham snapped.

"Nor will we," Doc Savage said. "Come on."

They took a native taxi to the airport—it was more of an air field—and were soon in the air.

The bronze man set a course due east. He found the branch line that led into the interior, and using the pilot's trick of following railroad tracks to a destination, flew at a moderate height above them, on the theory that this was the most probable route their quarry might follow.

Below, grassy savannah turned to impenetrable jungle and the tracks were lost for long periods of time. Mists arose, to be burned off by the climbing sun.

"You know," Monk was saying, "you think if there was a ruin called Novum Eboracum, some one woulda found it a long time ago. Africa's been pretty well explored by now."

"Not necessarily," said Johnny, who was perched before a window training a pair of field glasses on the rolling terrain below.

"Whatcha mean?"

"While it's true there has been a great deal of exploration, particularly in the last century, the advent of the airplane has had a curiously deleterious effect on the mapping of the continent."

"You mean," Ham interjected, "once it became possible to fly from place to place, there has been less exploration?"

Johnny nodded.

"Still, if there was the ruin of a Roman outpost down here, it should have been seen from the air."

"Not if the jungle overtook it. To this day, explorers

are still finding Mayan and Aztec ruins all over Central and South America that were claimed by jungle growth."

Monk brightened. "Then all we gotta do is find it."

"You make it sound simple," Ham sneered.

"Stanley found Dr. Livingstone all right, didn't he?" Monk countered.

"He got lucky," Johnny said blandly.

And that put an end to an incipient argument before it got started. Monk and Ham separated, Monk to play with his pet pig, and the dapper lawyer to daub anæsthetic onto his sword cane. He kept a supply of the sticky stuff in a secret compartment back of his wrist watch, and became busy with that operation.

They spotted a train around the middle of the afternoon. The jungle mists had burned off hours before and the train was not very impressive—consisting of only six cars, including the engine, coal car, and caboose.

Doc had spotted the black plume trailing behind the smokestack from many miles away and dropped the trimotor lower so as to get a good look at the train while he flew over it.

The train was moving with what seemed infinite slowness as they passed over it, their batlike shadow chasing jungle birds out of the tall raphia palms that poked sad, shaggy heads above the vivid greenery.

"What's that third car?" Ham wondered, taking the binoculars from Monk.

The car was long, cylindrical, and a round protrusion resembling a turret topped by a manhole cover bulged up in the center.

"Looks like one of them newfangled refrigeration tanker cars—you know, for haulin' chemicals and stuff that have to be kept cool."

Ham blinked. "Out here?"

"Why not?" Monk said. "It's hotter than blazes all year round. I can't think of a better place than Africa where one would come in handy."

Doc Savage brought the amphibian plane around for another pass as the train was approaching a trestle over a great winding river—the Congo River, Johnny Littlejohn informed them. It lay like a great mud-colored snake slithering along toward the horizon.

If the train had been creeping along before, it had slowed to a crawl now. In fact, two tiny figures dropped off and began running toward the trestle, as if to determine its soundness before crossing—a good idea in this remote area.

They had flown so far into the Congo region they could no longer be sure if they were still, technically, within its borders. No one had bothered with charts.

Their eyes were naturally drawn to the two figures when Doc Savage suddenly rapped, "Hang on!"

The advice was hastily taken. The bronze man, his aids knew, meant what he said. And the tri-motor abruptly banked. Ham lost the binoculars, which went out of the open window, and fought to hold his chiseled face from being mashed against the side of the plane.

Through the open window came a low cough. It did not sound loud, but they instantly knew that distance had diminished the noise, which must have been frightful at its point of origin.

"That sounds kinda like—" Monk began to say.

A noisy black flower blossomed in the air ahead of them. Doc Savage booted the rudder. The air giant banked sharply. It gave a convulsive shudder.

Then the port engine came apart!

XV

WRECK

The world seemed to reel around them. Earth and sky fought for position.

A fragment of duralumin propeller snarled in through the plane's fuselage skin and out again, fortunately harming no one.

It did, however, part control cables.

Immediately, the tri-motor began buffeting.

Doc fought the ship onto an even keel. Perhaps if one of the others—even burly Monk—had been at the controls, it would have ended in disaster. But Doc Savage, holding the control wheel, rigid as a statue of immutable bronze, kept the air giant from smearing itself all over the jungle below.

Monk put his nose to a window. The port engine was pitted and scarred, and the cowling had peeled off like the shell of an egg. The propeller was completely gone. The spinner spun, but without the constant-speed blades, it was a futile waste of horsepower.

Doc shut down the port engine to save precious fuel.

"What hit us?" Ham bleated.

Doc said, "Shell."

"From where?"

"Train."

"What's a cannon doin' on a train?" Monk wanted to know.

Then they fought their way to their seats and hung on as the bronze man, perspiration popping out on his metallic features, slanted the great sky wagon downward.

"There's nowhere to land," Ham said. "It's all jungle."

"River," Doc said. The word was an effort. It seemed to have been yanked out of him.

Distantly, they heard another cough. It was very far away. They waited, tensing.

A *crump* of a noise came. No violence resulted. They let out their breaths.

Then it came time to land.

The sinuous nature of the Congo River meant they could not simply follow it and alight. Nor did they have time to choose their angle of approach. Doc simply sent the big bus dropping lower, fighting the controls every step of the way.

A long scraping sound warned of the boat-shaped hull coming into contact with the treetops. Snapping on either side of the plane told of the great wing slicing and splintering branches.

The windows on both sides filled with whipping greenage, and a monkey could be seen bounding away in fright.

Ham, seeing this, got an idea. He gathered up Chemistry and forced him out an open window. The ape, frightened, took to the trees and was lost from sight.

Ham said, "That way Chemistry will survive if none of us—"

There was no time to get the rest of it out, because the snapping and snarling became a ferocious noise that went on and on and on until they were forced to clap hands over ears to keep out the awful racket.

After that, there was no knowing. Only chaos.

Monk Mayfair was the first to open his eyes. He peered around.

The plane, at least as seen from within, was intact and right side up. That was a miracle. Then Monk wrinkled up his nose. The cabin was filled with a pungent odor.

"Gas! We gotta get outta of here!"

An arresting voice said, "Monk—this way."

"Huh!"

The apish chemist looked back into the gloom of the plane. Doc Savage stood there. Over one shoulder was draped the stringbean figure of Johnny Littlejohn. Ham Brooks, equally flaccid, was a limp shape under the bronze man's other arm.

Monk clambered to his feet and scrambled to the bronze man's side.

"The door, Monk." The bronze man's controlled voice was steady, uninflected. He might have been requesting help with the door to a broom closet.

Monk undogged the hatch and pushed it open. Instantly, a warm blast of air smacked his homely face. He jumped out—and found himself hip deep in water the color of tea.

"Great blazes!" he squawled. "This water is hot!"

"Take Ham."

Monk reached up hairy arms and accepted the burden of the dapper lawyer—dapper no longer quite fit him now.

Wading carefully, Monk brought Ham to the bank of the river, deposited him on a mossy flank of grass, and turned to help the bronze man with Johnny.

Johnny was laid out beside Ham Brooks.

"They hurt bad?" Monk asked anxiously.

"Only stunned. It was necessary to get them out in case the plane caught fire."

Monk looked back at the great aircraft.

The Congo River is amazingly wide—only the Amazon in South America rivals it for sheer girth. Still, landing a craft the size of the tri-motor on such an expanse is a feat.

The wingtips—they ended in floats that could be cranked down to support the wings—were intact. In fact, the only visible damage was to the port engine, which had borne the brunt of the exploding shell.

Doc Savage's ships were invariably bullet-proofed, and this no doubt saved them from complete disaster. But the shell had done a job.

"It don't look as bad as it did from the air," Monk judged, speaking more from hope than certainty.

"The port prop was sheared off, as was the cowling," Doc offered. "Probably the substitution of a new propeller and some repair might make her airworthy again. Fortunately, we carry the necessary items on board for eventualities such as this."

While Doc Savage tended to Johnny and Ham, Monk waded back to the plane and sniffed around.

He called back, "Fuel line cut."

Doc nodded but did not look up from his examination of Johnny and Ham. He was feeling their bones for breakage, and finding nothing.

Monk clambered into the craft and climbed out again with Habeas Corpus under one arm and a long stick in his free hand.

He brought Habeas to shore and returned to the ship. The gas tanks were in the wing, and he got the caps off and began pushing the stick in and out.

"Tanks drained," he reported.

Johnny Littlejohn began stirring.

He sat up, looked around, and remarked, *"Cogito, ergo sum."*

"That sounds like Latin to me," Monk complained.

"It is," Doc said. "Johnny just said, 'I think, therefore I am.' Which might be his way of expressing pleasure at finding himself still among the living."

"I liked his long words when they came in English better."

Ham Brooks had to be revived with stimulants, oddly enough. Doc administered this by hypodermic needle.

The dapper lawyer was slow to come around, so Monk waded back and, dipping his furry paws into the river, began scooping up water.

"What is the meaning of this!" Ham howled, jumping to his feet.

"You're holding up progress," Monk said casually.

"Where are we going?"

"Nowhere," Monk grunted, cocking a finger back at the bobbing tri-motor. "We're outta plumb gas."

"We're stuck in this beastly jungle?"

"So it would appear," Doc Savage said. He slipped into the water and began an examination of the damaged engine. Monk joined him. They made grim faces and returned to shore.

"There's some good news, anyway," Monk said.

"Yes?"

"We can probably fix the engine."

"Capital," said Ham.

"But without fuel," Monk added, "we might as well have a wreck on our hands."

This did not noticeably lift the dapper lawyer's spirits, already dampened by the rips and rents that festooned his formerly immaculate garb. Abruptly, he snapped his fingers.

"Chemistry!"

"Forget that flea-paradise," Monk snorted. "That monkey has probably lighted out for parts unknown. He's in his element."

"You should know, you bush-ape," Ham said unkindly. He was looking around. Thick jungle surrounded them. Cupping hands over his mouth, the dapper lawyer began calling for his pet.

"Chemistry! Oh, Chemistry!"

Doc's voice, uncharacteristically sharp, called out.

"Ham!"

Ham ceased his calls.

"We need every hand to secure the plane. It is beginning to drift downstream."

They got into the water and salvaged lines. These they affixed to various cleats welded about the air giant's fuselage for this purpose, then secured the lines to stout trees.

There was an anchor in the nose and Doc dropped this electrically while the others went about their tasks.

In the end, the tri-motor resembled a frightened bronze bird caught in the web of some great jungle spider.

"Now what?" Monk wanted to know. "We got a plane and no dang gas."

"Fuel can be had," Doc stated. "It should be possible to distill from various vegetable products and grain an alcohol capable of suiting our needs."

Ham looked doubtful. "Are such plants found in this jungle?"

"We will find out," Doc stated.

"Well, what are we waitin' on?" Monk roared.

"First, Chemistry," said Doc.

"He could be anywhere," Ham murmured.

"Habeas might assist us," said Doc, dropping to the shoat's side. "Habeas—find Chemistry!"

Habeas Corpus had been trained to respond to simple

commands. He lifted his ears, kicked up some soil with his hind legs, and prodded the air with his inquisitive snout. Ham watched anxiously.

Then Habeas bounded into the jungle.

"There he goes!" Monk boasted. "That hog sure knows his stuff."

"If he can find my Chemistry," Ham promised, "I promise him an apple."

"Fat chance you got of findin' an apple out here," Monk snorted.

Monk and Ham took off after the ungainly porker.

Doc asked Johnny, "You have your supermachine pistol?"

"Of course."

"Stand guard until we return."

Johnny wore his unhappiness plain on his scholarly features as the bronze man melted effortlessly into the thick underbrush.

The jungle was an overpowering place of cedar, mahogany, rubber, and other exotic trees, their branches interlacing with suspended creepers to create a great cathedral of foliage through which beams of sunlight slanted downward, made green by passing through verdant leafage. It was hot. It was very hot.

Doc Savage soon caught up with Monk and Ham, who were struggling to keep up with Habeas, because the shoat had only to squeeze between tree boles. They lost sight of the porker several times, but his snuffling and squealing guided them.

"Habeas has the scent," Monk said proudly.

"Unlikely," Ham sniffed.

Monk started bragging on his hog again. "Habeas will find your chimp, if he has to climb trees to do it. That Habeas is a bloodhog like the world never saw before. He—"

Up ahead, came a frightful squealing.

Monk's capacious mouth dropped open.

"That sounded like—"

The squealing turned into a ferocious procession of cries and howls.

Doc Savage leaped into the nearest tree, balanced upon a thick branch, and launched himself into the next.

Seeing this, Monk followed suit. He was more monkeylike than Doc Savage, his arms longer and therefore better equipped for the task. Still, he had difficulty keeping up with the bronze man.

Ham, possessing neither Monk's simian physique nor Doc Savage's incredible strength, was left to fume on the ground.

Doc Savage had covered nearly two hundred yards when the fight sounds abruptly broke off. Monk, fearing the worst, redoubled his efforts. He soon overhauled the bronze man, who promptly dropped to the ground. Monk landed at his side with a gusty *oofing* explosion of expelled breath, his bowed legs cushioning the drop.

A furry shape lay on the ground in a welter of gore.

Monk's tiny eyes doubled in size. "Is that—Chemistry?" he gulped.

"No," Doc said. "Hyena."

Monk let out a sigh of relief. Then, blinking, demanded, "What got him?"

Out of the brush trotted Habeas Corpus, his tusks crimsoned.

"At a guess," Doc said, "Habeas."

For a moment, Monk Mayfair seemed lost for words. His eyes began popping.

"Habeas—"

"Evidently the stories you were told were true," the bronze man said dryly.

"No kiddin'!" Monk said, gathering up the ungainly shoat. He checked his bristly hide for wounds, found only scratches.

"I'll be danged!" he bellowed. "That Arab who sold you to me wasn't lyin' after all. You *are* a hyena catcher!"

Doc said, "It appears from this sign that Habeas interrupted the hyena as it was attacking another animal."

Monk looked up and began searching the overhanging tree branches with his gimlet eyes.

"You don't think—" he was protesting.

A chattering high in one cedar tree answered the

homely chemist's unfinished question. Crouching in the foliage, Chemistry, the rust-colored What-is-it, cowered.

Spying Monk, he let fly with something round and hard. It bounced off the homely chemist's nubbin head with an audible *bonk!*

Monk grabbed his skull in both hands and yelled, "Hey! What'd he brain me with?"

"Manoic."

"Huh?"

"Yam," Doc explained.

"Some gratitude he got—after my Habeas saved his mangy hide," Monk complained.

Doc, seeming to exert no effort, floated up the tree and collected the shivering Chemistry. The ape seemed suddenly soothed by the bronze man's presence and allowed himself to be borne to the jungle floor with a minimum of fuss.

They worked their way back to Ham Brooks, who, seeing the gore on Habeas's tusks and Chemistry's frightened condition, jumped to an erroneous conclusion.

"Bloodhog!" he howled. "Blood *drinker* is more like it. That rack of bacon tried to murder my Chemistry!"

Monk retorted, "The heck you say. He saved your worthless baboon."

"A likely story," said Ham, kneeling down to examine Chemistry for signs of injury. When his worst fears were confirmed, he jumped to his feet and unsheathed his sword cane.

For once, Ham Brooks actually looked ready to run Monk, or possibly Habeas, through. His face was reddening. He switched the glittering blade back and forth, as if uncertain on whom to inflict the first stroke.

Somewhere—it seemed all around them—came a horrible noise. The ground shook. A little, not much. But the noise was awful. Its duration was not protracted, but it included the shriek of metal and the splintering of wood.

"Our plane!" Ham howled.

"No," rapped Doc. "It came from the west."

"What was it?"

"Let us find out."

Doc returned to the trees. He used creepers to swing himself along where he could.

Monk and Ham settled for following on foot. They had a good run. It was forty-five minutes before they caught up with the bronze man.

They came upon the train, its engine lying submerged in the muddy Congo River amid the shattered wreckage of a trestle bridge. It was not the bridge the train had been approaching when they first spotted it from the air, but one farther along that crossed a switchback of the mighty river.

The coal car had also been precipitated into the river, as had a third car which had tipped over so that only its wheels were visible.

Doc was in the water searching for bodies. There was already a pile of them on the river bank.

"Blazes!" Monk said, jumping into the water to assist.

"No survivors," Doc told him grimly.

Still, Monk helped search. Ham, too. It was an unpleasant task. Train wrecks, perhaps more than any other sort of accident, show the utter frailty of the human form when modern machinery fails.

They pulled the limp, broken body of the engineer from the locomotive and took stock of the situation.

"Guess the trestle wasn't strong enough," Monk muttered to no one in particular.

"It was deliberately sabotaged," Doc Savage said, surprising them.

He pointed out sawdust where hardwood supports had been weakened.

"Who would do that—and why?" Ham demanded.

Monk said, "Must've been natives."

Doc shook his head. "Modern tools accomplished this." And to prove his point, he located a ripsaw that had been cast aside after the deadly work had been done.

"That still don't answer the question," Monk pointed out.

Doc said nothing. He got into the water, which was cooler at this point than where they had landed their plane, and fell to examining third car, the one whose wheels were sticking up out of the water.

Monk joined him. Ham hung back to keep an eye on the pets, which were unnerved by the dead bodies.

When the bronze man submerged, Monk followed suit. They were not under water long.

"Wasn't that thing the refrigerator car?" Monk asked, shaking water off his long, hairy forearms.

"It was."

"So where's the refrigerator tank?"

"Not here."

Monk grunted. "Musta broke loose and floated downstream."

Ham looked up and down stream. It was not possible to see very far in either direction, owing to the snake-track meandering of the river.

"That quickly?" he said in a doubtful tone.

They searched for the missing refrigerator car, did not find it, and then sought signs of the mysterious cannon that had brought them down. They did not find this either. A careful examination of the dead brought to light no faces they recognized. They did not expect any different. If Waterloo O'Neil had been on the train, it was he who had wrecked it—along with his new-found confederates.

In the end, there was nothing for them to do but bury the bodies and begin the silent trek back to their waiting plane.

Along the way, Ham resumed his argument.

"That hog of yours ought to be smoked alive and hung for bacon," he began.

Monk snorted. "Habeas saved your monkey from a hyena. He oughta have a medal pinned on him."

"You man-toad—"

A noise they all knew ripped across the jungle. A sound remindful a titanic bullfiddle being sawed.

"Johnny!" Ham clipped. "And he's using his superfirer."

"Maybe he's spotted a hippo," Monk muttered. "They like splashin' around in big rivers."

The bullfiddle bellow came again, and they began running as best they could. Monk pulled out his own superfirer and thumbed the safety.

A tortured shriek of metal made the sounds that had come before pale in comparison. It was a huge sound, and gave birth to a procession of other creaks and groans.

Doc sought a particular tree—a towering parasol tree —and went up it. It was the highest tree in the vicinity. He gained the top, clung there, and tried to sight through the thick foliage. Evidently the distance defeated even his sight, because he extracted his monocular and telescoped it to its greatest extent. The optical device came up to one eye and began to rake the horizon.

Monk called, "See anythin'?"

"No."

The awful noises continued. Splashings combined with the complaints of helpless metal, as if an elephant were tormenting a group of automobiles.

"Sounds something like those sea creatures we saw in Scotland," Ham muttered.

"Don't be a dope! They ain't got sea serpents in Africa—that I ever heard tell of, anyway."

The sounds trailed off to a final creaky groan and the bronze man, restoring his monocular to his vest pocket, rejoined them.

Ham asked anxiously, "What did you see, Doc?"

"Nothing," Doc admitted.

They continued on, moving at a rapid pace.

"That better not be our plane," Monk muttered, "or we're stranded for sure."

It was, they discovered not twenty minutes later, indeed the tri-motor.

When they had left it, it was securely tied to various mahogany trees. Now it lay mashed up on the high bank of the river.

Monk groaned. It was quite a groan and worthy of the occasion.

A giant might have stepped onto the tri-motor. The wings had been mashed down and the hull broken just back of the wing. The tail was not recognizable as such. The craft had taken on so much water that much of it was submerged.

There was no sign of Johnny Littlejohn, and the realization caused them all to plunge into the strangely warm river to seek him out.

Doc beat them to the open hatch. He swam in, because it was not possible to enter otherwise.

Doc moved about the water-logged plane interior with motions that betrayed his haste. Monk and Ham were more frantic in their search. They soon used up their oxygen and were forced to quit the craft.

A minute later, Doc Savage broke the surface and gained the shore. He was empty-handed.

"What coulda done this?" Monk said. "No hippo or elephant grows that big."

Doc Savage vouchsafed no reply. He found Habeas Corpus and said, "Habeas! Find Johnny. Go, Habeas!"

The porker went through the same routine as earlier. His ears came up and his snout tasted of the air.

He started off.

"Here's where Habeas shows his stuff," Monk said proudly.

Ham said nothing. He was concentrating on avoiding clothes-snagging nettles.

Habeas trotted along and stopped at the foot of a thick-boled baobab tree. He tried to climb it, but his hooves were not equipped for the task.

Doc, Monk, and Ham surrounded the tree. They looked up.

Something looked down at them. They could see tiny eyes high in the tree. The eyes were human, but the cluster of leafage was too small to conceal a human being.

Doc Savage's trilling filtered through the air then. It sounded, for once, like a perfectly natural sound. Perhaps the product of an African wind through the jungle's twisted branches and liana webs.

"Make no sudden movements," Doc Savage undertoned, suiting action to words.

"Why not?" Monk said, equally subdued of voice.

"Because we are entirely surrounded."

Carefully, Monk and Ham peered about. They saw nothing. Moreover, there was no place where a person could conceal himself.

"I don't see nothin'," Monk said, peering about.

"Nor do I," Ham added.

Then, in unexpected places all around them, still leaves began to stir and tiny heads poked up. Black button eyes regarded them with a wise scrutiny.

Monk and Ham took their cue from the bronze man. They stood perfectly still.

But Monk couldn't contain himself. He blurted out two words.

"Blazes! Pygmies!"

XVI

JUNGLE STRANGE

Doc Savage said in a perfectly natural voice, "Make no threatening movements. Their arrows are tipped with a deadly poison."

"Don't worry none. I ain't movin' a hair."

The pygmies began creeping forward. Their stealth was uncanny. Not a leaf moved at their passing. Even insects resting on leaves seemed oblivious to their coming.

Ham thought that their stealth was eerily like the bronze man's own. Every one of the little fellows had an arrow nocked in a tiny bow.

"If they want to kill us, they can do it," Monk muttered. "We're surrounded good."

"Doc," Ham breathed, "I think I can reach my superfirer."

"No. Under no circumstances go for a weapon."

"So what do we do—just let them take us?"

"Exactly."

They quickly found themselves surrounded. The pygmy who Habeas had treed came down from his perch like a nimble brown spider with a human face. He wore a scrap of antelope hide held about his waist by a length of creeper, and not much else.

The arrows that could inflict instant death were pointed unwaveringly at them. They might be loosed at any moment.

Then Doc Savage lifted his voice. His words were not loud. To Monk and Ham, they were not even understandable. Doc was not speaking Mayan, they quickly realized.

What it was became apparent when the pygmies began chattering among themselves excitedly.

Doc added something to his statement in the pygmies'

tongue, and the sternness of their arrayed visages was replaced by a ring of beaming grins. They suddenly resembled cherubic children of the blackamoor variety.

The nocked arrows were taken off strings.

"What did you tell them, Doc?" Ham wanted to know.

"My name," the bronze man said simply.

The fame of Doc Savage was far-flung. Monk and Ham were keenly aware of this fact. But this—

It seemed incredible, but it was true. The pygmies began reaching out for their hands and wrists, endeavoring to tug them in a certain direction.

"What are they saying, Doc?" Ham asked incredulously.

"They want to take us to their village."

"How do you say 'no thanks' in pygmy?" Monk grunted.

"We will go with them. It will simplify matters."

"What about Johnny?"

"I will ask them if they saw Johnny."

Doc lapsed into the peculiar pygmy lingo. The answer he got brought no hint of emotion to his metallic features. He told his aids, "They were attracted to this spot by the sounds of our plane being destroyed, and have seen no sign of Johnny."

"Dang!" Monk muttered.

The pygmies motioned them to one of their jungle trails. A comical scene ensued when the pygmies realized that the path—it was more akin to a leafage tunnel—proved too small to admit their captors.

This was demonstrated when Ham Brooks, clutching a chattering Chemistry, trampled the leafy tunnel flat as he attempted to negotiate it.

The pygmies began cackling what might have been profanity in their native tongue. At least, the vehemence of their words indicated that they were emitting verbal sulphur.

Doc Savage solved the impasse by suggesting a compromise. They broke a new trail. Doc borrowed Ham's cane—the blade was Damascus steel and therefore up to the task—and steadily chopped a path adequate to their needs.

Pygmies followed the bronze man and seemingly called encouragement. Monk and Ham made their way along, trailed by a darksome clot of the tiny fellows.

The way was long. Doc Savage seemed tireless as he hacked and chopped at lianas and creepers and whittled obstructing greenery away.

Once, Ham noticed a white orchid—they grew everywhere—attached to a cedar tree and reached out to harvest it, evidently with the idea of converting it into a boutonniere for his rather dilapidated coat.

Doc's sharp voice stopped him. "Do not touch it."

"Is it—poisoned?" Ham asked, shrinking from the flower as if it were some venomous butterfly.

"No," said the bronze man. "These fellows consider it a sacred flower. To touch one is certain to bring calamity upon the transgressor."

Thereafter, Ham avoided all flowers he met along the way.

As he hacked foliage, Doc Savage put to the pygmies certain questions in their own tongue. Answers came gobbling back. This went on for some time until Ham Brooks, impatient to know what was being discussed, demanded, "Doc, what are they saying?"

"They say one of their number went out hunting not long ago. When he did not return they went searching for him. They found him—dying. Shot. He told a story of seeing white men destroy one of their own trains. They called it a 'Smoking Snake of Iron.' "

"We kinda figured that part out, didn't we?" Monk pointed out.

"Before he expired," Doc went on, "the pygmy claimed that the ones who destroyed the train had first slipped it off and cut across the jungle to one of the switchbacks, where they sabotaged the trestle."

Ham said, "Waterloo O'Neil and his men, I'll wager! But why?"

"The pygmies have no idea. They say it is unusual behavior even for white men, whom they consider crazy to begin with because they wear too much clothing in hot weather."

Monk hooked a spoonful of sweat off his beetling brow, and said, "I got a notion they ain't half wrong in that. Man, it's murder out here."

"We are not far from their village," Doc said.

Monk looked interested. "They tell you that?"

"No, but I know this area well. I spent time with these people when I was a boy."

This so floored Monk and Ham that they said nothing for a long time.

Eventually, they emerged into a clearing dotted with beehivelike huts constructed of palm fronds and twigs. It was a surprisingly large encampment. The huts were arrayed about a spacious area of cleared jungle floor dominated by an iron cooking pot not unlike those popularly depicted in funny-paper strips, except it was reassuringly small.

The pygmy leader—they had no chiefs in the normal sense—was a wizened old man with the rounded belly common to his people. His hair was sparse and of the type called "peppercorn." At the sight of the bronze man, his dark face broke out in a pleased grin.

Then he took a bone whistle from somewhere on his person and blew a sharp, shrill blast.

This brought men, women, and children from the circle of untidy-looking huts that resembled beehives made of palm fronds. It was difficult to tell the adults from the children.

The pygmy elder—Doc explained that his name was Moyoga—made a speech. He waved his arms, pointed at his chest, then broadened his hands to include Doc Savage in his recitation. It was not necessary to understand his lingo to grasp what was being said. Moyoga was informing the others that Doc Savage was a friend from the past.

A fire was built and the women and children scattered to the jungle to seek food. Two pygmy warriors, clutching stout elephant spears, eyed Habeas Corpus with possible gustatory interest. Monk decided to put an end to their hopes before they got out of hand.

"Hey, Doc. Habeas would like to say somethin' to our hosts so they don't get the wrong idea about him."

Doc nodded, and offered the pygmies a rough translation of Monk's words while the homely chemist set Habeas in the dirt and gave a surreptitious signal. Instantly, Habeas lifted his winglike ears and began articulating his jaws in a fashion uncannily like speech.

Out of his mouth came a string of words in the clucking language of the pygmies.

The two pygmies with the elephant spears suddenly got round of eye and began backing away. Habeas, responding to another signal, started trotting after them, his curly tail bouncing. They gave a shriek and fled. The jungle swallowed them.

Moyoga, less credulous than the others, fell into a fit of laughter. Monk grinned amiably as Habeas returned to his arms.

Not so Ham Brooks. He yanked the hairy chemist off to one side and hissed, "All right, you chemical aberration, your ventriloquist trick fooled these natives. But answer this: Where did you learn pygmy talk?"

"I didn't," the homely chemist replied.

"Liar!"

Monk laid a paw over his heart and said, "Cross my heart and hope to die if it ain't the honest truth."

Ham eyed the chemist dubiously. He had known Monk long enough, he believed, to recognize when the hairy chemist was fibbing. If so, he thought, Monk appeared to be telling the truth.

A little later, Ham accosted Doc Savage.

"Monk claims he wasn't pulling his ventriloquist trick," the dapper lawyer said suspiciously.

"He was not," the bronze man imparted.

"What!"

"That was my voice you heard emanating—or appearing to emanate—from Habeas Corpus," Doc explained.

Ham flushed, rubbed his jaw. "Like all magic," he said grudgingly, "it's simple once they tell you how."

The villagers shortly returned, bearing baskets of food.

"Man, am I famished," Monk said enthusiastically, falling upon a covered rattan basket.

He pulled out his paw with sudden violence. It was covered with crawling black specks. "Hey, these are bugs!"

"Termites," Doc corrected.

Monk shook his hand free of the crawling things. "What are they doin' in here?"

Then, to the homely chemist's horror, pygmy fingers reached into the baskets, pulled out bunches of stunned and broken-winged termites, and began eating them like peanuts.

"They eat bugs?"

"Termites are usually better roasted," said Doc.

Monk and Ham decided to pass up the offering. They accepted some bananas and edible fruit, and dug in.

While they were filling their stomachs, a freshly captured turtle was hauled into the clearing, its shell broken off, and tossed, still living, into a cooking pot.

"I'm so hungry I might try some of that," Monk muttered, eying the steam rising from the bubbling pot.

Ham eyed the bubbling pot dubiously, and sniffed, "You first."

Twilight is brief in the tropical jungle. There was an appreciable transition from light to darkness, but as they ate and talked—Doc did the talking for them, rather—it seemed to Monk and Ham that night fell like a great sable curtain being lowered through the action of cutting the cords that held it up.

The peeping of frogs and jungle insects became a musical background to the feast.

From time to time, their bellies full, pygmy warriors slipped out into the jungle. After a while, they would return to whisper low words to Moyoga and take their places around the camp fire. Others would then enter the jungle.

"What's going on?" Monk demanded of Doc.

"They are searching for Johnny."

"No luck?"

"Not so far." Doc fell back into urgent consultation with the pygmy elder. His features in the crackling firelight evinced no expression, but Monk and Ham, alert to the bronze man's subtle changes in mood, detected interest.

At one point, he stood up and eyed the horizon. To the east, the range of mountains some romantic soul had dubbed the Mountains of the Moon loomed dark and distant.

Doc pointed to one and asked a question in the pygmy tongue.

Moyoga answered it and their exchange grew animated.

Monk and Ham waited for Doc Savage to translate the talk.

"In recent years, the chief tells me, this village has been raided by strange men who carry off any pygmy who has the misfortune to fall into their hands.

"Slavers. In this day and age?" asked Monk.

"Slavers, perhaps. But not Europeans."

Ham wondered, "Do Arabs get this far south? They used to conduct slave raids in times gone by."

The bronze man shook his head. "Not Arabs. But another people, a warrior group who hunt lions and wear metal skins and ride on wheeled platforms they call—"

Suddenly, a pygmy warrior duo burst into the clearing. They hopped about and chattered a fluent barrage of words.

Doc translated, "They are saying a creature unlike any other is in the river."

"Creature?"

"They describe it as having six heads and smoking skin."

"Six heads!" Ham blurted. "That sounds like—"

Doc switched to the pygmy tongue, eliciting a hesitant shuffling of feet. Moyoga broke in and gave the two reluctant pygmy warriors a lively tongue-lashing. They turned tail and reentered the jungle.

"Come on," said Doc.

Puzzled, Monk and Ham followed, taking no care.

The pygmies shushed them as they disturbed sleeping jungle birds, then gave it up as hopeless. Doc and the pygmy vanguard disappeared into the jungle. Monk and

Ham kept up as best they could. The dapper lawyer was forced to cut a path with his sword cane.

"Could that sea serpent thing have followed us all the way to Africa?" Monk said doubtfully.

"Don't be ridiculous!" Ham snapped. But he sounded unconvinced of his own words.

Up ahead was silence. They began to fear that they had lost the trail.

"I think Doc musta learned his jungle craft from these little guys," Monk muttered. "I can't hear a dang thing."

"How can you?" Ham complained. "You won't give your wagging tongue a rest."

"If you won't put any muscle behind that stick," Monk countered, "let a man try."

Then the pair froze. From somewhere came a clattery sound. It was hard to describe. Rattlings, drumming, and poundings mixed together. It had a familiar ring to it.

Monk, who had spent his youth in Oklahoma, said, "Danged if that don't sound like a buckboard to me."

"Buckboard!" Ham scoffed, "In Africa?"

"Yeah, that clatter is the wooden wheels turning, and the drumming must be hooves. Only the horses ain't wearing any shoes."

Ham Brooks was about to remark upon the unsuitability of the horse to the African terrain when from the general direction of the commotion, fighting broke out!

"One side, shyster!" Monk said, pushing past Ham Brooks.

The river was closer than they guessed, because only fifty yards along they came to its bank.

Once out from under the canopy of foliage, they were bathed in moonlight. It poured effulgence down upon a fantastic sight.

Doc Savage was surrounded by pygmies. And circling them furiously were strange two-wheeled vehicles of cedar and trimmed in polished brass—pulled by flashing zebra!

"Blazes!" Monk squawled. "Them things are chariots!"

XVII

TALKING DRUMS

Ham Brooks started to scoff. Then he got a good look at the tableau.

There was no question. The wheeled things were chariots of some sort. There were three of them and they were each pulled by a single boldly striped zebra. The zebras were running in a tightening circle that threatened to trample Doc Savage and the pygmy warriors under pounding hooves.

Monk and Ham yanked their superfirers from under-arm holsters and drew beads. Their fingers touched the firing levers.

Monk complained, "Dang! I can't get a clear shot that won't hit Doc."

"Me, either," Ham said worriedly.

Then, the issue was decided for them.

One of the shadowy figures in one of the wheeling chariots lifted a lance or spear of some sort. He tried to stab out at the most convenient target—Doc, who stood several heads above his pygmy friends.

The man was overconfident. He feinted. And Doc's great arms drifted out to snag the weapon. He wrenched it from the other's grasp. The charioteer—or whatever he was—lost his weapon and his balance. His chariot upset, threw a wheel. The wheel bounced along, struck another chariot, and caused that vehicle to swerve into the river. There came a splash and the pygmies, whose arrows had been nocked, let fly.

Doc's voice crashed—but it was too late. With small zipping sounds punctuated by ticking noises of impact, poisoned pygmy arrows found their targets—the charioteer and his threshing steed.

Doc plunged into the river. Monk and Ham rushed forward.

They arrived in time to take aim at the single fleeing chariot. Their machine pistols hooted. But the remaining charioteer, showing previous experience at evading pygmy arrows, lashed his zebra into a zigzag path until he careened around a bend in the river and was lost to vision.

Doc Savage emerged from the river clutching a limp form.

Monk got out his flashlight. When it popped light the pygmies, startled, retreated to the edge of the forest to watch from its leafy sanctuary.

The light disclosed the water-soaked figure of a man caparisoned in the leathern garments of a Roman charioteer.

"This guy is white!" Monk blurted.

Actually, closer examination revealed, his skin tone ran more to a deep tan. But his features were not Negroid. In fact, he had the classic Roman nose that they had seen on one side of the gold coin found on the lawn of distant Crowninshield.

His chest and back were feathered with tiny hardwood shafts. Doc frantically began extracting these, but left off when the man underwent a convulsive shudder. It was too late. The virulent poison had done its work.

Doc Savage got up, grimly silent, and sought out the other charioteer. He had managed to wrap his chariot around the thick bole of a baobab tree, with the result that his neck had been broken.

The zebra lay on the ground, tangled in its leathern harness, stunned, and wild of eye. Ham cut it free and it bolted into the underbrush.

Doc Savage fell into an examination of the two chariots, the shattered one and the other that had fallen into the Congo River.

Monk and Ham watched him and said nothing until he reemerged from the river.

"It is unfortunate that neither man survived," Doc said. "They could have told us much."

"The other guy went in that direction," said Monk, pointing downriver.

Doc swiveled his impassive head and stared off into the distance. For the first time Monk and Ham noticed that the direction was due east—toward the Mountains of the Moon.

"Back where he came from," the bronze man noted.

"Huh?"

"Unless I am very much mistaken," Doc said, "in that direction lies the city of Novum Eboracum."

"But it's a ruin!" Ham said.

Doc shook his bronzed head. "The pygmy elder has been telling me of a shrouded lake downriver where it is death to venture, from which come warriors riding the wheeled platforms."

"Lake?"

"The Lake of Smoke, they call it."

"But what of the sea monster they claim they saw?" Ham wondered.

"It was heading downriver in the direction of the Lake of Smoke."

Monk scratched his head. "None of this is making much sense."

"We must return to the village," Doc said suddenly. "There is much to be done if we are to reach the Lake of Smoke in time."

"In time to beat Waterloo O'Neil, you mean?"

"Exactly."

The pygmies shrank from Doc's approach, but he reassured them with clipped words couched in their own tongue. Then they followed him eagerly, bursting upon the village in a great humor and regaling the others with tales of their prowess.

From no certain direction came a drumming. The pygmies seemed to recognize the beats. Jungle drums. Relaying a message. They began chattering amongst themselves.

Doc Savage flashed to a hollow log, which was evidently the pygmy equivalent of a telegraph. He beat out an urgent message with a stick, paused for a reply, and replied with vigorous thunkings.

Then the drums fell silent. Doc stood in a listening attitude. He struck the log again, waited. Eventually, it became clear that there would be no response. The bronze man rejoined his aids.

"Waterloo O'Neil has Johnny," he announced grimly.

"The drums told you that?" asked Ham.

Doc nodded. "He says Johnny will be killed if we venture downriver. Evidently, he is being kept alive as a hostage."

"Blazes," gulped Monk. "What do we do?"

"What we have to," replied Doc.

It took some time to settle the pygmies down, but after this had been accomplished, Doc Savage made a speech. It was obviously a farewell speech of some sort, because the pygmies soon grew sad of expression.

Gifts were offered. Antelope-hide quivers filled with poisoned arrows. Elephant spears. Doc politely declined these. Baskets of food were tendered. These, too, were refused.

The farewells took nearly an hour. Even when Doc managed to break off and reenter the jungle, pygmies trailed like eager children. They followed Doc and his aids eastward for two more hours before growing disheartened. Some fell back. Others continued trudging along.

At last they came to a point along the river—they were following the burbling Congo—where spectral mists hung over the water like fading fingers.

The last of the pygmies emitted frightened squeaks and beat a hasty retreat.

"Is that mist?" Ham wondered as they pressed on.

Doc stopped and got down on his stomach at a place where the bank was lower and plunged a bronze hand into the water. He withdrew it with alacrity.

"Hot," he said.

Monk said, "How can a river be hot?" and got down on the spot Doc had just vacated. His hand was in the water for a fractional second.

"*Y-e-e-o-w!*" he squawled. "That ain't mist. It's steam! What would make a river steam like this?"

"Geysers," Doc said.

"They got geysers in these parts?"

"Active ones."

"Huh?" Monk grunted.

Ham asked, "Doc, what is that you have in your hand?"

The bronze man had been carrying the spear he had confiscated from the charioteer.

"Pilum."

"Eh?"

"It is a stabbing spear used by Roman legionnaires."

"All this talk of Romans," Monk muttered, "has me dizzy."

"Let us hope there will be answers found in Novum Eboracum," Doc said—and that was all he would offer on the subject.

The terrain changed. The river bank widened and the jungle thinned. Then vanished. It might be that the soil no longer supported life the farther along they got. Certainly that seemed to be the case.

In the night, they heard a furious hissing and spattering, like water splashing onto an immense and very hot skillet.

"Geysers," Doc explained. "We are approaching an area of volcanic activity."

Monk grinned, "I can't tell which of them mountains is volcanic and which ain't. All them clouds have swallowed the tops."

"Not clouds. Steam."

"Huh?"

"Unless I miss my guess," Doc Savage said, "the mountain with the greatest wreath of steam is Vulcan's Forge."

Monk blinked. "You mean the place that X Man talked about?"

"Vulcan!" Ham said suddenly. "He was the Roman god of fire and ironworking. It is from his name that we get the modern word, volcano."

"Exactly," said Doc.

They pushed on. Soon, the barren soil became black, gritty, and like a carpet of loose granular charcoal. This terrain soon gave way to an expanse that in the moonlight was weirdly like a sea of black glass whose waves stood still, as if frozen in time.

Monk knelt and ran a thumb along the stuff. "Slick as glass."

"Obsidian," Doc said. "Lava that has cooled to the consistency of glass."

"I getcha."

They walked along. From time to time, their feet made glass-breaking sounds. There were bubbles in the obsidian, some of which made tiny, fragile domes. Their feet broke these, easily producing the crunching sounds.

With the Mountains of the Moon before them, they felt as if they were crossing some lunar terrain. It was an eerie experience, uncanny when one realized they were somewhere deep in the Congo.

Ordinarily, the African air cools after the sun goes down. They had felt a little of that cooling, though not much. But now the air seemed to warm appreciably. It grew humid again.

They passed close to an erupting geyser. A wave of stiflingly warm air wafted in their direction, setting them to sweating.

The glassy smoothness of the ground grew cracked. They passed into a region of warm, loose-packed earth. Not soil; more like pumice. The air became like that of a steambath, except that steam is usually healthful to breathe. This exhalation was not. It reminded them of sulphur.

"Hades must be like this," Ham said, coughing.

From their pockets they drew the tiny gas masks that each of Doc's men by habit carried. This helped with breathing, but did nothing for the discomfort. They began shedding unnecessary clothing. Ham was forced to slice away the legs of his trousers to get relief.

As they picked their way forward, Doc used his pilum to test the ground for solidity. Once or twice, the spear head warned of ground that was treacherous to footing, and they were forced to circle.

They made no attempt to sleep that night. They could not have done so; the heat was terrific. And they were able to keep going—the grisly, hellish light from earth fissures furnished an unholy illumination, plus they had their flashlights. Fortunately, they were Doc's spring-generator flashlights, which used no batteries, hence could be used endlessly.

By dawn, they were two-thirds of the way across the fantastic place to the mountains. But a grim suspicion was growing on them. Even Doc Savage admitted it.

"There is only the rarest chance of crossing this place, unless by air," he said after removing his gas mask.

Monk, between gasps for breath, said, "I savvy—why they—rode in chariots—now." He fell to coughing and put his mask clip back in his mouth.

"We going back?" Ham yelled.

"We may have to," Doc replied.

They probably would have been forced to turn back had they not come upon a tributary of the Congo River. In the darkness they had not been aware of any water other than the occasional erupting geyser, which would send up plumes of superhot steam.

Doc moved toward the water, saying, "It may be possible to negotiate the river if the water is not too hot."

"It can't be any worse than this infernal place," Ham said fervently. Chemistry was riding on his shoulder. Monk was shifting Habeas from the crook of one long arm to the other.

Doc Savage exerted great care when he approached the river bank. To fall in might have meant an instant scalding if the river temperature partook from the surroundings, as it seemed it might.

Doc was in the act of kneeling when, abruptly, the water roiled and parted amid a great bubbling.

Doc veered off to one side, narrowly avoiding being splashed by a wall of water that hissed and sizzled as it struck the rocky river bank.

Then out of the water reared a great red-eyed head, followed by another and another, while rows of elephantine turtle's feet gouged up the soft river bank, pushing ahead mounds of mud.

The thing labored up, seemed almost about to slip

back, then made a final lunge and stopped level with the ground.

They stared at the hideous creature, which was exhaling smoking mist all over its dripping skin.

The foremost head regarded them balefully. Its mouth opened, revealing vicious teeth.

"I warned ye not to follow," it grated. "Prepare to die, damn ye!"

Monk howled, "It talks! *The blamed sea monster talks!*"

And from the creature's open gullet came a poisonously yellow jet of exhalation.

XVIII

THE VEIL OF SILENCE

Whatever the yellow stuff was, it had no effect, for Doc and his men kept their filter gas masks firmly in place. The stuff soon dissipated.

The apparition continued to shed white smoke as they absorbed the creature with their eyes. Swiftly, its outlines began to clarify. A long barrel-shaped body that was the exact silver of fish scales made up the greater portion of it. The feet were the green of grasshoppers, shiny and metallic, as were the six heads.

Before, they had thought the heads meant a herd of the things, but now they saw it was all of one unit, or creature. The first head was the largest and mounted at the front, reaching forward in a fashion that was remindful of the dragon prow of old Viking longships.

The remaining quintet of heads were arrayed along the flat spine. There was a fishy tail of some sort that was not clearly visible from the angle at which they stood.

Without warning, the main head fell over with a clank, and up from the stump of a neck popped two struggling figures.

The figures, it quickly developed, were struggling with one another. One appeared reluctant to emerge. This was Johnny Littlejohn. He was being pulled out of the innards of the metallic-skinned creature by the man they all recognized as Bruce "Waterloo" O'Neil. Johnny's efforts were hampered by the fact that his wrists appeared lashed to the belt loops of his trousers so that he could not pull them free without embarrassing his modesty.

As an additional inducement, Waterloo O'Neil was holding the muzzle of a Webley revolver against the skeletal archæologist's head.

"One wrong move, and I'll blast his brains out the other side of his head!" he gritted.

The muttonchopped Scot was eying Monk and Ham when he snarled these words. Abruptly realizing that Doc Savage was not in sight, he started to twist in his strange perch in the creature's neck, seeking sight of the bronze man.

Monk suddenly shouted, "You touch one hair on Johnny's head and I'll mess you up good!"

Waterloo jerked back again—which distracted him long enough for Doc Savage, who had dropped dangerously close to one row of those crushing legs, to pull a round cartridge from his gadget vest.

He pitched this upward. It described a flattened parabola and dropped down on Waterloo O'Neil's shoulder, bounced, and made the rattling sound of a marble down a tin chute as it fell below.

Hearing these distressing sounds, Waterloo O'Neil assumed the precise expression of a startled porcupine.

Doc's voice crashed, "Grenade!"

Monk and Ham threw themselves on the ground and covered heads with hands. The pets copied their masters' actions as best as they could manage.

Johnny Littlejohn strove frantically to throw himself away from his captor.

And from below, a frantic voice cried, "Fire in the hole!"

Waterloo O'Neil experienced a moment of understandable paralysis.

Then, fore and aft, other heads started tipping over to expose perches from which a frantic clot of men began piling out, pursued by roiling dragons of black smoke.

Among them were the Hindu, Goona Bey; the pilot, Mulligan; and an athletic young man they knew only as the spurious Matthew A. Nade. All three scrambled off the fantastic apparition with a frenzied alacrity.

The human animal is a susceptible organism. Waterloo O'Neil saw his comrades in roguery fleeing for their lives, and followed suit.

He landed, as it turned out, not a foot from the crouching figure of Doc Savage. The bronze man reared up like some metallic Nemesis and clamped hard fingers on Waterloo's neck. The Scot struggled briefly in the grip of something he plainly could not comprehend. Then he stiffened. Doc eased him to the ground, simultaneously barking out a quick command in the Mayan language to the others.

"Let's get 'em!" Monk yelled, jumping to his feet.

Ham unsheathed his sword cane and followed the apish chemist.

What followed was brief, violent, and noisy. Mostly it was chase. Goona Bey fled in one direction; Mulligan in another. The false Matthew Nade happened to run toward Ham Brooks. The dapper lawyer noticed the athletic young man was carrying his missing sword cane and challenged, "En garde!"

The other stopped, unjointed the cane, and a flashing duel commenced.

Meanwhile, Monk Mayfair pounced after Goona Bey. The Hindu was unarmed. His only recourse was flight. Monk ran low to the ground, his knuckles actually touching ground from time to time, to help propel him along. It was a comical sight—the fat Hindu waddling as fast as he could and Monk, knuckle-walking like a bull gorilla.

But it swiftly became serious when the hairy chemist caught up with the fleeing Goona and seized him by one ankle. Monk wrenched the Hindu off his feet. With a shriek and a floundering of limbs, Goona slammed onto his stomach and Monk jumped atop his foe's broad back. Thereafter, they gave an excellent imitation of an ape on a complaining trampoline—with Goona voicing the part of the hapless trampoline.

Doc Savage, meanwhile, was bearing down on his quarry.

Mulligan—he of the small eyes and protuberant jaw—was a husky man, and after a stab at flight he abruptly turned and threw up his fists in a manner that brought to mind John L. Sullivan in his bare-knuckled prime.

"I hear you're tough, Savage," he sneered at the bronze man. "Let's see how much sand you do have."

Doc Savage said nothing. He let Mulligan get off a

few jabs. The blows struck empty air. Doc seemed not to weave, but his head was never where it should be.

Glowering, Mulligan next attempted several body blows. A mistake. Doc shifted position twice. Then a frustrated Mulligan rammed one toward the bronze man's solar plexus and a smacking sound resulted.

Mulligan found that his punch had only gotten so far. A hand like an implacable bronze vise had seized the wrist in mid-blow. With no seeming effort, the bronze man raised Mulligan's helpless fist to the level of his chin and began exerting pressure.

Mulligan's case-hardened fist became a mass of writhing fingers, and his face became a twisted thing in which small eyes became smaller and squeezed out colorless strings of liquid pain.

"*Ah-r-r-r!*" he said. "I surrender! Honest, I do. Stop—hurting—me!"

Doc gave the man's captured arm a curious upward twist, and suddenly Mulligan was sitting on the hard ground, holding his injured wrist. The fight had gone out of him.

The bronze man turned his attention to the clatter and ring of steel on steel, which had been going on for some minutes.

Not far off, Ham Brooks was playing with his foe, driving him back to the river's edge. The dapper lawyer, of course, was the superior fencer, but he was overconfident. He was not pressing his advantage.

Doc moved in, grasped the fake Matthew Nade's arm from behind, and disjointed it with one hard pull. The sword cane fell, as did Ham Brooks's disappointed features.

"I was just about to nick him," Ham said in an injured tone.

Doc reached down and picked up the fallen sword cane. He brought the tip up to the light.

"Examine the blade," he invited.

Ham Brooks did. He noticed the tip was smeared with some waxy greenish substance. It was not the anæsthetic which the dapper lawyer invariably used. Its color was brown.

"What is—?"

"Poison," Doc explained. "Made from liana juice. The same type used by our pygmy friends."

"Fatal?"

"Invariably."

Ham paled. One scratch would have meant death. He realized how close to death his overconfidence had nearly brought him.

"Thanks, Doc," he said weakly.

Doc reached down and reset the false Matthew Nade's arm. The man groaned loudly, and then stayed put.

They turned their attention to Monk Mayfair, who was climbing off a thoroughly exhausted Goona Bey.

The Hindu allowed himself to be rolled over onto his back—not that he had much choice in the matter—and quailed at the vision of Monk's fierce face looking down on him.

"This side's done," Monk said gleefully. "Now to do the other."

Goona brought his fat hands up to protect his ample stomach. *"Nahin, nahin, sahib.* I am a lamb who bleats for mercy from the tiger. Have mercy!"

Monk set a foot on the mountain of flesh that was the Hindu's belly and pumped casually, as if feeding gas to an engine. Air began *whoofing* out of Goona's mouth and nostrils.

"Monk, enough," Doc directed.

Instantly, the homely chemist obeyed.

Doc Savage bent, collected the Hindu in his cabled arms, and bore him back to the sea creature, which stood on the river bank like some decapitated dragon.

They laid all four rogues out while Ham used his sword cane to slice Johnny Littlejohn wrists free of his bonds. Johnny had not gotten far, owing to a strap that secured his ankles together. Johnny dispensed with this himself.

"How ya doin', Sir William?" Monk asked.

"Veni, vidi, victus sum," Johnny said glumly.

"What'd he say?" Monk muttered.

Ham said, "I came, I saw, I was conquered."

"A crack worthy of a guy who keeps gettin' captured," Monk said good-naturedly.

Ham was studying the great sea thing, which had not moved since disgorging the inhabitants of its cylindrical innards.

Doc stepped onto the fixed centipedelike line of legs and clambered up to the thing's spine. Monk followed, as did Johnny. Their feet made hollow metal sounds as they stepped about the creature's flat spine.

Standing watch over the others, Ham saw them stare down into the necks of the cast-aside heads and then drop from sight.

"What is it?" he called up.

Doc Savage's voice bounced back, "Submarine."

Ham blinked. "It's not real?"

"Of course not," Monk snorted. "Who ever believed in sea serpents?"

Johnny, who had not descended, said, "Throw me your superfirer and see for yourself."

Ham obliged. Johnny used it to cow Waterloo O'Neil and his rogues as the dapper lawyer climbed up.

The heads that had been thrown aside were in the nature of fanciful hatches, Ham saw. One, still in place, had clear glass eyes. Suddenly, out of the glassy orbs peered other, more human, orbs.

With a metallic screeching, the head swiveled in Ham's direction.

"Boo!" it seemed to say.

"Monk, you hairy lunk! You almost scared me out of my skin!"

"That's what you get for believin' in sea serpents," Monk snorted.

Ham climbed below.

As submarines went, it was small. There was barely room for the four of them—five, counting the bound individual Doc and his aids all recognized, although he now wore tropical ducks.

"X Man," Ham breathed. Doc was untying him. The smoke—it was the product of smoke-cartridge grenade— still hung in the air, but had thinned remarkably. Fortunately for the helpless X Man, no more harm came from inhaling the pall than would have resulted from smoking a fifty-cent cigar.

"You recognized the symbol I left for you, Homo Metallicus?" X Man asked Doc.

"I did," Doc replied.

"It was the only opportunity I had, for I was kept a prisoner during the ocean crossing."

Monk was standing up, his head thrust up into the hollow of the serpent's head.

"Each of these dang things is like a combination conning tower and periscope," he said, looking about. "You just stick your head up, look through the glass eyes, grasp the handles that rotate the heads, and you're all set."

Monk ducked down. He began examining dials and other devices. There was a gasoline generator near the tail, which served to charge a series of storage batteries—kept under the floor—that powered the screws. One setup—it proved to feed off a small steam boiler—vented steam from concealed ports along the sub's hull, evidently as an aid to disguising the mechanical nature of the U-boat.

"Pretty slick setup, huh, shyster?" Monk said.

Ham frowned. "Obviously this is the thing we saw coming out of Waterloo O'Neil's boathouse back in Scotland."

"Evidently," said Doc Savage, who was untying X Man, "O'Neil had just completed construction when X Man escaped and Johnny got on his trail. After his escape, he piloted it to Southampton in preparation for the voyage to Africa."

Ham puckered up his forehead. "I fail to understand. How did he get it on board the *Numidia*?"

"It is demountable," said Doc. "Constructed in sections, which could be separated, crated for shipment, and reassembled at the end of the voyage. No doubt this was accomplished at the Southampton warehouse we investigated. Trucks conveyed it from there."

Ham noticed the sectional nature of the thing, as well as the clever clamp-and-rubber-gasket by which the joined sections could be secured together in such a way as to make the whole water-tight. It was a cunning arrangement, all told.

"So how did he get it inland here so fast!"

Monk snorted. "Dope. What do you think—by rail?"

Ham said in an injured tone, "The authorities insisted that the crates were set on a flat car. No such car was ever seen."

"It was," Doc said, standing X Man up. "In the rail spur, under cover of darkness, the submarine was partially assembled, stripped of the frightful heads and feet, leaving only the steel. We later saw it from the air."

A dumfounded expression crossed Ham's chiseled features. "The refrigeration car?"

"Exactly. It was a perfect disguise. After they had wrecked the train and murdered the crew to enable them to transfer the sub to the Congo River without leaving witnesses, they mounted the sea serpent heads and other decorative furbishments designed to give the craft its frightful aspect, and ran submerged."

"B-r-r-r," Ham said with a shiver. "Cold-blooded stuff. But how did they shoot down our plane from a moving train?"

Monk took up a pry bar and used it to heave a deck plate, exposing a deck gun like that on a military submarine, but much smaller. He seized an iron wheel and began turning it. The deck gun toiled up on a great worm gearing and reached a level where the barrel could fire out of one of the portholes once the monstrous conning tower head was thrown aside.

"This is what scragged our plane," he said unnecessarily.

Ham rubbed the side of his face. "But why fashion a submarine in the shape of a mythological Roman monster?"

It was X Man who answered that.

"Brutus covets the treasure of Novum Eboracum. It was his belief that my people would become cowed by the sight of his metal beast and surrender their wealth."

"Is Novum Eboracum near?" Doc wanted to know.

"In leagues, it is very near," X Man intoned. "But in years, it is very far, for it lies on the other side of time."

Digesting this morsel, they exited the fantastic submersible.

Once out in the hot African night, Doc Savage fell into an examination of the craft's underbelly. The two rows of turtle legs did not hold it very high off the ground, the belly dragging. Doc fell to uprooting the legs, which could be detached individually.

In doing so, he exposed the secret of the thing's ability to crawl along the ground.

"Caterpillar tractor treads," Monk grunted. "That accounts for them tracks we saw everywhere."

"It was this monster that crushed our plane," Johnny explained. "There was nothing I could do to stop it. Bullets bounced off its hull. I was forced to jump for my life. After the tri-motor was wrecked, Waterloo's men popped out, caught me, and made me prisoner. *Mea culpa*," he added, lapsing into Latin once more.

"When we were looking into Waterloo's past," the dapper lawyer recalled, "we came across talk of a submersible meant for exploring sea caves that O'Neil had been working on. It was supposed to be fitted with great iron wheels, or something. Perhaps this is it, with some modifications. But why Caterpillar treads?"

"Obviously," said Doc, "the goal of this machine cannot be reached by water alone."

"Kinda screwy, though," Monk muttered.

"A number of years back, a party of explorers crossed Africa in a convoy of Caterpillar tractors," Doc offered. "It was a very successful undertaking."

Monk spanked the side of the thing and asked Johnny Littlejohn, "Is this your time machine?"

Johnny looked abashed and said nothing.

Doc Savage strode over to the man they knew as Waterloo O'Neil. The burly Scot lay stretched out between Goona Bey and Mulligan, who were the pictures of defeat. The false Matthew Nade lay snoring, one arm hanging askew.

Waterloo O'Neil's eyes were jerking crazily in his head. He was as stiff as a pine plank otherwise.

Kneeling, Doc Savage reached up to the back of his skull and manipulated the man's spine.

Waterloo O'Neil might have been expected to seize the moment to lash out. Instead, he did a peculiar thing: He began scratching himself. He dug at one forearm, and used his free hand to claw his chest. Simultaneously, he began squirming like a dog trying to get at an elusive back itch.

"Damn ye, Savage!" he snarled. "This is all your fault!"

"Scratching only spreads the oily irritant that is causing your rash," Doc told him unconcernedly.

"Ye put that infernal poison ivy in that test tube I found on Prince Metho, I touched it, and now look at me!"

"A precaution," Doc admitted. "One which would enable me to keep track of X Man, should he escape. A man with a severe itch naturally attracts attention. As it turned out, it afflicted you. The results are the same."

"Bah!"

"A few questions, if you please."

"Ye go to hell!"

Ham rested the point of his sword cane against Waterloo O'Neil's Adam's apple and said, "I will be happy to scratch any itch you have with this, my good fellow."

"Is that the cane with the poison on it?" Waterloo wondered.

"I neglected to look," drawled Ham.

Waterloo O'Neil made a face and, except for his persistent scratching, subsided.

Doc asked, "You have constructed an ingenious vehicle, obviously to navigate through difficult terrain. Might we assume Novum Eboracum is your goal?"

"Novum Eboracum? I don't know him from Adam's off ox."

Ham dented O'Neil's chin with the point of his sword in such a way as not to break skin.

"How did you come to hook up with these men, Goona Bey and the others?" Doc queried.

"I heard over the damn radio that Matthew Nade had been found alive," O'Neil admitted. "I knew it was a lie."

"How did you know?"

"I crossed trails with Nade my last time in these parts. He died."

"You are certain?"

"A lion got him."

Doc said nothing. Then, "This does not entirely explain your presence at Crowninshield."

"I needed a crew to man the *Scylla*—that's what I call my sub—laddies who'd ask no questions and be willing to take risks. I figured the ones who were working this fake Matthew Nade job might be the sort I needed, inasmuch as they had come from Africa to start with. It happened I was right."

"He speaks the truth, truly," Goona Bey offered.

Doc indicated X Man, who stood a little off. "And this man—where does he fit into your schemes?"

"Him? He's Prince Metho—or so he says."

"Of Novum Eboracum?"

"Never heard of the place."

Ham said, "He's lying. Obviously attempting to cover up the truth."

Doc persisted. "The man you call Prince Metho was, until recently, an inhabitant of a Scottish asylum for the insane. He claims you brought him out of a place called Novum Eboracum and set him loose, whereupon he was captured and committed to Wyndmoor Asylum."

Waterloo O'Neil began scratching at his ample beard. It was looking rather scruffy, as if he had been worrying it for some time. It shortly became plain that he was scratching to avoid answering Doc Savage's pointed questions.

The bronze man shifted his attention to fat Goona Bey.

"Perhaps you might enlighten us," Doc suggested.

"Enlightenment, *sahib,* is my calling," Goona offered.

"Shut up, ye heathen!" Waterloo snarled viciously.

The Hindu winced. "What do you wish to know?" Goona asked Doc.

"Where were you bound?"

"A place of fabulous wealth and riches, *sahib.* Truly."

"Novum Eboracum?"

"This is the name I was told," the Hindu admitted.

"A ruin?"

"I was not told this. Rather, that some fighting might result during the course of our—ah—enterprise."

Johnny Littlejohn, who had been an avid listener to all this, chimed in at this juncture.

"I overheard them talking about it, Doc. They expected a battle of some kind. They had rifles and pistols of all types in order to battle some primitive people, whom Waterloo insisted would be armed only with swords and spears. I can only assume the ruin is guarded by these people."

"We saw some of them," Monk inserted dryly.

"Natives?"

"White as Presbyterians," Monk said. "And they were ridin' chariots."

Johnny blinked doubtfully. "Chariots? Chariots are not known in Africa."

"The chariots," Doc Savage informed a stunned Johnny Littlejohn, "were of a distinctly Roman character, and drawn by trained quagga, which resemble zebras."

The bony archæologist absently pulled out his monocle and began polishing it on a shirt sleeve. He said nothing for a long time. Then, "I'll be superamalgamated! The quagga is thought extinct!" His voice was very soft.

Doc gathered his men together.

"We have come this far. I vote we continue the journey Waterloo and his men started."

"To Novum Eboracum?" Ham asked.

Doc nodded. "If it exists."

There was no dissent. Not that any might have been expected. Doc and his men were bound by a love of adventure. They doted on danger, and the journey ahead promised it in plenty.

They set about preparing the *Scylla* for the voyage.

It was a simple matter to bind Waterloo and the others and load them into the fantastic submarine. Prince Metho—there was no reason to call him by any other name now—was allowed to board unimpeded.

Monk, Ham, and Johnny prepared the rig for a return to the steamy water of the tributary of the Congo. They dispensed with the many turtle legs, which were apparently useless, except insofar as they added to the fearsome quali-

ies of the apparition. At no time had they exhibited signs
of articulated locomotion, the aids realized. But in pushing
mud ahead of them, the illusion of a crawling beast was
striking.

Lastly, they dogged the dragon-head conning towers
back into place as Doc Savage familiarized himself with
the controls.

There was a little station in the prow that housed
these. There was a backless seat, with levers on either side
for guiding the Caterpiller tractor treads, along with
switches for controlling trim, ballast tanks, and the like.

Vision was possible from this station, thanks to an
ingenious periscope whose other end was disguised as a
saurian nostril.

"All set!" Monk called as the last hatch was dogged.

Doc, engaging the motors—they appeared to be bat-
tery-operated—threw both levers around. The tractor sub
jerked, and jockeyed about. Doc soon had the prow
pointed at the river. He threw both levers forward.

The craft began crawling. Everyone who could
grabbed for support as the sub tilted into the water. There
was a splash, an unsettling rolling sensation, and they were
buoyant.

"So far, so good," Ham murmured.

Doc engaged the screws. A whirring filled the tight
confines and forward movement resumed. There was none
of the constant and noisy chugging of a Diesel engine, such
as propel most submersibles.

Monk and Ham and Johnny took turns poking their
heads up into the various conning tower hatches. They
swiveled them about, reporting what they saw to their
bronze chief.

"A lot of geysers," Monk said at one point.

"This explains the hot river water," Johnny added.
"The geysers must feed into the river."

It shortly grew stifling in the tiny sub and hatches were
thrown. It was not long before they had to be pulled tight
again. They had entered a region where the geysers actually jetted scalding water into the river in great quantities.

Waterloo happened to catch a blast and set up a howl-
ing.

It was difficult to tell after that what tormented the Scottish rogue most—his burns or his poison ivy itch. His complaints were vociferous and unprintable.

After the forest of geyser plumes, vision became impossible. The surrounding air was a moist blanket of steam.

Hitherto, distant jungle noises could sometimes be heard. The trumpet of an elephant. A lion's throaty roar. Now these sounds had abated.

"We are nearing my home," Prince Metho said with no emotion whatsoever. He did not sound like a man returning to his people.

"What do you mean?" Ham demanded.

"We have entered the Veil of Silence," the other replied. "Here, time is not."

Monk looked at his watch. "Blazes!"

"What is it?" Ham asked.

"It's stopped! My watch has stopped dead!" The homely chemist's voice was a croak.

Ham Brooks brought his own watch to one ear. It was ticking.

"You dope!" he told Monk. "You probably forgot to wind it."

It was so. Still, the mood in the tiny sub had undergone a distinct change. All wondered if they were simply moving along a jungle river—or transiting time itself.

Silence was the predominent feature of the next portion of the journey. Gone was the hiss and sputter of superheated water. Only the whirling of the screws and an occasional cough broke the stillness. It made them feel strangely disoriented, disconnected from earthly things. This sensation went on for some time.

Doc maneuvered the periscope, to no avail. All about them lay writhing mist and utter silence.

"Hunt a flare," he told the others.

Johnny found one in a compartment near a cache of rifles and pistols amidships. Monk popped a hatch and scratched the flare to life. The illumination was yellow-red and made the steamy atmosphere lurid.

"I didn't see anythin'," Monk called down.

"Fling it as far as you can to one side," Doc directed.

"Which side?"

"Port will do."

The hairy chemist hauled back and let fly.

Johnny and Ham watched the flare, cometlike, describe an arc. Monk's throwing arm was good. The flare came down many rods distant.

Which was why they were all surprised when it landed with a splash and the hissing of its extinguishing came across the misty silence.

Monk muttered, "Either this river got awful wide all of a sudden, or—"

"Or nothing," Ham snapped.

Doc said it. "We have entered the Lake of Smoke."

They continued along. The mist lightened and they realized that dawn was breaking. The additional light did not assist vision appreciably.

After a time, Johnny said, "What is that sound?"

"I didn't hear anythin'," Monk said.

"Sh-h-h," Ham warned.

Silence resumed. And gradually the sound became clearer. Certainly the mists dampened it somewhat. It was a vague, mushy sound at first. But slowly they became attuned to it.

A watery sound. A splashing. Not playful, but intent. Rhythmic. It swelled. It seemed all around them, but actually the sound was concentrated off the starboard bow.

Doc Savage, hearing these sounds, abruptly cut engines. The screws fell still. A deeper silence descended.

And the sound became clearer and more insistent.

Whatever it was, it was bearing down upon them steadily, inexorably—a rhythmic sobbing that stirred the waters before them.

Dip. Splash. Dip and splash. Constant, gargantuan.

Out of the mists a shadow grew, darkened, and resolved into a looming, elongated shape. A second pushed into view.

Johnny Littlejohn was the first to recognize them.

Normally, the bony archæologist was not a user of profanity. Technically, the ejaculation that was jarred out of him was not profanity in the usual sense.

"*Ædepol!*" he exploded. Only Doc Savage understood

it to be Latin invective of a vintage some two thousand years old. But everyone recognized the growing shapes that were bearing down on them.

"Galleys!" Johnny howled. "Roman war galleys! I'll be superamalgamated!"

XIX

THE IMPERATOR

It was incredible, impossible. The eerie voyage through the Veil of Silence had worked upon their imaginations. Doc Savage and his men might have been forgiven for conjuring up phantoms out of the thick, writhing mists. But these were no figments.

Roman galleys, without a doubt. Long, gliding apparitions of polished mahogany and bronze railwork, bristling with oars.

They might have been emerging from the mists of history. Their prows reared up, curling back rather like the trunks of fabulously ornate elephants. The elephant motif was continued in great curved ivory tusks affixed to either side of each ship's rostrum. Set back of these tusks—each of which was capped by an iron protector—was a white-painted hull panel daubed with a staring black eye.

There were two of the long war galleys. Propelled by long banks of oars, twenty on each side of the craft, the ships were forty feet long from their curled prow to stern. Shadowy figures in ornate plumed helmets and clutching square shields lined the rails. Bare-chested individuals worked long-poled steering tillers at the stern. A gangplank with a great hook on the lifted end was being raised.

"Looks like they plan a boardin' shivaree," Monk warned.

Immediately, whizzing sounds came and with sharp metallic clanks, expertly cast grappling hooks began snagging reptilian projections along the *Scylla*'s ornate hull.

Johnny, his long form protruding from a hatch, ducked back in time to avoid decapitation. He pulled the hatch after him and vouchsafed another ancient Roman epithet.

"Mehercule!"

Doc Savage rushed to the controls. He engaged the electric motors.

There was no room to surge ahead, so Doc reversed the propellers. They churned. The craft abruptly reversed direction. It stopped with a jar, motors complaining.

Doc increased speed, but to no avail.

He leaned forward and put one flake-gold eye to the periscope.

"What's holdin' us up?" Monk demanded.

"The rowers are backing up on on their oars," Doc replied.

"Can't we out-Yank them?"

Doc shook his head. "Electric motors against eighty rowers distributed between two galleys—they have the advantage in sheer brute strength."

"Ye fool, Savage," Waterloo O'Neil ripped. "Donna try to escape. Ram them superstitious skurlies! Why do you think I built the *Scylla* the way I did? They fear their own demons. Ram them!"

Doc instructed, "Monk, take the controls."

The hairy chemist worked forward. As they squeezed past one another—space was that tight—Monk asked Doc, "Whatcha gonna do?"

"Endeavor to sever the grapnel lines holding us fast," Doc said grimly.

Ignoring Ham's offer of a sword cane, Doc Savage popped a rear hatch and began hoisting himself up. His feet, poised to take the deck, abruptly dropped back, bringing the rest of his tremendous physique with him.

A javelin of some sort clanked its iron head on the spot under the open hatch where he had stood. The bronze man had gotten out of the way in the proverbial nick of time.

The spine of the submersible began thudding with the arrival of more iron-tipped projectiles.

They had come in a short, violent rain and Doc, employing a pry bar, angled the hooked end up and got the hatch clanging shut once more. A second rain of javelins began denting the submersible hull after that.

Moving forward, Doc rapped, "Submerge!"

Switches for blowing air tanks were distributed through the craft. These were thrown.

Amid a great percolation, the sub began to sink.

"We'll probably pull those ships down with us," Ham warned.

"They will cast off before they allow themselves to be dragged down," Doc returned.

At the stern, Johnny Littlejohn was swiveling one of the monster conning tower heads. He had said little since the galleys had appeared.

"O, Juppiter," he gulped, watching the war galleys respond to the sinking *Scylla.*

"He said, 'Oh, Jupiter,' " Ham translated.

Then Johnny switched to English.

"They're not casting off. A tall man in a white toga on one of the decks is egging them on."

Doc turned to Prince Metho.

"If they have to swim for it, would they survive?"

"When I was last in the Veil of Silence, to be dunked into the Lake of Smoke was to cook while living," he related.

His features grim, the bronze man poked his head into the dragon head aft of Johnny's station.

Outside, the galleys were wallowing amid the steam. They were a fantastic, barbaric sight, partaking equally of ancient Rome and darkest Africa. Soldiers in the scarlet-and-bronze uniforms of Cæsar's legionnaires stormed the decks under the exhortations of a man who towered over them. He was dressed in a flowing toga, white but edged in purple. His fists shook. And the rowers put their backs into retreat.

It was anyone's guess who would win the contest of wills, Doc Savage realized—the war galleys or the submersible.

But it no longer mattered. Doc Savage had long ago pledged to cause no deaths by his own hand. It was an inviolate vow. He could not drag the galley crews to a terrible, scalding death.

"Blow tanks," he clipped, his voice metallic.

A gurgling all around them told of compressed air expelling water. The sub became lighter, rose.

* * *

Doc Savage urged Prince Metho to take his place under one of the heads and asked, "Do you recognize them?"

"All of them. Legionnaires. *My* legions, until I was exiled from this place and time."

"The man in the white-and-purple toga—who is he?"

"My greatest enemy, Imperator Kizan. It is he who cast me out of Novum Eboracum."

"Will he accept our surrender, if offered?"

"It is likely."

"Then we will surrender," said Doc.

Monk gulped. "Doc!"

"We have no choice."

Waterloo O'Neil bit out harsh words. "Savage, ye be a bigger fool than I thought. They'll throw us all to the lions, and that'll be the end of us."

Doc got a hatch partially open. Arrows rained. He shut it, tried to shout through it.

His Latin was impeccable. Scholars say that ancient Latin, although identical as written to the variety taught in modern schools, may not entirely resemble the spoken Latin of Imperial Rome. Too, there are two kinds of Latin —the classic tongue practiced by the high-minded, and the common, or Vulgar, Latin of the people.

Doc tried both. The classic variety seemed to get his point across best. Words volleyed back through the writhing mists.

Doc looked down. "Prince Metho, they have agreed to take us alive. Can they be trusted?"

"To take us alive, yes," Prince Metho said dejectedly. "To keep us alive, in captivity, probably not."

Doc called back his response. His voice was a thunder in the sub's tiny confines.

A final answer ripped back and Doc told the others, "We will begin exiting the submarine."

Monk Mayfair jumped up. "What about our superfirers? Can't we just mow them down and take their ships!"

"Not enough ammunition between us for that. We will have to rely on our wits."

"No wonder Monk is worried," Ham cracked. "He hasn't any."

Ignoring the caustic comment, the hairy chemist indicated Waterloo O'Neil and his villainous crew. "What about these mugs?"

Doc seemed to consider briefly. "They can only complicate matters. We will leave them here for the Romans to discover."

"Alone?"

"Prince Metho will guard them," Doc suggested.

Prince Metho looked infinitely relieved not be be included in the surrender.

They started up. Doc went first. Then Johnny. Monk cradled Habeas Corpus under one arm and Chemistry clung to Ham like a frightened—if hirsute—child.

"We will raise our hands," Doc said when they were on deck. "They should get the idea. It is a fairly universal gesture."

Doc had to say it twice for Johnny Littlejohn's benefit. The bony archæologist was goggling at the galleys as if he had stepped through the Pearly Gates and been confronted by dazzling angels.

"Mirabile visu," he breathed. "Wonderful to behold."

"Snap out of it, Sir William," Monk taunted. "This ain't no field trip."

Frowning, Johnny flippered up his long arms. His ogling continued unabated. He swallowed often, an action that made his bony Adam's apple bob like a cork in water.

The rowers began their maneuvering. It was tricky stuff. One galley crew cast off lines and put distance between the sub and themselves while the other beat closer, pushing aside hot billows of steam.

The approaching war galley surged in at a slanting angle and as the curling elephant tusks drew close, oars on the near side were hastily shipped. Thereafter, it was up to the two men at the tillers to complete the docking maneuver.

A long scraping of timber against steel signaled contact, and poised soldiers stepped across. The submarine deck was slippery and one lost his footing and fell in. His scream was short and when he bobbed back to the surface, his visible flesh was already turning a cooked-lobster scarlet.

He was still alive, although in a bad way. They fished him out and laid him on the galley's narrow deck.

"Guess that water ain't as hot as it used to be," Monk noted, with more than a trace of disappointment. The hairy chemist was inclined to be bloodthirsty.

Surrounded, Doc and his men were searched for weapons. Ham had clung to his sword cane, which he had kept sheathed in the hope—it turned out to be futile—that he might be allowed to retain the seemingly innocent stick. This was taken from him. Doc's gadget vest was carefully felt and two legionnaires tried to remove it. They seemed unable to fathom the zipper.

In Latin, Doc offered to accomplish the task himself, and this was allowed. The Romans blinked in surprise at the speed with which the zipper fastener parted.

Monk gave a low groan when the vest was surrendered. They were entirely without weapons now.

The legionnaires goaded them onto a hooked gangplank laid across the gulf between sub and ship, which was widening, despite two men pulling hard on the grapnel lines.

They crossed and found themselves face to face with the Roman-nosed individual whom Prince Metho had identified as Imperator Kizan, the emperor of Novum Eboracum.

Ancient statues of Julius Cæsar depict a proud-featured individual with a garland in his hair and a fringe of short curls hanging over his forehead.

Imperator Kizan's own face brought to mind the classic features of Cæsar's. They were proud and strong, combining youth and maturity in an agreeable combination. Although there was no garland of ivy adorning his close-shorn skull, he did wear the Cæsarean white toga whose hem was dyed purple, and pinned up, like the original, on one shoulder so a slanting stripe crossed his chest.

But there the resemblance—if in truth there was one —ended.

Kizan's face was more elongated in aspect. The top of his head was rounded, much like a pale pumpkin's. Below the brow, it began to narrow, pausing only at the bulge of high cheekbones before coming to a point. There were points at the tops of his small ears and the lobes dropped to points as well.

The features, though strong and intelligent, could in no wise be termed noble. Crafty was the impression that came to mind. This was not a man to be trusted, regardless of his high station in life.

Imperator Kizan regarded them with dark, steady eyes. His frank glance met that of Doc Savage.

"Ex pede, Herculem," he stated, his voice somewhat harsh.

Monk nudged Johnny. "What'd he say?"

"From the foot, we recognize a Hercules."

Evidently, he next asked the bronze man his name.

Doc replied, "Medicus Sævus."

"Doctor Savage, or close enough," Johnny undertoned to the others.

Imperator Kizan lifted an interested eyebrow, seemed to doubt Doc's answer, and stepped over to Monk Mayfair.

"Quis es simia hic?"

Monk recognized the question. Prince Metho had put forth the identical query. Who is this ape?

Monk cocked a thumb at his barrel of a chest and said proudly, "Simia *sum.*" Then he added, indicating Ham Brooks, "Porcus Rivulus."

Imperator Kizan appeared cruelly amused by the rendering of the dapper lawyer's name into Latin. He indicated Johnny, and looked to Monk hopefully.

"Him? That's only Sir William. He's kinda tongue-tied right about now."

Imperator Kizan cut Monk off with a gesture and asked, *"Quis es?"*

Monk screwed up his homely features in thought, grinned, and offered, "Ossa."

"Bones!" Johnny howled and lapsed into fluent Latin. Evidently he was attempting to give his true name and something of his erudite background and learning. But the imperator was having none of it. He cut off the apoplectic archæologist with a curt slash of a hand that brought spears pointing toward Johnny. Johnny subsided.

"Thanks a lot, Monk," Johnny said bitterly.

"Don't mention it—Sir William," Monk said blandly.

Doc Savage began speaking. Johnny translated the exchange when it was over.

"Doc just told the imperator that evil captives are tied up in the submarine and they should be treated with utmost caution."

"Good," said Ham.

"But I don't think the imperator is buying it. He just ordered Waterloo and the others to be hauled out of the sub."

They were. But it was the appearance of Prince Metho which brought loud cries from the legionnaires.

Imperator Kizan strode over to the high rail, peered through the swirling mists, and ripped out harsh commands.

Prince Metho was brought across the plank. There was nothing gentle about his treatment. Spear points dug into his flesh.

When he stood before Imperator Kizan, the former madhouse inmate they had known as X Man and then Prince Metho, showed spine. He did not flinch from Imperator Kizan's cold, imperious glare and gave back as good as he got.

From his cruel lips, Kizan hissed, "Regulus Metho Antonius Nævius." His voice dripped with a cold sarcasm that required no translation.

Johnny took care of the rest. "He just called him Prince Metho Antonius Nævius."

"Eh?" Ham said.

"Romans typically had three names—a prænomen, nomen, and cognomen. Metho Antonius Nævius is the prince's full name."

Ham grunted. "So he *is* a prince, after all. A Roman prince."

"Isn't that obvious by now?" Johnny said testily.

"Nothing about this adventure has been obvious since it started," the dapper lawyer retorted.

Prince Metho was ungently tied with plaited vines.

The Roman leader then ordered that Doc and the others be likewise bound. Only Monk struggled. The Romans were trying to take Habeas away from him.

"Monk, do not resist," Doc admonished. "Our only hope is to talk sense to these people."

"I don't like the way they're looking at poor Habeas," the apish chemist growled.

Kizan looked up. "Habeas?" he asked.

"Habeas Corpus," Monk corrected.

"You shouldn't have said that, Monk," Johnny said. "Habeas Corpus is Latin, remember? It means 'have the body.'"

"Oh, yeah. I kinda forgot. What're they jabberin' about?"

"They wonder if they throw Habeas into the Lake of Smoke whether or not he'll pop back up boiled."

"Ye-e-o-w!" Monk squawled. "I'll murder 'em if they—"

Doc interjected. His lips did not move, but his words were plainly heard. They seemed to be coming out of Habeas's mouth. The shoat appeared to be speaking impeccable Latin.

"Habeas has just told them that he is a magical pig, a kind of swinish oracle," Johnny said dryly, "and they'd better treat him right."

After that, the Romans did treat Habeas with an utter respect. There was no more talk of boiling him alive.

Doc and his men were herded to a covered section of the galley deck and made to sit. From this shade they had a pretty good view of the attempt to haul Waterloo O'Neil and his cohorts out of the submarine *Scylla.*

It did not go well. Bound men are awkward and the submarine hatches were small. Doc Savage had tied the Waterloo crew so their elbows protruded, effectively making it impossible for them to exit the weird U-boat while so fettered.

The legionnaires realized this after they failed to pull, squeeze, kick, or otherwise prod fat Goona Bey out of the sub. The Hindu howled, cried, protested, and eventually fell to blubbering before they finally gave up—as much to stifle his ungodly moans as anything else.

Goona was untied and allowed to exit on his own. He emerged at spear point and stood aside as Mulligan and the false Matthew Nade came next.

Lastly, Waterloo O'Neil levered himself up, snarling and bristling. His inability to scratch his poison ivy itch had not exactly mellowed his demeanor.

He was recognized then. The words came out of Imperator Kizan.

"Brutus Otho! *Et tu, Brute?*"

Waterloo O'Neil—or Brutus Otho, to give him his Latin cognomen—fell to roundly cursing his captors.

"Ye think ye killed me that time—me and that Prince Metho of yours. Well, ye can't scrag Waterloo O'Neil that easy. I'm back and I aim to get your damn treasure."

This tirade, of course, fell on deaf ears, being couched in a thick Scottish burr, as well as modern English.

Imperator Kizan signaled for the rogues to be brought to the waiting war galley.

A legionnaire pointed to the galley with a short sword called a gladius. It was he who had appropriated Ham's sword cane and, evidently prizing it for himself, still clung to the elegant stick.

It happened to be within convenient reach of Waterloo O'Neil.

Doc was the first to realize this. His voice crashed in a one-word warning.

"*Cave*—Beware!"

Too late. Waterloo snagged the cane, threw off the hollow sheath, and slashed the hapless legionnaire with the tip. Whether it was the blade tipped with anæsthetic or deadly poison no one knew for certain. Either way, it did not matter. The legionnaire grabbed at his throat and fell overboard. A splash and the roiling of smoky steam told that he had fallen to a horrible fate.

"Now I've got ye!" Waterloo raged, slashing furious arcs about him.

The legionnaires seemed uncertain what do to. Their own blades were of the short chopping style—designed for close quarters. But the blade they faced was so slim it seemed invisible in motion.

It licked out, split a forearm here, cut a cheek there. The wounds were obviously slight, but the results definitive. Legionnaires fell, began sliding into the water or simply lay still.

"Follow me!" Waterloo shouted, cutting a path.

Goona Bey and the others jumped for open hatches. There were plenty available. Still, the Hindu and Mulligan found themselves fighting over access to the rearmost hatch.

Imperator Kizan ripped out orders. Javelins were brought from somewhere. The Roman soldiers were snappy about executing orders, but they were not quick enough.

The spears began thudding after the last hatch clanked shut. They struck, but their crude iron points made no impression on the steel hull and they clattered and slipped into the lake.

Immediately, more legionnaires leaped for the sub's spine.

Doc called out a warning.

It went unheeded.

For the submarine began to submerge. The Roman soldiers were fighting with the hatches when this began happening. They seemed not to notice or care.

They started caring when steaming water began lapping at their sandaled feet.

Howls went up. Feet hopped. Some tried to swim. Some did swim—but for not more than a stroke or two.

On the galley deck, there was no one manning the grapnel lines to hold them fast. They were strong. So the lines broke their cleats—they were of iron but secured to wood—and took the anchorage with them.

The row of dragon heads sank in a frothy bubbling. The last sight of the *Scylla* they had was of one of the fearsome conning towers swiveling in their direction, from which a raucous laughter echoed hollowly.

It was the laughter of Waterloo O'Neil.

The suggestion of a monster from the deep mocking them was marked.

Then the *Scylla* was lost to sight.

The frustrated Roman legionnaires hurled more spears into the water, garnering a few unsatisfying thunks. They continued throwing until their efforts brought no more sounds.

XX

TRIBUNAL

A profound silence fell over the galleys. They might have been sitting in some sound-deadening mist. The water was calm. The craft neither rose nor fell, and did not bob. Sails hung limp on their masts.

Then with a roar, Imperator Kizan ripped orders.

There was no need for a translation. Instantly, the great banks of oars were manned. On each ship, a man squatted before a drum of some sort and began beating out monotonous time.

These Romans were masters at their shipcraft. Oars dipped in unison, propelling the war galleys into a half circle until they were side by side, their elephant-tusked prows pointed in the same direction—deeper into the Veil of Silence.

Then, increasing tempo, the drummers set the pace.

The war galleys knifed along, tearing rags of steam out of the smoky atmosphere.

They traveled a surprising distance. It was hard to judge for certain, vision being inhibited, and their past experience traveling in Roman war galleys not exactly lavish.

But after a time, the mists began to thin somewhat. It was just in time. A gobbling as of thunder sounded to the east, and rain seemed imminent, because the rumble was followed by another, somewhat more loud.

The air cooled, which was a relief. And suddenly they could see their destination.

It left them speechless at first.

They had been peering through the mists, aware that it was thinning, eager to sight their destination. Each man formed a different idea of what to expect. Perhaps some

207

thought they were nearing a ruin. Others, a primitive village of some sort.

Novum Eboracum was no town. It was a city. But it was more than a city. It was a metropolis. Stonework came into view. There were standards capped by the eagle of Rome.

It was grandeur carved from limestone and stucco.

And it drew a reverent comment from no less than Prince Metho Antonius Nævius, who had surely seen it before.

"Ecce Novum Eboracum," he breathed. "Behold Novum Eboracum."

Johnny Littlejohn went him one better.

"Ecce Roma," he said.

It might have been Rome, too. The Imperial Rome of Cæsar's day. Pennants flapped from staffs, unreadable in the misty exhalation.

They were coming up on the city from a side. It was a walled side, the walls perched on the barest lip of stone shelf that held back the lake water.

The galleys changed course smartly, began to run parallel to the sheer walls.

Once they passed a tiny lanteen-rigged fishing vessel —although what sort of fish could live in the steamy waters was a question.

When they rounded a bend, they came to a realization.

"Hey!" Monk exclaimed. "The dang city is set on an isle!"

"Yes," said Prince Metho. "An isle where no time exists."

"Bosh!" sniffed Ham.

Stone jetties came into view, and there were people waiting. An honor guard of Roman soldiers, holding pennants, could be made out now. They read: IX HISPANA.

The other war galley slowed with the braking action of dipped oars, and the ship on which they rode began maneuvering for the jetty.

Lines were thrown off, caught, and secured around decorative posts in the shape of uprearing war elephants.

A gangplank was lowered, and Imperator Kizan stepped off.

He was greeted by a figure in blue, an elderly man, entirely bald save for some snow that fringed the back of his head, garland fashion.

Imperator Kizan and this figure conferred for some time.

"That is Mikan the *haruspex*—the soothsayer," Prince Metho offered. "Another wicked one. Kizan and old Mikan were co-conspirators in the plot to deny me the throne of Novum Eboracum."

"They look to me like they're scheming again," Monk muttered.

Ham asked Doc, "Are we really back in time?"

"Everything we see smacks of ancient Rome," said the bronze man in a careful tone. He was watching the two schemers intently, so his aids did not pursue questioning.

"We are going to be tried before the imperial senate," Doc said suddenly.

Prince Metho started. "How do you know this? They are speaking far from the hearing of an ordinary man."

"Doc ain't exactly ordinary," Monk boasted.

"Lip-reading," the bronze man explained.

Prince Metho looked blank, so Johnny explained it to him. The explanation left a dubious expression on the prince's face, but he did not outwardly scoff.

Then it was time for them to disembark the war galley. The other galley had just docked and disgorged its complement of legionnaires. These came to assist in escorting them, inasmuch as a goodly number of the first galley's crew had been lost in the struggle for control of the *Scylla*.

"Offer no resistance," Doc admonished as they were goaded to their feet.

A crowd was gathering as they stepped into the stone jetty. Children predominated. Cries went up. *"Simia! Simia!"*

Monk grinned, and waved at them. He may have been the homeliest man alive, but it was the pleasant kind of ugliness that caused dogs to wag tails and children to follow him.

These Roman urchins were no different.

"They have your number even here," Ham said pointedly. "You ape."

"Oink, oink!" Monk snorted. Ham colored.

They were made to form a single file. A phalanx of legionnaires grouped in front of and behind them. Three rows of them took positions to either side.

They were marched through a great triumphal arch on which was carved "NOVVM EBORACVM," and then into the city of that name.

It was even larger than they imagined it would be. The skies were not clear, but the air had clarity to it. Evidently the steam of the Lake of Smoke drifted over the time-lost metropolis continually, obscuring it from aerial observation.

"Explains why this place ain't been seen from airplanes," Monk commented.

"If there *are* airplanes in this era," Ham said doubtfully.

They had the feeling of having stepped into an extravagant costume epic such as were popular before the advent of talkies. It was a little unreal.

There were houses, ships, paved streets. Even barking dogs.

Ham pointed out a sign over a modest home that said: CAVE CANEM.

"Beware of Dog," he said.

"Some things don't change much," Monk grunted.

"Credo quia absurdum," breathed Johnny, who seemed a little dazed by it all. He craned his long-necked head every which way, as if his eyes could not drink in enough of the vision at one time.

"Novum Eboracum is quite real," Prince Metho countered in reply to Johnny's dumbfounded expression. "It has not changed in nearly two thousand years. It will not change for two thousand more years."

They passed, much to their surprise, an amphitheatre. It was not of the proportions of the original Colosseum of Rome—which still exists to-day, albeit in a ruined state— but for the heart of Africa, it was an impressive sight.

"I wonder if they still throw Christians to the lions here," Johnny murmured dreamily.

"Not a lot of Christians around here," Monk said.

"This being Africa," Ham said, "they shouldn't lack for lions."

"Think of something cheerful, why don't you," Monk complained.

Along the way, there were temples to various Roman dieties and statuary of a high type. Once, they passed a statue whose Roman-nosed profile was familiar. Incised on the stone base, was a legend:

DVX LVCIVS OPTIMVS DENTATVS AFRICANVS CONDITOR

"That's the guy who was on the other side of the gold coin!" Ham exclaimed.

"*Conditor* means founder," Johnny supplied.

Doc asked Prince Metho, "What can you tell us about that man?"

"General Lucius Optimus Dentatus Africanus did indeed found this city. It was long ago, even as time is measured here."

The procession at last came to the senate of Novum Eboracum. They climbed the steps, where their escort surrendered to a much more elaborately caparisoned group of soldiers in plumed helmets and purple cloaks.

"The imperator's Prætorian Guard," Prince Metho told them.

Inside, they were made to stand in the center, surrounded by rows of stone seats.

The senate began filtering in not long after.

Prince Metho looked to his feet. Doc Savage noticed this.

"You have been through this before?" he asked.

"I was tried for treason, along with Brutus Otho, although I was innocent of the charges. My fate is sealed."

"Musta had a bad lawyer arguing his case," Monk murmured, eying Ham. "Not that all lawyers ain't bad."

The dapper lawyer fumed.

From the entrance came a cry of some sort. It mixed delight and fear, with perhaps a little astonishment, too.

The one who had spoken came through the door. Both Monk and Ham drew in breaths so suddenly that they made slight whistling sounds. It was a girl.

She came rushing in, holding her long, full skirts off the stone flooring. Her togalike garment was topped by a linen hood which half covered her head.

"Metho! Metho!" she cried.

Monk Mayfair was a connoisseur of feminine pulchritude. Tacked on the wall of his laboratory in New York were cut-outs of magazine cover girls and movie queens. He had often bewailed the fact that these beauties in person never quite lived up to their pictured charms. This one did. She equaled anything on his laboratory wall. He made a mental note to add her picture to the collection—if he ever got a chance to garner it.

The girl rushed between the lines of Roman soldiers and threw herself into Prince Metho's waiting arms.

They embraced warmly. Tears ran down the girl's tender cheeks.

She could not have been more than twenty years old. Her eyes were very dark, and her ebony hair hung in ringlets that appeared to have been oiled. Either these Roman girls were the equal of American women in the cunning art of make-up, or her complexion was a perfect olive hue.

"This is Princess Namora," Prince Metho said after they had disentangled themselves from one another.

The princess seemed not to know what to make of Doc Savage and his men. Chemistry walked up to her and began chattering.

Ham was quick to point to the runt ape and say, "Chymia."

The girl seemed not to know what to say to that. Then a Roman centurion bustled up to yank her away.

Prince Metho got in his way. The centurion lifted his gladius and Doc Savage would have fallen on the man had not the princess thrown herself between the blade and the object of her affection.

She walked away under her own power, thus avoiding violence.

Monk nudged Ham. "Whatcha think?"

"She's beautiful," Ham breathed.

"Anyone with eyes in his head can see that. I meant, what is she to that prince? His sister? His cousin?"

"Maybe his wife."

"If she was his wife, they would've kissed."

"They didn't have time to kiss."

"Remind me to talk to Prince Metho about this," the homely chemist muttered. "I might want to declare my intentions, sort of."

"I will race you to that particular goal," Ham said.

The senate chamber was filled now, as were the spectators' rows. Imperator Kizan occupied a seat of eminence. At his right hand sat the wizened old soothsayer, Mikan. Princess Namora was on his left. Her attractive face was strained.

Arguments began. Doc, Johnny, and Prince Metho took turns translating, but soon left off. The more the senators talked, the more Monk and Ham's schoolboy Latin shook off the rust of disuse.

It soon became apparent that they were on trial for their lives.

Not every senator was against them. Most were, true. But a few argued on their behalf. One or two seemed inclined to filibuster, but were roundly shouted down.

"I kinda lost track after that last windy guy," Monk muttered. "What's he sayin', Doc?"

The bronze man replied, "We stand accused of being enemies from a foreign land, allies of Brutus Otho, come to pillage the treasure of Novum Eboracum."

"Can they make it stick?"

"We were seen with Brutus—or Bruce O'Neil, to call him by his right name. Apparently, Waterloo was caught attempting to raid the Roman treasury the last time he was here."

"I take it we're not doing so good?"

"No so far," the bronze man admitted, grim of voice.

Came the turn of the old soothsayer, Mikan. He was windy in his own fashion. He reviled them as—and this was funny in its own way—barbaric Britons. He insisted that the gods were against Doc Savage and his men, and if there were any skeptics in the audience, their doubts were quickly dispelled, because a rumble of thunder rolled through the chamber at that point.

"Jove!" Ham exclaimed. "I mean, *O, Juppiter!* Talk about poor timing."

As Mikan ran on, more thunder punctuated his ranting.

"Storm brewing," Monk muttered.

But no storm came. Just thumping thunder that made it seem as if the stone roof would come crashing down on their heads.

After a while, Mikan the soothsayer ran out of breath or words or both. He sat down, his exhortation completed.

Imperator Kizan stood up at the last. His words were brief, harsh, and final.

"We have just been sentenced to death," Doc Savage told them.

The bronze man might have saved his breath. They all knew the verdict when Princess Namora buried her face in her hands and began shaking uncontrollably.

They all looked to Prince Metho. His handsome face was stone.

"Dum spiro, spero," he shouted suddenly.

"While I live, I breathe," Johnny said in admiration.

Then the Prætorian Guard moved in on them.

Monk put up his fists.

"I'm for fighting it out here and now," he gritted.

"Me, too," said Ham, assuming a pugilistic stance.

"Ditto," said Johnny.

"We will go peacefully," said Doc Savage.

They all stared at the bronze man, aghast. Doc added, "We are weaponless, hopelessly outnumbered, and if by some miracle we can gain temporary escape, it would be at the cost of much bloodshed."

"We can't just let them execute us," Monk howled. "Not without puttin' up a scrap!"

"We are not being taken to an execution," Doc said.

"No?"

"They are going to put on gladiatorial games. We will be allowed to fight for our lives."

"Things are startin' to look brighter," said Monk, over a peal of distant thunder.

"Not really," Johnny put in dryly.

"Whatcha mean?"

"We are expected to fight *leones.*"

Monk grunted. "Who's he—the local champion?"

"*Leones* is not the name of a person. It is a Latin word."

"Latin for what?"

"Latin for lions," Johnny said.

XXI

GLADIATORIAL COMBAT

They were immediately taken to the great round amphitheatre, where they were placed in a dark room lit only by sunlight streaming in through a barred grate of immense size.

Monk went to this and peered outward.

"I guess they just raise this grate and herd us out when the time comes," he said. "They got one of them—what do you call it?"

"Stadia," Johnny said absently. He was examining the stonework with his monocle, apparently oblivious to the direness of their situation.

They were made to wait for some time. Distantly, strident trumpets blared, calling the hoi polloi to the spectacle. It took some time for people to begin filing in to occupy the ranks of stadium seats.

In the meantime, the captives were brought weapons and costumes.

Pygmies lugged these in, much to their astonishment. They did not appear to be very friendly pygmies. None apparently recognized Doc Savage, although they were startled when he put a simple question to them in their own tongue.

One of the little brown men gave a dispirited one-word reply: *"Bo."*

After the pygmies had departed, Ham asked Doc the logical question. "What are these fellows doing here?"

"Slaves," said Doc.

"The ancient Romans kept slaves," Johnny intoned. He had joined Monk at the grate and was drinking in the sight of the many-columned amphitheatre.

"Supermalagorgeous!" he breathed.

"That?" Monk jeered. "It looks like a wedding cake skeleton—if there was such a thing."

"Philistine," Johnny sniffed.

Monk went over to examine the pile of weapons and garments. There were helmets, arm and shoulder guards, cuirasses, greaves for the legs, etcetera—in short, the accoutrements of the Roman gladiator. He bent a critical eye to the heaped clothing.

"Heck, none of this stuff would fit me," Monk snorted. He stepped over to the weapon pile and selected the shortest, most vicious-looking stabbing sword he could find. He eyed it lovingly and made a few chopping strokes in the air, testing heft and handleability.

"No lion is gonna eat me as long as I got this baby," he said fiercely.

"They do not always unleash the lions," Prince Metho said forlornly. "Sometimes, it is war elephants who have been made mad by inserting barbs in their hides."

Ham, who had picked out the shiniest metal and most colorful garments and had begun donning them, asked curiously, "What did you have when you went through this before?"

"Lions." And he shuddered.

They all remembered then the story told them of Prince Metho's unreasonable fright at the sight of a common cat—the incident that had triggered the events that led them, step by fantastic step, to this place in the mists called Novum Eboracum.

"Tell us more of your story," Doc inquired. The bronze man was stepping out of his shoes, which had become ruined during his travels, and began lacing sandals about both feet.

"I was condemned to die in the arena," Prince Metho said, selecting a long spear. "I was fortunate: There was only one lion. Others had died in previous games. With Brutus Otho's help, I was able to—prevail."

Monk remarked, "So it's ain't hopeless after all."

"If we emerge victorious, will our lives be spared?" Doc asked, removing his clothing and donning a kirtlelike garment. He left his chest bare and ignored the plentiful supply of helmets.

"In our case, a rumble of Vulcan's thunder came after we had vanquished the lion," said Prince Metho. "The soothsayer Mikan called this an augury and we were put on a raft of wood and sent into exile, in order to appease Vulcan, who had been chilling the Lake of Smoke. It should have been fatal, but the gods were with us that day."

"Are you up to this?" Doc asked the man.

"I—I do not know," admitted Prince Metho, who removed his tunic and donned armor. They all saw the long gouges on his back then and understood what they meant.

Ham finished buckling his cuirass and asked of no one in particular, "How do I look?"

"Like a metal peacock," Monk cracked. Then, noticing Johnny still at the grate, he called over, "If you're plannin' on joinin' in the games, Sir William, I'd grab a frog sticker if I was you."

Johnny stepped away from the grate and snapped, "I do not like to be called that!"

Monk threw him a helmet in the shape of a fish and said, "With that on your noggin, you'll look like Sir William of Rome."

Johnny fell to examining the helmet's detailed workmanship and had seemed to entirely forget their surroundings when from out in the amphitheatre, came the strident blare of trumpets.

Monk and Ham rushed to the grate.

"The house is pretty dang full," Monk said.

"It will not be long," said Doc, joining them.

After the trumpet blare stopped, the murmur of the crowd became the only sound.

"Normally," said Johnny, struggling to find accoutrements that fitted his beanpole physique, "they put on chariot races in order to warm up the crowd."

When the grate commenced toiling upward, the skeletal archæologist redoubled his efforts.

"What happened to the chariot races, Professor?" Monk wondered.

"*Sicce,*" said Johnny.

"Eh?"

"Johnny just told you to dry up in Latin," Ham chortled.

When the grate had finished its upward march, it locked into place with a dull click.

Doc Savage moved to his discarded clothing and went through them, extracting small objects the others could not discern in the gloomy space. One he took from the hollow of a shoe heel.

"Whatcha got there, Doc?" Monk asked curiously.

The bronze man seemed too preoccupied to answer. He took from the pile of weapons a long artifact of iron that a Missouri farmer might have mistaken for a pitchfork. It consisted of a three-prong affair at the end of a ridiculously long pole. A trident.

Doc knelt, the trident's tines resting on one knee, and Monk saw that he was holding a single phial in one hand. He unstoppered it and, careful not to spill a drop, poured out the contents, distributing a greenish liquid among each sharp tine.

Noticing this arcane action, Ham asked Monk, "What is that Doc has?"

Monk shrugged. "Search me."

"You're supposed to be a chemist. Can't you guess?"

Monk frowned. "Well, it's probably some kinda anæsthetic, or maybe something more potent."

"You mean a poison?"

"Not poison so much," Monk allowed. "There are chemicals which, if placed on the human skin, will be absorbed, carried to the brain, and produce a kind of mental depression which is susceptible to fear. In other words—well, I'll illustrate. One time, I took a full-grown lion in my laboratory, treated him with some chemical depressants, and got the lion to the point where, instead of being a hell-raiser afraid of nothing, he was actually afraid of an ordinary alley cat. I sold that gag to a curious animal trainer, and he cleaned up with it."

"And you probably split his earnings with him," Ham grunted.

"Well, I got mine."

Doc Savage abruptly stood up. "There is no point in

postponing the inevitable," he said, and started out into the great dirt-floored arena.

A rumble of thunder attended his entrance. Trailed by Monk, Ham, Johnny, and a dispirited Prince Metho, Doc strode to the exact center of the arena.

He stopped, facing the imperial box in which Imperator Kizan, Princess Namora, and the wizened soothsayer Mikan sat, muscles distinctly graven under his fine-textured skin.

"Form a circle facing outward so that everyone can see each of us clearly," the bronze man directed.

They did so. And waited.

Doc Savage was normally not a demonstrative individual. Indeed, he was genuinely modest. He was not wont to show off, which was why it seemed uncharacteristic for him to have entered the arena bare-chested. Not to mention reckless, inasmuch as there was good armor to be had.

Yet the bronze man now threw up his great muscular arms, showing his Herculean build off to advantage. He was holding the trident over his bronze head and getting a reaction from the crowd.

There were gasps of astonishment. Oohs from the women. Even a few from some of the male members of the audience.

Doc turned so that all could see what an unusual specimen of humanity he was, take in the permanent bronze of his skin and hair, and, for those in the front rows, catch a glimpse of his arresting golden eyes.

A few excited souls started to shout.

"Homo Metallicus! Homo Metallicus!"

Arrayed about the arena were great bronze statues of gods and heroes out of Roman antiquity—fellows who were so agile and mighty that the world still talks about them, two and three thousand years later.

The resemblance of Doc Savage to some of these statues was not lost on the crowd.

Monk, not exactly shy about his simian physique, threw caution to the winds and grabbed a spear that Ham Brooks had selected as a substitute for his appropriated sword cane and bent it double.

The crowd went wild. So Monk grinned, straightened

it again, and handed the restored weapon back to the dapper lawyer.

Now the mob was shouting, *"Simia! Simia!"*

"What was that all about?" Ham growled.

Monk grinned broadly. "Just givin' the folks a show."

Johnny Littlejohn, up until this point a man in a dream from which he appeared unwilling to awake, advanced a few paces toward the imperator's box and raised his long sword.

"Ave, Imperator! Morituri te salutamus!" he shouted. "We who are about to die salute you!"

Hearing the familiar invocation spoken by Roman gladiators to their emperors, the crowd jumped up in their seats, cheering.

"Speakin' for myself," Monk growled after a grinning Johnny had rejoined the circle, "I ain't exactly plannin' on dyin'."

"I have always desired to speak those words," Johnny said dreamily.

Situated all around the lower level of the stadium proper, under the lowermost rows, were barred grates such as they had emerged from. The chambers beyond were dark, like maws.

As the crowd settled down, sounds could he heard coming from some of these. Throaty roars.

"Lions," Ham said grimly.

"We can take 'em," Monk boasted. "Ain't that right, Habeas?"

The pig raised its hackles, giving the lie to a boast Monk had often told. Namely, that Habeas was a lion chaser as well as a hyena catcher.

Chemistry hunkered down behind Ham Brooks, resplendent in his gladiatorial outfit. His chattering brought a response from another grate.

"What was that?" Johnny wondered.

"Not a lion, that's for sure," Monk muttered.

Then the grates began lifting, all of them at once. They saw then the other purpose the bronze man had in ordering them in a circle. There was no telling exactly which grate barred animals—indeed, if all of them might not. This way, they stood an equal chance of confronting danger and protecting one another's back.

As it turned out, every second chamber was inhabited.

A lion stepped forth, moving languorously. Its amber eyes blinked. Its padding approach seemed unthreatening at first.

A second lion came padding out, tufted tail switching.

Then a third. One let out a low growl of warning.

Cautious pygmies stepped out of the dark spaces behind them to prod the great cats along with long spears. One pygmy was forced to beat a hasty retreat when his lion abruptly turned and swiped at the lance point. It snapped just back of the point.

Monk Mayfair happened to be facing the remaining space, the one from with the decidedly unlionlike growl had come.

Something came out of the space then. It was large and hulking and entirely covered with very dark hair.

Chemistry immediately climbed up Ham's costume and squatted on his plumed helmet, shrieking in fear.

The crowd roared, *"Simia! Simia!"* Only they were not cheering Monk Mayfair now. Or if they were, it was no longer clear.

For the hairy thing coming out of the dark alcove was a bull gorilla!

The ape and Monk saw one another at the same time. Their tiny eyes locked and whatever bestial impulses ruled the gorilla's dull mind sprang to life in Monk's!

They began roaring at one another.

Dropping to his knuckles, the gorilla bounded toward the homely chemist. Habeas Corpus, seeing the threat to his master, lunged for the ape, tusks bared.

Monk Mayfair went wild then. He jumped to the rescue of the shoat.

Doc's voice crashed. "Monk! It is stronger than you!"

"I don't care," howled Monk. "I got my sword!"

Waving it high, Monk Mayfair charged.

Doc Savage shifted position. His intent was to use the trident to impale the gorilla if necessary, but the lions had begun to close in, all three of them.

"Ham! Johnny! Help Monk!" he clipped.

Ham hesitated. "What about you?"

"I can handle the lions."

"All three?"

"*Go!*"

The bronze man's voice was a crash that pierced even the swelling murmur of the mob. Then, like an ocean wave on rocks, the murmur broke into a thousand cries.

And the games were on!

Monk came in, sword held low. He got a surprise. The gorilla evidently had experience facing swords. His features were terribly scarred and there was a cicatrix on one forearm where fur no longer grew.

Ignoring the pig snapping at his feet, the beast swiped up a paw and caught Monk's wrist. The sword jumped out of the startled chemist's grasp.

Then Monk found great hairy arms sweeping up and around his thick chest.

"*Y-e-o-w!* It's got me!"

It did. Monk roared. The gorilla snarled. The hairy chemist tried kicking with his feet. It was a good tactic, but his sandaled feet had no effect. Deciding to fight fire with fire, Monk wrapped his long, simian arms about the gorilla's chest.

Monk squeezed. The gorilla responded in kind. The crackling of rib cartilage came like a fire starting. Explosive grunts alternated from the wide nostrils of both combatants.

And the gorilla promptly lifted Monk off his feet.

"This is humiliatin'," Monk complained as he was surrounded by Johnny and Ham.

"Don't just stand there, you ape," Ham urged. "Break loose!"

"Break loose? This monkey is stronger than me!"

"It's also making a monkey *out* of you," Johnny snapped, prodding it with his sword.

The gorilla howled. Ham, swapping the pointed end of his spear for the other, brought the blunt end down on the gorilla's bullet head. This brought a reaction. From Monk.

"Watch it—you almost brained me with that thing!" Monk howled.

"It's hard to tell which ape is which," Ham complained, rapping the gorilla again.

The second time produced results. Snarling, the gorilla abruptly released the hapless chemist and charged Ham.

Ham Brooks was strong, as ordinary men go. But he was not in Doc Savage or Monk Mayfair's class. Should those animal-strong arms wrap around his chest, Ham knew, his ribs would be crushed in a trice.

Ham started to feint with his spear, instantly realized the futility of trying to frighten off a charging gorilla, and took flight, with the ape, Monk, Johnny, Habeas Corpus, and Chemistry in pursuit. In that order.

It was quite a spectacle, but by that point virtually every eye in the stadium—some thousand or so excited Romans—was on the bronze figure they were now calling *Homo Æratus.* Man of Bronze.

Doc Savage, moving with a feline grace which matched that of his leonine foes, maneuvered himself so that he had the attention of all three lions. All were males, with great hay-colored manes.

They took notice of the scene of combat. Evidently, they understood what was expected of them, because they padded toward the bronze man unerringly, seeming in no hurry. Nor did they appear especially enraged.

Doc Savage knew, however, how lions in the wild behaved. As a part of his youthful training, he had observed the so-called King of Beasts in his own element, studying it as he had other animals and adapting its techniques of hunting and stalking to his own repertoire.

They would pounce when they were ready—all of them or only one or two.

Doc used his trident to hold their attention. No fear showed on his metallic features. Or in his confident motions. This did not go unnoticed.

The cheering had now taken on two characters. *"Leo! Leo! Leo!"* some yelled.

Others were shouting, *"Homo Æratus! Homo Æratus!"*

So far the lion fans were outshouting the supporters of Doc Savage.

Doc had maneuvered the lions into a clump. Their tails switched angrily, just as will that of an ordinary house cat when annoyed.

Doc understood this signal. They were gathering themselves up to pounce.

The bronze man did not wait to be pounced upon, however. He drove in, the trident held low.

The lion whose back and shoulder muscles signaled the most readiness to pounce was his target. At the last minute, Doc flipped the trident and smacked it on the nose —a very sensitive portion of a lion's anatomy—with the blunt end.

The lion howled and took a swipe at his tormentor. Doc had already backpedaled. The tension went out of the lion's crouching pose.

The others, cowed, retreated slightly.

Doc reversed the trident again, bringing the three tines in line.

He started in. The lions were crouched in a tighter clump. They showed frightsome dental work. If they expected the bronze man to retreat, they were disappointed.

Their tufted tails began switching again. They sank into nervous crouches, bones and muscles sliding easily under their great tawny pelts.

The crowd was yelling, *"Leo! Leo! Leo!"* in a frenzy. They wanted blood.

They got it.

A lion pounced. It was unexpected. Doc Savage's frantic attempt to dodge the fury of its leap told that. The bronze man, intent upon one of the other cats, missed the signal.

He tried to get his trident up and under the lion, for a plunge into its soft vitals. But the weapon was too long and the bounding lion too swift.

Padded paws slammed into the bronze man's bare chest. Extended claws raked. Doc was slammed onto his back. He lost his weapon.

The weight of the great beast, the velocity of its leap, would have been enough to stun an ordinary man—certainly would have made him helpless from the moment he went down.

Doc Savage took the full brunt of the lion's attack and instantly brought his great arms up. Bronze fingers reached into the profusion of mane, seeking the sinewy neck.

Teeth bared, Doc Savage expended all effort. It showed in his face, in his set teeth and the perspiration that broke out over his straining features, his corded body.

Pound for pound, the strength of a wild animal—any wild animal—is far greater than that of any human being. This might have been the case here.

But as the lion snapped its yellowed fangs at the bronze man's throat, Doc Savage wrestled it off its feet, simultaneously wrapping his strong legs up around the lion's tawny flanks.

He got it over on its side.

The shouting changed. There were more cries of "Homo Æratus" mixed in now.

Straining at every sinew, Doc Savage pushed the snapping, snarling fangs away from his throat. His legs exerted pressure. His hands might have been vises.

The lion found itself helpless. It roared. The roar came again. It was weaker. Doc Savage was strangling the lion.

The crowd took up the cry: *"Homo Æratus!"*

Doc pushed the lion's head inexorably back. His muscular back was a river of sweat. A paw swiped feebly. Weak as the strike was, it left four red stripes across the bronze man's broad back.

Then there came a crack. Perhaps only Doc heard it. The crowd cries were thunder now.

With a convulsive shudder, the lion went limp.

Doc stepped off the tawny beast, found his trident and then his feet.

He lifted the weapon to the crowd and the cheering swelled. No expression showed on his face.

Then, walking with a steadiness that belied the ordeal he had been through, Doc Savage padded over to the two remaining lions, which had watched the entire procedure with winking amber eyes.

Doc brought the tines toward their noses. He simply held it there.

They sniffed. And sniffed again.

Doc pulled the tines away—not by much.

One lion reached up to swipe at the points, to hold it. It sniffed some more. The other joined in.

Doc pulled the tines away, back walking backward.

The lions followed him, sniffing actively.

One reached up to paw at the tines, seemingly oblivious to the razor-sharpness of its points.

Doc led the lions to the center of the arena. There, he calmly set the weapon in the dirt and retreated a few paces to watch them.

Their behavior became amazing.

They sniffed at the dangerous end of the weapon, licked it experimentally, and took turns dragging it around the dirt. To the astonishment and approval of the crowd, they rolled over on their backs, first one and then the other, like dogs in something malodorous.

Doc Savage lifted his bare arms, and the cries now were: *"Medicus Sævus! Medicus Sævus!"*

Evidently, word of his true name had filtered through the mob.

After acknowledging the roar of approval, Doc directed his attention to the others.

They were having a time of it.

Ham was up on a statue of some ancient hero, out of reach of the gorilla, whose weight precluded his scaling the thing. Not that the ape hadn't a mind to do exactly that.

But Johnny and Monk were doing their best to distract him.

Even Habeas and Chemistry had gotten into the act. The runt monkey was throwing stones and Habeas was snapping at the gorilla's vulnerable heels and retreating with alacrity whenever a hairy paw reached for him.

"You stay out of this, Habeas," Monk called.

But Habeas seemed intent on getting his piece of the fighting. He trotted around and went for the neglected ankle. His tusks sank in.

And the roaring gorilla swept him up!

That was too much for Monk Mayfair, who dropped

his sword and leaped on the gorilla with both feet. They landed on the ape's back, knocking him to the ground. Habeas scampered away.

Then the gorilla bounced to his feet. He swiped a loose-fingered paw at Monk.

Monk returned with a scientific jab.

After that, it became interesting.

The gorilla fought as animals do, by making a great deal of unnecessary blood-chilling noise, throwing dirt, and waving his talons wildly about.

Monk dodged expertly, until he found an opening. He threw a solid punch that rocked the ape's head back.

Doc drifted in, and assumed a similar fighting stance.

"Ham! Johnny! Stay clear!" he directed.

They did.

Fully two thousand eyes watched what followed.

Doc and Monk, working as a team, began to wear down the gorilla. They danced around him, throwing jabs, uppercuts, and other well-timed blows. The gorilla flung his arms about and bounced in place. He could not touch his foes. But they kept connecting with him.

Blows rained. The gorilla staggered backward with each one, gore leaking from his mouth. Neither man was swift enough to deliver a knock-out punch. But working in tandem, Doc and Monk succeeded in wearing down the hairy anthropoid.

He became disoriented, began weaving in circles. His blows grew hesitant. None connected.

When it became evident that the gorilla was, in prize fighter parlance, out on his feet, Doc Savage reached up and found the spinal nerve centers that exist in apes as well as men, and began his chiropractic manipulations.

There was no resistance. The ape, his eyes on a weaving Monk Mayfair, seemed oblivious to the bronze man's touch.

He fell forward on his flat face, kicked up a slow cloud of dust with his feet, and did not move after that.

Ham clambered down the pole.

"We did it!" he puffed.

"No thanks to you, you flagpole sitter," Monk jeered.

Doc led them to the center of the arena, where they lifted their arms in recognition of the mob's hoarse salutes.

"Remarkable," Johnny said. "We have survived an actual gladiatorial circus."

"We are not yet out of this predicament," Doc Savage cautioned as the cheering washed over them in wave after wave of sound. From the expression on the faces of Imperator Kizan and the old soothsayer, Mikan, they were not pleased by this turn of events.

Monk noticed the two surviving lions, who were rolling in the dirt. Lions do not purr, but if they did, these two would have been purring.

"What the heck got into them?" Monk wanted to know.

"Nepeta catari," Doc said.

"Huh?"

"The British call it cat mint," Johnny said dryly.

"What on earth is cat mint?" Ham wondered.

"Catnip," said Doc. And there was a rare trace of satisfaction in his tone.

"Say," demanded Monk, looking around, "where'd Prince Metho get to?"

They found him cowering behind a statue, shaking as if from ague.

"Brave, ain't he?" Monk grunted.

"Bravery has nothing to do with it," Doc explained. "He is suffering from ailurophobia—fear of felines—the result of his earlier ordeal in this arena. And we owe him our lives."

"How so?" Ham wanted to know.

"Had he not cultivated the catnip, whose scent has a soothing effect on all cats—an extract of which I placed on my trident—this combat might have had a different ending," Doc pointed out.

The bronze man gestured for Prince Metho to join them. The olive-eyed man emerged from hiding to a vehement booing and hissing of the crowd. He looked very unhappy.

XXII

THE CONQUERORS

Their elation over their victory in the Roman arena was short-lived.

Doc Savage had cautioned that the ordeal was not over just yet. This was proven when Imperator Kizan gathered his flowing toga about him, and stood up. His strangely tapered face was a thundercloud. A grumbling reverberation in the distance might have been a product of his Jovian expression.

He raised his fist. Two thousand eyes went to it. Out popped the imperator's thumb, at right angles to his fist and parallel with the ground.

Roman soldiers came down off the stands, swords in hand. They wore the stony expressions of executioners.

A cruel smile wreathing his features, the imperator of Novum Eboracum began to rotate his fist, tilting his thumb inexorably skyward.

The soldiers began to advance.

"We are doomed," Prince Metho whispered.

So it appeared. But then, thousand voices spoke up. From a thousand throats issued a single word.

"Mitte!"

Over and over, the word was repeated.

Johnny Littlejohn spoke up, "They are beseeching the imperator to spare us."

"I kinda got that idea," Monk muttered uncertainly. "But will he do it?"

At first, the imperator seemed fully prepared to ignore the swelling calls for mercy and risk the wrath of his people.

But Princess Namora leaped from her seat and began to plead with him. That alone might have produced no change of mind had the shriveled old soothsayer, Mikan, not slipped up and begun whispering in Kizan's other ear. His wizened face was very worried.

The imperator's thumb froze. Doc and his men held their breaths. The shouting grew louder, more insistent.

His features displaying no happiness whatsoever, Imperator Kizan grimly jerked his thumb downward.

The mob broke out in cheers that would have done a World Series audience proud.

Then, gathering his purple toga about him, Imperator Kizan stalked off, old Mikan trailing after him like a faithful dog.

"Huh!" Monk exploded. "I don't get it. Didn't he just give us the Indian sign?"

"Thumbs-down," Doc Savage explained, "is the signal to spare our lives. Popular misconceptions have reversed the meaning."

Johnny said, "I thought everyone knew that."

"How about that?" Monk said happily, gathering up his pig.

There was a silver bowl in a prominent position in the imperial box. Princess Namora lifted this up and brought it to the edge of the box. Smiling, she offered it to the bronze man, who stepped forward to accept it.

Doc immediately retreated, walking backward, holding the silver bowl high over his head. His face was impassive, his flake-gold eyes very animated.

Ham said, "Looks to me like Doc is enjoying this spectacle himself."

"Don't be a dope," Monk said. "Doc's just trying to play to the crowd, keepin' 'em on our side."

If so, it seemed to be working. The Roman citizenry of Novum Eboracum began pouring out of the stands, and rushed the victors. The grim soldiers sheathed their swords and joined in.

Doc and his men were quickly lifted up on strong shoulders and borne in a triumphal procession out of the amphitheatre and into the city proper.

They shouted his name, *"Medicus! Medicus Sævus Herculeum!"*

Evidently, they considered the bronze man a latter-day Hercules. He was deposited into a waiting quagga-drawn chariot, and the procession began to wend its way to the city.

"Wonder where they're takin' us," Monk, clutching Habeas Corpus, wanted to know.

"Typically," Johnny said, "victors are given their freedom, a fine villa, slave girls, and the like."

Monk grinned. "That so? Sounds like somethin' I might get to enjoy."

Ham, looking over his shoulder, noticed Prince Metho walking dejectedly at the end of the procession. He was all but ignored after his poor showing in the arena. Even Princess Namora kept her distance.

"Our prince does not appear very pleased with the turn of events."

Monk snorted. "Him? He hardly did any fightin' a all."

"If his story is true," Johnny put in, "he acquitted himself well enough the last time he was thrown to the lions."

"Says you, Ossa."

"I prefer to be called Johanulus," Johnny said in a superior voice.

"What's that mean?" Monk wanted to know.

"Little Johnny," supplied Ham.

"Well, you'll always be Sir William to me."

Johnny happened to be carried directly behind Monk Mayfair. At the sound of the name Sir William, he lashed out a bony fist that struck the hairy chemist on the shoulder.

"I told you to stop calling me that!" he said testily.

Monk tried to swipe back, but to no avail.

"You know," Monk said pointedly, "this kinda reminds me of that time we came across an island in the Indian Ocean where there was a lost people who lived just as they did in the days of old King Solomon. Johnny, you missed out on that expedition, didn't you?"*

Johnny made a long face. He had, in fact, missed out on the past adventure, and it had been a deep disappoint

---

* Python Isle

nent when he'd learned of the experience. But he quickly
rightened. Novum Eboracum more than made up for that
nissed opportunity.

"That brings us back to the unanswered question—are
ve in some lost time, or in our own?" he wondered.

A rumble of distant thunder seemed the only reply.

Monk looked skyward worriedly. "I wish it would just
p and rain," he complained, "and stop threatenin' all the
ime."

They passed at one point what must have been the
oyal palace. From a balcony, Imperator Kizan and his ad-
iser, Mikan, stared down with cold eyes.

"Don't look now," Monk said, "but look who's givin'
s the evil eye."

At last, the procession came to a quarter of the city
hat was, by outward appearances, the Roman equivalent
f Sutton Place or Tudor City in Manhattan. It was domi-
ated by a street of fine homes, bountiful gardens, and
nmaculate paving stones.

Doc Savage was let off in front of the finest villa in
ight. A door was opened for him.

The bronze man stepped in, the others trailing.

The place was no mansion. There was little in the way
f furniture other than a few stools and benches, but it was
arge by the standards of the city and well kept up.

They took a turn about the place. It was constructed
n the shape of a rectangle, surrounding a patiolike affair
hich Johnny explained to them was an atrium. There was
garden, very African. Orchids predominated. They
eemed to thrive in the natural hothouse atmosphere.

With a short speech, addressed to the crowd—fully
alf of Novum Eboracum seemed to jostle outside his door
–Doc Savage gracefully accepted the new home.

But the fine villa was not the full extent of the Ro-
ans' gratitude. Fine garments were brought and laid at
he bronze man's feet. Also sacks of gold coins. Most wel-
ome of all, Doc's appropriated gadget vest was produced.
hese he accepted with simple, heartfelt words.

Next, fettered pygmies were brought before him.

Doc astonished the crowd by undoing their bonds and
roclaiming, in words loud enough to carry far, that he

would have no slaves. And further, that slavery was a thing which should be abolished.

This was met with some surprise, even a dash of skepticism.

Doc pressed on that it was his desire that the pygmy slaves standing before him be carried across the Lake of Smoke and set free to return to their homes.

A few shouts of approval were voiced, which picked up some support, and a consensus was reached.

Doc seemed out of the woods then. But the Romans were not done with him just yet.

Beautiful women—olive-skinned, dark-eyed Romans instead of pygmies this time—were given to him to do with as he wished.

The bronze man looked abashed. He hesitated.

Johnny hustled up and said, "It wouldn't be a good idea if you refused them."

Doc nodded. He accepted the women, who filed into the villa with shy expressions.

Then, along with a last gesture of gratitude, Doc Savage asked that he be left alone to recover from the day's activities.

Reluctantly, the Romans started to drift away. Some remained, most of them children. Novum Eboracum was a bustling city and merchants and metalsmiths and the like had business to be about.

One who remained was Princess Namora. She stared at Prince Metho for some moments. The prince, noticing this, strode over to speak with her.

But the princess quickly stepped onto the waiting chariot. It bore her away.

A few hoots of derision came from the remaining spectators, aimed in Prince Metho's direction. He slunk into the villa like a bedraggled puppy.

Finally, Doc was able to close the door and they were left in relative privacy.

Ham and Johnny immediately fell upon the garment and for once got into an argument. They were fighting over a toga.

"I saw it first, you dandified pettifogger!" Johnny snapped with surprising vehemence.

"But it won't fit you!" Ham retorted. The dapper lawyer obviously coveted the garment for its fine workmanship.

"You do not even know how to put it on," Johnny pointed out.

Which, as it turned out, was correct. Ham ended up with the toga and utterly failed to get it to adorn his body correctly. He tossed it aside unhappily.

Johnny pointedly refused to help him into another even after sheathing his gangling form in the discarded garment.

For his part, Monk climbed into a simple tunic that left his hairy arms and legs unencumbered. Surveying the lavish appointments, the apish chemist remarked, "Swell digs, huh?"

"We will not have long to enjoy them," Prince Metho said morosely.

Monk stepped up to him and said, "You got a bad habit of throwing cold water on everything, you know that?"

"He is right," Doc interjected. "Imperator Kizan and the soothsayer Mikan desired our deaths. Only fear of angering his people changed the imperator's mind. No doubt the two are scheming to be rid of us in some fashion once the ardor of the citizenry cools."

"How long do you think that will be?" asked Ham, eying the demure Roman maidens who stood off in one corner. They were watching Doc Savage steadily. The bronze man, in turn, was ignoring them.

"Long enough for us to locate the *Scylla* before Waterloo O'Neil and his men embark upon their plan to loot the city's treasury."

He turned to Prince Metho.

"Where is the treasury?"

"In the southern part of the city."

"Well defended?"

"Yes."

"After dark we might take a look."

"It will be dangerous," Metho warned.

Doc ignored the warning and asked, "Have you any influence over the citizens of this place?"

"I am still the prince of the city, now that I have returned alive," Metho said.

"Kin to Imperator Kizan?"

"No," said Metho. "Imperator Kizan has no sons. He is the brother of the last imperator, who died years ago. I was to succeed Kizan upon his death, along with Princess Namora."

Doc stared at the young prince at some length.

"Born here?"

"Yes. Of course. Why do you ask?"

Doc made no reply to that. Instead, he said, "When we have settled in, it might be a good idea if you were to use any influence you might have to promote our use of a war galley."

"To hunt the *Scylla?*"

"Exactly."

And with that, Doc Savage repaired to a room—they all thought—to rest.

Instead, he left the door open, and they could see him launch into the two-hour routine of exercises which in part explained his more-than-human abilities.

The exercises were intended to develop alertness, observation powers, the senses, and the muscles. Since he did not have with him the equipment that was a part of the faculty-strengthening portion of the regimen, Doc concentrated on the physical exercises, which were similar to the accepted methods of physical culturists, in that they involved the pitting of sinews against one another. They were so intense and unusual that they made Monk, who never took any exercise, tired just to watch them.

This strenuous activity drew the young Roman maidens to watch. Doc Savage continued to ignore them. He had donned a casual short-sleeved tunic that allowed for freedom of movement, but sacrificed modesty. He seemed very self-conscious about the coyly appreciative stares he was collecting, and ultimately exiled the maidens to quarters on the other side of the villa.

* * *

That night, after they had rested, Doc Savage and Prince Metho donned dark, hooded, waterproof garments not unlike Mexican ponchos and went out into the misty night. The city was patrolled by centurions, much the way a cop might pound a city beat back in the United States.

And like their American counterparts, the centurions were bored and, as often as not, inattentive to their duties.

Time and again, Doc Savage, using stealth and a tossed, distracting pebble, was able to slip past them, until at last he stood on a roof with Prince Metho and gazed upon the treasury.

It was a fine building, well guarded.

"It will be difficult for Waterloo and his men, no matter how well armed, to fight their way to this corner of the city, Doc ventured."

"He knows that," said Metho guardedly. "He dwelt among my people for many months, learning all he could. Almost every way into the city is known to him."

Doc nodded. "You came to know Waterloo well?" he asked suddenly.

"He was the first outlander to successfully cross the Lake of Smoke. His arrival created a sensation, for he told wonderful tales of the outer world. We became friends, and I petitioned the senate to make him a citizen of Novum Eboracum. A mistake. He was a mere thief—one who betrayed us all."

"Did he at any time mention a Briton known as Matthew A. Nade?"

Prince Metho seemed to give this name some thought. Finally, he said, "I have never heard that name before."

"We will go now," said Doc Savage suddenly, and he helped the prince to scale the building's face. Together, they made their way back to the bronze man's fine villa.

XXIII

CAMPAIGN

The next day, Doc Savage and his men had an opportunity to explore Novum Eboracum at their leisure.

It was, they discovered, an almost completely self-contained city. Vegetables were grown in backyard gardens. There were, additionally, plots of land where farmers tended crops.

Meat, mostly elephant and cattle was hunted beyond the Veil of Silence and brought back dressed, to the islet city, via chariot and galley, as were captured lions and zebra like quagga that provided entertainment in the gladiatorial games.

Slaves—exclusively hapless pygmies—were harvested in like fashion.

Wherever Doc Savage went, he attracted a retinue of hero worshipers. He found his name scrawled on walls by children, much as is still done to-day. The popular name for him was "Scriba," Latin for clerk and thus a suitable approximation of his actual first name of Clark.

Since he bore the title of "Medicus," the sick sometimes came to him for relief. Their ills, fortunately for Doc, were slight. Most he was able to cure with a little common-sense advice or first aid. Dispensing headache pills from his gadget vest gave him a reputation as a miracle worker.

When he had attracted enough of a crowd to make it worth his while, the Man of Bronze would make a speech. The theme was always the same—that men were born free and should never suffer the yoke of slavery. He exhorted the Romans to release their slaves and restore them to their families in the outer world.

It came out that the slave-taking was not a one-sided matter. That in centuries past, Novum Eboracum had been beset by Black Ones—*æthiopes,* the Romans called them—who continually sought to overrun the city and plunder it. Thus, the need for isolation and their distrust of outsiders.

It was also the reason for a growing concern that the daunting waters of the Lake of Smoke were losing heat. Should it cool completely, it was generally feared, the Black Ones would soon be upon the city.

Upon questioning, Doc discovered that these much-feared black interlopers were not pygmies but from other tribes plentiful in this part of the Congo.

Doc countered the Romans' arguments with these facts and from time to time, pygmy slaves were offered to him to keep or release as he saw fit.

By that afternoon, the bronze man had collected a goodly number of the bewildered little fellows.

Around that time, a messenger came, saying Prince Metho had secured a war galley for Doc Savage's use.

Doc led his slaves to the stone jetty and coaxed them aboard.

They rowed out onto the Lake of Smoke and Doc put his men to dropping grapnels into the water and dragging them along.

They directed the galley to the opposite shore, where they let off their pygmy cargo. Then, reversing, they returned to the monotonous task of dragging the lake.

If the *Scylla* lurked under the steamy waters, the grapnels did not demonstrate this fact. They came up clean, bereft of even weeds. Apparently no life existed in the boiling lake waters.

At one point, Doc clambered down the galley's side and clung just above the waterline. Removing a long steel instrument not unlike a fountain pen from his gadget vest, he dipped this into the hot waters, careful not to scald his fingers. He did this repeatedly, each time lifting the device to his flake-gold eyes and studying it intently.

"What is it, Doc?" Monk asked when Doc Savage clambered aboard.

"The lake waters are definitely cooling."

"Mikan will blame this upon my return," Prince Metho said.

A rumble of thunder almost drowned out his prediction.

"Perhaps it might be advisable, if we cannot locate Waterloo O'Neil, to find a way to discredit Mikan," said Doc, looking to the steamy skies.

They gave up for the day. The threatened rain did not come.

Over the next several days, Novum Eboracum provided them with a great deal of pleasant diversion.

Johnny discovered that the place boasted an authentic Roman bath, a multichambered place where one could pass from a steambath-style environment to successions of cooler and warmer rooms, and hied his bony frame to the public place.

The others went with him. Doc did not partake, but instead spent some time studying how the place was set up. It turned out that under the isle lay a hot spring; this was tapped in some ingenious fashion and the steam directed to the appropriate rooms.

They emerged at the end of an hour, refreshed and invigorated.

Naturally, there was a crowd waiting.

The citizenry, and these included some senators, were engaged in animated discourse. Doc went among them. Johnny, too, since his command of classical Latin made it possible to overhear and converse freely.

Doc Savage returned to his waiting men, somewhat grim of mien after listening to the talk.

"They are saying that Imperator Kizan is growing jealous of our popularity."

Monk snorted. "Heck! We ain't bothered him none."

"Our freeing of the slaves is setting an example the imperator does not wish to follow," Doc added. "He has many slaves himself, and is unwilling to relinquish any. There is talk that he may have to let some go as a gesture to public sentiment."

"So?"

"There is also talk of installing Medicus Scriba Sævus as the next in line to be imperator," Doc said dryly.

"I do not think Kizan will take to that idea with a lot of enthusiasm," Ham said, rather understatedly.

Johnny Littlejohn put in an appearance and said uncomfortably, "Doc! People are talking about putting a bill through the senate calling upon Imperator Kizan to offer the hand of his niece, the princess, to you. In marriage," Johnny added in a dry croak. The thought plainly horrified the bony archæologist. It was the first sign of discomfort he had evinced since his arrival.

"Let us hope," Doc said fervently, "that is all there is to that notion—just talk."

They continued their perambulations about the city. Prince Metho had joined him.

There was a library, and when Johnny Littlejohn—or Johanulus—laid eyes upon it, he all but fainted with joy. He raced the others up the wide steps.

The library was well stocked with papyrus scrolls relating to the history of Novum Eboracum. After the custodian welcomed them, he brought whatever items they asked for.

Both Doc Savage and Johnny requested histories of the city.

They sat on small stools, the brittle material in their laps, and read intently. Monk and Ham from time to time peered over their shoulders, struggling to turn the familiar Latin alphabet into understandable thought.

Johnny began reciting.

"During the reign of Imperator Hadrian, the Ninth Hispana Legion was called from their fortress at Eboracum. Hadrian had had built a great wall, called Hadrian's Wall, designed to protect Roman Britannia from the untamed barbarians of Scotland. He believed that the Ninth Hispana could better serve him in Cyrenaica, where his subjects were in revolt." Johnny wrinkled up his brow. "We call it Libya, these days."

"Hadrian," mused Ham. "Wasn't he the emperor who spent most of his days traveling the empire?"

"He was," said Johnny. "This was at a time when the Roman Empire was at its height, stretching from Britannia to Mesopotamia. It seems that Hadrian was eager to expand the empire even further. He saw his chance when the Ninth Hispana disgraced themselves in failing to put down this revolt. He offered the general who commanded the legion, Dentatus, a choice between subjecting his troops to decimation or pushing south to found a colony deep in the African interior."

"Decimation?" Monk said.

"A custom by which disgraced Roman military units atoned for their transgressions," Doc supplied. "Every tenth man was put to the sword. It was an indelible lesson to the survivors."

"It says here," resumed Johnny, "that the Ninth Hispana Legion, along with their wives and children, drove south out of ancient Cyrenaica, seeking the southernmost point of Africa. At that time, only a thin strip of the northern continent was known. They had no idea how long a journey they had embarked upon.

"Along the way, they suffered decimation by wild beasts and marauding tribes, enduring great hardships until their leader, General Dentatus, heard jungle tales of a place recorded here as *Velum Silentii*—the Veil of Silence. He brought them through the mists to the Lake of Smoke, where they built rafts and paddled to the isle on which they founded this city, which they called Novum Eboracum after the British fortress where they had last seen glory. The hot waters kept them safe from the Black Ones they considered savages. Unfortunately, they were also cut off from Rome." Johnny paused, his face aglow. "Remarkable! One of the great mysteries of ancient history, and it is all explained here."

"Yeah?" said Monk. "How long ago was that?"

Johnny read along. He started and his shaggy head came up.

"According to this, in the Roman year of 877—our 124 A.D.!"

"So?"

"So, you dull ape," Ham inserted. "That means that nineteen centuries have passed since the founding of Novum Eboracum. We haven't gone back in time at all!"

"You mean that Waterloo was just running a job on us?"

"Yes," said Doc. "So anxious was Waterloo O'Neil to conceal the existence of Novum Eboracum and its treasure that he concocted that fantastic story about traveling backward through time to prevent us to seeking out this city."

Monk indicated Prince Metho with a hairy finger. "What about him? He told some fibs, too."

"I told no lies," retorted Prince Metho indignantly.

"You said time don't exist here," Monk reminded.

"It does not. Novum Eboracum exists to-day just as it did in the beginning. We do not mark the passing years."

In that, they could find no fault. For all the difference that it made, they might as well have stepped back through the mists of the ages into a hitherto-unknown outpost of ancient Rome.

They learned more facts. Evidently, the people of Novum Eboracum had, from time to time, acquired Arab wives, thus assimilating a noticeable strain of Arab blood. This explained the swart coloration of some of its inhabitants.

Doc's trilling came at one point. They all looked to him. He had a fresh scroll in his bronze hands.

"This is a listing of every ruler of Novum Eboracum since its founding," he said. "It includes the lineage of all imperators, princes, and princesses. I find Princess Namora's name inscribed here, but there is no Prince Metho. No Metho Antonius Nævius at all."

All eyes went to Prince Metho.

"How do you explain this?" Doc asked quietly.

Prince Metho seemed at a loss for words, "I—I cannot," he stammered out. And he looked very confused.

They left the library. Johnny had to be practically lifted off his feet and carried out bodily.

Outside the building, they received confirmation that they resided firmly in the twentieth century.

Down from the eternal mists of the Lake of Smoke, a drone could be heard. Even though it was muffled by the thick, steamy blanket, there was no mistaking it.

"Airplane!" Ham exclaimed.

Doc Savage said, "Probably a mail plane on its way to the coast. The pilot, if he chances to look downward, would see only mist."

"Well, that settles it," Monk said. "We ain't gone back through time at all."

Looking around at the splendor about them, Johnny Littlejohn murmured, "That is a matter of opinion."

Their perambulations eventually took them back to the stone jetty where the two barbaric war galleys rode at anchor. Doc walked down a flight of limestone steps and knelt to test the waters with his penlike device.

He did this several times, at five-minute intervals, pausing each time to hold the device in the air in an expectant fashion.

"Is that some kind of thermometer?" Ham asked Monk.

The hairy chemist nodded. "Natch."

Ham frowned. "Wouldn't the mercury explode in this heat?"

"Naw, it ain't a mercury thermometer, but one that works electrically, like a thermostat."

After a time, Doc Savage left off this testing of the waters and rejoined them. They stood in the shadow of a group of bronze statues. The likeness of Doc Savage to these bronzes was marked.

It had been a pleasant day. It had not rained exactly, but the air was moist with a warm mist—a gentle precipitation caused apparently by the steam that blew over the city and, meeting cooler air, condensed, falling back to earth. Their clothing had acquired a not-unpleasant dampness to it, but by no means were they wet.

The inhabitants of Novum Eboracum had by this time grown accustomed to their presence. Doc and his aids were greeted by stares, waves, smiles, and more exuberant hails. But they were not accosted.

"Guess fame is fleetin' every place you can go," Monk observed.

Doc Savage, however, happened to notice a figure skulking in the shadow of an imposing building.

"We are being watched, brothers," he cautioned.

Doc's men were too canny to suddenly turn and look.

"Which direction?" whispered Ham.

"South."

Ham, pretending to notice that his leather sandals had

come unlaced, knelt, ostensibly to attend to the things. He thus was able to glance in the right direction, and spot the skulking man.

The individual lurked in an alley. He wore one of the Roman costumes that serve as raincoats and resemble the Mexican poncho. The hood was up and around his face.

"I don't recognize him," Ham undertoned.

"His hood is perfect for concealing features as well as keeping the head dry," said Doc.

"He is probably a spy sent by the imperator," Prince Metho offered.

"He appears too nervous for that."

"Then who—"

"Let us find out," said Doc, abruptly stepping out of the circle his men had formed around him.

The skulker—that was the only word to describe him —saw the bronze giant stride purposefully forward and came to an unavoidable conclusion.

Gathering his garment about him, he retreated into an alley.

Doc was already running by then. He flashed down the alley, which was—like alleys throughout history, it seems—choked with refuse. The bronze man bounded over a sack of spoiled vegetables, and the leap brought him to the other terminus of the disreputable alley.

Some sixth sense seemed to make him pause. In truth, it was no attack of clairvoyance, but common sense. Doc's acute hearing came into play. His quarry had been running, but now there was no detectable sound of flight.

Easing up to the alley's end, Doc took a chance. He stuck his head out and, without waiting to register impressions, brought it snapping back.

He was one flash second ahead of the bullet that knocked a chip out of the building corner.

Monk and the others arrived at that point, sliding to a stop.

"Was that a gun shot?" Ham hissed.

Doc signaled for silence. He was digging into his gadget vest. It was not easy, inasmuch as his tunic boasted no convenient openings designed to admit hands.

Out came a simple firecracker of the dime-store type.

Ham Brooks was in the habit of carrying a jeweled lighter —an affection, inasmuch as he did not smoke. Ham scratched the flint wheel and offered flame. The bronze man ignited the firecracker's long fuse, and it commenced hissing and shedding busy sparks.

Doc flung this overhead so that it would drop in the vicinity of the spot from which the shot had come.

There was an entirely satisfactory howl that followed the short pop of the explosive.

Sandaled feet whetted the ground, and Doc pitched out of the alley.

Their quarry was in sight. He was running fast, Doc hard on his heels. The man stopped, and wheeled to snap off another hasty shot.

"Down!" Doc shouted.

Instantly, his men flattened. Doc dodged the bullet— he had time to recognize that it exploded from a British Webley pistol—and kept going. His reflexes were unbelievably coordinated.

But no man—no matter how skilled—can dodge bullet after bullet when there is no shelter, as was the case here.

Doc saw the Webley come up again and threw himself flat. Bullets sparked stone chips into his bronze features. His arms lifted protectively.

Then he leaped to his feet and made for the wall.

By that time, the man was balanced on the wall. They got a good look at his face then.

Monk yelled, "Hey! That's Matthew Nade—I mean the guy who was pretendin' to be Nade!"

They had no more than a moment to register this discovery. Then the erstwhile Matthew Nade turned and leaped into the sea!

Ham shouted, "He jumped! The utter fool!"

"He'll be scalded!" Johnny added.

But he wasn't. There wasn't even a splash.

Doc reached the wall. There were handholds and he used them to advantage. Monk joined him a moment later.

Below was a shelf of sand. And footprints going into the water.

They stood watching the escaping figure. He was in a

tiny boat of some sort. It was rather round and he knelt in the prow, where he seemed to be using an oar to pull the little cockleshell along.

"What kinda boat is that?" Monk grunted.

"English coracle," said Doc, and then he was running along the top of the wall. He got to the stone jetty, Monk not far behind.

Doc clambered down to leap for one of the galleys. There was a skeleton crew aboard—five men. Centurions. That was all. No rowers were at hand and there was no wind to speak of. Without wind and rowers, the fleet warship might as well have been a log. Worse. A log could have been propelled with a long pole. It was useless.

Doc and Monk were watching the little cockleshell vanish into the mists with grim expressions when Ham and the others found their way back to the stone jetty.

"Looks like he was spyin' on us, all right," Monk growled.

"No doubt," Ham said grimly, "he has gone back to the *Scylla* to report to Waterloo O'Neil." The dapper lawyer looked to Doc Savage. "What do you suppose his game is?"

"Waterloo O'Neil has come a long way to loot the treasury. He will not leave until he has succeeded."

"Wonder what that guy's real name was?" pondered Monk.

"His name," said Prince Metho, "was Leo Corby. I learned this when I was a captive of Brutus Otho."

XXIV

PLOTTERS

Leo Corby, the erstwhile Matthew A. Nade, was sweating as he propelled his tiny coracle along. His manner of doing this would have astonished a seaman not familiar with the properties of the coracle. Kneeling in the bow and leaning forward, he simply stirred the short oar back and forth, creating pull. Steering was accomplished by an intricate manipulation of the paddle.

Leo Corby stirred the hot waters of the Lake of Smoke for twenty minutes and stopped. He tried to see through the swirling mists, but they defeated his sight.

Stowing the oar, he cupped hands over his mouth and gave a shout.

"Hallooo?"

No answer. He tried again.

"Hallooo! Waterlooo!"

A raspy voice called back. "This way!"

"Say it again!"

"Come this way, damn ye!"

The bellow was sufficient for Leo Corby to fix the voice's position, and he resumed stirring the lake waters.

His shell soon bumped the *Scylla,* which lay at anchor.

Clambering from the coracle to the sub's deck took some ingenuity, but Corby managed it without mishap.

Mulligan and fat Goona Bey helped him to drag the fragile cockleshell out of the water and shake the hull free of too-hot water. They disassembled the thing until it was compact enough to fit into a forward hatch. It consisted of a canvas hull fitted over a folding framework of wood, and made waterproof by a coating of pitch.

Waterloo O'Neil minced no words when Corby faced him.

"Well, what did ye learn?"

"Doc Savage and his men are alive."

"Damn them!"

"It's worse than that, Waterloo. They've got the Romans buffaloed. There's talk of making him a prince or something."

"A prince?"

"That's what I overheard while hanging about the markets."

Waterloo O'Neil scratched at his whiskers. Then, realizing that would only spread the virulent poison ivy that still afflicted him, he left off. His face and hands were mottled and red.

"I wonder what Prince Metho would say about this turn of events," he muttered.

"We're not going to be able to get to the treasury with Savage on deck. He knows what's what."

"There is only one thing to do, laddies."

Everyone looked to Waterloo O'Neil.

"If I know Imperator Kizan—and I do—he's none too keen on Savage being so popular. Maybe we can do business with him."

"I thought you said the imperator likes to throw people like us to his lions?"

"He likes keeping his throne more." Waterloo looked up. "Leo, ye're going to slip back into Novum Eboracum after sundown."

"And do what?"

"Take a message to that dried-up old soothsayer, Mikan."

"Isn't that asking for trouble? It was risky enough that I—"

"Never ye mind! Mikan is a skulking dog who likes to bring bones to his master. He'll take the message I give ye and leave ye be. Mark me on it."

"If you say so, Waterloo."

"I say so. I hired ye on in spite of the fact that ye're but a miserable Thespian. 'Tis a good thing yer acting skills have come in handy."

Leo Corby fetched his fragile coracle from storage, looking none too happy about it.

* * *

That night, the *Scylla* stood at anchor, her hatches open. It was not appreciably cooler after dark. But it was more eerie. Moonlight filtering through the strangely still mists made it seem as if the submersible was afloat in a universe of shimmering ghosts.

Mulligan the large-jawed pilot stood guard, along with fat Goona Bey.

Squatting on the U-boat's spine, the two rogues passed the time in swapping complaints.

"This is a long way to come for nothing," Mulligan groused.

"*Sach Bat!* Indeed! Perhaps a mutiny might be in order."

"Count me out. That damn poison ivy has made Waterloo meaner than a mamba snake."

"It is true. Still, I fear a place where the stars of the night sky cannot be seen." The Hindu wrinkled his swart face and looked heavenward. "If there are evil portents they will go unheeded."

Then, off in the stillness, came the dip and gurgle of oars. Many oars.

Goona Bey picked himself off the hull and, straightening his turban, crawled to the handiest open hatch.

"Waterloo! They come!"

Waterloo O'Neil poked his bristled features out of the hole like an annoyed hedgehog. He listened.

"O.K. Ye know enough to keep yer tongues still."

"*Han, Sahib* Waterloo. We do."

They waited.

Out of the mists, the elephantine prow of a Roman war galley glided.

"Ahoy there!" Waterloo called.

A voice rapped out a sharp command. Instantly, oars were lifted, dropped, and pushed in reverse.

Water roiled noisily. The war galley's eerie gliding motion slowed. It began to circle, losing even more speed.

Then, after some careful oar work, it drew to a stop.

The two ships—representing two different eras of nautical craft—stood off from one another.

"*Ave,* Imperator!" called Waterloo O'Neil.

From out of a tower set forward of the mast emerged a figure in blue robes. Mikan, the old soothsayer. He scuttled to the rail, regarded them coldly, and turned.

Imperator Kizan stepped into view then. Imperious, his cruel face a mask, he strode into the moonlight. He began speaking Latin.

"Brutus Otho, I have your message. Speak, you *furcifer*."

"That's a fine way to talk to the one who is going to rid ye of Doc Savage," Waterloo shot back. "Callin' him a gallow's rogue."

"Medicus Sævus is very popular with my people."

"I hear that said. I hear they want to make him a bleedin' prince of the realm, too."

Imperator Kizan scowled darkly, and offered no comment. None was needed.

Mikan spoke up. "The gods are angry. Vulcan's voice speaks loudest. In fury, he hammers at his forge day and night, angry that Novum Eboracum is defiled by outland barbarians. You, Brutus Otho, are the worst of them."

"Ye won't be saying that once that bronze devil steals the throne out from under ye. I know his kind. I know his weaknesses, too."

Imperator Kizan called, "Speak, Brutus Otho."

"Not unless ye give me what I want."

"What is your price?"

"Half the treasury of Novum Eboracum. Not a gold coin less."

Imperator Kizan's strong features betrayed suspicion. "How do I know your advice will work?" he demanded.

"Ye don't. But if ye pay me one-half and my plan works, ye'll be rid of two thorns when the deviltry's done— me and Medicus Sævus. And ye'll still have half of the treasury. Any other way and ye stand to lose everything."

Mikan the soothsayer lifted up on his toes to whisper counsel into the ear of his emperor.

"*Sahib*, I think you have overplayed your hand," said Goona Bey.

Waterloo O'Neil scowled. "Not me."

A moment later, Imperator Kizan spoke again.

"I will do this. Now, speak your counsel."

"Not a chance. Leave the gold on an unguarded ship and after I have it on my vessel, I'll give ye the advice."

"Give it to me now as a gesture of good faith."

"Ye're a fine one to talk of faith, good or bad. But all right. Ye know if ye double-cross me, I'll not rest until I have that gold. Listen. There's talk of Doc Savage taking Princess Namora in marriage."

"I will never allow this!"

"Offer her hand to Savage. Make a big show of it."

"Are you mad?"

"Savage will turn her down. That ought to start a big ugly ball rolling."

"I do not understand."

Waterloo O'Neil lowered his voice conspiratorially. "Listen, this is what we will do—"

The burly Scot spoke for some time. A thin-lipped grin came over Imperator Kizan's tapered face. Even Mikan's wizened features were wreathed in smiles when it was over.

"I will do this, and your gold will be at the appointed place," promised the imperator.

Then, turning in a swirl of white garments, Imperator Kizan returned to his tower.

The oars were extended and dropped. Under the force of its forty synchronized blades, the galley began to back away. Then, the way cleared, it surged forward. It was soon gliding away, a fantastic sight in the moonlit mists.

After the writhing mists had swallowed it, Goona Bey said, "It is a wise man indeed who settles for half of something rather than risk all and end up as a snake or a toad in his next life, *sahib*."

"In that case, call me a bloody fool."

"Eh?"

"Because I want it all. Not just the half. All of it."

"You will go back on a bargain?"

"With Doc Savage out of the picture, there'll be nothing standing between us and the damn Roman treasury," Waterloo O'Neil said fiercely. "All we have to do is run the *Scylla* up that jetty and through the streets while their damn spears and arrows bounce off her hull, until we're at the treasury building itself."

He fell to scratching his face, and then cursing voluably for forgetting himself.

"I fear a man who does not know when he has a bird in his hand," intoned Goona Bey.

"Ye won't be saying that once this sub is filled with gold dinarii, will ye, my fine fat heathen?"

"Gold is a very precious commodity," said Goona Bey softly. "Almost as precious as one's life."

XXV

SKY TALK

Dawn came the next day with that particular opalescence that marked the advent of a new day in Novum Eboracum. Slanting sunlight turned the overhead mists the hue of smoky brass.

The Roman people rose with the sun. The din of human activity soon grew so loud that it became impossible to sleep on.

Doc Savage was already up, deep in his exercises, when the mob began clamoring for him.

"Scriba! Medicus Scriba Sævus!"

Monk stumbled out of his bedroom wearing the tunic in which he had slept. It barely contained his apish physique.

"What are they sayin'?" he muttered sleepily.

Doc replied, "They are calling me to the senate."

Monk screwed up his homely face in concern. "You know what happened last time we got haled before those bed-sheeted politicians."

Johny poked his sleepy head out the door. He listened a moment.

"They do not sound angry."

"We will do as they bid," said Doc.

A chariot, it turned out, awaited them. This presented a problem, inasmuch as there was only room for two passengers in addition to the driver. Doc solved this problem, in part at least, by taking the driver's place. Johnny hopped on with alacrity, beating both Monk and Ham, who immediately fell into a vociferous argument over the remaining spot.

Monk offered to flip a coin. Ham protested that Monk's coin was of the two-headed variety. Monk replied

at Ham, being a lawyer and therefore two-faced, was
ardly one to talk.

Johnny offered a Roman coin he had pulled from
omewhere in his toga and they flipped that. Monk won.
Iam was forced to run along behind after Doc chucked
1e reins, sending the chariot rattling along the narrow
vways of Novum Eboracum.

"This is worse than a buckboard," Monk complained
: one point. "No dang springs!"

For his part, Johnny Littlejohn was grinning like a
1ild on a merry-go-round. Once, he actually gave out with
whoop of pure pleasure as the chariot careened wildly
round a corner.

"When we finally leave this place," Monk growled, "I
ope you remember to come along."

Johnny just grinned. The skeletal archæologist was
lainly infatuated with this lost survival of ancient Rome,
1d was in no hurry to leave.

They drew up before the Corinthian columns of the
:nate building, and stepped off.

Panting, Ham Brooks caught up with them just as they
itered.

"On the way back," Monk offered, feeling his back
eth for looseness, "you can have my place."

"Not on your life," snapped Ham, instantly suspicious.

They entered. The senate was in session. In his ornate
1air sat Imperator Kizan, on either side of him the prin-
:ss and the soothsayer, Mikan. The expressions distrib-
:ed among the trio were of a type—unhappy.

A Roman senator stood up to speak. He declaimed
)r the better portion of forty minutes. Doc and Johnny
stened attentively at first. After a while Johnny began to
1wn. Even Doc began to look rather tired.

"Must be one windbag of a speech," Monk said to
am. "Can you make any of it out?"

"Mostly it is praise for Doc Savage. Otherwise the
an is not saying much."

"I guess Republicans ain't changed much in two thou-
1nd years," Monk scoffed.

At last the senator came to the end of his speech.

They could tell because Johnny let out a sharp oath an Doc stiffened.

"They want to make Doc Savage prince of Novun Eboracum."

"Looks like our campaignin' done too good," Mon grunted.

Another senator stood up and launched into a long windy oration. Soon, it began to appear as if the better pai of the day was thus to be expended.

Seven or eight speeches along—they had lost track–Prince Metho burst into the senate chamber and shoute something.

All heads turned to him. He took the floor. His exhoi tations were emotional.

"He is pleading for the hand of Princess Namora," Doc translated. "He is making a prior claim."

Imperator Kizan suddenly stood up. Pointing a lordl finger at the prince, he shouted the man down.

In the silence that followed, the imperator arrange his regal toga and began speechifying himself. It was not long speech. Doc, Johnny, and, to a lesser degree, Mon and Ham were able to follow it.

It was a proposal. Of marriage. Specifically, Imperatc Kizan was offering his niece to Doc Savage, and with it th title of Prince of Novum Eboracum.

Midway through the speech, Prince Metho storme from the chamber and out of the senate building.

The imperator wound up his speech. He sat dow Then all eyes were on Doc Savage.

Monk muttered, "This has gotta be the tightest spot ever saw Doc in."

"And how," said Ham.

"Ditto," added Johnny.

This giant bronze chief of theirs was an amazing fe low, and he had a great many of the qualities of a supe man. But in one respect, he was just like the next guy. H could not handle a woman with any great success.

Not that members of the feminine sex, even the mo ravishing ones, seemed to make any impression on th bronze man. He was woman-proof, as far as anybody ha been able to learn. There was a reason, of course. H strange profession made it too dangerous; any woman with whom he fell in love would have been a target for enemies, who would strike at the bronze man through her.

Marrying anyone—be it a Roman princess or an American beauty—was out of the question.

Doc Savage stepped close to the imperator's seat. He began speaking. His voice, which so often brought to mind a mighty engine at low throttle, now swelled to its full power. Oddly, he barely seemed to raise his voice. But his words rang like bronze bells as they fell into the stentorian cadences of ancient Latin.

As he spoke, the bronze man made a promenade of the room. In his tunic, he might have been a hero of ancient Rome, returned from some distant war.

His speech was spare, gracious, and utterly riveting, as much for the way it was delivered as for the words themselves—although they hung in the memory long after they were uttered.

In the end, the bronze giant graciously declined the offer of Princess Namora's hand and, incidentally, made pointed references to Prince Metho's prior claim.

The princess blushed a deep red. It might have been embarrassment or humiliation. It was hard to judge. The imperator turned stiff of countenance and Mikan the soothsayer brought the hem of his toga up to his dry lips, ostensibly to wipe them—but it was possible to detect a crafty smile on his wizened lips before the obscuring cloth fell into place.

A low, ominous mutter raced around the senate chamber.

Monk scratched a hairy arm. "I don't like the sound of this."

"Nor do I," added Ham, who knew how to read the faces of juries and saw dark portents in the senators' expressions.

Johnny, one ear cocked to collect fragments of the talk, said, "They are angry. To decline the honor is being seen as an insult."

The mutters went on for some time. One could see the various factions of the senate take shape as groups of senators paired off to exchange strong opinions.

Imperator Kizan just glared at Doc Savage, who was politely waiting for the buzz of conversation to abate before addressing the senate further.

It could be seen that old Mikan had one ear cocked to the ceiling, as if in anticipation of something.

The something came. Thunder, it sounded like. But the sound was short, without the cannonading rumble of the occasional thunder that had punctuated their days in Novum Eboracum thus far.

"Cannon," Doc said, rejoining them. "No doubt the deck gun of the *Scylla* being tested."

"These mugs don't seem to recognize it for that," Monk muttered.

Another report came. There was no whistle of falling shell or detonation. At least, not that they could hear.

Doc and his men went to the doorway and looked out. The city was as before. Peaceful. They returned.

Old Mikan was speaking now, his voice shrill and accusatory.

Johnny began a running translation.

"Mikan is claiming that Doc's refusal has angered the gods once more, erasing our victory in the arena."

"That old reprobate!" Monk snorted.

"He is further claiming that the gods are about to give him a sign of their anger. Three rumbles in a row."

"Three?"

"He said three."

Mikan continued speaking. His harangue grew tiresome, even to those of Doc's men who could not follow it. The upshot of it appeared to be that the lake waters were cooling because of the continued presence of Medicus Sævus and his followers, who were sowing dissension and discontent among the good people of Novum Eboracum. Already slaves were growing scarce. Work was going undone. Two thousand years of peaceful existence was threatened.

A senator intruded with a few words on the good that Medicus Sævus had done. His healing of the sick especially.

His acclaim was not seconded and Mikan resumed his litany of complaints, most of which came in the form of ire predictions of a tepid lake in which any of the black avages from beyond the Veil of Silence could navigate ith impunity, and thus conquer Novum Eboracum at will.

In the middle of this, a cannon report thumped, fol-owed by another. Then a third.

The senate came to its feet then.

"Three claps of thunder!" Monk howled. "Just like he redicted. How is that possible?"

"I detect the fine hand of Waterloo O'Neil," Ham pat.

"Waterloo O'Neil," agreed Doc grimly. "He and Mikan must have reached an agreement. The first shot was nquestionably a signal for Mikan to make his prophesy."

Johnny tightened his bony fists. "Our gooses are ooked!"

"I'm for bustin' out of this joint," Monk grunted. "No nore fightin' lions for this baby."

Doc quieted them with a gesture. He stepped up to he spot below which old Mikan was continuing his tire-ome oration.

Doc talked over Mikan's words. Eventually the sooth-ayer was forced to shut his mouth. His raspy throat, lready hoarse from declaiming, was no match for the ronze man's powerful vocal cords. He sat.

Once more, the bronze man used no more oratory han was absolutely necessary to get his point across. When e was done, he stepped back, waiting.

Once more, the senate was abuzz. While this sound ominated the chamber, Doc spoke to his men.

"I have just told the senate that Mikan is a liar. That is message from the sky is false. And further, that a true nessage will come at the noon hour—from the sky."

"Think that'll give us time to get off this wart of an le, Doc?" Monk asked nervously.

"That is not my plan."

"Huh?"

"At noon, Imperator Mikan and Kizan will hear a nessage from the sky they will not soon forget."

And that was all the bronze man would tell them. Vhen the buzz had died to a persistent murmur, Impera-or Kizan stood up and made his voice loud.

"We will convene at the noon hour in the courtyard before the Arch of Dentatus," he announced to all assembled.

And that was that. They were free to go.

Outside, Doc Savage wasted no time leaping on the waiting chariot. He gave the reins a shake. Monk and Johnny leaped onto the open back just in time. Ham Brooks, hesitant, was once again left to his own devices.

The bronze man urged the fine quagga to a speedy gallop. There was a grim urgency about his movements. No questions were asked of him, not even when he pulled up before his villa and surrendered the reins to the still-waiting charioteer.

For the rest of the morning, Doc Savage toiled in the seclusion of his room. Once, he called Johnny in for a consultation.

Monk and Ham paced the floor.

"Dog-gone if I see how Doc is gonna get us out of this fix," Monk ventured.

"I have faith in Doc," Ham sniffed.

"Listen, shyster, I got just as much faith as you, but if that imperator has gotten himself in cahoots with Waterloo O'Neil, our troubles just had cubs."

Ham frowned. He could not think of a retort. It was true.

Less than twenty minutes before the noon hour Johnny Littlejohn emerged from Doc's private room clutching a bundle of cloth. It appeared to be a toga, not unlike the one which flapped about the archæologist's bony shanks. They had the impression it concealed some item or items.

"Where are you going in such a rush, Professor?" Monk called after him.

"Errand." And that was all Johnny would say.

Doc appeared a number of minutes later, grim of visage.

"We will go now."

There was no chariot waiting for them this time, so they walked in a silence that was sepulchral.

The day was calm. Little wind seemed to blow across

the Lake of Smoke, possibly because the Mountains of the Moon served as a break to the winds. The air had a glassy clarity to it, nonetheless.

Their course took them to the open court before the stone jetty that was dominated by a great limestone arch. A crowd was already waiting for them. It parted to allow them to step into an open space in the center.

There, Imperator Kizan waited, his face a sneer. Mikan looked nervous. The princess stood a little behind them, her dark eyes downcast.

"We are waiting for your message from the sky, Homo Æratus," Imperator Kizan said in Latin.

Doc replied, "A message from the sky cannot be gotten without first sending a message *into* the sky."

The imperator blinked. "How is this possible?" Mikan interjected.

"Where I come from, this is customarily done with fire and smoke." Doc addressed the crowd. "Who will bring a small pot of charcoal so that Vulcan may be beseeched?"

Someone went off to fetch the desired object.

Doc and the others waited calmly. There was no sign of the missing Johnny Littlejohn.

When the pot was brought, Doc knelt before the charcoal and made certain passes over it with his hands. He raised one hand, chanting in Mayan so that no one except Doc's own men would comprehend. He was saying, "Get ready." Monk and Ham swapped blank glances. The bronze man had given them no instruction.

Doc threw a black powder onto the fire. Instantly, the white smoke turned black.

"Simple gunpowder," Monk said to Ham. "Probably from a firecracker."

The dapper lawyer nodded. He was watching intensely.

As the black smoke billowed around him, enveloping his giant form, Doc Savage plunged his hands into it, evidently adding more gunpowder, which he had no doubt palmed from his gadget vest.

The smoke soon obscured all but his head and shoulders. From the play of his shoulder muscles, Doc's hands were busy. Suddenly, there came a hissing sound. Abruptly, Doc stepped back, getting to his feet.

And from the pall of smoke a great smoky blackness bloomed, expanding rapidly. It took their breath, so quickly did it blossom. An evil genie coming out of a corked bottle was Monk and Ham's predominant impression.

Almost at once, it shot up into the air, trailing a tail like an ebon dragon.

Signs of alarm and surprise were wrung from the crowd. The imperator looked startled. Old Mikan visibly paled. And all heads craned upward as gazes followed the rapidly rising comet of smoke. They could not see what was making it smoke, only that it was ascending like a startled black ghost fleeing the domain of mankind.

Then, down came thunderous words.

"Audite, O cives Novi Eboraci!"

Roman citizens, absolute believers in gods and goddesses, were struck dumb by the Jovian voice from the sky. It had instructed the people of Novum Eboracum to listen.

It spoke again. The words were Latin, thundering, classical Latin.

"Medicus Sævus is a true friend to the gods!" decreed the voice, still speaking Latin. *"He will be treated well! He will not be harmed! I, Vulcan, have spoken!"*

The smoky ghost continued its unerring rise. No more words rumbled forth. Every eye was fixed on it, wide and expectant.

When realization that the gods had spoken their Olympian piece began to dawn, Roman heads dropped. Their gazes returned to the waiting figure of Doc Savage.

Imperator Kizan, as pale as the smoke had been black, opened his mouth to speak.

Then, came a distinct crack.

"Rifle shot!" Monk exclaimed.

Doc looked up. Above, the smoky apparition abruptly changed direction, jumping sideways as if stung. It popped.

The worm of smoke began to spiral back to earth like a wounded thing.

It landed, by ill luck, in the square smack between Imperator Kizan and Doc Savage.

It continued smoking, but it was a gray, weak exhalation now. The smoke was coming out of a cartridge Monk and Ham recognized as a smoke grenade invented by Doc Savage. It was affixed to the exploded remnants of a small balloon, which had obviously been filled with helium; the balloon and a tiny supply of helium under pressure were items that Doc often carried in his remarkable vest.

Also attached was one of the compact radio receivers which all of Doc's men carried. It had landed intact, by some miracle.

And out of the speaker came a stunned bleat: *"I'll be superamalgamated!"*

XXVI

RETREAT

Everyone within earshot of the fallen balloon, it seemed, heard the unmistakable sound of Johnny Littlejohn's startled voice. It was recognized.

"Johanulus!" old Mikan spat. "It was a trick! Vulcan did not speak. Their message from the sky is false! The gods spoke truly when their anger came in threes."

Monk bellowed, "They're on to us, Doc! What do we do?"

Doc had another smoke grenade. This jumped into his hand, and he flung it. Black, boiling smoke erupted and mixed with the remnants of the sputtering cartridge. People began to flee wildly.

"This way!" he rapped. And the bronze man plunged into the heart of the ebony pall. The others did not tarry.

Inside the concealing smoke, they linked hands and their bronze chief led them on. They encountered some bodies, but the spectators were more interested in flight. And in the blackness one body was indistinguishable from any other. They were not molested.

They emerged on the stone jetty moments later. Johnny was there to meet them. He was profuse in his apologies.

"This is all my fault," he moaned. "I had forgotten to turn off my radio when the shot came. I'm sorry."

"Never mind," Doc said grimly.

Only one warship lay at anchor. The other was evidently patrolling the lake. They made for it.

A head popped up from the deck. It belonged to Prince Metho.

Monk said, "Uh-oh."

Prince Metho waved them on. "Hurry!" he called in English.

Doc surged forward, the others following at his heels. They clambered aboard the galley. It was occupied entirely by pygmies, who were hunkered down at the oars. It was now the custom of the citizens to make the pygmies row themselves back to freedom, and this was no doubt another consignment of the little fellows.

"I heard that you had renounced all claim to Princess Namora," Prince Metho said quickly. "I knew what that would mean. So I prepared for this moment."

"Good," said Doc, casting off lines. Johnny and Ham took to idle oar banks. Monk and Doc laid hands on the great tillers.

The oars slid out, not exactly with the military precision of the trained rowers, but quickly enough to dip into the steamy water and begin to stir it.

They left the pier amid a ragged splashing. The smoke was drifting toward them and this, along with the commotion of hundreds of people fleeing in all directions, kept their actions from being noticed.

A voice called through the confusion.

"Metho! Metho!"

Doc turned. Through the pall, he could see Princess Namora stumbling in their general direction. She went down. Panicky feet began to trample her.

"She'll be killed!" Monk howled.

The warship had not yet cleared the jetty. Doc Savage started to go back. Ahead of him flashed a gold-and-white figure. Prince Metho.

The prince launched himself, landed hard, and made for the princess. He reached her, despite the onrushing crowd. He fought hard to protect her, but trampling feet proved too numerous. He threw himself down on the princess and let the feet trample him instead.

Doc Savage appeared at their side, flung blindly milling bodies this way and that, gathered up the duo—one under each cabled arm—and reversed direction.

The galley continued its slow slide.

At the end of the jetty, Doc launched himself into space. From a standing start, weighed down by no less than two hundred and fifty pounds of dead weight, he cleared a dozen feet easily and landed on deck. His knees bent, but he retained his balance.

As he relinquished his grip on the prince and princess, his metallic features betrayed no sign of strain or emotion.

The bronze man took hold of his tiller and the oars began pulling anew.

Princess Namora picked herself off the deck. She looked around. Her eyes fell upon the imposing figure of Doc Savage in the boat's stern.

She had no eye for the bronze man, however. She ran toward Prince Metho, who was himself coming to his feet, and their embrace was all the more passionate for its utter silence.

"Guess we know where things stand between them," Monk said in a disappointed voice. He put his back into his tilling.

They began beating out onto the lake, where the squirming mists were thickest.

Back on shore, the legionnaires of Imperator Kizan were getting organized. A javelin chucked into the water— too far short to be of concern. Another came, even farther back of their wake.

"Guess we're out of the woods," Johnny breathed.

"The remaining galley is still out here," Doc warned.

"But they don't know what is going on, do they?"

"Not yet," Doc said, and his tone conveyed concern that that particular condition might be short-lived.

It was. A booming came from the city of Novum Eboracum. It resembled the jungle drums of the pygmy tribe, and might indeed have been an adaptation of it.

Doc listened intently.

"Can you read them, Doc?"

"No." The bronze man looked to Prince Metho.

"It is a call to find us and ram us."

Ham said, "Ram?"

Doc said, "There is a brass ram affixed to the bow of these craft, below the waterline where they are not visible, and where they can do the most damage to an enemy vessel."

Monk looked interested. "That mean we got one, too?"

"It does."

Monk's grin split his face along the bottom like a melon dropping into unequal halves. "Then if I was them, I'd watch out for us!"

Lapsing into their language, Doc urged the pygmies to increase their rowing tempo. When they had mustered sufficient speed so that they were freely gliding along the lake surface, he ordered oars shipped. They came up smartly. Thereafter, the majestic galley skimmed along in silence, except for the steady gurgle of the prow cutting the water.

Silence fell over the deck. Every ear was attuned to the slightest change in their aural surroundings. No words were spoken. They knew what they were listening for—the lap and sob of many oars in motion.

After a while, it came. Off to the bow, starboard. The other warship was moving at a brisk pace.

"Sounds like they're comin' this way," Monk muttered.

Doc gestured for silence. His keen hearing was busy, hunting sounds. He paced the narrow deck, switching positions often, trying to ascertain the other ship's exact course.

When he thought he had it, the bronze man rushed back to his tiller.

"Port, Monk! Hard!"

They bent their weight to the tillers. The long paddle-shaped things carved boiling wakes of foam. The long galley responded, cutting a shallow arc.

It was in the nick of time.

Out of the mists reared the long ivory tusks and curled trunk of the other galley. Cries went up as its crew sighted them. The warship looked poised to cut them in two.

Doc rapped, "Starboard, Monk!"

The hairy chemist matched Doc's abrupt shift.

The galley shuddered with the abruptness of the course change, but was soon sliding in a new direction. The other galley was busy with activity. Shields were plucked off rails and the long hooked boarding gangplanks called corvi were readied for boarding.

These actions proved to be premature.

The galley manned by Doc's men was now poised
pass safely to the rear of its opposite. The other crew
rowers were holding their oars flat to the water in order
break its forward momentum.

"Looks like we're gonna make it," Monk said, h
squeaky voice strained.

It was not to be. From the look of it, Doc had time
things so that the prow of their galley would skate behir
the other by a narrow but comfortable margin. Just as th
other stern began slipping away, a shudder shook bo
craft.

"What happened?" Ham howled.

The other galley began behaving as if it had bee
smacked by the tail of some undersea denizen. It began
turn on its middle axis. Oars, forced backward by resistir
pressure, were lost overboard. Confusion reigned on dec

Monk guessed the truth and called it out. "Our ram
It nipped them on the tailbone!"

"Man shields!" Doc called. In English, and again
the pygmy tongue.

On Doc's galley, oars and tillers were abandoned. Th
crew leaped to the port rail, where the square shiel
called scuta were set in a row. These were lifted high.

Lances and javelins began arriving. The shields we
of bronze, and stout. They were able to fend off the wor
of the rain of death. Some of the missiles splashed into th
water. Others embedded themselves into the deck wit
blunt, ugly noises.

Monk collected a handful of these and began re
turning them, point-first.

"Monk!" Doc admonished.

"What's wrong with fightin' fire with fire?"

"They are only soldiers. Let them be."

Then the other galley, damaged but not in danger c
sinking, skated out of spear-throwing range.

The mists soon swallowed both ships, concealing ther
from the sight of one another's crews.

From across the silencing mists, they could hear th
sounds of the other crew of rowers getting reorganized.

"What do we do now?" Ham asked.

"We have momentum. Silence will serve us best for ow."

As usual, the bronze man was correct. By keeping the ars out of the water, they maintained a stealthy advan-ge. The other ship's rowing could be heard. Sometimes, ices of crewmen.

When Doc Savage judged it prudent, he and Monk djusted the tillers to steer a departing course.

In time, the sound of oars was very much distant. heir progress was slowing alarmingly, but it seemed ardly to matter anymore. Safety lay in concealment.

Doc went to the rostrum and wrapped an arm around s fanciful elephant trunk bow. He was peering ahead. The ists were thick writhing billows. Visibility beyond a few ards was impossible.

Johnny joined him.

"We should be nearing the shore," Johnny said.

"Not yet. But soon."

"Oars?"

"No. Drop grapnels. Try to find the bottom."

Monk and Ham brought the grapnels and they made oundings as best they could. So far, the water seemed very eep.

Doc allowed the galley to continue its silent glide.

Then Monk gave out a yell. "I snagged somethin'!"

The line had anchored to a cleat. Still, the cleat was lmost torn loose. Monk had a firm two-handed grip on e line and was all but yanked off his feet and into the ater. Doc joined in, tightening bronze fingers on the line. Ie pulled.

"Snagged on something," he said.

"We must be nearing shore then," Ham suggested. He ished up to add his strength to Doc and Monk's efforts. hey waited, braced for the moment when the line was autest.

The galley glided on. Then, with a jar, it was brought p short. The line held. They let go.

Doc Savage moved along the rail, trying to see over-oard. Worry creased his ordinarily unmoved features.

He dropped another grapnel overboard. It failed to

find bottom. The bronze man tried sounding at differen points.

"If we ain't touched bottom," Monk said plaintivel "what *did* we snag?"

The answer came amid a furious bubbling and blow ing not many rods back of their stern.

"Lookit!" Monk howled.

There, like a row of hideous ducks seen through primordial mist, reared the six dragon heads of the su mersible *Scylla*!

XXVII

FULMINATION

The *Scylla* broke the steamy lake surface amid such an upflinging of hissing water and roiling mist that for a breath they momentarily forgot it was but a fanciful machine and not some saurian denizen of earth's prehistoric past.

The U-boat righted itself, and the hot water on its silvery skin quickly began turning to steam, giving it an appearance of unreality that disguised its manmade origins.

A hatch popped—the center hatch. Up poked Waterloo O'Neil's thick, bewhiskered features. More than ever, he resembled some bristly, burrowing varmint.

"Savage!" he called. "Ye hear me?"

Doc called back. "I do."

"I see ye got yerself chased out of town!"

"No thanks to you," Doc returned. "What do you want?"

"The gold of this forgotten outpost—and ye're all that's standing between it and my lads."

"You are forgetting Imperator Kizan and his legions," Doc reminded.

"Roman armor ain't much of a match for the modern rifles I brought along."

"The butcher," Ham said. "He plans a slaughter!"

"Your scheme cannot work, O'Neil."

"Why the hell not? I spent over a year planning it."

"Have you tried firing your weapons lately?" Doc asked.

"What do ye mean?"

"During our trip through the Veil of Silence," Doc

271

said, "there was time to remove the gunpowder from you
supply of bullets."

"Ye did no such thing! I had my eye on ye all th
blasted time!"

"There were four of us, you forget. Each taking h
turn could have accomplished the task surreptitiously."

"We'll see about this!" Waterloo howled and droppe
out of sight.

Instantly, Doc Savage flashed to the line and yanked
loose, cleat and all. He tossed it overboard.

He called, "Row!" and fell onto an oar himself.

The pygmies, frightened by the sight of the *Scylla* an
not understanding English, were only too happy to cop
Doc's action.

As they pushed, the galley surged into motion. Johnn
said, "I do not recall anyone tampering with the rifle sup
ply."

Doc said, "No one did."

"Eh?"

"Recall I told Waterloo there was time to accomplis
that task, not that it *was* accomplished. In truth, we ha
more important things to do. But while he is checking h
armament, we should be able to get out of rifle range."

"I'll tell a man!" Monk exclaimed, grunting with eac
oar stroke.

But if Doc Savage's deceit offered hope, it did by n
means mean they were out of peril. They were travelin
blindly, with no clear expectation of what lay ahead. Th
knowledge that death hovered close gave strength to the
exertions. Mists swirled as the elephantine prow slice
them, like a woolly mammoth negotiating a prehistori
realm.

Up ahead, they heard blooping—a thick, liquidlik
percolation.

"Sounds like oatmeal cookin'," Monk ventured.

"Maybe it's hot lava," Ham added.

Doc said, "Lava is superhot. We would feel such in
tense heat even at this distance."

"Do we keep rowin'?" Monk asked.

"We do."

They rowed. The mists congealed and they could n

longer see the top of their mast above them. The queer blooping continued. It was not a pleasant sound—all the more so because it was so mysterious.

The keel of the galley began making a noise. An ugly sound like a blunt knife gutting a very large fish. It had a mushy, meaty quality that chilled the blood.

While they were pondering its meaning, the crack of a rifle came from the stern.

A bullet passed over their heads. Had any one had the misfortune to be standing on deck, he might conceivably have acquired the slug as a permanent souvenir. They were all hunkered low in the rowing benches, which were set so that the rowers could not see above deck and be distracted in their work.

"Looks like Waterloo discovered you were runnin' a bluff on him," Monk said.

Then a terrible sound came from the vicinity of the bow.

"Ship oars!" Doc directed, pulling his out of the water.

The others obliged. Johny started to rise in his bench. Doc sat him down again with an irresistible hand.

"Hold tight!" he rapped. "We are about to run aground."

The galley did just that. A continuation of the ugly noise became evident. The galley lurched, continued on, and from either side they were aware of the weird blooping percolation that could not be identified.

Then the bow ram struck something hard and immovable. With a jar, they were thrown backward on their bench seats.

Monk, naturally the most curious, poked a head up and peered over the rail.

"For the love of mud!" he shouted.

"Untie that knot in your tongue and tell us where we are!" Ham snapped.

"What I said. Mud. We run into some kinda bubbling mud flat, or somethin'."

It was that. An expanse of mud, kept in a perpetual state of lazy bubbling by underground hot springs or some other source of subterranean heat.

Another shot came. This one struck the mast; the thick pole cracked in response. But it held.

"It is time," Doc said, "to abandon ship."

"Ye gods," Johnny said. "Where?"

"Over the bow. We appear to have struck a rock ledge."

Doc went first. The others clambered onto the bow, and there saw the truth of the bronze man's words. The great brass bow ram was out of the mud, having ridden up on a flat expanse of stone. There was enough room for them to get down and not be much spashed by the distressingly hot mud that was continually agitated.

The rock was more than warm, but tolerable if they lifted their feet often. The pygmies had the worst of it, lacking footgear. Still, it was preferable to dodging flying lead.

The lead started arriving in earnest. It banged shields off the rails, gouged the polished mahogany lines of the hull and did other damage.

Fortunately, the galley was very long. No slug could penetrate it longitudinally.

Waterloo O'Neil seemed to conclude that because soon, the sound of the *Scylla*'s electric engines could be heard.

"He's comin' this way!" Monk bellowed.

"He will not make it," Doc said. "The mud."

Before long, they heard the toiling of the Caterpillar tractor arrangement that was set in the submersible's belly. The sound it was making in the mud was indescribable.

Doc had out his tiny optical device and had converted it into a reasonably efficient periscope. He angled it around the galley's curving hull, and after a moment said, "They are stuck fast."

"Hah! Serves 'em right!" grinned monk.

Doc continued to observe.

"Now they are throwing hatches," he reported.

"Rifles again?" Ham inquired.

Doc shook his head. "They are lifting the deck gun into place."

"That's bad news for us," Monk said. He looked behind him; the pygmies were squatting, plainly miserable, eyes wide, not quite sure what to make of their predicament, but understanding it could not be good, what with everyone cowering.

Prince Metho sat in such a way that his body protected Princess Namora. She clung to him, saying nothing, but showing no obvious fear.

"At least Habeas and Chemistry are safe back in the villa," Ham whispered.

"My Habeas may be, but by now he's probably chewed off your baboon's arms and legs and is draggin' the rest out into the trash," Monk said with ill-disguised pleasure.

"If any harm befalls my Chemistry," Ham raged, "I will pursue you all the way down to the hot place if I have to!"

Monk looked around glumly and said, "I think the hot place has gotta be more cheerful than this fix we're in."

Johnny asked Doc, "Why haven't they fired?"

Doc opened his mouth to speak.

The thump was not as loud as they expected. Everyone crowded down. Everyone, that is, except Doc Savage. He seemed unmoved by the sudden sound. In fact, he kept his eye to the periscope and continued to manipulate it.

The whine of shell did not come. There was no explosion. What there was was another thump. It was then they realized it was not that close—certainly it could not have come from the *Scylla*'s compact deck gun, which was perhaps two hundred yards distant.

"Why ain't they fired?" Monk said in exasperation. "What are they waitin' on?"

"You ape! Do you want us to be blown to smithereens?"

"Beats waitin' for somethin' that's gonna happen anyway to happen," said Monk, rather illogically.

"What about it, Doc?" Johnny asked.

"They cannot fire the deck gun," the bronze man said calmly.

"Why not?"

"No shells left."

"Huh?"

"Remember when they fired four shots to simulate the sound of thunder?"

"Yeah?"

"When we abandoned the submersible, they had only four shells left. I had counted them."

"You mean you knew all along they couldn't fire!"

"Yes."

"Then what are you watching for?"

"The other galley. Its crew could not help but hear all this shooting."

It did not take long for the splash of oars to reach their alert ears.

That prompted an immediate response from the *Scylla*. It began backing up. Electric motors whined. The Caterpillar treads spun mushily, sputtered, and tried again.

The second time, it met with success. With a sucking sound, the submarine began backing into deep water.

Another sound came in the distance. It was followed by a second, and after a long pause, a third.

Doc stowed his periscope away and brought out the silver penlike thermostat. Carefully, he reached around and dipped it into the bubbling mud. The bubbling seem to pick up tempo.

The bronze man lifted the thing and shook it clear of mud. A calibrated dial showed the temperature. He dipped it again, repeating the operation. The second time registered an increase by five degrees.

Doc came out of his crouching position, and rapped, "Into the galley!"

"What good will that—"

"*In!*"

Doc clambered back into the long craft, and reached down to help Princess Namora. She accepted the assistance with a warm smile, but when Prince Metho joined her on deck, she clung to him.

Through the mist they could see a little—the *Scylla* was once more afloat, the troubled waters around it dark and muddy. Waterloo O'Neil was standing on deck. His hands were cupped over his mouth. His shout was directed at the galley looming out of the mists, but all could hear it.

"Medicus Sævus—*hic!*"

"He is informing the others that he has us cornered," Doc translated.

A voice came back. They all recognized it as belonging to Imperator Kizan.

"That ship musta gone home to check their damage and picked him up," Monk said, unhappily.

Shouted words volleyed through the mist. Johnny did the translating.

"They have agreed to share in our execution," he said.

Monk cracked his knuckles noisily. "They gotta get within executin' range to do that," he growled.

A moment later, it was clear how that was to be accomplished.

The galley had slowed and was warping alongside the *Scylla*. Roman legionnaires stepped across as Waterloo, Mulligan, and the others were unfolding their ingenious little coracles and slapping them into the water.

There were four coracles in all. Enough to bear eight men, all told. Imperator Kizan and Mikan the soothsayer distributed themselves among the boats. Kizan wound up with Waterloo O'Neil. Two legionnaires took their places in the other coracles.

Then they all began rowing in the peculiar leaning-forward fashion of the tiny craft.

"If we only had our superfirers," Johnny mused.

Doc was at the stern. He called out.

"Waterloo! You'll never get through the mud," he warned.

"Donna have to, damn ye!" Waterloo snarled. "We just need to get in rifle range to put ye down."

His last few words were drowned by another tremendous peal. It was not of short duration. It kept on rumbling.

Monk asked, "What's that noise? Thunder don't growl like that."

Johnny started to say, "It appears to be—"

The sky turned red. That was the first thing. They had become so accustomed to the bubbling of the surrounding mud flat that they were only subconsciously aware that it began bubbling faster and had become quite busy.

"Volcano erupting!" Doc rapped, and the splitting of

the very air around them might have been a response to his warning.

Immediately, there came a breath of heat. The steam, thick and hot, was literally pushed ahead of the blast of superheated air that attended the top of Vulcan's Forge coming off.

Evidently, the entire surroundings—the Lake of Smoke, the mud flats, all of it—were tied in together by some common source of earth heat. The bubbling became furious. And all of the Lake of Smoke's vast expanse was visible for the first time, once the water had commenced boiling.

The bubbles were large and when they broke, smelled of sulphur.

The coracles, unstable craft at best, and built for negotiating gentle English streams, were tossed about and sent whirling. One upset and the cries of fat Goona Bey in distress came. They were cut short. The Hindu's weight tipped him out of his boat, and only his turban marked the spot where he had slipped from sight.

Waterloo, kneeling in his coracle, kept his wits about him. He was stirring the craft about and was making for the waiting sub.

He might have made it, but for the fact that the skin of the thing was held together with pitch. The boiling water naturally softened the tar. The shell began coming apart.

Waterloo and Imperator Kizan saw their fate coming. That was the terrible thing. The fate of some of the others was horrible, but swift.

These two saw that there would be no appeal to fate and turned their rage upon each other. Fingers flew at throats, faces, eyes. They scratched, they struggled.

And locked in a mute death grip, they dragged one another down to a boiling conclusion of their roguery.

Doc Savage stood in the stern, his hands fists, his face a metal mask of sweat. The others had gone below to escape the heat. The bronze man seemed to strain in place, as if he ached to rescue his enemies, evil as they were.

But there was no possibility. He could only watch.

The bubbling was terrible now and the sulphur stink all but unbreathable. Two coracles remained—Mulligan's and the one belonging to Leo Corby, whom they had known as Matthew Nade. They were tossing and whirling in place.

Then came a great eruption, as if a pocket of subterranean gas had been released from the lake floor.

It broke the surface with an ugly pop and splash.

After that, the last two shells were gone and the Lake of Smoke continued to boil, but with less fury than before.

Then came the long-promised rain. It was black, and not wet. It sent Doc scurrying down to the rowing pits with the others.

It was not until some three hours later that the worst of it was over. The earth heat that had been released seemed to abate. The bubbling of mud and water had settled down to a steady simmering. A fine coating of ash, thrown up by the eruption of Vulcan's Forge, lay over the great lake. It coated the galley, as well as the moist skins of its crew, until they resembled living cinders.

The sticky stuff would no doubt have burned them severely except for the fact that it had had to fall through great moist billows of steam. The steam moisture reduced the hot ash to a warm powder. It was not pleasant, but it did not burn much.

When it was all over, Doc Savage stood up and tried to see through the regathering mists.

"Galley of Novum Eboracum!" he shouted.

A reply came back. Then a question. They were asking after Imperator Kizan. Evidently the climax had been lost in the sulphurous mists.

Doc gave a one-word reply. *"Obiit."*

Silence greeted that revelation.

"But Prince Metho and Princess Namora have survived," Doc added in Latin.

A moment of silence followed that announcement, too. Then came shouts of gladness.

"Sic semper tyrannus!" they proclaimed. Thus perish tyrants.

Monk looked to Prince Metho, and cracked a grin like a snowman in reverse. "Looks like your day has dawned, guy."

XXVIII

REVELATIONS

It was the work of another hour to get them all off the beached galley. This had to be done carefully to avoid loss of life. The water and mud flats were scaldingly hot.

Prince Metho did the directing. Doc Savage stood off to one side to give the new ruler of Novum Eboracum a chance to exercise his new-found authority.

He did not do badly. The galley was brought in close and a line was thrown, and made secure.

Doc Savage tested it for strength and realized it would not bear his weight.

"I will go," said Prince Metho, and demonstrated not only his courage, but his balancing skills, by walking the makeshift tightrope back to the other galley.

From there, he directed operations. The other rowing crew commenced sculling backward.

Doc had his men and the pygmies do the same. They lost a few oars in the thick muck, but after a time their galley squished free and was once more afloat.

The first thing Doc Savage did was to row to the abandoned U-boat, *Scylla*. He jumped across and examined the submersible's innards.

When his head resurfaced, Monk called over, "How bad is it?"

"Serviceable. I will follow."

It was a pensive journey back to Novum Eboracum. No one knew what awaited them there.

In fact, the jetty was virtually deserted when it came into view. It was also covered with a fine film of volcanic ash. Everything was. The volcano whose eruption Doc Savage was able to predict by its warning rumbles and a sud-

280

den increase in the temperature of the lake had deposited a darksome coating of pumice on every rooftop and byway. The city had the unpleasant aspect of having been scorched by the wrath of some infernal diety.

This, they decided once they had dropped anchor and entered the place, was pretty much how the citizenry had interpreted events. They were for the most part huddled in their homes.

The appearance of Prince Metho, Princess Namora at his side, brought them out of doors. News of Imperator Kizan's demise was met with a stunned muteness. He had been a cruel and harsh ruler, but still he had been their lawful imperator. The word that Mikan the soothsayer had also perished was greeted with applause. No one had liked old Mikan.

That night, the senate was convened again, although there were a lot of pumice-blackened faces in evidence— mere washing seemed insufficient to eradicate the stubborn stuff. Prince Metho was invested as the new imperator with a minimum of oration and a maximum of approval. Princess Namora became Queen Namora.

Doc, Monk, and Ham, not exactly conversant with the customs of Novum Eboracum, did not realize the pair were being married right before their eyes until the ceremony was nearly complete.

"I guess," said Monk, after the assembled notables had repaired to a great hall for the wedding feast, "this about wraps up everything."

Johnny made a long face and said nothing.

"We will stay a day or so longer," announced Doc.

Johnny immediately brightened and began to wax enthusiastic about his postponed lecture before the Fellowhood of Scientists.

"Wait until those stuffed shirts hear about the true fate of the Ninth Hispana Legion, and our adventure here!" he enthused.

"This?" snorted Monk. "Nobody's gonna believe this in a million years." He fed a piece of fruit to Habeas Corpus, whom he had found in their villa. Ham peeled a banana for Chemistry and the ape ate half of it and tried to jam the other down the back of Monk's tunic when the hairy chemist wasn't looking.

Thereafter, the wedding entertainment consisted of Monk and Chemistry chasing one another about the great feast hall, throwing food, and both trying to evade an apoplectic Ham Brooks, who was flourishing his recovered sword cane.

Queen Namora shyly approached Doc Savage, Imperator Metho at her side.

She spoke two heartfelt words: "Thank you."

Evidently, Imperator Metho had taught her that much English for the occasion.

Doc Savage smiled one of his rare bronze-and-ivory smiles.

Two days later, the *Scylla* was being readied for the journey home.

Monk clambered out of the sub's entrails and said, "Not a lot of juice left in these storage batteries, and the gas for the generator is about all gone, too."

"We will go as far as we are able," said Doc, "and then distill grain alcohol for the engines."

Monk brightened. "That should get us to civilization, all right."

The gold of Novum Eboracum was discovered stowed away aboard the submersible and Doc Savage presented this to Imperator Metho, saying, "This rightfully belongs to you."

Imperator Metho was sincere in his gratitude.

"I cannot thank you enough for restoring me to my people," he said.

Doc Savage opened his mouth to speak, hesitated, and simply nodded. He walked off.

Imperator Metho frowned.

Some time later, he approached the bronze man.

"Is there something wrong?" the new imperator asked.

The bronze man fixed him with his steady gaze. "Do you understand hypnosis?" he asked.

"Hypno—"

"A kind of benign magic. I would like to see if hypnosis might clear your mind."

Imperator Metho appeared puzzled by Doc's suggestion. "My mind is perfectly clear," he protested.

"No mind is so clear that it could not be made clearer," said Doc.

Imperator Metho frowned more deeply.

"It is in your best interests," added the bronze man.

"I owe you much," the new imperator admitted.

Indicating Queen Namora with an inclination of his head, Doc said, "This is best done in private."

The submarine proved to be the most private place available. Its frightsome aspect kept most of the superstitious Roman citizens at a discreet distance.

Not that they were alone. Monk, Ham, and Johnny were there to watch. They did this in silence, understanding what Doc was doing, but not his reasons for resorting to the practice, which he usually did when he needed to extract information from an unwilling person during those times truth serum was not available.

Most hypnotists employ a prop—a timepiece swinging on a chain or some other bright object—to focus the subject's mind. Doc needed only the continually whirling depths of his aureate eyes to hold Imperator Metho's attention long enough to put him into a trance state with soothing words.

Soon, Imperator Metho sat with closed eyes and blank face.

"Think," Doc said in a sonorous voice. "Think back, before Britannia, before Wyndmoor Asylum, before Waterloo. Before Novum Eboracum."

"Before Novum—"

"In Novum Eboracum, you were known as Prince Metho."

"Yes," Imperator Metho intoned dully. "In Novum Eboracum, I was known as Prince Metho."

"By what name were you known prior to that time?"

Imperator Metho frowned, his mind obedient to the bronze man's hypnotic spell.

"Before—?"

"Do you remember before?"

His face began to twist, his brow to contort. It looked like a face at war with itself. "Remember . . . I remember. Yes. I was Meth—Matthew. . . ."

"Matthew!" Johnny exclaimed. "That is not a Roman name!"

"What was your full name, Matthew?" asked Doc.

"It was . . . Matthew . . . Anthony . . . Nade. . . ."

"Do you remember your father, Lord Nade?"

"Yes. . . ."

"Do you know what happened to your father?"

"Yes. He was poisoned. Goona Bey boasted of this. He . . . murdered him. . . ."

"When I snap my fingers, you will awaken from your trance," said Doc, "remembering your life as Matthew Anthony Nade."

Doc snapped his fingers. The other's olive-black orbs snapped open.

He looked about the cramped submarine interior, blinking.

Doc inquired, "Do you remember who you are now?"

"Yes," said the other firmly. "I am Imperator Metho Antonius Nævius."

Monk blurted, "I don't get it!"

"And," said the new imperator, "I wish the world to believe Matthew Nade died in Africa, which in a way is the truth."

"In other words," said Doc, "you wish to continue your existence here in Novum Eboracum undisturbed?"

The imperator nodded. "My father is dead. I have no other family. Back in Britannia, I would merely be Lord Nade. Here, I have a wife and am imperator of a proud people. What more can a man desire of life?"

"Wait a minute!" Ham shouted. "How can this man be Lord Nade's son? Matthew was a chubby sort with blond hair."

"The rigors of his ordeals were more than enough to shrug off excess poundage," explained Doc Savage. "As for his hair, Matthew Nade was a very young man when he set out for Africa. It is not unheard-of for a young man's hair to darken as he approaches his majority."

"But Waterloo said Nade was killed by a lion."

"Not killed, but certainly it is true that Nade's fright-ful experience fighting the lions of the gladiatorial arena caused him to snap, to lose himself to amnesia."

Johnny asked, "Exactly how long have you known all this, Doc?"

"Recall that my original purpose in journeying to Great Britain was to meet with Lord Nade, Matthew's fa-ther. When I beheld the photograph of Matthew A. Nade on his father's mantel, I noticed certain resemblances to the individual we knew as X Man, or Prince Metho, partic-ularly in the shape of the ears."

"Ears?"

"Like finger prints, ear contours are, if not unique, certainly distinctive. Also, recall the newspaper accounts that had reported that when he was first found in the Ro-man ruin—where Waterloo O'Neil had obviously depos-ited him to make it seem he was delusional—X Man was reciting Marc Antony's speech from Shakespeare."

"I don't follow that."

"Marc Antony. Matthew Anthony. The similarity of names was striking. It is the British custom to pronounce Anthony the Roman way, as you know, with the *h* silent."

"But he didn't remember who he was then!"

"The subconscious workings of the human mind are a great mystery," explained Doc. "Matthew Nade suffered from a kind of traumatic amnesia. Nevertheless, he re-tained enough of his former identity that it would betray itself in strange, small ways."

Monk was making comical faces of confusion. "One thing I don't get," he asked Matthew A. Nade. "Why did you call yourself X Man?"

Confusion troubled the former scion of British nobil-ity's lean features. "I—I do not know," he confessed. "I had forgotten by then that I had ever been Prince Metho, never mind Matthew A. Nade."

"The answer to that is deceptively simple," said Doc Savage—and even Matthew Nade looked to the bronze man for an answer.

"A person who is formerly with the navy is sometimes

said to be an ex-sailor," stated Doc. "That was the firs
clue. The X stood for the prefix ex."

"O.K., but he was still a man, wasn't he?"

"In this case, the word man did not mean what it ap
peared to. It represented not a word, but initials."

Ham said, "M . . . A . . . N . . . ."

"Matthew Anthony Nade!" Johnny exclaimed.

Doc nodded. "His subconscious mind clung to his for
mer identity even after it had forgotten his alter ego o
Prince Metho Antonius Nævius—a Latinization of his rea
name, which provided another clue. Recall that Bruce
O'Neil also Latinized his name, becoming Brutus Otho."

Monk grinned broadly. "Pretty good figurin', Doc."

Doc continued. "If I had not deduced the truth be
fore, I would have become suspicious upon reaching thi
place. Of all the Romans we have encountered here, th
only one who had the traditional three Roman names wa
the man we knew as Metho Antonius Nævius."

Imperator Metho nodded. "That was a custom tha
was allowed to wither over the centuries. Novum Ebora
cum had been cut off from all contact with the outer worl
when I stumbled across it six years ago. I was welcomed
fell in love with Princess Namora, and we agreed to marry
But Imperator Kizan, knowing that he would have to abdi
cate the throne to his niece's husband, schemed to dis
credit me. The cooling of the Lake of Smoke and th
treachery of Bruce O'Neil, who came among us only to
steal, made it possible for Kizan to exile me."

"You have had an incredible experience," said Doc
"But it is over. I am certain you will rule these people with
wisdom."

"Now that we are known to moderns, I fear for ou
future," admitted the new imperator of Novum Eboracum

"There is no need for the world to know this plac
exists."

"What do you mean?"

"I mean," said Doc Savage, "that the outside world, i
it learns of Novum Eboracum, will only spoil it with it
curiosity and greed. The mists have returned to shroud th
city from being seen from the air, and the Lake of Smoke

s once again hot enough to inhibit marauding tribes from
venturing across in their primitive dugouts. When we leave
here, I will prevail upon the pygmy tribes to form a protec-
tive guard around the Veil of Silence so that no white man
ever penetrates it again."

Imperator Metho Antonius Nævius nodded gratefully.
"That would," he said softly, "indeed be a treasure out of
time."

"It will be."

"What about my lecture?" asked a disappointed
Johnny Littlejohn.

"What had you been lecturing on?" Doc queried.

"Pterodactyl diet."

"Give that lecture."

Johnny's long face got longer, but all knew that there
would be no further argument from the gaunt archæologist
on that particular score. He understood the bronze man's
reasons for the decree, and beneath his profound disappointment, agreed with it.

With these matters settled, they prepared to cast off
the lines of the strange submarine that had brought them
to this fantastic realm in the heart of the African Congo.

The people of Novum Eboracum crowded the stone
jetty and lined the city's high walls to see them off. The
galleys were already out on the Lake of Smoke, ready to
escort the *Scylla* to the tributary of the Congo River and
civilization, and incidentally drop off the last of the pygmy
slaves, all of whom had been freed in Doc Savage's honor.

"I will certainly miss this place," Johnny sighed.

"Not me," scoffed Monk. "I'm hot to get back to
where people speak my kinda lingo."

"I, too, look forward to dwelling among those who
speak the King's English," drawled Ham.

"I guess we're going to two different places then,"
cracked Monk.

"I, for one, will not miss those rogues Imperator
Kizan, Waterloo O'Neil, and their confederates," Ham
added thoughtfully.

Johnny intoned, *"De mortuis nil nisi bonum."*

Monk winced. "Think you can try gettin' back to English, Sir William?"

"In reference to the deceased, let no maledictions be enunciated," murmured Johnny. Taking a last wistful look at the lost survival of Imperial Rome, he added sadly, *"Vale, Novum Eboracum.* Farewell."